I0556810

The Promised Land

A novel by

Mary Elizabeth Morin

The Promised Land

Copyright © 2014 – Mary Elizabeth Morin

All rights reserved. The copyright laws of the United States of America protect this book. No portion of this book may be copied or reprinted for commercial gain or profit; however, the use of short quotations or occasional page copying for personal or group study is permitted and encouraged. Permission will be granted upon request.

Credits/Permissions:

All song lyrics by the Grateful Dead are used by permission from Ice Nine Publications.

Special thanks to the songwriters for graciously sharing your inspiring words and insights! You are amazing...

Scriptures are the author's own paraphrase.

Published in the United States by Promised Land Media and Createspace

vCS5/21/14

ISBN-13: 978-0615939643
ISBN-10: 0615939643

I dedicate this book to Avraham of Ur – the Chaldean moon worshiper who left his familiar life to follow the Unseen God to his celestial city.

To others who have lived as pilgrims in this life: thank you for the writings that like Hansel and Gretel's breadcrumbs, lead us home, and away from the witch's house.

To loyal friends who have believed in me and encouraged my experiences with the supernatural:

Veronique Bennett : you and Tim helped me in those early days, and were such attentive, giving, and challenging friends – thank you.

Liz Adams: you welcomed me, a stranger.

Laurence-Mark, my faithful husband, and best friend: we've been in dark valleys, walked through the wilderness, and He has been our light. You are my hero. Thanks for believing in me.

To my children, Abby and Josh: you are amazing! Such awesome rewards…I love to see how you are walking out who you were created to be.

To my parents and family: you are wonderful and beautiful to me. I love you.

To the pearls hidden in the fields – fear not, little flock, for it is your Father's good pleasure to give you the Kingdom.

I want to make special mention of the prophets and poets, writers, thinkers, artists and revolutionaries of the Church, who have mined the "riches of the wisdom of the knowledge of God" for us to build the house on.

And I would be remiss if I neglected to thank Rich Bullock, a great writer and friend, who has worked so hard to format this book, and help me learn how the publishing process works.

Finally, to the Light-bearer, and Captain of my soul. Lead on…

Mary Elizabeth Morin

Promised Land Dictionary

Ba'al Aruni - Lord of the Cursed Ones

Brit – covenant

Chag – feast, celebration

Chevah - living one

Chevar korbanim – "band of brothers" friends who serve Korban

Gefani – vineyard

Gibbor – mighty one

Gibborim – mighty men

Kadosh – holy

Korban – sacrifice

Malkah - queen

Masos – bliss, exaltation, joy

Minmar - deceitful

Mogen – ruler, king

Nohedim - lost wanderers

Tikvah - hope

Tziyon – Zion, the City of The Three

yada - intimate knowing

The Promised Land

The joy, the triumph, the delight, the madness!
The boundless, overflowing, bursting gladness,
The vaporous exultation not to be confined!
Ha! Ha! The animation of delight
Which wraps me, like an atmosphere of light,
And bears me as a cloud is borne by its own wind.

Percy Shelley, "Prometheus Unbound"

Prologue

"Now, then, raise your cups as we celebrate plans for our newest creation!" The queen and prince smiled broadly and nodded, raising their glasses, as the king glanced around the room, his heart swelling; all eyes shone with joyous anticipation, so united were they in spirit, to promote the will of their beloved king Glaurius.

He squeezed his wife's hand, as she stood to join him on the platform, her black and silver hair cascading over the gold-trimmed, deep purple and crimson gown she wore. Her beauty was extraordinary, and her presence irresistible, with undercurrents of power, mystery and fiery love pouring out in waves over the crowd. The king kissed her impulsively, and turned back to those assembled in Glaury Hall, "These *adamah* will be our finest creation yet!"

Serafs standing beside the draped figures tugged at the coverings, and as they slid off, unrestrained applause and thunderous cheering erupted. The innumerable crowd of serafs and gibborim began to toast, and sing, and dance, and walked around and around the life-size models of the new creation, awed by the majesty they exhibited even in statuary.

The serafs were themselves quite extraordinary. These inhabitants of Tziyon resemble men, women, and children, but they are neither male nor female, and have extra eyes hidden all over their bodies. They possess the ability to speak telepathically, and can move at will throughout the air, or

1

through any kind of material, and appear deep inside the ground, or far below the sea; they can also travel through space, and even disappear into granite mountain sides.

Fully corporeal - that is, having bodies - their substance is of nothing that can be understood on earth. They cannot be injured, or grow old, and cannot get sick, or die, because they possess the power of immortal life, and are perfect by virtue of their allegiance to Glaurius, Sofia, and Korban - the gods of Tziyon.

As long as they remain in the love and fellowship of The Three, eating of the eternal fruit, and drinking of the water of The River of Life, they can never diminish or suffer in any way, so great is the power of that realm. They are also geniuses in intelligence, and work as farmers, vintners, cheese-makers, and craftsman in clothing, fine jewelry, and furniture; others are weavers, chefs, and poets, and serve The Three.

The other class of creature - the gibborim - are human-like as well, but are taller, and very strong and muscular. They practice all manner of athletics and competition, create new inventions for the kingdom, compose music and art, and serve as watchmen, overseers, generals, captains, lieutenants and corporals in the army of The Three. They also speak telepathically, and move at will throughout the universe, and possess towering intellect and skill - particularly in leadership, technology, government, and strategy. Many are scientists, lawyers, and engineers. There are classes and levels of authority among the gibborim, and three top generals oversee the thousands of gibborim: Chag, Masos, and Tikvah.

Chag (whose name means "celebration") is the chief of all who play instruments, and possesses music inside his wonderfully crafted body. He understands every kind of melodic combination and harmony, and is constantly creating new ones. He is the poet laureate of Heaven, and his words can move an entire crowd to ecstatic delights, deep love, or awesome revelations of the glory resident within The Three. His oratory is matchless; with his words and music, he can hold a crowd in thrall for hours at a time, taking them on an emotional and spiritual journey wherever he desires, so great is his power. Perfect in every way, his beauty is the stuff of legends: his curly blonde hair, stunning white teeth, and chiseled physique reflect the wonder of his inner reality.

Masos is the chief protector of the Presence – that ineffable and unspeakable power of The Three: Glaurius, Sofia, and

Korban. His primary function is to watch day and night for any signs of offense or diminishing of honor toward their Majesties - this is his bliss, which is what his name means. With his flashing sword ever ready, he never ceases to hunger for the glorious presence and worship of The Three. He is also the chief lawyer and mediator of Tziyon.

The general overseer and chief engineer of the realm is Tikvah, whose name means "hope." Not the kind of wishing hope we have here on earth, but the eager anticipation of good that is absolutely guaranteed. He is always building, always planning, imagining and envisioning the future, inspiring and delighting the happy residents of Heaven.

For weeks, there had been talk among the serafs and gibborim of a major announcement. Rumors abounded of late-night meetings in the palace, and the kingdom was by now filled with anticipation. Even the the three gibborim chiefs had been excluded from the planning, which was a very rare thing.

However, earlier in the week of the much-anticipated announcement, Chag, Masos, and Tikvah were invited to afternoon tea at the palace. The Three greeted them with great affection, as the great generals entered the game room of Glaury Hall. Oak logs radiated delightful warmth from the fieldstone fireplace, and shelves of artfully bound books, paintings, and tapestries covered the walls. The generals took their seats in the ornately-carved wood and leather chairs around the drawing table. The room was heavy with exotic scents, and in the corner of the room, a handsome, red-haired gibbor plucked a harp, and sang a mysterious tune.

Glaurius began. "This week, we will be meeting with all the serafs and gibborim, to present something very, very special, but we first wanted to share it with the three of you." He could barely contain his excitement as he spoke, twirling his thick, snowy curls, while staring into space at something he saw with great clarity.

"We have decided to create another world, and to populate it with a new kind of creature."

"The new world will be called 'Earth,' and will have beautiful skies and tall mountains, oceans and seas, rivers and lakes, an abundance of gold and gems, and all kinds of new animals."

He leaned back, now stroking his wooly beard, his eyes sparkling. "They will also have something called 'night,' that will be illuminated by planets, a moon, and stars, which I think

3

you, Tikvah, have been playing around with – a 'solar system?'"

The gibbor flashed his milk-white teeth, and nodded.

"Excellent, my son. The views of the sky at night will be breathtaking - your artistry is magnificent."

Tikvah blushed charmingly at the compliment. Masos and Chag poked him, grinning at his discomfort over the attention.

"Yes, dear brother," they teased. "You are *very* magnificent indeed!"

They all laughed good-naturedly, and suddenly, Prince Korban stood, and walked to the fireplace, lost in thought. He stared deep into the flames, playing with something in his pocket. After a moment or so, he turned back to them, his dark eyes filled with emotion.

"The greatest part of this plan is that we will make new creatures, who will possess our own nature: they will have the capacity for immortality, and have the creative power power of speech and belief, for we will breathe our very nature into them. They will be male and female, and will reproduce, and rule over this new world, answerable only to us."

There was silence as the chiefs listened thoughtfully.

"And what will be our role in this, Father?" Masos wondered at the complexity of numerous beings possessing the divine spark.

"There will be a multiplication of our Spirit and power, which is obviously different from how we function now. But we feel it is a perfect expression of the love and vision that dwells at our core, and under the watchful care of the serafs and gibborim, our honor will only be enhanced." Korban answered.

Tikvah nodded his head vigorously, and began to shake with laughter, beating his beefy fist upon the table, in sheer awe and delight.

"Hahahahahahaha," was all he could manage, as he thought about the grand experiment.

But Chag's face was cloudy with doubt, and his radiant smile was dim. In his eyes was a look of anxiety - something they had never seen before. The others waited for him to explain.

"Did you say that they will be *rulers* over this earth, answering only to you? Does this mean also that *we* will serve *them*?" There was the faintest hint of displeasure and resentment in his voice.

Puzzled, Sofia looked at Glaurius, and then at Korban, all

4

sensing the dark force emanating from the gibbor.

"Why Chag, it seems you are troubled by this idea of ours. What is the matter, my son? They will not rule *over* you, of course, but will summon you to help them. This is a great promotion for you, and you will be highly honored among them."

Chag didn't seem at all moved by the reassurance. In fact, he began to drift away in his imagination for several moments, considering what this all might mean, and as he thought, he grew increasingly agitated. Images began to swirl in his head, as he saw the prominent position these new creatures would hold in the rulership of Tziyon, and in the heart of The Three.

A world of their own, where they rule? This is a great injustice! I have faithfully served the Prince, the King, and Queen for millennia, and yet I have received no such reward! And they? These new creatures have done nothing to deserve such authority, and yet, they receive a greater crown than I; Masos, Tikvah and myself have earned this position, this reverence. I will speak to my generals in private, to find their true thoughts on the matter.

As he pondered all these things in his heart, The Three spoke wordlessly to each other, shutting off their thoughts from the two chiefs, and from Chag, who was too preoccupied with his perceived humiliation to notice. *This is a terrible, terrible development.*

Masos and Tikvah squirmed in their seats, uncertainty etched on their faces.

Glaurius cleared his throat. "Chag, there is much here for you to consider, and I urge you to think carefully about what is happening in your heart and mind; you have always served us, and lived within the parameters that we have set, and have been perfectly happy in every way, is that not true? The esteem in which you are held, and the authority that you possess is very great, but it seems that you feel it is not enough. Perhaps you need some time to think it through - please let me know your thoughts when you have searched your heart."

He stood, indicating the meeting was over.

Masos and Tikvah, watched helplessly, their minds racing as Chag stormed out of the room, war in his eyes. The chiefs looked at The Three, completely dumbfounded at what had just occured.

"What is going on with *him*?" Masos blurted out, feeling the threat to The Presence, but looking for direction, since he had never encountered an enemy like this before.

Glaurius, Sofia, and Korban looked grief-stricken, but Sofia responded with a resolute calm.

"This is the darkness of pride: clearly Chag has been meditating on his own greatness, and dreaming of opportunities for greater authority."

She whispered the next words, as the horrified gibbors listened closely. "In fact, he has created a world where he himself is the supreme ruler - in his imagination. He has been at it for some time, and our announcement exposed the secret desires of his heart; he is enraged that we have other plans."

Korban answered their unspoken question. "We didn't know, because we have no need to invade the thoughts of serafs and the gibborim - but we have been aware that something has not been quite right about Chag for some time."

He went on. "It would seem the great applause he receives for his talents has gone to his head, and now, he is in a very precarious place; he must choose whether he will turn away from self-exaltation, or pursue his fantasies of ultimate glory."

Glaurius added, his compassionate face clouded with emotion, "Yes, he has imagined that things are other than what they truly are. He is seeking to benefit only himself. Freedom has this potential; it can be used to produce the greatest good, or it can be used for personal ambition. And any dream that doesn't have Love as its motive - and Ourselves as the chief objects of worship - will never come true. This is the crossroad at which Chag now stands, and it will be a very difficult task for him to return to The Way. Let us pray that he will find the courage and humility to do so."

He placed his hands on Tikvah and Masos' shoulders, and met their eyes. "We may have war on our hands, and an Enemy like nothing we have ever experienced, but we will match every threat against the kingdom with fierceness, and our victory is sure. We must prepare for battle; keep a watchful eye on the gibborim, for Chag will seek supporters. In his rebellion he will appeal to those who have less authority, and draw many into his scheme."

"What do you mean, Sire?" Masos' hand gripped the hilt of his sword, which flashed with lightning as it responded to the mounting danger.

"It is very plain that he wants to rule over the new world." The Three nodded, seeing clearly now into the mind of the gibborim general, as he writhed in anger outside in the courtyard.

"But we will create nonetheless!" Korban joined them in a

circle, and they grasped hands; spirit to spirit, the five warriors gained strength. After several moments, they dropped hands, as a cruel, threatening darkness loomed on the horizon.

They looked at one another, contemplating the things that would soon take place, and finally, with fire in his eyes, Glaurius acknowledged and challenged the unwelcome reality.

"And so it begins!"

Chapter One

"Light, be!" Glaurius stretched his massive arms far apart, and shouted into the empty, formless void at the far end of the kingdom.

Starting as small vibrations, streams of light suddenly exploded with a roaring sound from inside his body, and shot out into the black, fathomless space around him. Luminous orbs, filled with the strings of life, began to float all around him in the trembling, expectant emptiness.

The King closed his eyes and smiled, rocking gently back and forth for a long time, reveling in the freshness and joy of light. Then soft and low, he began to sing - a comforting and sweet lullaby.

Appearing from the darkness came Sofia, who joined the song in perfect harmony. As they sang together, brilliant shafts of light poured forth from their mouths and bodies, and flowed into the swirling waters that now were visible below them, the light driving away the shroud of blackness.

Colorful, multi-dimensional crystals, minerals, and the other building blocks of matter, manifested from the song, and started dividing, multiplying, and intermingled in this abundant, flowing sea.

Watching in wonder and delight, Korban, sat singing and

laughing, astride a spotless white stallion that grazed in the sweet grass at the periphery of the realm of Tziyon.

Sofia, radiant in a shimmering gown, danced, and with her hands stirred the luminous fragments of light above the sea.

Iridescent colors sparkled: violet, rose, emerald, sapphire, yellow, sage, teal, navy, indigo, umber, carnelian, and gold, each with a distinct life-force. They trembled with energy, and joy, and raced off into the vast reaches of the universe, only to return a second later to swirl around Glaurius' face, affectionately rubbing against his bare arms and legs. Whenever they did this, kaleidoscoping sparks of color and light shot off like fireworks, illuminating the remaining darkness.

Everything - the colors, the light particles, the waters, the mist, the crystals and minerals quivered in ecstatic delight, as the song continued.

"We will separate this light from the darkness, and give it definition and measurable qualities, to initiate 'time.' But light and this universe - like us - will ever increase." Walking hand in hand with Glaurius to join Korban beneath a vast, spreading oak, she explained further.

"We will go in and out of time – this new reality."

"Sofia, my dear, we are all ears."

She spread her hands apart to display a hologram illustrating the complexities of the time-space continuum, the concepts of future, past, present, and how these things would function inside the never-beginning, never-ending reality in which they had always existed.

"Time is necessary, because as we now know, there will be reason to end this world one day; it – and them - cannot be eternal until..." Her words trailed off, and she closed her eyes, pain etched across her face.

Glaurius and Koban nodded soberly, but said nothing further, still hoping Chag would change his mind.

Sofia continued. As she spoke, Glaurius and Korban connected her ideas, comprehend easily the overarching systems of the new earth: gravity, thermodynamics, electro-magnetism, and the like. The flawless logic of the operational laws Sofia had devised, and the beautiful complexities of the systems elicited awe and admiration from both husband and son.

Smiling, Korban wobbled his head absorbing the new information, appearing slightly drunk. "Mom, you're a total *nerd!*"

Glaurius, grinned and closed his eyes, as if savoring a good wine. "Yes, knowledge is good, learning is good, *creating* is good! Hahahahahaha! Well done, Wife!!" He stood, and picked her up, twirling her around. Sofia beamed at the compliment, smiling into his radiant face.

"Let's go home, and return 'tomorrow.'" She waved goodbye to the swirling light, the churning, busy waters, and turned toward the palace, whose high towers dazzled in the sunshine, and the crimson banners with the three golden lions snapped in the breeze. Tziyon stood magnificent beneath the snowy peaks of the holy mountain that vaulted over the glorious, jeweled City.

"Tomorrow, then!" Father and son erupted again in laughter, jostling and wrestling each other to the ground. Breaking free, Korban let out a victory holler, leaped onto the placidly patient Brit, and raced off to the palace grounds. Glaurius took Sofia's hand, and they gazed once more at the expanse of happily buzzing light, until they turned to walk to Glaury Hall.

So the dark and the light were separated into the first Day, and the first Night.

* * *

Early the following day, The Three returned to the colossal blue planet that had formed overnight from the swelling, colorful sea. It resembled a sapphire, and was wrapped in a misty, watery veil. On the mown grass at the edge of the kingdom, Glaurius, Sofia, and Korban sat and feasted on warm, sweet rolls and fruit, and sipped aromatic dark coffee, laced with cream from the dairies of Glaury. Serafs flitted around serving, filled with wonder and excitement, and honored to be so near to the place where their new lord and lady would soon appear.

Korban wiped his beard with a cloth napkin, and took a final sip from his mug. He jumped up, and reached into the pocket of his linen shirt, retrieving a silk bag tied with a scarlet cord. He poured out the sky-blue stones into his hand, and tapped them. In the area between he and his parents, a holographic screen appeared, with diagrams, and a blueprint.

"The division of upper and lower waters is next, Father."

Korban pressed one finger to his lips in thought, and smiled warmly at Sofia. "Brilliant idea, Mother. I love the

10

economy of your plan – to utilize the existing water - it's virtually effortless; they will only have to speak out the command, and the humidity will be adjusted. Every kind of fruit, nut, vegetable, grain, grass and tree will receive the proper amount of moisture.."

He turned to his father. "Let's do this!"

Glaurius grinned, nodded, and stood up. Taking several steps away from them, he paused for a moment, inhaled deeply, and spoke, his voice like thunder.

"Let the waters above, separate from the waters below!" Instantly, the swirling mist stretched itself over the arc of the sky, and formed a rosy canopy, dripping with moisture, while the crystals and other elements continued to mingle together in the seas below; this was Day Two.

On Day Three, Glaurius and Korban spoke, and dry land appeare, to divide the waters: craggy mountains, gently sloping hills, and sheltering valleys. They spread out large areas of water on the adamah - earth and created the great oceans, seas, rivers and lakes.

Then, in silvery notes, the words came from the tongue of Korban.

"Let there be leafy green trees, vines, and small plants bearing every kind of fruit, vegetable and nut." And so juicy, red apples, fragrant mangoes, meaty walnuts, crunchy macadamia nuts, crispy lettuces, hearty wheat, carrots, and colorful potatoes cam forth from the ground.

Sofia took note of the progress; the food was every bit as abundant as the gardens of Glaury. Along with Korban and Glaurius, she took turns speaking each species of plant into existence, laughing at their "ooing, and aahhing" over the myriad manifestations.

At the end of the day, the new earth burst with color, and the scent of ripening food. Every kind of tree and grass - towering bamboo, and spreading sycamine, fragrant cinnamon, and gracefully draping elms, bear grass and cane, willows and alders, and the mighty cedars, began to release oxygen into the atmosphere to purify the air. They were glorious to look at, and would provide shelter for the animals that were to come.

And in the midst of The Garden, Glaurius made two trees: The Tree of Life, and The Tree of Independence.

On Day Four, Korban set up the diagrams again, and The Three consulted.

"Their solar system is next."

In the mind of Glaurius, he saw it all: the brilliant furnace at the center – a blazing star – that would provide warmth, proper gravitation, and light for plants to grow; next, a great moon that would light the night sky and clean the oceans, and he saw the other planets and their moons. Finally, there would be innumerable stars to mark off seasons, and which they arranged in configurations to reveal secrets, riddles, and prophecies of the Kingdom. The Three marveled at the slow revolution of the planets and stars, as they hung suspended throughout the deep recesses of space, like diamonds on velvet.

On the fifth day, The Three took nitrogen, sulfur, and phosphorous, and spoke life into them, creating animals for the water, and the sky.

"Be," they said to each one, and stood back as the creatures appeared.

Great whales, rays, sea lions, dolphins, jellyfish, turtles, sea snakes, every kind of large and small fish, and all the urchins, algae, plankton, and shelled, crawling creatures came forth, from the water, bowed before their Makers, and plopped happily into the sea.

With a cacophony of sound and whirring wings, the creatures of the sky lowered their heads in respect as they came before Their Majesties – then sprang joyously into the rosy expanse of the heavens. The Three smiled and laughed, peering into the water to see the creatures swimming about, showing off their wonderful skills.

The birds circled overhead, screeching for attention, delighting with joy in flight. All day long, the animals and The Three basked in the perfection of new life, and the sights and sounds of sky and water. When the day drew to a close, the sun set over the waters, and the birds flew off into the sheltering trees for the night, to rest under the watchful eye of the moon.

On the morning of Day Six, Glaurius woke with a bound, to find Sofia seated in the over-sized wicker rocking chair in their back garden. It was a favorite spot for her to muse and dream, because the canopy of leaves, vines and flowers sheltered her, creating a private space. He approached quietly, and just watched her; she smiled as she worked, the super-fine knitting needles clacking together as her fingers flew in expert, happy design. Sofia endlessly created from the depths of her magnificent being, whether it was items of clothing, tapestries of woven mystery, or stunning laws and concepts, or vast, complex universes; she was Wisdom personified.

Sensing she was being watched, she glanced up, affectionately perusing her husband's passionate face, her own mysterious sea green eyes imponderably deep with love and and compassion. Glaurius reached out for the garment she was working on. The silk and linen tunic, the pants, and gown fell as water through his fingers; he held them to his face, closed his eyes, and breathed in the scent of morning and evening - fresh grasses, lilacs, roses, myrrh, jasmine, cassia, pine and cinnamon.

"You – and the silk worms have certainly outdone yourselves, my Love. Mogen and Chevah will look magnificent in these."

He handed the apparel back to her, and they locked eyes. The look was blissful at first, but then a shadow passed between them. Sofia, caught his arm, and pulled him down to her in the seat. They held each other in silence for a long moment. Sofia spoke first, "Weeping may remain for a night, but joy comes in the morning."

"But we could save ourselves from great sorrow."

Sofia leaned against him, stroking his bare forearm. "That is true, but the Two Trees must exist, so they can choose freely to trust and obey."

Just then, Korban came bounding with the gibborim chiefs, and leaped over the low wall into the courtyard. He embraced and kissed his parents, while the chiefs too greeted their lord and lady with a kiss - even Chag, who acted as if his outburst the other day had never happened. "We will be with you shortly," Glaurius said with a hearty laugh, and the generals retreated to gather breakfast from the vines, trees, and bushes in the yard, returning soon with arms and hands full of fragrant fruit, their beards and shirts stained with juice.

"You'd think you had never eaten before!" Korban laughed and grinned at them, with no shadow of suspicion toward Chag.

"New every morning, hahahahaha!" Chag erupted in song. "It is my favorite thing about eternity – nothing is old, boring, or tiresome, but always a delightful adventure! He added dreamily, "So much to be happy about!" He sang a captivating melody, his body shining with jeweled colors, and perfumed spices exuded from within, scenting the air all around.

Masos, Tikvah, Glaurius, Korban, and Sofia gazed in rapt admiration, at the beauty of his gift, and his presence. The music spun an entrancing covering around him, and within this, light and power radiated.

The Three spoke silently to one another. *It appears he has had a change of heart after all!*

But Glaurius probed a little deeper, pulling his attention away from Chag's appearance, and gazing into his heart. When he had plumbed its depths, a shadow passed across his face. He glanced at Sofia and Korban, and they locked eyes, their spirits speaking. Masos and Tikvah took notice and looked at each other, and then at Chag. But Chag remained oblivious, caught up in the splendor of his personal adoration and delight. The two chiefs looked quizzically into the eyes of Glaurius, who spoke wordlessly to them. *Trust me.*

Korban smoothed his tunic, a blood-red tattoo visible inside the slit. Written in the calligraphy of Tziyon, the word 'Kadosh' was emblazoned on his lean, well-muscled leg.

The king addressed Chag.

"Have you had a change of heart, my son about our new creation, and your new lord and lady?"

With all eyes on him, Chag smiled broadly and lied, without an ounce of shame.

"I am completely ready to serve you in this, as in all things, my King." He turned to look directly at Glaurius, his eyes like daggers for just a second, before he bowed.

Korban looked at Glaurius, who said nothing except, "Then let's prepare ourselves for what we are about to do." The six clasped hands, and began to express in rapturous melody, their hopes and dreams for the thing that would be created next. Only Chag's spirit had spaces that were closed to the others.

Their voices and ecstatic harmonies shook the ground below and the sky above as the song rose and joined with the music of the stars, planets, moons and suns.in a symphony of unseen instruments. From Chag's body flutes warbled, guitars rang, trumpets pealed, and drums thundered and resounded into the far reaches of space.

After a long time, Chag broke the spell by clapping his hands together "Hahahaha! This is going to be good!"

Sofia looked at the others and lowered her gaze to the path before her; Glaurius whistled, and six horses cantered up from the lower meadow, neighing and leaping, to stand proudly before their masters. Climbing on a magnificent ebony stallion, Chag bolted out ahead.

"I will race you all there," he cried, and thundered off.

The others mounted their horses, and formed a circle.

Glaurius spoke first.

"As I feared, there is no change in our dear Chag. His gifts are extraordinary: he is wondrous in appearance, and has power to create and shift emotions and direct the imagination into new realities – and with these, there was always the possibility that he would become entranced with himself and with his talents, and this, he has done." He looked at Masos and Tikvah.

He looked at the figure of Chag, galloping hard away from them.

"What will you do, my Father?" Masos asked, struggling for answers.

"He denies his self-absorption and pride, and has chosen to trust his own perception, and create his own truth. He is just pretending right now, but in his heart and mind, he is busy making plans to turn serafs and gibborim against us. You must strengthen the bonds of love and loyalty with the rest of the gibborim, for it will happen quickly; I will not allow rebellion to foment here."

Sofia nodded in agreement. "I will warn him of the consequences of his actions - which will be very terrible - but at this point, I don't think he cares."

Up ahead on the grassy plain, Chag stopped and turned around, a small figure in the distance.

Sofia waved to him. "We must go now. Do not attempt to persuade him harshly, and do not alienate him. He is your brother, and your most powerful weapon is love. If he is not moved by fear, perhaps he may still be changed by love. And if he will not be changed by love, he will not be changed at all, please remember that."

She pressed her heels into the silvery mare, and sped off in the direction of her beloved gibbor, and the new world. The two chiefs followed, their hearts burdened with a sadness they had never felt before.

Glaurius turned to Korban. Pain and joy mingled together as they held each other's gaze. Powerful, conflicting emotions penetrated their hearts as visions passed between them of things yet to come. As thousands of years flew by in seconds, they stopped at a scene of gore and death – an altar in the midst of a massive temple hewn of rough, stones.

What would it take to heal the wounds of the coming war, and its unsuspecting victims?

Blood ran over the sides of the altar, down the steps and

into the street, from the body of the man who lay on the altar, his heart pierced in two. The sound of the blood was like a babbling stream, as it flowed endlessly out from the temple.

Glaurius looked at Korban's handsome, eager face, and the son responded with a broad smile. The visions started again between them, ending with a blinding flash of color and light. From the sky, a city of magnificent proportions and architectural form, descended amid the euphoric roar of an innumerable crowd gathered below. Music, joyous laughter and shouting continued as the people danced with all their might. Suddenly, The Three appeared in the midst, and the vision ended.

Glaurius clasped Korban's hand and cried, "Onward!" The two heeled their mounts and galloped off to the adventure that awaited, their hearts steeled for what was to come.

"We will triumph in the end, my father!"

Korban and Glaurius were one as they careened in the direction of the others, to fulfill The Great Dream for which they had so long prepared.

Chapter Two

When all had arrived at the edge of the clearing, they stepped into a glittering portal that transported them to the garden of the new earth.

As they walked between fruit trees and beds of flowers, Sofia began to explain the plan to the gibborim chiefs.

"We will use the same elements that are in the earth, to create the *adamah*. They will look like us in physical form, and have emotions as we do – affectionate love, deep familial connection, hope that is endless, and joy to crown their happiness and contentment."

She continued. "They will have an intellect that can configure complicated puzzles and equations, and decipher mysteries. As they eat from the Tree of Life, they will be eternal, immortal, divine, and filled with creative power in speech and thought. There is no gift or quality we embody that will not be theirs in abundance and their authority will be comparable to ours over this new world."

Korban saw the troubled look that passed across the eyes of the beloved gibbor of worship and the arts, while Masos and Tikvah responded, "We will gladly serve them, Mother."

"Wonderful! Your skills and gifts will be indispensable to them, and the love will be deep between you."

Korban looked at his father, for evidence of his thoughts. The struggle remained indiscernible on Glaurius's face, but Korban read his heart. *If only I could keep him from the path he has chosen! Oh, the folly of pride, and the covetous desire for that which is not ours!*

Sofia also spoke wordlessly, undiscerned by the gibborim.

We dare not interfere with this supreme grace of freedom of will; it is this that separates them from the inanimate world.

But setting his thoughts on the joy before him, Korban's face spread into a glorious smile, and he burst into laughter, with the rest joining in, setting aside their concerns over Chag for the moment. Raising a silver horn to his lips, Tikvah blew upwards, and soon, a shining cloud of serafs and gibborim filled the sky: small and large, young and old they came to the garden.

The crowd gazed in awe and deep admiration at the wonderful world of colors: the pink and pale blue sky with its brilliant sun, the dizzying variety of emerald-green trees, the turquoise sea, leaping black, grey, and multi-hued fish, sandy-brown lions, orange tigers, striped zebras, shiny giant lizards and dinosaurs, and red, blue, and yellow birds.

Sheep grazed beneath heavy-laden fruit and nut trees, amidst winding vines full of luscious grapes, as long-eared rabbits and deer nibbled nearby.

Lost in admiration, the three generals turned toward a sound in the grass at their feet. Approaching them in an undulating motion padded a large, mesmerizing serpent, every color of the rainbow present in its glittering skin and soft feathers. Its movements captivated them, and the eyes of all were riveted on it.

"Why, this is the most magnificent creature of all, truly beguiling." Chag reached down, and took the creature up into his arms, where it stretched out across his massive shoulders. "I think it likes me!"

Delighted, he began to play a song, which perfectly expressed the animal – an alluring violin that coaxed, and a soothing flute, which caressed the ears; it prompted the desire to surrender, to respond, and to dance.

One, now with The Minstrel of Song, the serpent made its way down to the ground, and possessed by the music of Chag, entertained and delighted its audience – which now included many of the animals – for some time.

Finally, Glaurius interrupted. "Thank you, Serpent, you were in fact inspired by our love for Chag, and created as a reflection of his beauty. We look forward to enjoying more of your entertainment in the future."

He turned away to address the creatures gathered in the garden. "We have a very great surprise for all of you."

Rebuffed, Chag grimaced at the curtailing of his performance, and reached down again for the serpent.

Glaurius continued. "To all of this new creation: you are perfect and glorious, and there is nothing missing in you, nor anything neglected for life and joy; we love you, and you are *good!*" At this, plants, trees, animals, birds, and fish erupted with quivering, shaking, sqwawking, bleating, roars and neighs of delight, and splashing and pounding of tails on the ground.

"We will create a king and queen for you, to care for you, and help you, and you will serve and help them. They will rule over you, and you will obey them, but they will love you, so there will be no burden."

He called to Chag as the gibbor played with the serpent. "Chag, please bring me a mound of soil from beneath The Tree of Life."

Chag petted the head of the creature, and put him down, bowing to the king. He walked past flowing fountains, and roses, and as he drew near to the Tree of Independence, he stopped for a moment, gazing up into the beautiful, leafy branches that were heavy with fragrant fruit.

"Such a wondrous tree! What is your secret?" He whispered in awe. Its power dazzled and allured him; the urge to take and eat the fruit was very strong, and he reached out, but recoiled suddenly. *I will not be mastered by anything.*

Taking note of its strange power, he spoke to it.

"There is something deeply mysterious about you, Mighty Tree, and I will discover this great power you hold, for you could be of value to me."

The gibbor scooped the dirt, and returned with his apron filled with rich, dark, sun-warmed earth. He dumped it out on the ground in front of Glaurius and Sofia.

Glaurius placed his hands on Chag's shoulders, locking eyes with the mighty chief. "Thank you, my son."

Chag shifted uneasily, and then flashed his radiant smile. "Of course, Your Excellency."

Unable to penetrate the mask, Glaurius turned to address the crowd. "Serafs and gibborim, we have modeled and taught you the power of independent will and thought, which is the source of your creative originality. With that, you have freely accepted the limits of freedom, recognizing that your talents, powers, and your very existence come from us."

"The beings we now create will have this same freedom, and they, too, will have to maintain the truth by daily practice; the two trees that stand in the center of the Garden will be a visible reminder: The Tree of Independence, and The Tree of Life. They may freely eat of all the trees in the Garden, except this one - he pointed to The Tree of Independence.

"For if they eat the fruit of this tree, they will die."

Suddenly an idea of great evil sparked in the mind of Chag, and he smiled cunningly to himself.

Glaurius looked around at the innocent faces, savoring the peace and unity of the moment, but fully aware of the intentions of Chag's heart. Still, he knelt to scoop up some of the fragrant loam, declaring,

"Watch, now, as I create your new master!"

With every eye riveted, he began to create the adamah. Adding water to the dirt, he worked skillfully, like a master potter, and shaped the skeleton, attaching muscles and tendons to the bones, and then hid the internal organs and blood vessels under a covering of skin. He sang a passionate melody, a tender smile wreathing his face, as he worked with precision and care.

The genius and artistry of the chest, shoulders and back were like the chiseling of a marble statue, the hands were expressive and useful, and the belly rippling with muscles.

Between the legs, he fashioned softer, curious organs, and modestly shaded them with soft, curly hair. Below, he formed powerful brown thighs, hips, and calves that sloped down to the more intricate work of the feet, which held the weight of the frame. But the masterpiece – the head - was the most wondrous of all.

They had chosen an average height of six feet for this new creature. Tikvah, amazed, stepped closer to admire the masterpiece. "Father, what is he called?"

"He and those from him are *adamim* – beings made from the earth, the adamah. Their connection to this world will be very intimate, for they are part of it. Therefore, it will be natural for them to nurture and care for it and for all the creatures here. As we are of celestial and invisible attributes and our authority and activity works in the invisible realm, so the adamim will operate from the core of themselves in their oneness with the material world."

Glaurius, Korban, and Sofia gathered around to gaze on the adam with pride and satisfaction, while Tikvah, Masos, and Chag stood slightly aside. Glaurius wiped his hands, and smiled at the inanimate man.

"I have waited a long time for you, my son,"he said affectionately. Then taking the face gently in his hands, he took a deep breath and exhaled into the mouth of the creature.

"LIVE!" he commanded, the earth shaking with the sound. Suddenly, the creature came to life, a brownish-red glow spreading through his face, and down into his body. A bright light appeared in the dark brown eyes, and he stood majestic, magnificent before them.

Standing back, Glaurius marveled. "Now he is of one spirit with us, can understand mysteries, and create with his words, as we do. He has all authority in this place." He spoke to the creature. "We respect your will, and your works here, as do all the serafs and gibborim."

Masos and Tikvah bowed before The Three, the chief engineer, greatly impressed. "You do all things well, my lords. But Chag averted eye contact, nodding his head, and motioning almost flippantly with his hand. "Your will be done, Father."

Glaurius addressed the adam. "Hello, my son. Welcome to life, to your people, and your home. I am your Abba, and this is my wife and your Ama. Korban is your brother, and these are your brothers Chag, Masos, and Tikvah."

He paused for the introductions to sink in. "The world you see is a gift we have made; all is yours to possess, cultivate, train, and enjoy." Sofia stepped forward with the garments she had made for him. Korban helped him put them on, drawing the jeweled belt around his waist. The fabric shimmered and flowed over his strong body, draping him in comfort and covering him with honor.

Korban signaled to the animals to come near, and they rushed forward bleating, squawking, roaring, honking and trumpeting. The adam laughed with delight.

Sofia smiled warmly. "We have named you Mogen, for you are the king of this realm. And in the hours and days to come, we will enjoy seeing you name the animals, plants, and features of your world, and call them into order."

Masos disappeared, returning with several gibborim who spread a large tapestry on the lawn beneath the almond trees.

"Sit, Mogen, my son." She took his hand. He had not yet said anything, but carefully observed everything that occurred around him.

Mogen took the goblet of new wine that a young, golden-haired seraf offered him, and other serafs set out golden bowls of fruit, and platters of cheese, baskets of fresh bread, and plates of olives, grilled peppers, tomatoes and eggplant, along with crisp salads. When they had finished serving, and all were seated, the animals came around, and Glaurius lifted his goblet to Mogen.

"A toast. You are our beloved son, Mogen. May you increase and fill the Earth with goodness and abundance!"

"Here, here!" went the refrain, and the toasting and feasting began in earnest.

"Mogen, we have withheld nothing from you in the way of wisdom or abilities. You will learn in days to come the kind of powers we – and you – possess, and this knowledge is all you will need to conduct your realm."

Sofia raised her glass, "To you."

Korban leaned over and embraced his new brother. Mogen smiled broadly, showing perfect white teeth. They raised their cups together. "May you cherish the love of family and friends, and never doubt your value to us."

But glancing at Chag, The Three saw the tightening of his temple, the only sign of the conflicting emotions in his heart.

And Masos and Tikvah kept a close eye on Chag throughout the meal, as he remained aloof and preoccupied with the serpent, almost rudely ignoring Mogen. The Three communicated their wordless thoughts to them. *Let nothing mar the joy of this day; we will face what comes as it comes.*

Little by little, the wine began to warm hearts, and the entertainment with music, jokes and riddles began, along with contests of skill in tumbling, juggling, and dancing. Chag played every instrument in his repertoire, and for many hours, the party and laughter continued. Others demonstrated their skill in song, while Mogen mingled with the animals, observing their mannerisms and qualities.

His first words he spoke to Glaurius as they walked together down the lanes of fruit trees, flowers, and vines in the cool of the evening. "Thank you, Abba. This is good." Glaurius reached out and held him close, savoring the warmth of his body, and the scent of his hair.

They returned to the others who had lit a bonfire, and the feasting, drinking and laughter continued into the night, with Sofia leading the crowd in dancing. As darkness fell and the moon came up, she finally collapsed giggling into a happy heap onto the carpet of cool, aromatic grass, her disheveled hair covering her in a silvery mass. Glaurius and Korban joined in, and soon The Three erupted in uncontrollable laughter.

Each time they glanced at one another, it started up again; even the birds came to watch, twittering cheerily and chasing one another in the trees and sky overhead, while the enormous whales, struck their tails on the surface of the sea, sending geysers of foam and spray high into the air. After some time, Glaurius, Sofia, and Korban lay peacefully reflecting, fully satisfied with their play, watching while Mogen walked among the animals and serafs.

Just then the sound of whirring air announced the arrival of serafs carrying bundles of puffy comforters, feather mattresses, pillows and quilts for sleeping under the stars, and they got to their work quickly. Freshly made ice cream and cherry, peach and still-warm apple pies were set out for late-night snacking during hide and seek, and catching lightning bugs.

Still basking in the glow of the new world, The Three sighed happily, until Sofia broke the spell. "I wonder how much time we have."

Korban reached for his mother's hand, and sat up to look at her, the sadness in her lovely eyes touching him deeply. *So much wisdom, hope and love has gone into this – all she ever desired, and all she has ever done is good.*

He looked at his father. "Yes, it will be a great fall. One day, they will forget, and deny that we - or this place - even existed." Glaurius closed his eyes and looked into the future where he saw kings, professors, scientists and clergy – all the great men and women of the earth – standing in their places of influence, teaching the masses to ridicule and hate him.

* * *

For a long time after, Mogen discovered the world around him. He learned about the gold and precious stones hidden in the ground – freely given for all to use and enjoy. He learned from the serafs and gibborim the art of translation – of reappearing in a different location. He could also move things and relocate tools he needed simply with his mind (imagination) and speech. Everything came easily to him, and great was the joy he shared with The Three, the animals, serafs and gibborim.

But when Glaurius told him about the Tree of Independence, he determined to place a wall around *both* of the

Trees, so none of the creatures would go near them - ever.

Glaurius spent many hours with him in the Garden, and Mogen visited the palace. Together, they named and played with the animals, hiked and explored the rivers and mountain crevasses, and slept together under the stars, and The Three together instructed him in his role as caretaker and protector of the earth.

But despite all the beauty and creativity, the companionship of The Three, and the fun he had with the animals, his heart longed for a companion of his own.

Chapter Three

As dawn spread its rosy fingers along the horizon, Glaurius and Mogen sat together in the fading shadows of the night, beneath the Tree of Life. An owl swooped overhead and alighted in the topmost branches. Refreshing water flowed from lush canyons in the towering mountain above the garden, and branched out in three directions. Along the banks of the rivers, jewels shone in the first beams of sunlight.

"So then, I will cause you to fall into a deep sleep, and remove a rib to create a lover and friend for you," Glaurius explained. Mogen stroked his side, and smiled.

"As you breathed life into me, I will give of myself to bring life to her - and it looks like a pretty safe place to get parts from."

Glaurius laughed, pleased at the heart of this adam. *You are so like your older brother.* But his countenance saddened for a fleeting moment, as the premonitions of destruction came to him again. *If only you would remain innocent forever.*

"But please hurry, Abba. I don't like being inside the wall, near the Tree of Independence."

"I know, my son, but there really is no benefit to this fear, and walls only fuel curiosity and temptation. It's far better to master yourself: you have the will to overcome any temptation, no matter how strong. I know you were determined to enclose the trees, and it wasn't my place to stop you, but it is not the best way."

Glaurius kissed him on the head, and twirled the wiry curls in his fingers. "I love you, Mogen. Now then, stretch out on the grass for a nap. When you awake, you will have your companion and friend."

Mogen reclined, stretching out his long frame in the warm spot of sun beneath the tree, and looked up into the beaming face of Glaurius. *You are such a treasure, dear one. So fair, full of affection, passion, curiosity, and …trust. Trust.* The word hung suspended in his brain and heart like a pendulum. *Will he, won't he…*

Mogen's voice broke through his thoughts. "Father, can I ask you why you made me first – and alone?"

Glaurius smiled again, savoring each moment they had together. "I wanted to have time with you before, um before," but he stammered. Mogen's heart responded with a stabbing pain as he reached out with compassion, seizing Glaurius's strong forearm. He looked with concern into the clouded face of The Magnificent One.

The king shook his head. "It is nothing, my son. You are perfect in my eyes, and all my hope is in you. Now sleep, and soon, you will have something – someone – *very* good! Hahahahahaha!"

Like a child turned from sadness by a delightful promise, Mogen lay down and closed his eyes. "I love you, Father. There is nothing that could ever come between us in this beautiful garden you have made. We will be together forever."

Glaurius's chest heaved with sorrow at the words, the love and longing for Mogen so strong, he felt he would break in pieces. He passed his hands gently over the eyes of the waiting one, and soon Mogen fell into a deep sleep. The king gazed at him for some time, as he lay in repose on the ground, and the desire grew within him to interfere, to remove Mogen's free will as he lay unsuspecting in sweet sleep.

Now would be the perfect time. After all, we made him, and can do what we like. What harm can it do? He will know nothing but pain and devastation - he and all his offspring – for thousands of years unless I stop it now!

The voice of Korban broke through the battle in his mind. *Father, I have already determined my course of action. You know it must be this way.*

He also heard the voice of Sofia, *Darling, there can be no breaking of this law, or else they could never know the voice of their own hearts, nor learn to trust it. And we would never know if their love was true, or freely given.*

Glaurius sighed, and rose to his feet, steeling his mind and emotions against the visions that paraded before him - a future that would bring sorrow never before known in his kingdom. *Better to have loved and lost...*

He bent over the prostrate form, and feeling along Mogen's right side, he gently spread apart the skin with his hand, reached in, and took a slender rib, re-sealing the opening. He placed the still-warm bone on the ground, and began to mold and fashion it into legs, arms, neck, head, organs, belly and pelvis of a similar, but different body than Mogen's.

"Woman - Isha," he spread long, dark curly hair over her shoulders and back, created full breasts, and a triangle of soft mystery between her legs. Her brown skin had a golden tinge, and above her lips and nose, he made warm, brown eyes like Mogen's. "In our likeness - male and female – with attributes of both, we have created them."

He admired the beautiful, inanimate creature before him.

I could stop this right now. Mogen has all that he needs with us – he doesn't need anyone else. Her curiosity and trust will be greatly tested, and she will fail.

But she does have the power to obey – she will always have that, Father. There are no victims – at least not yet.

Glaurius thought of his own sweet companionship with Sofia. *He will never choose us over her, and he will need her – they will need each other.*

He trembled with fury. "Fantasy is the child soon to be unleashed from the twisted imagination of Another."

He looked down at Mogen, and saw into the future.

"Instead of bouncing on my knee, your children will be afraid of us, cut off from us, and powerless against the evil spirits loosed upon the earth. They will serve these cruel and capricious 'gods,' and inhabit a world of lies, stumbling all their miserable days in the chaos of ignorance – and they will kill and steal for crumbs of self-exaltation, and the praises of men."

Glaurius already knew those who Chag would use to construct his alternate kingdom: the list of names adorned the schools of philosophy, higher criticism, science, mysticism, religions, music and literature, and their ideas, over the millennia would construct a City of Man, woven from strands of truth - here a little, there a little - cobbled together in a house of many tilting rooms that reached ever higher into the blackened air of humanity, warring for the souls of men.

This vast, world-wide web of beautiful-sounding words,

human reason, imaginative and lofty arguments, flowing together with provocative images, and gripping music connected these lies to ever more intricate layers of thought and rhetoric, science and logic, until at last it stood: a colossus, stark and shiny, linking the beliefs of the whole family of man, in the utter blackness of deception - terrifying and monolithic at The End of Days. No one could withstand it, unless they knew the real truth.

Yet with the truth, even the smallest enlightened child can, with the gentlest whisper, deconstruct it all into a pile of dust that will go out with the trash.

It made his head hurt just thinking of it all. But the sweet, comforting voice of Sofia broke in through the tumult of his mind and heart.

Dear One, foreknowledge is a painful burden, but think of the many that will choose truth, and receive the secret knowledge. For Love is the essence of life, and never fails to find its home in an honest heart.

Chapter Four

Glaurius rose decisively, wiping the tears from his cheeks.

Reaching down, he took the woman's beautiful, lifeless face in his hands, and released his breath into her. She trembled as he held her lightly in his arms, opening her eyes wide in wonder as she came to life. A bloom of color rushed to her face, and she smiled at him.

"Hello, my dear," he spoke gently, and stroked her hair, puling her close to kiss her on the head, inhaling the scent of her. "I love you, Cheva, you are my beloved daughter, and I am your abba, your Daddy."

He set her in front of him. Though naked, she felt no shame. "You are beautiful, and so powerful." He took the shimmering gown Sofia had made, and offered it to her. "Slip it over your head, like this." He helped her put it on, and it dropped from her shoulders, falling just below her knees.

She enjoyed the feel of the silk and linen against her skin, and twirled to flare the bottom, laughing and dancing in the cool grass. "I also have these for you." Glaurius held out drop earrings of deep blue sapphire, set in gold, with a matching bracelet, and ring. The necklace held a single large sapphire, with rubies as large as peas on either side.

"Oh, they're beautiful," picking up the word he had used to describe her.

"They're not as beautiful – or as valuable - as you, Darling.

They're shiny and pretty, that's all - just a nice gift from the richness of the earth, to enjoy, and to accent your beauty."

He helped her put on the jewels, and she hugged him, kissing his furry cheek. "Hahahaha, that feels nice, Abba. Or do I call you Daddy?"

"You can call me Abba, Daddy or Father, whatever you like. I am the father of all that you see – the Maker." He paused, and toyed with a curl on her shoulder, smiling at her with great love and affection.

"We have made you, for we desired a daughter to love."

She cocked her head, "We? Father, I see only you!" He chuckled at her innocent grasp of reality - that it was only what she could see.

"Beautiful One, you have a mother and brother, and many others who love you and are waiting to meet you." He grinned mischievously, sweeping his hand in Mogen's direction. "And this magnificent creature here, is your husband, Mogen."

She turned her face to the figure at the base of the tree beyond them. "Husband? What is that, Abba?" He took her hand, and as they got closer, her eyes widened in admiration at the sleeping form. "Is he mine also? Another gift?"

"Hahaha, he certainly is a gift, my love, and he is yours in a very important way – just as we all belong to one another here. He is yours for companionship, affection, sharing secrets, dreaming, and for designing and creating things for the Garden and the earth. And…" He paused, smiling mysteriously, patting his chest.

"And for making love, Cheva."

"Making love, Father? What is that?"

He explained it to her, adding. "Cheva, while there is a splendid physical aspect to lovemaking, an unbreakable emotional and spiritual oneness also occurs. We designed it to provide joy and happiness for body, soul and spirit, just as in our kingdom there is bliss in everything!"

Cheva practiced this word. "Bliss, bliss, blisssss!" She danced, leaped, and twirled around him as she sang it.

"Bliss is the love of my Father, and all his kingdom is bliss, ahahahahaha!"

She grabbed his hands and pulled him into a spin, which they continued until they flew apart, landing in a heap on the soft grass. Cheva crawled over to Glaurius, and collapsed onto his chest, leaning back against him for support. Her lungs heaved from the exertion, and sheer delight spread in the flush of her face. They laughed together for a long time.

As their breath returned, Glaurius continued. "Cheva, in lovemaking you will discover *yada*, and Mogen and you will come to know each other as you know your own selves. Along with your work, and your relationships with us, you have all you need for life." Here he broke off, and leaned forward to caress her cheek, and look intently into her eyes. "In the kingdom, you will have need of nothing. Complete wholeness in everything is yours, my darling. You can trust me in this."

"Yes, Father. It sounds good – it all sounds *so* good!"

He kissed her on the forehead, and held her fiercely. "Yes, Cheva, it is good, it is *very good!*"

He let her go, and suddenly the memories of planning and creating Mogen and Cheva, and this new world, came rushing back, with joy and passion, tenderness and anticipation. All the elements, planets, and stars, the animals, and all of nature were nothing compared to the value and feelings he had for these two. Yet, mixed with the incomparable pleasure he found in her affectionate, innocent and enchanting presence, sorrow and pain gripped his heart.

For in his imagination, he saw her reaching out, to take of the tree...

Stop! The struggle within subsided, as he turned to Cheva who was babbling happily about yada, and knowing Mogen.

"Oh, wake him up, Daddy, please!" She teased, but was startled at the look of dread in his eyes. "Father! What is wrong?" An ache pierced her heart, and deep distress etched her lovely face, reviving him.

He smiled and moved to rise, helping her up. "It is my concern, Cheva. All you need to remember is to always trust me. Can you do that, my darling?"

He turned away from the tree under which Mogen lay, and walked over to the Tree of Independence. "Do you see this tree, Cheva?" She tore her eyes away from Mogen, and came to the king. Looking up into its verdant, overspreading branches, she caught her breath at the luminous leaves and fruit that hung on it. There was an air of mystery and enticement, and Cheva found herself irresistibly drawn to reach up and touch the luscious fruit.

"Cheva, no!" The force of his command caused her to tremble with fear. "I asked you if you *see* this tree, Cheva. What do you see?"

"I see it is beautiful and attractive, and I want to eat its fruit. It looks good."

"You have seen well. This is the Tree of Independence; though this tree has the *appearance* of good, it possesses a very dangerous power, and death is in its fruit. Failing to obey me in this will unleash forces you cannot control, which will take you far from me, and from this place."

A puzzled look spread across her face. "But I do not understand. How can something that looks so desirable be so bad? And why did you make the tree, if it is bad?"

Glaurius rubbed his chin. "Cheva, the tree has enormous power – but if you eat from it, you will die. It will release the darkness of selfishness, greed, hatred, envy, which will destroy you and your children."

Cheva's eyes widened. "You can duplicate all the ways and laws of the kingdom in some form - because we made you in our image, you can create with words and ideas. You can create order, subdue this earth and make it beautiful for all the people and creatures yet to be born. You can do this now by the power of love, but the fruit of this tree will open your heart to another power – the power of evil – which will cause you to use your power and authority to control others, and take their freedom away."

Cheva listened, astounded at the authority and godlikeness which she possessed.

"Ultimately, Daughter, we made the tree so that you could freely choose what is good."

She looked again at the tree, and shuddered at his warning. How different it looked in the light of truth. "Abba, you are the King of Life, and the King of bliss and love. I will always listen to you and trust you. I will do only what you tell me to do."

He looked at her with a wistful sadness, but smiled bravely. "Well, Cheva, I have already explained about the Tree, and now you must tell *yourself* what to do, as far as that is concerned. We have placed wisdom and truth inside you, so there's no need for rules."

He went on. "I don't tell anyone what to think or do, just as I do not need anyone to control me, I have given you the same freedom; you are a powerful being who can choose what you will think and do, and you can command yourself. That's how it works. *That's* what freedom looks like."

"I am powerful, I can choose, I command *me*!" Glaurius laughed at her furrowed brow.

"Don't work too hard, Cheva. You'll get it. There's no

hurry, just relax and enjoy. Bliss, remember?"

"Yes, Father, I just want to learn now! I want to learn many things."

He smiled at her thirst for knowledge, and the curiosity that the Three had hardwired into the their new children. How twisted these remarkable gifts will one day become, and what devastation will be released by them. Oh Cheva, my Cheva!

To be powerless to protect his creatures from harm, assaulted his very nature; the presence of rising evil disturbed the harmony and perfection of his being, and of the Kingdom, battering his peace, demanding new and perplexing responses, unprecedented in the long span of eternity.

"Well, don't be too curious. You will learn all you need to know little by little. I wanted to tell you a couple of other things, before we wake up Mogen. I told you that in yada, you will become as one person, and you will make a new reality shared by only you two. But – and this is important – you will always be distinct and unique people. Your ideas and qualities are indispensable to Mogen, your children, the animals, the earth, and to us. We made you male and female – with characteristics of both sexes, because we are that way."

Cheva's smiled and nodded her head, as she thoughtfully processed what he had said.

Glaurius went on. "Others will observe, learn, and enjoy what you create with your life, and you will learn and grow as you discover their gifts and uniqueness, too. This creative love is the foundation of our kingdom. We are love, and all you see is the fruit of love, expressed in visible reality."

They walked hand in hand into the meadow.

"Mogen will be a wise friend and companion, someone to hold you at night, and work alongside you to envision new ideas and bring form to the earth; together you will create children, and they, too will take their place in bringing forth the best the world has to offer."

His hand swept the breadth of the Garden, "All that you see, we have created for you. It is a gift for your pleasure, and all that you need to build your Paradise is in it."

He whistled, and the animals began to come: birds, giraffes, zebras, lions, to admire their queen. She walked beside Glaurius, and touched each one affectionately. They responded with shrieks, grunts and purring of delight. Glaurius threw back his head, and began to sing – a haunting, moving song that caused the world to spin around them, and colors to explode, as all of creation replied in song, each element and creature vibrating to its individual, unique frequency, in a symphony of praise and ecstatic joy.

Glaurius took Cheva in his arms and began to dance with her across the cool grass, as the sun rose over the trees, illuminating the party gathered there. Her gentleness and sensitivity to Glaurius, the animals, and to the atmosphere exceeded Mogen's, and she began to release her own song, to which the earth responded with a sigh of comfort, and peace. Glaurius surrendered in rapt attention to her beauty, affection, and innocence; he was clearly smitten with his little girl.

"Cheva, you are everything I could ever hope for in a daughter. All I have is yours, and all my hope is in you." She smiled, and ran to his arms.

Looking over his shoulder shyly, she turned back to him. "Father, can we *now* wake Mogen?" Glaurius felt a pang of jealousy, longing for more time alone with her. *Maybe if she just knows us better, she will never doubt…*

"Yes, Cheva, we can wake Mogen." He took her face in his hands and looked deeply into her eyes.

"You are my daddy. I will never forget, and I will *always* trust you." He let her go, anguish in his heart, watching as she walked to the sleeping *adam*. *How long will always be, my love?*

Glaurius smiled through the pain, observing her desire and admiration for Mogen. "He is beautiful, Father."

He nodded in agreement, "He is indeed. Made just for you – well, not entirely for you. He is my son, too of course."

"Of course! He is ours, and we are his. And we are yours, and you – you are ours, too?"

"Hahahaha, that's exactly right, my dear!" He pointed to a path outside the wall.

"Cheva, I want you to wait down by the waterfall. I will bring Mogen to you soon; I want to surprise him."

"Yes, Abba, but don't be long!" She kissed him, and dashed off in the direction of the noisy water, waving as she ran, twittering birds leading the way.

Glaurius touched Mogen on the shoulder, and he shook off sleep, looking around in alarm. "Father, have I been sleeping long? I-I had a bad dream, it was something dark and terrifying, but I cannot remember it now."

"No, Mogen, it has only been a short while." He furrowed his brow, "I'm sorry for the dream, Mogen. But sometimes these are warnings, so while you should not be afraid, you should pay careful attention." He pulled Mogen to his feet.

"But Abba, everything is so perfect here, and good. Where is the danger? I do not *see* it!"

"No, my son. For a long, long time, things have been perfect. But there is no guarantee that it will remain so. There is a threat to my rule from one of my generals, so you must be aware that he does not deceive you, for he desires to have this planet." He went on. "He has no authority here, and cannot harm you, except by your disobedience. Beware of believing things that aren't true."

Mogen felt the familiar stab of fear.

"Yes, I am talking about the tree. Trust me when I tell you that if you eat from it, you will die." Mogen began to tremble.

Glaurius drew him to his chest, hugging tightly. "Do not fear, my son, for you are far more powerful than he: only trust and obey."

"I will, Father! I do not want to die, or ever be separated from you – or from this place." He pulled away, gazing with admiration, and a sense of ownership around the Garden. "This is *mine*, and I will protect it!" His face flushed with anger, as he faced invisible adversaries.

"Yes, Mogen, that is good. All this is yours, and only you can lose it."

Chapter Five

"Mogen, let's go now, your new companion is waiting!" As they walked to the gate, the king continued. "I have named her Cheva, which means 'Life-Giver,' for she will be the mother of all the living."

Mogen locked and checked the door, turning to Glaurius. "Wonderful! And me, what am I?" He pounded his chest. "I am the *father*. Hahahaha! And Abba, I remember *all* that you told me about lovemaking!"

"Refresh my memory, son. I'd love to hear what you know." Glaurius chewed on a grass stem, waiting, a proud smile plastered across his face.

"Well, I remember that we will have strong feelings for each other sometimes that will bring us close, and we will kiss, and then, well it's kind of private, Father." He blushed.

"Yes, it is, my son, it is private."

Mogen went on, "We will have pleasure, and fun, and it will feel good; we will have yada, and be best friends. I will love her, and she will love me. Is that it?"

"Yes, very good, Mogen. It's very simple. You will know her strengths and ways, and she will know yours, and you will have great honor and value for each other. You will find great joy in your children, in work, in the animals, and with us."

Suddenly, Mogen seized the king's arm. "Abba, did you tell Cheva about the Tree of Independence?"

"Son, I explained very carefully to her that it was deceptive and powerful, and what the consequences would be. I am confident she understands, and desires to trust." He hesitated, "But as soon as she saw it, she was drawn to it, and reached out to eat of it."

Mogen recoiled in anger. "Father, I am done with this tree! Please take it away!"

Glaurius waited, as he vented. Mogen slammed his fist in his hand. "No, this place is *mine*; I will cut it down and destroy it." He wrung his hands as if to choke the neck of an unseen enemy, desperate to fight.

Glaurius twirled the grass in his fingers, and tossed it to the ground. "Mogen, that is not the way. You are ruler here, but I am King of all. The tree cannot be destroyed, but must always be an option."

Mogen dropped his hands, and lowered his head, the adrenaline slowly receding. He kicked a stone at his feet in frustration. "I know, I know, that's what makes free will free. I'm tired of hearing that!"

Glaurius pulled him close. "Yes, Son. Rule over yourself, love Cheva, and do not fear. She is intelligent, and powerful; honor her freedom."

He sighed resignedly, "Yes, Father, I will do these things."

"Well, now, let's not look so glum – don't want to keep Cheva waiting – come meet your bride!" Glaurius laughed, and began to run swiftly in the direction of the water, while Mogen rushed to catch up. He overtook him, and they jostled one another on the way, wrestling on the grassy banks, to see who would arrive first. Glaurius scampered like a deer up the sides of the hills, and leaped atop the rocks, with Mogen close behind.

Finally, the king stopped, and they gazed down into the canyon below. A stream of water flowed from the springs in the mountains, fell over the rocks, and poured into a turquoise pool. Beside the small lake, stood Cheva, her golden-brown body radiant in the sunshine. A variety of birds and a small menagerie of monkeys, otters, foxes, lynx and bobcats played in the water, and at the water's edge.

Cheva dove in, and clambered out onto the rocks, tossing pebbles into the pool. Hibiscus flowers as large as a hand grew amidst dark, shiny foliage, lacy ferns and waving bear grass. Fragrant, speckled lilies bloomed in the shadows of the cliffs, and water droplets formed from the cascading spray, sparkling like diamonds in the in-breaking shafts of afternoon sun.

Graceful willows bowed elegantly, brushing their long, trailing branches on the smooth, wet rocks, and the wind whispering a soothing hush. Doves cooed in the tops of the mountain mahogany, oak, and maple trees that dotted the hillsides.

Mogen stared as the magnificent creature before him plucked a soft pink bloom, and tucked it into the curls behind her ear; his mouth involuntarily dropping open. Glaurius grinned, and reached over to lift his chin and close his mouth. "What do you think?"

Mogen turned to look at Glaurius, and with all seriousness, responded, "That is *very, very* good."

"Hahahahahaha! Yes, my son, she is very good!!! Let's go see her!" He clapped Mogen on the back, and leaped down to follow the path to the water.

Mogen let out a whoop and Cheva glanced up, but the two became partially hidden by the trees and tall bushes; she could only catch a glimpse every now and then. But as they came closer, she heard an unfamiliar voice that sent a shiver of excitement through her body. She sat with anticipation, until finally they burst into view. Mogen appeared first – tall, with muscles bulging, his brown skin, eyes, and curly hair a perfect complement to her own. He smiled and looked directly into her eyes, and she returned the friendly overture. He hesitated for a few seconds more, transfixed.

"I'm Mogen, it is my honor to know you, Malkah Cheva." Instinctively, he bowed his head at the majesty radiating from her.

She rose and bowed to him as well. "My lord, Mogen. I welcome you to know me."

Glaurius smiled at her directness, and confidence, watching the meeting from the path. *Naked, and unashamed – and the reverence they show one another! It is a good sign.*

The king stepped forward, and spoke to the animals scampering around, and watching the interaction between their lord and lady. "Here I come!" he said to a tiny monkey who chattered at him to chase him up the cliff. Stripping down to his shorts, Glaurius ran, leaped, and hit the water in a cannonball that sent waves over the side of the pool.

Mogen, now completely soaked, laughed with Cheva at his antics. "Our father is such great fun – care to join him?"

"Oh, yes!" Mogen shed his clothes, and Cheva took his

hand.

"Come with me!" She led him up a steep, short, grassy path, took an overhanging vine, and handed him another. Cheva stepped up the hill for momentum, and sailed out into the air, dropping at the midpoint into the water below. Mogen followed, laughing as he tumbled into the lake.

The three played for the afternoon, stopping occasionally to snack on fruit along the banks of the water. Blackberries, raspberries, succulent strawberries and blueberries stained their faces and hands, and they refreshed themselves with cool water from a fountain nearby. As they lay in the soft grass, their clothes drying in the warmth of the sun, the three talked about many things, and then later, walked together up the path, and back to the center of the Garden.

"I have so enjoyed this day – and there is more to come! Your mother and brother, and all the gibborim and inhabitants of Tziyon have prepared a feast, and are coming here shortly to celebrate you, Cheva. But a question – my children, is it your intention to be husband and wife? What do you say?"

Mogen looked at Cheva with an ache of desire unlike anything he had ever felt before, but he took her hand, and gazed into her eyes for her answer, before he ever spoke a word. There in the depths of honeyed-amber, he read her heart. Smiling, he touched her face, and gently brushed back a stray curl.

"Cheva, you are more beautiful to me than the hills of spices that rise above this garden; you are like the rich perfume of the flowers by the lake that release their scent in the evening and morning. You are the brightness of the stars set in the backdrop of the sapphire night sky. Your insights and wisdom are profound; your spirit is captivating, and fun. My life is complete because I am no longer alone, but have the perfect companion. Will you be my lover, my friend – my wife?"

Cheva responded to his expressions of love and honor, and the words of admiration with openness and gratitude. "Mogen, I am deeply moved by your passion for me; your authority is impressive, your judgments and vision are deep. You are like the strength of the mountains, mysterious as the canyons and glens. Your beauty is like the sun rising in its glory, and though we have only just begun our friendship, I could imagine no other life but by your side. I desire you, and accept you as my lover, my friend, my husband."

They placed their palms together between them, and

entwined fingers, drawing closer to look deeply into each other's eyes. Glaurius reached out for a plump-breasted dove perched above him in a low-hanging branch. He stroked her head and back gently, then whispered something, and released her in the direction of the city.

Chapter Six

Within a few minutes, the air swelled with the sound of birds, and the music of the spheres, preceding the arrival of thousands of serafs and gibborim. Some came from the sky, and some came on foot, or on horseback, and some from the unseen realm. In the center of the throng rode Sofia and Korban, in a carriage drawn by dappled grey Arabian mares. They came to a stop in the orchard where Cheva, Glaurius, and Mogen waited.

Korban helped his mother down from the carriage; she never took her eyes off Cheva, and Cheva responded to her alluring influence, coming straight into her arms. "My daughter...you are beautiful, truly awe-inspiring." She whispered to her gently, and held her close. "How I've longed for this day, my darling one."

Cheva looked up into Sofia's ancient and love-filled eyes. "How is it I feel like I have always known you?"

"I am your mother, my love, your Ama. I helped create you, and part of me is in you, so you do know me." Cheva sighed and remained in her embrace a few seconds longer. Finally, Sofia kissed her, and turned to Korban.

"Cheva, this is your brother, Korban."

"Cheva! How delightful to have you here with us at last." He gave her a bear hug, and pinched her cheek. "Let me look at you. You are beautiful, that's true, but I think you have other gifts as well, as I recall."

He winked at Glaurius and Mogen. "C'mon, woman, let's see how fast you can run. Hahaha!" She didn't hesitate but took off in the direction of the meadow. Korban followed and caught up with her, and they soon returned – at the same time.

Korban slapped his thighs, and laughed through his labored breath. "Not bad, not bad at all! We will try your hand at archery later – and drinking!! Hahahaha!" He turned to the bartender gibborim who linked arms and toasted with their mugs. Cheva smiled at their antics, and Korban's teasing.

"*Drinking*? What is that?" At her question, everyone fell silent, and looked around, giggling, and jostling each other, wondering who would explain one of the most foundational and revered realities of Tzyion.

"Well, son, why wait??? Hahahaha!" Glaurius's eyes glimmered, and he took a cup from the tray held by a seraf who instantly appeared at his side. Crystal clear water turned into ruby-colored wine as he tilted back his head, taking it all down in one drink. He wiped his beard and sighed happily, laughter filling his eyes.

Joy and glory began to manifest from within him, like a wave building in the sea, and with all eyes expectantly on him, his chest began to heave with increasing mirth; he poked one, then another, until the bliss had spread to all. Everyone took a cup as the bartender serafs came around, and drank. A roar of laughter filled the air.

Try as they might, they could not control the billowing waves of rapture and happiness that crashed over them. In fact, trying to stifle the hilarity became a game that caused even greater manifestations of joy. Eventually, the entire crowd surrendered and collapsed into a superb, intoxicated heap on the ground. For almost an hour everyone laughed and soaked in the joy, and the animals, too, lay with them, enjoying the petting and attention they received from the inebriated party.

At one point, Cheva lifted her head above the crowd and crawled to her knees. Lifting her hand in a toast, she addressed her family, slurring her words. "Well, Abba, Ama, and dear Brother, I am delighted to be here, and I thank you for making me amazing! Hahahaha!" Unable to stay upright any longer, she collapsed in a fit of laughter onto Sofia's lap.

Glaurius elbowed Mogen. "Oh, Son, she's got it *bad*!" The comment spread through the entire crowd until everyone cheered and clapped, and toasted in thunderous approval. Sofia stroked her hair and replied without a hint of jesting, "This, my dear Cheva, is *drinking!*"

Eventually everyone regained composure, and returned to the work of the wedding holiday. As the last stragglers wobbled off, Sofia took Cheva by the hand, and with a well-supplied basket of warm bread, cheese, olives and pastries, invited her to a picnic near the spring just past The Vineyards of Table Grapes.

Strolling arm in arm down the rows of grapevines and luscious grapes, the sweet, honeyed scent bore them along in the last rays of the sun, accompanied by the sound of buzzing bees. Their heads touched as they conversed and giggled like girls, with Cheva affectionately hugging and kissing her mother without reserve as they walked along. Reaching a flat round of turf near the bubbling spring, sparrows and starlings took the padded picnic cloth and spread it out. As they set out their meal, their grateful hearts and eyes mused on the delights all around them.

"Ama, it seems like all there is to do here is *enjoy* – there is abundance everywhere I look, and every need is satisfied."

Sofia laughed. "Yes, Cheva, it is true. There is only abundance and pleasure here, and nothing that any of us need. Work and play, it is all one thing." She popped an olive onto her finger, and nibbled on bread topped with a slice of buttery cheese. Cheva cut a thick slice of bread, and made an open-faced sandwich with olive oil, and tomatoes sprinkled with rosemary. Each drank from a simple wooden cup filled with fresh water, white tea and honeyed blackberry juice.

Cheva clapped her hands with delight as Sofia brought out warm hand pies, glazed and raspberry-filled donuts, and chewy, bite-sized brownies. The scent of apples and cinnamon, and warm peach and ginger competed for her affection, so she chose one of each. Washing them down with iced coffee, she chose a walnut-topped brownie, and popped it into her mouth.

"Mmmm, Ama! These are heavenly" She faked a swoon, and fell over onto the blanket. Glancing up at Sofia, who smiled at her with great affection, she propped herself onto one arm, and watched as Sofia cleaned up the meal, and made room for her to lie down beside her.

They lay on their backs in dreamy silence, gazing up into the pink and blue of the sky, admiring the wheeling of eagles far above. After a while, Sofia began to speak.

"You know, Cheva, this covenant into which you are entering with Mogen is very special indeed. Glaurius and I are husband and wife, and your relationship with Mogen is patterned after our marriage. It is a union of equals, and is for pleasure. Mogen possesses qualities of leadership and authority that will bring definition and direction to all you do together, in making a habitable, productive, and blissful world here. You have ideas, creative genius and wisdom that is different from his and both contributions are indispensable."

She paused, and then continued. "Just as everything in Tzyion flows from within the three of us, and is influenced by the serafs and gibborim, so it will be that you, Mogen, your children, and their children will determine the kind of world in which you live.

Sofia took Cheva's hand, and gazed penetratingly into her eyes.

"Cheva, you are very powerful, and all wisdom and authority is available to you. You must remember to choose connection and unity, and submission to the truth whenever you find you are presented with a choice. In this way, you will maintain peace and security in your marriage to Mogen, and safety in your domain. You are the queen here, Daughter. Do you see?"

Cheva's eyes grew wide at the knowledge entering her heart. "I see that you have given me great authority, favor, and responsibility, as well as unending pleasures. My one desire is to fulfill the purpose for which you created me; to increase and fill this place with beauty and people who love you and will enjoy this abundant life forever."

"Yes, Cheva. That is the plan. May you always be as committed to it as you are at this moment."

Sofia pulled her close, and stroked her hair, burying her face in the thick curls, stifling the sobs that threatened to erupt.

"Soon you will begin your new life with Mogen, and there is much to do. We can talk anytime you wish, my dear. Now, let's go return to the wedding grounds."

Cheva bolted impulsively from her arms, and gathered up the basket and picnic cloth, chattering excitedly. "I hope Mogen finds me pleasing, Mother, and that I will know what to do. Will he know what to do?"

She hadn't noticed Sofia staring, her eyes brimming with tears, and her hand over her mouth. But she spun around at the sudden cry. "Cheva?" Sofia stretched out her hand to Cheva, who came quickly to her side.

"Ama, what do you see? What is it?" As soon as Cheva

touched her hand, Sofia tore herself away from the vision, then clutched Cheva's face with both hands. Confusion and pain gripped her heart, as she saw the look on Sofia's face.

"Be careful, Cheva of what you believe, and remember that you alone choose your path – every moment of every day. You must always be self-aware, sensitive to truth, and wise. All the ways of Tziyon lead to wisdom, so above all, set yourself to know and follow them, searching for them, as for the greatest of treasures, because nothing is automatic. You must fill *yourself* with truth and wisdom."

She smiled, kissed and patted her cheek one last time, then dropped her hands. "Come, let us go."

Chapter Seven

The serafs delivered presents, food, decorations and bedding for a massive, weeklong feast to the badminton fields. Outlining the field, they hammered golden posts into the ground every 15 feet, attaching braided cords of scarlet, blue, and gold to the tops of the poles, connecting them to each other.

Next came the tents, with sides that could be rolled up or tied down. The bridal tent went up in the middle of the field, and many serafs encircled it, ornamenting the inner and outer walls, and the top with ribbons, jewels, flowers, and greenery. Inside, others prepared the furniture, and laid out clothing, food and presents. The bed they prepared with a thick mattress of scented grasses and soft wool, linen, and cotton into which they infused oils of myrrh, pine, cassia, and frankincense. All this they sewed inside a cover of spun linen, with pillows of scarlet, purple, and gold arranged invitingly on top.

The return of Sofia created a stir among the serafs and animals, and they stopped their work, eager to discover the surprises in the wagons she had brought earlier in the day. Korban ran up to greet them, and climbed up onto the tallest wagon, whistling loudly for attention. "All right, all right! It is a great day of celebration – and a week of festivities for the marriage of my brother Mogen, and his bride. You are working beautifully, and making a party fit for a king - so of course, we have presents for all of you! Hahahahaha!"

In his excitement, Korban leaped off the wagon, sailed over the tops of the littlest serafs, and into the arms of half a dozen quickly assembled gibborim. This sent the smaller birds and animals twittering into the brush for safety, and left Sofia and Cheva shaking their heads in amusement. The gibborim clapped him on the back and shoulders, set him on his feet again, and the creatures slowly returned to the throng that now surrounded the wagon.

"My son, the crowd-surfer!" She smiled indulgently at the fun, and climbed up to direct the giving of gifts, rising elegantly and strong, her hair tumbling down the back of the pale turquoise and yellow outfit she wore. Animals and serafs looked at her admiringly, patiently - clearly soothed by her presence. The air buzzed with excitement, as assisted by several helpers, she passed out the presents of clothing, paintings and sculptures, illustrated books, gems, and different kinds of new devices, to 'oohhs and aahh's' of delight and wonder.

Setting aside their treasures, preparations continued, and took several days, with everyone working, eating, and playing together, and sleeping under the stars at night. Carpenters fashioned tables and chairs from wood harvested from the ever-replenishing Forest of the Builders, the pungent aroma of cedar permeating the festal grounds. Young serafs set the tables with china plates, newly hand painted and double-fired with mysterious signs, and floral patterns from the House of the Glaziers.

Alongside the settings were gold forks, knives and spoons, and crystal goblets rimmed in gold. Artisans from the glaziers and other houses placed elaborate centerpieces of wood, brass, or glass art on each table, complete with continually changing scenes of nature, stars and planets, or the world under the sea, animated and fitted with music for the delight and enjoyment of the guests. Some of the art responded to the personality and interest of the person watching, inspiring their imagination with new ideas, and fresh vision as they gazed on it.

During the work, Korban, Sofia, and Glaurius helped alongside the others, hauling lumber, decorating, or preparing food at mealtimes. Mogen and Cheva spent time together and apart, unloading provisions, playing bocci and badminton on the manicured lawns, and enjoying the arrangements for their wedding celebration. Masos and Tikvah supervised all the serafs and gibbors, while Chag arranged the music.

One evening, at the time the owls hunted, Tikvah and

Masos walked into the forest to take pleasure in the moonlight illuminating the darkness, and the soft shadows of the night. As they came to the edge of the grounds, there was a small bonfire, with several gibbors seated around it. Chag stared into the flames while strumming his painted mandolin, but the approaching chiefs never did hear the words of the plaintive ballad he sung, for he abruptly stopped singing and playing as soon as he saw their faces.

"Hello, my brothers! Please, won't you join us?" An involuntary flash of anger in his eyes betrayed the welcoming words; they two chiefs instinctively reacted to confront the challenge, but Chag soon began to laugh, and plucked a happy dance tune. Tikvah and Masos looked confusedly at each other, then back at Chag who feigned friendship, and mocked them with his song.

"How happy are we, the servants of the great King, who now will serve his children?"

Just like Glaurius had warned, jealousy toward Mogen and Cheva had shifted his affection away from Glaurius and the kingdom; they had no need of rumors, they could now see for themselves. And whatever Chag had said to those around the campfire, it was clear he was succeeding in building an army, which like hungry wolves would strike at the opportune time.

"Yes, Brother, we are the honored servants, and we bless our new lord and lady. We cannot stay now, but urge you to join the others in the main area. Shalom."

Chag waved his hand around those gathered there. "Yes, yes, my friends, we are just finishing our little gathering, and will do as you suggest. All is well on this wonderful night." Chag smiled conspiratorially at the gibborim around the fire who nodded in agreement, and then all turned menacing eyes on Tikvah and Masos.

But Masos sent his words like a knife as he turned to leave, "Is it true, Chag – that all is well? I think we will soon find out."

Abandoning their plans for a tranquil evening - and full of anxiety and rage over the treachery they felt brewing - Tikvah and Masos went back to the wedding grounds to tell Glaurius all they had seen.

As they walked along, the happy sounds of dancing and laughter rose into the night sky above the sparks of the campfires, and here and there, groups of serafs lay sleeping, telling stories, or rocking the young ones to sleep. The gibborim chiefs seethed within over the threat they felt, as they surveyed the peaceful life of Tziyon around them.

In front of the tent of Glaurius and Sofia, a tall gibbor leaned on a staff, tapping his boot in time to the flutes and guitars.

"Where is my Lord Glaurius, Brother?" The gibbor met the steely gaze of Tikvah with surprise, and concern.

"He is here within, my friend, playing chess with Lord Korban."

Saying nothing more, the gibbor pulled aside the outer curtain, through which Masos and Tikvah passed. The inner curtains were parted and pulled back, giving permission to enter, and this the generals did, approaching Glaurius and Korban at their game in the center of the room.

"Greetings, Abba." Glaurius looked up, and received the kiss on his cheeks. "Lord Korban, Lady Sofia." They bowed toward their majesties.

Korban's eyes narrowed as he discerned the agitation in the gibbors. Sofia glanced up from her writing, then at her husband and son, waiting. Korban played with a tiny menagerie of porcelain animals on his lap, distracted from the game. A seraf came in with a tray carrying two cups and set them before the gibbors. Tikvah lifted the mug to his lips and drank.

"Mmm, honey ale. Thank you, it is very good, Leon. My compliments!" Masos also took a deep draught, and nodded in agreement. The seraf departed, and turning to the King, Tikvah began.

"Abba, there is disloyalty, just as you suspected; we came upon Chag in the forest with a band of gibborim. Envy has taken hold of him, and he is shape-shifting - he shows one face and then another."

Tikvah paused, and Masos continued. "Yes, it's true - as we spoke, he said one thing, but his eyes and heart said another. He is filled with an anger and hatred that increase as we wait – those gibbors and seraphim are clearly committed to him, Sire, so we dare not delay!"

Tikvah spoke again, with a smoldering fire in his voice. "I feel the danger in the atmosphere – it is unsettling and disturbs my peace. I fear if it is left unchecked, there will be war in our land."

Glaurius held the white queen between his fingers, rolling it back and forth, as he listened to Tikvah and Masos, occasionally glancing down at the board, considering his next move. Without a word to anyone, he moved the queen into position against the black king, who he had hemmed into a corner.

"Checkmate, Son." Korban stared unbelieving at the move, then burst into laughter.

"What? I never saw that coming!" Glaurius smiled at him.

"Indeed!" He erupted with joy and laughter, and the chiefs finally relaxed, joining in with relief and admiration. They talked, and The Three revealed to them the coming war, sharing the plans which they had prepared in advance.

"But Abba, if you knew what they would choose, why did you put the Tree of Independence in the garden?" In frustration, Tikvah crossed his arms across his chest, and leaned in toward Glaurius.

Sofia responded, "Tikvah, my son, as the seraf of science, you understand better than anyone that the spirit and fundamental nature of all life is for infinite increase, to express and expand its influence and glory – for all things are wonderful and beautiful and valuable. Life is abundance, reproduction, perfection, order, and harmony in the myriad manifestations of all things. We cannot control the freedom of serafs or man, without violating the very laws of existence; freedom by definition must be free."

Korban picked up the conversation. "There are, however, consequences for violating the laws of science and of life – operating by any other spirit besides selfless love, peace and trust releases a force which will eventually stop the activity and the one who violates the Way. The Law of Entropy is the polar opposite of the Law of Life. If Mogen and Cheva choose to explore the knowledge of good and evil, and peep into realms of dark power, they will unleash this; we have given them authority, but if they surrender that right, whatever they yield to will become their master."

He looked intently into the eyes of the chiefs, seeing the struggle and sorrow within. Masos spoke softly, the dagger twisting in his heart. "You are talking about Chag, aren't you, Brother?"

Korban's eyes, too, reflected deep pain, as he nodded sadly, then turned away to gaze into the fire burning in the brazier at their feet. Silence fell upon them all as they pondered these things and with fire in his eyes, Glaurius explained the events that would soon unfold.

"He will amass a third of the gibborim against us, so we

must prepare the others. There will be searching of hearts, and broken friendships that will bring upheaval to our peace for a season, but in the end, those who make themselves our enemies will be driven out forever, and will wish they had never seen life."Rage burned in his eyes.

"How do we inform and discuss these things with the serafs and gibbors not knowing who can be trusted?" Masos played with his staff and flipped it behind his massive neck, wrapping his arms around it, rubbing the smooth cedar with his calloused hands.

"It will not be that hard to maintain secrecy, as Chag's narcissism blinds him to all but his desire for power," Glaurius interjected. "Pride and ambition replace his love and loyalty; he thinks very little now about his betrayal, fueled as he is by the intoxicating flattery of his followers. And frankly, since he has never seen any, he expects no consequences for his actions."

He continued. "But in this, he is most deceived, for his passions will dig a pit for him from which he will never escape.' He added, thoughtfully, "And something else: there is a timing issue here. His sin must become fully formed, and clearly manifested before we can respond, or we will forever be accused of dealing harshly; Chag's rebellion must be evident to all, and then we will cast him out."

Despite his intensity, tears rolled unchecked down his cheeks, shining like diamonds in his wooly beard, while satisfied now with a strategy, the gibbors fell silent.

Glaurius wiped his face with a linen cloth, and rose to say goodnight. With his cup lifted high, he smiled broadly at each one.

"Now, we must put these concerns to rest, for the time is not yet come upon us. Let's turn our attention instead to the joys of love, because we have a wedding to celebrate tomorrow!"

The others rose also, and joined in the toast. "Here, here, bless the happy couple!"

Chapter Eight

The horseshoe and volleyball pits were raked, and the grass on the badminton and bocce lawns mowed. The tennis courts were rolled, and Glaurius ran around the bases of his newly chalked baseball diamond, sliding into home – just to test it out. Sofia – in pigtails – checked off tasks on a clipboard, while Korban strode up with a gang of young serafs carrying croquet mallets. Sofia smiled as he approached, and he kissed her on the cheek. The serafs quickly organized their wickets on the spot, and throwing down the colorful wooden balls, began to play.

Dance music came from the musicians nearby, as the serafs pogoed around the field.

"They are so competitive, it's crazy," Korban said, laughing at their antics.

"Have you seen your brother yet?" Sofia regretted her question when she observed the ache in his eyes, and reached out to push back the curls from his beautiful face.

"It's hard to see Mogen wed, while you must wait, isn't it?"

"Yes, Mother." She kissed his cheek, and pulled him near. "You are my dearest treasure, Son, and your heart of humility and patience, your mercy and goodness, is so sweet. The fullness of time will bring her to you, and it will be well worth the wait."

Korban nodded thoughtfully, looking into the future. He sighed wistfully. "You are right, Mother. But sometimes a day feels like a thousand years."

"I know, she said sympathetically. And yes, I've seen Mogen – he and Father are hiking Mount Yehudah. He's totally goofy over Chevah and needed to burn off some energy." He chuckled as he returned to the croquet match. "We're going to get ready together in the lake house after a swim and breakfast." He nodded at the serafs as he hit several balls with his, and they groaned as their balls flew across the field.

"They're not the only competitive ones," Sofia laughed, and returned to her work.

As the day wore on into late afternoon, everyone retired to nap and then dress for the ceremony, and the food was delivered to the dining tent. Matronly serafs in aprons with pleasant, chubby cheeks supervised the unloading of the food onto tables, that groaned under the weight of the dizzying array of juicy pears, peaches, grapes, berries and tropical fruits of every kind (fresh and glazed), and every kind of cheese – including the nutty Edam and buttery Gouda for which the creamery was famous.

Baskets of hearty rye and caraway loaves, crunchy wheat and oat baguettes, and fat rounds of kalamata olive and rosemary, and bowls of creamy butter filled the tables, along with platters and bowls of grilled vegetables and salads, lasagna, macaroni and cheese, Shepherd's Pie, and quiches, snowy mashed potatoes, and red-jacket potatoes with chives and garlic.

Lastly, set onto long tables at the back of the tents, came the still-warm pies, fragrant cobblers, dense chocolate cakes and brownies, cheesecake with raspberries, rice pudding made with coconut milk and plump raisins, vanilla bean, peach, butter praline, coffee and chocolate ice cream that chilled in oaken, hand-cranked freezers. The serafs filled pitchers of water from the Stream of Life, and by early evening, they had finished all their work.

Meanwhile, in the tents of the gibborim, a fight was brewing, as Chag's poisonous lies took root in the fertile soil of pride and self, found in the hearts of the faithless. Conversations became bolder, questioning the foundations of love for others, and serving, humility, and honor on which Tziyon was built.

"But Chag, we must attend the wedding, and be careful to be seen as helpful, and supportive. Maybe there is a misunderstanding. Certainly we can talk to Glaurius – he is kind and just."

"Shut up, you maggot. Who are you to address the chief of the gibborim?" The trooper raised his fist to Aiden, a scribe, who backed up several steps in utter shock. Chag nodded his approval at the assailant, and cast a disdainful smirk at the astonished gibbor. Softening, he approached him, and placed his massive hands on his shoulders, looking into the frightened eyes in a fatherly manner.

"It's a new day, son. I am sorry to break the terrible news to you, but The Three – Glaurius, Sofia and Korban – well, we have evidence that we gibborim and serafs were originally created to be co-heirs and rulers here in Tziyon – just like the adam - but because The Three fear sharing that authority, they have kept this knowledge and privilege from us."

Aiden's eyes widened in disbelief.

"I know, I know," Chag responded. "You cannot believe it – neither could I. But with my revelatory gift, I saw it all clearly the morning Glaurius presented the adam to us. Surely something resonated within you, too, when he said they were to be rulers and gods of the new earth, and that *we* would serve *them?*"

Aiden continued to gape at Chag's fanatical ramblings.

"Yes, that's when I knew. I knew that though we have faithfully served The Three for millennia, this new creature was not a gift – a reward – for that service, but rather a power play! I have a growing number of the clans who will follow me, and we will take control of this new earth, and rule over it, with the adam as our servants. He rubbed his hands together, and stared at the vision before him. "I only have to get them to give their authority to me, and then The Three will have to accept it; it will be mine by law!"

"*What?* What kind of perverse plan is this?" The scribe angrily pushed Chag's hands away from him, and thrust his finger in his face. "You feel that because Mogen and Cheva were given rule and authority over the new earth and that we are to serve them, we are somehow diminished? What is higher than *serving*, Chag? You are the angel of worship and music, of the arts - your songs create atmospheres that influence the entire universe! Your beauty is beyond compare, and your position is secure for all eternity - how could you ever be dissatisfied or envious of anyone? And Glaurius *made* you! How could you betray him?"

Chag smiled wanly at the praise, and then responded

condescendingly to the reminder of Glaurius's supremacy. "Scribe, there are some things beyond your ability to comprehend. Better left to wiser heads. But trust me when I say that things are about to change, and if you wish to keep any shred of pride and position, you will join me."

Aiden was on his way out the door, as Chag turned to the gibborim who now encircled him, their arms crossed decisively across their chests. He called after him.

"Join us, little scribe - for there *is* something far greater than serving; it is called *ruling*. Oh, and don't worry, we'll be at the wedding. After all, I am The Muse."

The mob erupted in shrieks and grunts of mocking laughter, as rage burned in the heart of the loyal scribe.

Chapter Nine

K orban approached the cascading waterfall the serafs
had created as a backdrop for the wedding ceremony.
To the side, Chag attended to the musicians, who were
busy tuning their instruments, and vocalizing. The
seraf of song released the strings, horns, percussion and wind
devices inside him, the sound swelled and billowed,
resounding with power, but Korban felt only rebellion and
violence in the music.

The two locked eyes, and Korban saw mistrust and hatred
in the one he so loved, and had fashioned with his own hands.
Keeping his gaze on Korban, Chag spoke to the musicians. "I
will not be playing, but only directing this time - you all know
your parts." The cheerful serafs smiled and nodded,
unsuspecting. "Yes, it is your opportunity to shine - apart from
me."

Korban, relieved to get away from Chag, walked to
Mogen's tent. "Permission to enter, Brother?"

"Permission granted!" Laughter spilled over him as he
entered the tent. He found Mogen on the floor, wrapped in ivy,
with flowers in his hair as several young serafs tugged on him.
A tickling contest erupted, and soon the screaming serafs were
running wildly around the tent. Korban quickly scooped up
two and leaped with them onto the bed where they jumped and
flipped - since all mattresses in Tziyon double as trampolines
and tumbling mats.

"Brother, help me - it's time to get dressed!" Mogen
crawled over to the sofa, and pulled himself up, shooing off the

little serafs. "Outta here," he said as he held aside the heavy fabric door, prodding the last stragglers in their behinds.

When he returned, Korban lay with his head hanging over the end of the bed, looking upside down at Mogen. He jumped up and grabbed Mogen, wrestling him to the floor, where they battled for several minutes. They finally stopped, and leaned against each other, panting for breath.

"So, Mogen, it's the big day. You must be pretty excited."

"I am, Korban, but I admit to feeling some anxiety about ruling the earth, the animals, and making something of it all. What if I fail?"

Korban smiled at his serious tone, but put his strong arm around him. "Mogen, nothing comes without risk, and risk is always uncertain in terms of outcomes. *But* you have everything you need, and you are never alone." He paused, and played with a tassle on the rug. "And there is always faith – the ability to believe in good - and hope. Always have hope, Mogen, even if you feel disappointed or if somehow things go terribly wrong."

At this, Mogen looked up, but in Korban's eyes there were no answers, fear, or judgment, just a steady calm, like the blue of the sky on a summer day.

"You're talking about the tree again, aren't you?" Inside Mogen screamed for direction, but Korban remained silent about it.

"And most important of all, is love. Mogen, love is the seed from which we created you. It is the one thing that will never fail, and by which you will always know – deep down inside – whose you are. He took Mogen's face in his hands.

"And love always rescues."

Mogen cocked his head, puzzled, but seeing no explanation forthcoming, sighed, and rose to his feet. "Thank you Korban – for everything. I am so grateful for this life, for Cheva, for our home, and the trust you've placed in me – in us. I find the weight of responsibility quite a burden, and feel afraid of things I cannot control – like whether or not Cheva – or our children or anyone will eat from the tree. I spend a lot of time thinking about how I can keep everyone from it. But it grows alongside the Tree of Life, which we need."

"Mogen, always listen to the truth in your heart. As you study the Way of the kingdom, temptation will disappear. *That* is the legacy you can pass on to your children. You will become what you focus on."

Mogen brightened up at the encouragement. "All right then, Big Brother – let's do this!" He grabbed the linen wedding shirt Sofia had made for him, and slipped it over his head. It fell open at the neck, and the sleeves flowed over his strong, tanned arms.

"Alright, turn around now, Korban while I put my pants on." Korban laughed at his modesty, waiting while Mogen pulled on the knee-length pants, and slipped on a pair of sandals. "You can look now."

Korban spun around on his heel, assessing the outfit. "You look pretty handsome, but here, I have more gifts for you." Korban reached into the pouch in his shirt, and pulled out gold earrings, and a gold bracelet with a large piece of turquoise, and offered them to Mogen.

"I made these for you – a gift for your wedding day." Mogen took them, smiling, and slipped them on. The turquoise responded to Mogen as he spoke, and light shone when he touched it with the palm of his hand. "What is this, Korban? What does it do?"

"It's a stone of prophecy – from the Mountain of Yehudah. With it, you can communicate with any of us when we're not around, and we will answer you." Mogen took off the bracelet, and studied the other side. "The writing here Korban – what does it say?" Korban took it from him, turning it over and over.

"It is the secret name of Glaurius, and some day you will know what it means." He laughed at Mogen's furrowed brow, as he attempted to figure out the strange figures. "Forget it, Mogen, it's time to go!"

Mogen brushed back the errant curls that fell over his eyes, and stood radiant before Korban.

"You are awesome in majesty, Brother. Abba will be here shortly, and we will escort you to your bride." He smiled broadly at Mogen and clapped his shoulders. "This is truly a wonderful day."

Just then, laughter from the friends of the groom drifted into the tent, as Glaurius and twelve gibborim warriors came down the grassy lane. Korban glanced around the tent, and then at Mogen, "Are you ready?"

Mogen set his face, and nodded. "Yes, I am!" For a split second, Korban saw the suffering Mogen would face, and he marveled. *Such a courageous spirit…how I love him!* "Well, they're here, so let's be off."

Mogen bounded to pull aside the opening for Glaurius.

When the king and the gibborim saw him, they paused in their revelry, drinking in the splendor of the young prince. Glaurius went to him, and hugged him tight. "My beloved son, you are like the sun that rises in the east, and your power like the planets in motion. Such perfection and beauty."

Taking the jewel-studded crown from the seraf at his side, he placed it on Mogen's head, blessing him. "You are altogether wonderful. You will rule the earth we have created, and then all things will be made new."

At these last words, the gibborim looked puzzled, but remained silent, wondering what he could mean about "all things will be made new." But Mogen did not pick up on the prophecy.

Korban came out and joined the group, and soon they were jostling one another, and singing loudly, carrying Mogen on their shoulders to the wedding grounds.

Meanwhile, Sofia and several serafs attended to Cheva. Her gown of white linen was woven with gold, scarlet, and blue thread, and on her head, they placed a garland of red roses, with ribbons streaming down. As a seraf helped, Cheva arranged the garland, and cried out. "Ouch! What was *that?*" Sofia took her hand, and wiped away the droplets of blood.

"A thorn, my dear. That was a thorn." Sofia took a rose from a nearby vase, and brought it to show her, lifting up the leaves to reveal the sharp barbs along the stem.

"I thought we removed them all from your garland, I'm sorry."

"Ama, why are there thorns on the flowers? They're so beautiful, but if you don't know about them, you can get hurt."

"Indeed, Cheva. Thorns are there to protect the roses from being overrun by animals, or destroyed by birds – the thorns give the creatures respect for flowers, which are here to beautify the earth. Flowers are for your enjoyment, but if they are trampled underfoot, or eaten, what joy would they bring to you?"

"Ama, you are so wise."

Sofia smiled at the compliment.

"Cheva, you have a protection of your own – words of wisdom within you – to keep you from harm." She came near to stroke the long, dark curls. Tipping Cheva's chin up to look into her eyes, she smiled, caressing her face. "You are altogether lovely, my darling. Like a rose among the thorns, so is my love among all others." Cheva closed her eyes, and placed her hand over her mother's. Sofia began to sing a lullabye, and Cheva drifted on the waves of peace.

They heard the sounds of the groom's party as it approached, and a seraf entered, announcing Glaurius had arrived. Cheva trembled with anticipation and excitement, and ran to greet him as he entered her tent. His radiance hit her, and the two embraced in a blaze of glory. When they released, all the attendants lay prostrate on the floor, laughing and soaking in the deep peace and contentment.

"See how you are, Abba?" Cheva asked and kissed his cheek with great affection. Glaurius stood over Sofia, who lay lost in joy on the divan. She reached for his hand, and stood unsteadily to her feet. They held each other and watched Cheva as she stood before the mirror, finishing her preparations. Glaurius came and stood beside Cheva, and a seraf appeared with a tray of jewelry - gifts which the king had commissioned for her wedding day.

She turned to him, and he took up the gold crown studded with stones in every color of the rainbow, and accented with diamonds.

"I crown you with glory – the same glory we have – to rule over our creation." He placed it on her head, and she turned to look at Sofia, and then at her reflection in the full-length mirror. The serafs and attendants all bowed as she turned around, the flash of majesty felling them at once.

Sofia took the matching necklace and clasped it behind her head, the stones slipped into place together adorning her strong neck and shoulders. She took the bracelets – one for each arm, and slipped them high around her biceps. Two rings – a ruby, and jasper fit on her index fingers.

Her attendants stood beside and behind her, as Glaurius, with Mogen and his attendants went ahead to wait for them at the wedding site.

Outside, the colors of day faded into soft evening, streaks of violet, gold and scarlet painting the sky, and the crescent moon hanging like a lamp, with the evening star at the lower tip, a brilliant diamond.

A band of gibborim and serafs led the procession with violins, flutes, guitars, clarinets and drums. The crowd swelled to thousands in the field, with many thousands more serafs and gibborim filling the skies overhead. Animals and birds thronged the trees, and the outskirts of the fields. Cheva rounded the corner of the tent city, astonished at the scene before her. Cheers erupted and the sound was deafening, in the light of a thousand torches.

But perched high in the forbidden tree, glaring at the throng, Chag cursed all those gathered there. Then hearing a sound below, he spied the glittering serpent climbing up to him.

"Well, Serpent, how is it that an unthinking creature like you is exploring this tree? He looked into the vacant eyes, but could comprehend nothing there. The serpent's beguiling tongue and undulating movements captivated him, and as he reached out, it quickly clambered over to him, and caressed his face, like a cat. Suddenly, a thought came to him. A very sinister thought.

"Serpent," he said, stroking the reptile. "Would you like to be *very* close to me?" It responded wordlessly by standing on its hind legs and nodding its head. "Well, then, I have an excellent idea. Close your eyes, open your mouth wide, and I will come inside of you!"

With that, the gibbor entered into the serpent, and the eyes of the creature snapped opened and shut, as Chag now looked out from inside.

Chapter Ten

Ruby-red roses and snow-white lilies festooned the grassy lane along the processional route, which was outlined by scented olive oil torches that illuminated the velvety black night. Stars sparkled in the heavens, and the planets in their orbits sang the love-song of eternity, the echoes of the ethereal music drifting down over the serafs and musicians, who joined in singing.

At the head of the throng, Glaurius and Sofia, Korban, Masos and Tikvah waited with the friends of the groom. Magnificent in royal splendor, their robes of gold and purple, scarlet and blue, and their glittering crowns and jewels shone in the flickering lamplight. Mogen stood transfixed, as Cheva nobly strode the length of the field, the train of her dress carried by her attendants. Cheva took Mogen's hand as they came together under the linen canopy, and they turned to face the crowd. Wild cheering erupted as they waved, and when it died down, Glaurius moved to stand in front and lead the couple in their vows.

"With the founding of this imperial race, we offer our devotion, our help, and our unending love. Receive our blessing to expand in limitless ways throughout the ages, and may the sons and daughters born to you, dream and create with boundless freedom, a happy, adventurous, beautiful, and peaceful world."

Turning to Mogen, he asked, "Mogen, what is in your heart for Cheva, and for those assembled here?"

Mogen spoke to Cheva, "Cheva, you are part of me, and

my love and desire for you is immense. I promise to keep you as chief among my pursuits, that our friendship and pleasure would be foremost in my heart. I promise to share all that I am with you, so our connection will bring wholeness to us both, and vision to our children. I vow to love you always." With one hand, he took her fingers to his lips and kissed them, and caressed her face with the other.

Cheva looked adoringly into his eyes, and then at Glaurius, who nodded for her to speak. "Mogen, you are king of this realm, and I am honored to be your companion and queen. I promise to excel in the gifts I possess, to advise and support you in all we do here. I will be devoted and sensitive to your heart, and loyal in friendship. With Father, Mother, and Korban, as our helpers, I will look to them, and work with you in unity and love. And I will teach our children well in the ways of wisdom and trust."

Sofia and Korban came forward with a long garland of red linen, and weaving it around their necks and across their hearts, they tied it behind Mogen and Cheva, who stood face to face. "With this act, we solemnize your covenant, and declare you husband and wife." Mogen kissed Cheva for the first time – a long and hungry kiss – then turned to the crowd and let out a shout of elation. Cheva trembled with anticipation and desire. The couple turned to face the crowd, and addressed them.

"Gibborim, serafs, animals, Earth and Heaven, as your king, I vow to treat you always with honor and in consideration of your highest good. I – we – with your help, will seek to create a world of maximum pleasure and perfection for all. Trust in us, and we will care for you, and love you always."

Masos released the garland and wound it up, handing it to Cheva, with a bow of his head. "My lady, Cheva." She took it from him, and after thanking and hugging The Three and the attendants, took Mogen by the hand, and led him to the bridal pavilion in the center of the field. Almost there, Mogen swept her up, and grinning to the crowd, ducked inside the folds of the tent.

* * *

Hearing every word from his lookout in the Tree, Chag shook with rage, and climbed with nimble serpent feet to the ground. "Their happinessssssss will not lassssssst one harvest year, or I am not the Sssssson of the Morning!" He again cursed

The Three, the serafs and gibbors, Mogen, Cheva, and the new creation, coveting bitterly the authority given to the man and woman.

But his conscience, growing faint, spoke one last time, its voice barely audible now above the inner clamor of pride and anger. *But you are so loved, and Tziyon is your home – there is none like you...*"Ssssssilence!" he shrieked. "There isssss no going back – I have made up my mind. For I can now sssssee the truth sssssso clearly. No, I will be like Glaurius, and I will exalt my throne above the heavens of Tziyon. I will be king of this new world order!"

Chag slipped unseen into the undergrowth and deep into the woods, to wait for an opportune time. "They will come some morning - to walk with Glauriusssss in the cool of the day - but I will meet them firssssst."

* * *

The feasting and merriment continued for days, and afterward, the newest creation settled into life as the lords of Earth. Days turned into weeks, and then months, as Mogen and Chevah enjoyed life in the garden, tending and researching every kind of fruit tree and vine, and every type of vegetable, bean, seed and nut that would grow in the rich soil, under the vibrant sun.

The water canopy above the planet kept the soil perfectly hydrated each night, and every morning, the pair rose from their slumber in the midst of the orchards to eat, tend the animals, and begin their work. And Glaurius would visit, often with presents, or delightful treats from the bakers of Glaury Hall.

Everything was perfect; they had no worries, and every day was better than the day before.

Mogen usually woke before Chevah, and spent several seconds just staring at her beauty, thanking Glaurius in his heart for her. "Abba, you have given me such a perfect friend and lover. She is everything I could ever want and need in a companion, thank you."

He heard the king's response in his heart. "It was our good pleasure. Now be fruitful and have lots of sex." Mogen laughed, waking Chevah, who glanced over at him with an adoring, sleepy grin. "Mogen, what are you *doing?*" though she knew perfectly well. She reached out and pulled him to her, laughing, and they disappeared under the fluffy covers for some time.

When they finally stepped out from the tent, the sun was already well up, and it shone on their brown bodies, warming them, and imparting life. A black panther that slept with its mate outside their entrance at night, stretched itself, and rubbed against them.

"Umgar, you are such a big kitty!" The big cat nuzzled them affectionately, and padded off to the crystal stream running through the garden. The other animals grazed, and played throughout the garden: giraffes with new babies plucked bamboo leaves from the upper branches in the marshy lowlands, and lions snoozed or wrestled in a large group, in the big field beyond. Monkeys rode zebras, and dogs and cats played together with hippos, and alligators. Chevah glanced up the hill at Glaury Hall, the pinnacles of the palace sparkling like jewels in the morning air. The hundred crimson banners with the three gold lions floated in the breeze, and she saw Glaurius bounding down the hill toward them.

"Here comes Abba," she cried, and ran off to greet him, flanked by eager animals and colorful squawking birds. His snowy-white hair and beard made a cloud of wool around his face and head, and his smiling blue eyes were filled with delight at the sight of his daughter. But none was more attentive to his presence than the serpent, who now shared the tent with the royal couple, so dependent had they become on his affectionate loyalty, wisdom and skill.

"Darling, girl! How are you on this fine day?" Glaurius scooped her into his arms, and they enjoyed the embrace for a long moment. He savored her expressive love and unguarded affection. A fluttering bluebird appeared, and settled on his shoulder, then flew a short way off. Suddenly Sofia stood before them, radiant in a lavender gown, her hair braided with gold, scarlet and blue thread, interwoven with jewels.

"Ama, good morning!" Chevah withdrew from Glaurius and moved into the arms of Sofia, who stroked her hair, and kissed her face, smiling over Chevah's head at her contented husband.

Mogen had caught up to the three, and hugged Glaurius impulsively, lifting him off the ground a couple of feet. When he set him back down, Glaurius grabbed him, but Mogen slipped away, and started running down the hill, toward the mown fields. Glaurius, quick as lightning, overtook him, and ran beyond, leaping and dancing on the carpet of emerald-green grass.

Dozens of animals and birds joined in the play. Sofia and Chevah held hands and walked back through the orchards, picking fruit and eating breakfast as they strolled along, the serpent dutifully trotting behind Cheva, like a little dog.

Chevah pointed out the work she and Mogen had begun yesterday on the thinning out of the trees, and when they arrived back in front of their tent, she opened up the blueprints they had begun, pointing out the plans for the various groves of trees.

They had begun months ago to tackle the orchards and large trees first, and then moved on to the bushes, vines, and smaller plants. They also continued to discover the talents of the animals, and how they could be used to help in the work of the Garden. Obviously, some were larger, and were used for bigger projects, like digging, moving earth, or toppling trees, and the smaller ones could trim or organize, and clear away branches, but each one had something they could do.

"So we are now going to make a number of groupings - forests - with the trees. I like the idea of a large forest filled with beech, oak and elms - a deeply shaded grove where our children can play hide and seek, and the nocturnal animals can hide and rest during the day. Mogen also wants to have a Grove of Giants filled with redwoods and the slightly smaller cedars."

She turned to the serpent. "And thanks to this little guy, we realized that the larger animals and reptiles can use these for scratching, and sharpening their talons and beaks. They will also find privacy in the recesses of these woods, to have their young." She petted the serpent's head, and looked up at Sofia, who beamed with pride.

"Excellent ideas." She pointed to a colorful mass of trees in a corner of the diagram. "And what is this?" Chevah nodded excitedly.

"Oh this is one of my favorites! Here we will have a meadow of every color of tree blossom - white, yellow, pink, purple, blue, red, lavender, and orange. And none of these has perfume so there won't be scent overload. Instead - twelve types of scented trees - or some combination based on complementarity of scent - will be planted together in groves, and will bloom and give off their odors for one month, consecutively, so there will be perfume all year long."

"Just brilliant, Chevah, I can't wait!" Chevah pointed out the conifer forests, and the incense groves, and the groves of exotic trees.

"Yes, Ama, we are so glad you made the big reptiles that can help in this work. They're truly magnificent." Sensing she was referring to it, the male stegosaurus rose to its full height, and shook out its plated armor in the warm sun. It lowered its head majestically, and Chevah patted his rough cheek. He closed his eyes, and sighed happily.

"You are such a lover, Samson." Sofia kissed his forehead, and he lumbered off, pounding his legs in glee, and shaking the ground with his antics. "Hahahahaha, he's just a big baby!"

Chevah nodded in agreement. Sofia turned to her, with a happy smile.

"Speaking of babies, what have you and Mogen discussed about them?"

Days passed pretty much like this, for weeks, and then months, with the daily visits from The Three to the Garden, where they worked with Mogen and Chevah managing the animals, plants, water, and food. Every Saturday, the pair spent the day at Glaury Hall, and outside with the serafs, eating, hiking, exploring and playing.

* * *

Meanwhile, Chag's army was growing, as he worked his poisonous betrayal into the ranks of the serafs and gibborim - just enough to start the wheels of dissatisfaction turning, but not too fast, lest he reveal his dark plan prematurely, and miss his greatest opportunity. And in and out of the body of the serpent he went, while Mogen and Chevah knew nothing of it.

But finally the time came to move against The Throne, and he assembled his followers in the Valley of the Winds. Led up a low hill by his inner cabal of high-level officers, he stood above them all, and began his speech on a rocky outcropping.

"Greetings, Brothers! My heart swells as I look at your vast numbers, stretching to the horizon. I have been informed that a third of the Mighty Ones have now fled from the false love of Glaurius. I applaud you for your great courage, and wisdom!"

A roar of approval erupted from the crowd. Chag continued. "I have decided that is is the hour to present our demands to Glaurius. He must grant our request, or we will oppose him by force. *We* demand to rule over The New World, and receive the honor and glory that is rightfully ours. There we will establish the headquarters of our kingdom, and rule over mankind; we will be their gods."

Every voice was silent as he explained, awed at his audacity, but also anxious at the very real possibility of losing. A low-ranking gibbor stuttered out the thoughts of the rest.

"And what if Glaurius refuses, my lord Chag, and we fail? The Three are sovereign, no one can oppose them." Chag stared him down, before turning back to the crowd.

"Generals, captains, and lieutenants, my kings and princes, if The Three will not comply with our request, we will do battle against The Throne. And if we lose, we will likely be banished, but I have a plan." He puffed out his chest.

"There are great possibilities for us in the unexplored darkness. In the event that we are cast out, we will still rule over men and women, and they will be our slaves - make no mistake."

He squared his shoulders. "I have already made my decision – regardless of the outcome - I want no part of this nefarious kingdom any longer!"

His voice trailed off, as he envisioned the scene in his diabolical mind. "They are so foolish and trusting of Glaurius, so innocent..." He closed his eyes, sighing deeply with cruel satisfaction. "Yes, everything is so perfect in their little world; they will never suspect the danger. Very soon now, I will make my move, and they will give their authority to me by their own weakness and transgression."

He grinned wickedly, rubbing his hands together."It will be especially sweet to tempt the woman - such a silly, inferior creature."

He bellowed again to the crowd of worshipers at the foot of the mountain, his fist raised to the Heavens.

"And we will crush them, and use them, and mar the image of The Three in them; we will expunge all knowledge of Their Infernal Majesties from their memories, forever!"

At this, he began to laugh insanely, leaping around in a manic dance, joined by the iniquitous horde; he carried on, whirling, shrieking, and playing jarring notes on stringed instruments, producing loud buzzing on zithers, and endless staccato drum beats, making songs of war; and for hours, the throng of rebels joined in, filling the skies with violence and dread, and making their declarations of loyalty to Chag, bowing before him, hailing him as "Ba'al Aruni" - Lord of the Cursed Ones - in a mockery of the fellowship of the blessed.

And finally they withdrew to prepare their terrible

instruments of war.

And when the hour had come, they approached the City, assembled in their ranks before the gates of Tziyon; down into the canyon, snaked the long, black line of reprobate gibborim, like a river of filthy water.

The Three came forth from the palace, with Masos and Tikvah on either side. Power radiated from them, and as the messenger of Ba'al Aruni stepped forward, he was thrown back by the force. Tikvah reached out for the scroll that contained the dark lord's demands.

Suddenly overhead, a rushing sound moved the air, and Chag appeared before them on a magnificent black horse. Dressed in a white robe of the finest silk, his radiance shone forth like the sun. His minions held their breath at his beauty, as he waited, his face twisted in a mocking sneer, for a response from the King.

"Here is our response, Chag." Korban signaled to a seraf on the wall above them, and as the seraf lifted the silver trumpet to his lips and blew, the sky was filled with an innumerable company of gibborim, all armed with terrifying weapons, and fierce in appearance. They filled every empty space, and the hordes of Aruni began to tremble and quake, hemmed in on every side.

And the stars themselves shook with horror, as their Great King stood opposed by his most magnificent creature. But with one word from Glaurius's lips, the faithful gibborim engaged, and threw out The Pretender and his evil army, whose falling was like lightning from the sky.

And the innumerable multitude of gibborim followed hard after them, driving the wicked traitors out from the Presence, and the City, leaving them forever to wander in the waste places of the spirit.

* * *

One very early morning when it was still dark, Cheva and Mogen rose to go out into the orchards, to see the new growth on the trees. Aruni, having accustomed the serpent to his presence, had entered the creature in the night, and when he saw they were awake, the creature lifted his head and shook his glorious plumage out, preparing to follow them.

"No, my Precious One, you cannot go with us just now. Sleep tight and we will return later." Cheva smiled and kissed him on the head.

The scent of honesuckle, jasmine, and juniper hung in the air as they slipped quietly out of the tent, and strolled hand in hand down the lane between the almond trees. Clouds of snowy blossoms released their intoxicating perfume, white petals glistening in the moonlight, as the lovers passed by, whispering, and nuzzling, and pausing to kiss. Finally, Mogen pulled Cheva down beneath a tree, and hidden by the screen of flowers and low branches, they made love in the silvery light of the fading moon. Afterward, they dressed, Cheva putting on her pale yellow gown, and silver sandals, while Mogen slipped a soft cape over her shoulders, to keep out the slight chill.

And gliding along in the underbrush was the Serpent, silent as death, watching and listening...

After they ate their fill from the basket of bread, and cheese, and drank the honey-wine they had packed, light appeared at the edge of the horizon, and violet, blue and pink streaks spread across the sky.

"Oh, Mogen, let's please go inside the wall, to the Trees. I want to eat from The Tree of Life."

He gaped at her in horror.

Cheva quickly added. "Mogen, I have been thinking. Our life is so perfect here. But I know that we are not yet eternal, and I don't want anything to ever stop what we have. The fruit of the Tree of Life is the most desirable of all, and I wish to eat it and live forever! Then we can forget about the wall, for the other tree can never harm us, or our children. I find I am thinking about the Trees more and more - and Abba said we could eat from every tree except the Tree of Independence. So why do you stop me?"

Mogen looked at her earnest face. "Cheva, there is nothing I would ever deny you – and there is nothing for us to fear in this place. All is ours, and all is good. But it is better to stay far from the trees, so let's forget about them for now."

Cheva pouted, and stood apart from him, determined to press her case. "The truth is, Mogen, you are afraid, but I am not; Glaurius has said we can eat from the Tree of Life, but you have walled it up. She softened a little, and came closer. "Come on, aren't you at all curious? What could go wrong? Abba never said we couldn't go near the trees."

Mogen's resolve melted away; he couldn't argue with her

point. Fear was taking its toll, anyway, as the bad dreams had increased, because he thought about the Tree all the time. He sighed, and reached for her hand, pulling it to his lips, and kissing her fingers lightly. Pushing back a stray curl from her face, he answered.

"Of course, My Love, you are right. There is no reason to avoid the Tree of Life. Come; let's go face this temptation head-on."

Chevah squeezed him, dancing with delight as they walked on together, and came to the barricade. Mogen ran off, and came back with a box he had hidden in the underbrush.

Removing a large key, he turned it in the lock, and thrust aside the heavy oaken door.

As they stepped inside, the rays of the sun burst over the wall, and they stood entranced as the Tree of Independence shimmered like a precious jewel; it began to release the fragrance of its fruit, caressing their nostrils, and seducing them to taste of it.

The more they stared, the greater grew the desire to eat. "What a beautiful tree - and the fruit looks delicious!"

Mogen ripped his eyes away from the tree, but the desire for the fruit was strong. Still, as soon as he looked away, the power was less overwhelming. Confused, and nervous, he took her hand. "Let's just eat from the other tree, and get out of here, Cheva I feel perplexed by this tree."

The struggle on his face frightened, and then irritated her, but she was momentarily distracted by a rustle in the bushes. Undulating rainbow colors appeared, and the quick-moving serpent scaled the tree, popping his head out from the deep green leaves above her. The creature laid his head on his forelegs, next to an enormous ripe peach, looked at her and exhaled: the scent of the fruit hit Cheva, almost knocking her over. Longing and uncertainty churned in her heart, while Chag made his move.

"Hello, my Lady! How delightful to sssssee you and Massssster Mogen here thisssss beautiful morning." The reptilian eyes opened and shut, and the serpent slid down a little closer to Cheva. Mesmerized, Cheva stood mute, while Mogen also remained transfixed by the seductive speech of the serpent, and his eyes kept returning to the fruit covering the tree.

"Yesssss, I have prepared a gift for you. You sssssee thisssss issssss *my* tree, and the fruit isssss mine to give – there

71

isssss no fruit ssssso lussssscioussssrs and dessssssirable in the entire Garden."

Cheva stammered a response, "Wait a minute! This isn't your tree, and Glaurius warned us that if we eat from this tree, we will die!" For effect, she added, "He said we shouldn't even touch it!" She glanced over at Mogen who shook his head vigorously in agreement.

"Not even touch it? Nonsense!" The force of the Serpent's words startled her, but he suddenly vanished, and reappeared on another branch, leaning down to gently whisper in her ear. The ever-moving scales mesmerized her, and the sweetness of his melodic voice drew her in. She closed her eyes.

"The reassssson Glauriussssss told you that, issssss becaussssse he knowsssss when you eat of the fruit of thissss tree your mindssssss will be open to the Truth, and you will be like him – like *them*." Chag almost spat out the words in venomous anger, but calmed himself. He could see the wheels turning inside her head, as she considered what this could mean. Doubts about Glaurius, Sofia and Korban popped into her mind, and her heart battled to speak.

Don't listen to him! As the war raged, a juicy peach fell, and bumped against her feet. She reached over instinctively, while Chag sighed contentedly, and Mogen remained immobile, helplessly watching nearby, his thoughts racing about Glaurius, and all that the Serpent had said. Cheva held it up, and turned it around and around in her hands, inspecting it for signs of danger.

"Mogen, I see nothing wrong with this fruit. What is going on here? What is Abba keeping from us?" She glanced at the Serpent who now lay on his back, playing a tune on a small wooden flute. The tension built within her, and as the music closed in, she suddenly, impulsively plunged her teeth into the soft-firm flesh of the peach. A blissful smile spread across her face, as she handed it off to Mogen.

"It is the most incredible thing I have ever tasted! Here, My Love, take it and eat. Trust me." Mogen glanced guiltily around for a sign, or for help, but seeing the look of joy and innocence on his wife's face, he took the remaining fruit from her, and ate.

Chapter Eleven

Mogen gaped in stunned disbelief, at the image of Cheva before him; what he feared most had indeed come to pass. The Serpent jumped to a higher branch, anticipating the wrath of the man, but as he swallowed the intoxicating fruit, Mogen stood immobile, unable to respond.

The powerful light which had radiated from within her, disappeared as suddenly as a candle snuffed out; the look of ecstasy slowly giving way to horror, as she cried out and tried to flee invisible dangers. Dark, sinister, and terrifying images and thoughts flooded into her mind, and choked her heart with fear.

Mogen had not yet noticed what was happening to him, but she covered her mouth and pointed at him, beginning to faint. He rushed to her side, as she screamed and beat the air, begging him to help her, but he quickly discovered he no longer had the ability to respond with wisdom and love; her plight created a tortured mixture of compassion, disgust, fear, and anger inside him, and he lost patience, grabbing her wrists with one hand, while roughly slamming his other hand over her mouth to stifle the maddening sounds.

She cowed in panic, going limp in his arms, but her eyes told all. His heart broke, while his fragmented mind raced to find a solution to the crazed activity. For now, Cheva stood still as a statue, though trembling with adrenalin, and her colorless face showed growing exhaustion.

"Cheva, my darling! What have you done? He reached to stroke her face, and she ripped her arms away from him.

"What did *I* do? What did *I* do? You were standing right over there listening to the whole thing, but you never said a word!"

Mogen felt as though he had been slapped across the face, and it took all his self-control to not hit her. "Cheva! How dare you? I had no time to do anything – you took the fruit and bit into it before I could stop you!"

"That's your interpretation, Mogen. You should have known that I was in danger, and pulled me away from this damned tree!" But suddenly frightened at her words, her anger vanished as she searched his face, and came close for him to hold her. But his newly-acquired pride was ignited, and her nearness and accusations enraged him; he stood immovable, willing his body, soul and spirit to reject her, disgusted at her neediness. He rubbed her shoulders without feeling, then pulled her head back by the hair, making her wince in pain as he poured out his resentment in a lustful kiss. She tried to pull away, and he softened, wanting more, and took her in the dirt beneath the Tree.

Her desire for him burned, but a wall she could not scale now rose between them. Afterward, shame welled up inside her heart, as Mogen refused to look at her, and left her alone without explanation. Several hours later, he returned, and she ran to him, but stopped when she saw the cruelty and hardness in his eyes. Anxious that the anger in him might erupt again, she remained silent.

Staggering into the lane, she began to tear at her hair and clothes, pouring out her grief in sobs that wracked her whole body. She collapsed in the grass, and wept until her strength was gone. Mogen listened impotently to her tormented cries, but a thought soon dawned on him, and he began to slowly pound his fists into the ground.

"Abba, how terrible a thing you have done by placing this tree in the Garden." Bam!

"No, no - I no longer call you Father; you are cruel and terrible, and have destroyed us." Bam!

"Where are you now, great Father, great King? A great king are you? A loving king, are you?" Bam!

"No, you are nothing but a liar, and I will hate you forever for what you have done." Bam!

At this, Chag left the serpent, which forgotten by the two, awoke to the terrible drama it had precipitated. Chag slipped into the forest where he could hear yet remain out of sight, while the serpent, uncomprehending in its simple understanding, scurried off into the underbrush.

Suddenly, the familiar voice of Glaurius broke into the dreadful atmosphere.

"Mogen, Cheva, where are you?"

Cheva bolted up from the ground as if shot from a canon, and ran back to Mogen, who stood in the lane, legs spread apart, his eyes smoldering with rage. But when he saw the cloud which hid Glaurius, his fury melted into dread, and the two held each other tightly, terrified. They stood mute, confused and shaking, as the Presence came toward them. Their eyes darted frantically for a place to hide, as his presence felt terrible to them, though in his heart was only sorrow and pain at the evil now unleashed.

In a pitiable show of courage, Mogen placed Cheva protectively behind him, and faced the king. But before he could say a word, Glaurius spoke.

"Mogen, what have you done?" Oblivious to the turmoil in Glaurius' voice, Mogen steeled himself to answer. His bluster fled, and he turned and pointed accusingly.

"The woman you created gave me fruit from that tree."

Cheva's stunned look spoke the betrayal that gripped her heart.

As the cloud turned to her, she hissed, "That is not true! It's not my fault – I ate the fruit because the serpent lied to me!"

The creature had returned, and when Cheva pointed to it, it scurried hastily to hide behind the broad leaves of a fig tree. From within the veil, Glaurius looked at the misery on the faces of the three, sighing deeply.

The sound of rushing wind and a stirring of the grass at their feet signaled the arrival of Sofia, Korban, and the two gibborim chiefs. All surveyed the solemn scene, but they could no longer be seen by Mogen and Cheva.

Living now below the "light line," only physical reality was visible, and though Sofia approached Cheva with open arms, the barrier kept them apart. Cheva clung to Mogen, and turned her head away in shame.

"Cheva, my darling. It is I; do you not know me?" Tears burst from the corners of her tightly shut eyes, as she tried to bury her head in the unpitying hardness of Mogen's chest.

"I cannot see you, Ama, and I don't know anything anymore," she choked out pitifully.

Korban, walked toward Mogen, searching his face with deep compassion, but Mogen glanced hastily away, holding more tightly to Cheva.

"Dear Brother, what has happened here?"

Mogen snapped at him, "Isn't it obvious? We ate from this evil tree that you put here, and now we are lost, and dying." Korban's heart broke, and he reached out to touch him, but Mogen pulled away.

Glaurius spoke first to the serpent, which had yielded to Chag. "Because of what you have done, your body will act in response to this great folly; even now, your legs are shrinking and you will crawl in the dirt, on your belly, and you will be unable to hear the sounds of laughter, or of singing – you will be deaf. Your dazzling colors are replaced by markings representing the danger you possess, and there will always be hatred and fear between you and human beings."

He reached up to stroke the beast, whose legs disappeared, even as it came forth, slithering down the tree. Before their eyes, its brilliant appearance and plumage dropped off, and it became spotted with simple black and white bands. Glaurius shook his head, as the snake now stuck out its tongue seeking to navigate with inferior skills.

"It is truly dismal that this magnificent creature should come to such a fate. You were deaf to danger, and so now deaf to all sounds, you will be." All watched with sadness, as the reptile vanished silently.

Glaurius turned to Cheva. "Cheva, you had knowledge and power sufficient to resist this test, but not enough trust. Chag went into the serpent, and spoke to you, because he has rejected us and wants to be worshiped. He wanted your devotion, and now he has it; he is the new ruler of this world, because you chose to listen to him, and not to me."

In stunned horror, Cheva looked around slowly - first at Mogen, then at the cloud that hid the others, as the truth dawned on her, shame and despair pouring down like freezing rain, encasing her soul. Mogen's face tightened, as he steeled himself to this new reality. He turned desperate eyes to Glaurius. "Is there no hope, my father?" He cried out in spite of himself, all anger and pride, subsumed in anguish and need.

Glaurius turned pitying eyes to them both. "Cheva, because of this choice to seek your own truth, there will be no protection from us any longer. You see, we are the source of all your life; although your bodies will continue for a time, your essence no longer connects to ours. Our life is divine, immortal, perfect, all-wise, and the well of existence; you still have the memory of what is good, and the knowledge, but not the power to do it. Your ability to access this place, this reality is broken because your nature has been altered."

Cheva hung her head, bracing for more. Glaurius reluctantly continued. "You will have great pain in delivering children, and you will desire yada with Mogen, but he will now rule over you, because you have lost the ability to govern yourself fully. There will be fighting and struggle between you, as there is now, and that same battle will continue to your children, and their children."

Misery hung like a heavy stone around her neck, as she sunk to the dirt.

"Mogen, there is more. This creation will no longer respond to your voice, your commands, your administration; it doesn't know you or trust you any longer. Chag is the master here now, and under him you will work hard, and your body will ache until you return to the ground from which you came. I am so very sorry." Mogen just stared silently, as if envisioning what Glaurius had said, until finally a sense of resignation came.

"All this Garden of Paradise, we will seal up. The day is coming when we will be united again, but corruption must have its time."

Korban was careful not to speak of dates or times, desiring to inject hope into their disconsolate spirits. "When mankind groans under the weight of failure, the Answer will come. In the meantime, we will be watching over all things, for although Chag has legal authority to rule here, we are still lords over all. And he – and all the wicked - will meet his fate, rest assured."

"Although you don't believe it right now, we are for you, and are near, though you will not always sense it."

Mogen woke from his stupor, and spoke to Glaurius.

"Are you leaving us? How can we survive without you? Where will we go?"

"You will indeed leave here, and soon experience separation from us, but we will never leave you. It will seem to you that we are gone, however, because the death unleashed by this tree does not permit you to perceive us as we are, or to perceive Tziyon as it is. What happened here, you will pass on to your children, and they will pass it on to their children, but soon it will become the stuff of myth and legend, disbelieved except by children, and full of distortions and false impressions."

Glaurius sighed. "Natural, rational, logic and "science" will replace the truth, until only what is seen is believed. Many will be the tales of origins, and cruel will be the religions and self-appointed 'authorities' that seek to order, explain, and control the world, and the minds of people. But those who believe in the Spirit, and search for wisdom with a humble heart will always be free, though they are hunted down in an attempt to silence the truth, for the song of Tziyon that lives in their hearts, will prevail."

Mogen turned to the cloud which obscured Sofia, and though he could not see, she smiled through her pain.

"Son, there is always hope. Though it tarries long, and you suffer much, you are made of greatness, and help will always come. Be strong, and call to us in your time of need. Though we remain unseen, there will be serafs to assist and comfort you. And one day, we will again be face-to-face."

He reached out to her, and she to him, but he felt no substance. But he caught the scent of her garments - honeysuckle, fresh grass, and endless, sun-washed days; he drank in the deep comfort of her presence one last time.

Glaurius opened his arms to Cheva, and called her name softly. Pathetically, she ran inside, sobbing, begging for forgiveness. "Cheva, you are already forgiven. You are my precious one, my dove, and I love you with an everlasting devotion. Nothing you could ever do will change that."

She could not feel him, but hung her head in shame and disbelief at the absence of judgment and condemnation; for she surely felt them weighing on the inside of her.

"Cheva, my darling, those are not my thoughts, and they are not my ways. I will make sure to send you messages of my love, only remember your temptation to disbelieve, and trust instead. I will never leave you, or forsake you – never forget!" His heart broke as he longed to wrap her in the protection of his strong arms, and embrace Mogen just one more time.

Sofia spoke to Cheva. "My princess, I promise to be with you through all of your trials and pain. You will produce kings and queens who will break the grip of Chag and his lies. Though some perish in the process, in their time of testing, they will overcome. Now, let your shame go."

Cheva smiled weakly, as Sofia stretched out her hand to stroke her hair, but all Cheva felt was a stirring of air, and an evanescent sense of love and comfort, which fled as quickly as the breeze.

Finally, Korban spoke to Mogen and Cheva, and laying his hands on their heads, released protection and perseverance. "Though the battle rages, you will prevail to see your revenge on our enemies." He reached into his breast pocket, and removed a silver key, on a simple rope, which he placed in Cheva's trembling hand. "Pass this on to the worthy women of your lineage. One day, you will know why."

She furrowed her brow at him, and then looked at Mogen, but tied it around her neck where it warmed her skin. A seed of hope and the promise of future victory lodged in their hearts and spirits, as they heard in his voice, the oath that would one day destroy all evil, and restore the Garden. A fiery radiance blazed in the mist that surrounded The Three, and courage rose in their hearts.

"I have placed you like a brand on my arm; my desire is for you, and I will come back.Korban looked at them, but also through them - down the ages - to another day. They looked at each other, puzzled at the meaning of the words, but drawn by his passion.

Masos and Tikvah had waited patiently throughout the farewell, but now appeared in a shimmering light, speaking to the exiles.

"Master Mogen, and Lady Cheva we are at your service. We will manifest in different form from time to time. Chag – though powerful – will not ultimately prevail, and there will still be joy amidst your sorrow."

They bowed low, and stepped to the Tree of Life, one on each side. The Three looked with deep affection and care at the grief-stricken couple, who smiled bravely at each other. Turning back, Sofia, Glaurius and Korban began to grow faint before their eyes, and the last thing they remembered was a flash of light before the Tree, the Garden, and The Three vanished from sight.

An eerie silence hit them, as they surveyed their surroundings. Blighted trees and plants, and colorless rocky ground assaulted their vision, and animals began to run chaotically in every direction howling, and attacking each other – the strong overpowering the weak. A hyena crept up to a family of rabbits huddled together beneath a scraggly oak, and pounced on the smallest, sinking its teeth into the back of its neck, its lifeblood pumping out into the thirsty ground.

Cheva took Mogen's hand, and with deep remorse, searched his face. "Mogen, I am so very, very sorry. Can you ever forgive me?"

His hardened features softened; he remembered the first time he ever saw her – her beauty, authority, and perfection were so compelling and admirable. Now, she seemed marred, fragile, empty. He sighed, as he felt the weight of responsibility settle on his shoulders, but said nothing. She had made a terrible mistake, but didn't deserve to be utterly scorned. Besides, she was the only other person alive, and he needed her, though he hated to admit it now.

"Cheva, I forgive you." He held her close, mildly repulsed by the scent of sweat, and dirt until he buried his face in her hair, where the faint aroma of roses and paradise lingered; he let his body respond to the urges which now cried out louder than his soul or spirit, though every fragmented part of him wailed like an orphaned child in this vast, broken wasteland.

Chapter Twelve

hag and his followers unleashed endless misery down the long parade of centuries on the descendents of Mogen and Cheva, as people multiplied, and slowly spread out across the earth. With the genetic material of man now corrupted, Chag and the iniquitous gibborim and serafs – known as nohedim - influenced the minds and hearts of all. Ba'al Aruni reveled in, and perfected the dark arts and sorcery.

By his power, brother rose against brother, and though Mogen and Cheva faithfully recounted the story of the Garden to their children and grandchildren, before many generations had passed, it was as Glaurius predicted, almost pure fiction. There was no time for stories of a lost Paradise, as by brute force, and using ever-more diabolical armaments of war, men fought for power, and the strong enslaved the weak.

All the innate creativity Glaurius had put into Mogen and Cheva came to serve this one purpose: ruthless rulers, imitating Aruni, and filled with pride, subjected women, children, and smaller nations, as well as the land, water, and animals to futility and despair until the creatures returned to the dust from which they came. For millennia, nation rose against nation, and great powers dominated the others, each more brutal and systematic than the one before, survival of the fittest replacing the divine power given to man and woman.

However, there were those who believed in the ancient

stories, and to some of these, Glaurius revealed himself. They kept their connection to Tziyon by living simple, nomadic lives, in areas remote from the rest of the nations, and Cheva's key was carefully guarded and passed on.

Finally, Glaurius appeared to a simple, and honest man named Avraham, to reveal The Way that had been lost.

With his family and a few servants, this old man crossed the vast land-bridge, and settled in a fertile area near the great sea. Over succeeding centuries, this once-tiny group of people flourished, but eventually, in the growing shadow of the empire of Romu, the knowledge of Glaurius again faded, as Avraham's descendants prospered and intermingled with the surrounding people. Desiring to be included with the nations, they encouraged their children to marry the sons and daughters of the people, went into business with them, and embraced the arts, politics, education, medicine and science, and even the religions of the people.

Human society became increasingly complex, and centered in bustling cities with Aruni and the nohedim exercising influence in every area of life - with power to bring famine, or plenty, life or death to any person or enterprise they chose. These fallen creatures frequently appeared to people, and in an endless variety of forms. These gods of the ancient world were many: there were gods of gold and silver, gods of commerce, gods of law and order, gods of streams, rivers, lakes and oceans; gods of barley, wheat, fruit and fields; multitudes of gods ruled over air and forest, marriage and childbirth, flocks and herds, war, building, and healing, city and country.

Aruni passed his time devising strategies of conquest, and the nohedim carried out his will in politics, trade and commerce, the arts, music, and religion.

By Aruni, men created vast empires, always seeking domination of the world, as he operated from the top down, through strong, charismatic leaders who demanded obedience and loyalty. Many of these kings communicated directly with him, or with nohedi, or through the religious leaders - high priests - who also oversaw the various rituals, facilitated the instruction of new priests, and spread the teachings throughout the community. Great temples were constructed by the forced labor of the unfortunate people, who often died from exhaustion, disease, starvation and abuse of the overlords.

There were a variety of elements involved with the worship of Aruni. As the former seraf of song, he well knew the power of music to open up spiritual pathways, and it became an integral part of the cultic services. He longed to hear the swelling sound of instruments, and words of praise from those who cried out his name. In gatherings, the priest and his assistants would use a variety of plants - dried and mixed with wine - to induce trances, and open their spirits to the nohedim, or in some cases, to Aruni himself.

Once intoxicated by the pharmakeia, the nohedim would easily enter into their defenseless bodies, or influence their minds. Through spells, they pronounced blessing as they willed, or released words of destruction. Wild dancing and unbridled sexual behavior then followed, with screaming, riotous drinking, and drunkenness far into the night.

The blood sacrifice (usually of an animal, but sometimes not), and the partaking of a meal together to affirm devotion to the gods completed the worship service; when it was a person, the morning cast an incongruous light on the grisly scene, and wailing would soon take up from the dwelling of the poor wretch who had paid with his life, to satisfy the demented and evil desires of Ba'al Aruni.

A similar system of worship to Glaurius also developed, centered, too, on a magnificent temple, with a priesthood and hierarchy of its own.

However, the Glaurius they worshiped bore little resemblance to the true king, who was wise and good. No, this king was the anti-glaurius - demanding, aloof, angry, unpredictable, violent and merciless. He governed with an iron fist, and required great sacrifices of time and wealth, with the priests culling the best of the people to serve the demands of this god. This religious system had many laws, and the leaders sought to rule nations, too.

The temple and priestly homes were constructed using the forced labor of the young and strong, and the wealth of the merchants was extracted through fear of divine retribution. Those who gave themselves most fully to Glaurius were rewarded in the short-term with their names inscribed on buildings and furnishings, given prominent community positions, the favor of the powerful, and after death, promises of eternal life and rewards. Glaurius the Great, the figurehead of their new religion, possessed all the qualities of the ones who imagined him, and money, or daily animal sacrifices were offered to appease his greed and wrath. The altars were flooded with the endless blood of goats, bulls, and sheep, and mandated offerings from all the people. And this was exported to the whole world.

But there was always a remnant, a small but devoted group, to whom The Three appeared, and nurtured in The Way. They would speak to the leaders and give direction, and by the power of The Three, droughts were broken, the sick were healed, and those afflicted by nohedim were freed from madness. Believers in The Way released words of blessing, and cared for the sick and the poor, and preached a God of love. In all of this, they succeeded in greatly weakening the evil powers of Aruni and the nohedim, since by the force of love many people believed and encountered The Three for themselves.

But Aruni inspired the Glaurianists, and Ba'alists to oppose The Way, and war broke out. The followers of The Way were either imprisoned, killed, or driven into exile, including women and children. Aruni showed no mercy, but try though he might, he could not extinguish the flames of true devotion, nor the longing the people had to know this good God. And although he had great power over those who followed him, he could also do nothing when Glaurius intervened to protect his own. The chief nohedi could only writhe in confused rage; and though he suspected, he never could know the plan that his arch-enemy had created long before the world began.

For wherever they went in the earth - in the teeming cities, or in the quiet fields, in tangled jungles, or vast deserts, in palaces and prisons - the prophets of The Way announced the restoration of all things, and declared the coming of the One who would break the power of Aruni in the earth once and for all.

And many were those who believed.

For in all these places, if one had eyes to see, there were traces of light, the footprints of The Three.

And the key continued to seek its rightful owner...

Chapter Thirteen

In a small village in the land of Eyre, a young girl slipped unnoticed down the mossy banks at the head of the inland sea. Just past the waterfall and below a massive, overhanging oak tree lay her hiding place. Invisible behind an impenetrable tangle of willows, cat tails and marsh grasses, Lailah, daughter of Ferin, nimbly scaled the beaver dam, and scampered through the dark tunnel into her hiding place, her bare feet padding silently on the cool mud floor.

She tapped her little foot impatiently until her eyes adjusted to the light in the cave; the sun found its way through openings overhead, small holes worn into the rocks by water. Lailah sighed with satisfaction as she surveyed her private kingdom: a stool, a large wolf skin on top of a bed of straw, a small wooden table, an oil lamp, a ceramic pot for water, a wooden plate, and a crude vase with flowers adorned the place.

The girl struck the tinder after rubbing the flint, and lit the lamp with the little flame. She removed the leather pouch from her back, spilling the contents onto the table, carefully arranging dried meat, bread, and a small piece of cheese on the plate, then bowed her head in a prayer, and ate hungrily, washing it down with water.

Lying on her back on the straw pallet, Lailah stared at the strange figures on the roof and sides of the cave. She shivered in the dampness, and hugged the fur around her small body, savoring its warmth. Carved and painted into the rock were panoramic scenes of people dancing, playing instruments, and eating and playing, surrounded by trees and animals, and several winged, man-like creatures flew in the sky.

In the next scene, a woman and two men with light rays shooting out from them stood beside two trees. Around the trunk of one, a snake coiled, and another man and woman stood before a gate, their faces covered with their hands.

After this, she saw the couple and the snake, and an unknown object in the woman's hand.

She lay very still, memorizing every detail, trying to absorb the message of the pictures. But as always, her mind wandered into dreams of a far-off land before she could see the full story, and she fell fast asleep to the rhythmic hush of the waterfall. A seraf stepped out from the shadows, and leaning over, placed a small object next to the sleeping child.

* * *

She woke to find the light much the same as before, and knew she had slept just a little while. In the half-light, her fingers searched for her little flax doll. As she floated between wakefulness and sleep, she heard a voice, "He is coming."

She found the doll, and as she hugged it to her, a shiny object dropped from it, into her hand. She leaped up and plunged it into the narrow shaft of light streaming down into the dark cave. A silver object glinted; Lailah's eyes widened in disbelief and wonder as she stared at the key, turning it over and over to learn its message.

Suddenly, she remembered the object in the hand of the woman in the painting. She grabbed the stool, and stood on it, holding the oil lamp up to the drawings. Her eyes surveyed the rest of dramatic story told there, especially one panel that always caused dread yet inexplicable longing. Etched into the reddish grime, was the stark image of a man hanging on a tree, blood running from his body. But from the blood grew a tree full of fruit, and through an open gate she saw fields and sunshine, an endless sea of people like heads of grain, the winged creatures, and the shining woman and man.

Moving on, she gazed at the illustration of the man and woman, who now had crowns on their heads. They always appeared to smile at her, and she believed they had a message just for her, which is why she alone knew about the cave and the drawings.

Lailah looked back to the diagram of the couple and the snake, and standing on tiptoe, brought the lamp closer for a better look. Suddenly, the key began to strangely warm, and as she held it up to the cave art, she gasped as she saw that the silvery object in the woman's hand was identical to the key that now burned in her hand.

* * *

Life passed slowly in Innisfallen, as Lailah grew restless with the endless monotony of the village. Now that she was older and could work more, it seemed there was nothing much to look forward to except early marriage and having lots of children. Though her heart was still invested in her secret world in the cave, years had come and gone since the day she had received the key and heard the strange words.

And the world around her was filled with violence, war, disease, superstition, poverty, and uncertainty, and while she was more affluent than most, it wasn't enough to satisfy her heart's cry for meaning, or provide the security she longed for. The dull ache never went away, like the mist from the sea. *Why am I even alive? There must be more than this.* In the revolving seasons of life in an agricultural village in the Middle Ages, it seemed that sowing, reaping, calving, shearing, weaving and small celebrations of birth and death were the sum total of life; and what made it even worse was that no one else asked such questions but were content with their lot - even if all they had was surviving from one day to the next.

But in the hushed darkness of a recent late-summer night, the still, small voice spoke to her again.

"He is coming."

Now not a day came and went, without her glancing up the rutted cart road that led away from the town, in anticipation of this mysterious Someone. And lately, there was no lack of activity, as strangers passed though, hawking their potions, magic rocks, feathered amulets, tall tales, exotic animals, spices, and gadgets from around the expanding world. Every cry that preceded these travelers, caused Lailah's heart to leap, but so far, all she'd seen were shiftless thieves, and greasy charlatans ogling her beauty, dowry, and virginity.

Lailah had made a shrine in the cave, and set her hope on the coming of the man on the tree. Over the years, she had come to see a progression in the panels on the cave walls, and wove a story line from endless hours of viewing and contemplating the mysterious figures. It bore a slight resemblance to the story the old Glaurianist priest told - about the first man and woman from whom all mankind descended.

But there are so many religions, and so many ideas about god and man, life and death.

The old priest's god had a terrible temper, and many rules, and the secret ceremonies of Cernunnos scared her. But now new ideas set the marketplace abuzz, disseminated by way of the travelers who sought to propagate their strange teachings. Even her family had its own story - a story of Glaurius appearing to her great-grandfather that painted a very different picture of The Unseen God. It was hard to know what was true.

After a breakfast of flax meal, currants, nuts and warm milk, she carried the tied-up bundles of soft sweaters, scarves, socks and mittens of crimson, green, brown, and orange to the wagon. Dependent upon fine harvest weather, the Connel clan anticipated good sales of the clothing before the winter snows fell.

This year, Cernunnos - the Horned God - did not disappoint, and the yield from the flocks and herds, and fields and orchards was plentiful. Lailah's father had bragged just last night about how the offerings he had made throughout the year had paid off, to the dismay of his wife. Miriam strongly defended The Way, and carefully protected the scrolls that had been passed down to her.

But Ferin, her father wavered between serving the pantheon of local gods, and following The Way. Furthermore, Lailah knew the prophets of The Way foretold of The Coming One, and the mysterious cave drawings seemed to confirm that. Still, she was confused, and curious. *What really happens in the sacred groves? And what of the native gods our ancestors served? Where is any sign of Glaurius, and where are other followers of The Way?*

These and many other questions filled her waking hours - hours she spent in the market, selling warm garments made from the wool of her family's abundant flocks of sheep and goats, and from linen spun from the fertile flax fields.

Into the wagon bed, Lailah heaved the tightly woven capes, blankets, tunics, and leather boots, and piled the linen dresses, shirts and undergarments alongside the baskets of walnuts, pecans, apples, and potatoes. Wooden boxes filled with squashes and pumpkins lined one side, and when she finished, she recorded everything in her leather-bound parchment book, scratching out figures with a goose quill.

"Alright, 5 capes, 10 tunics, 4 pairs of boots..." Whatever she sold would be registered in black ink; anything left over at the end of the week went into the ledger in red.

Ferin employed two dozen men and women in making boots, shoes, sandals, and clothing for the people of Innisfallen. His 100 acres of inherited land produced what some folk swore was magical. The truth fell on the side of those who said there was a blessing on the Connel tribe, and a secret blessing indeed played a part, but there were no leaders who could work and inspire others like the sons of Connel.

For this hand of favor that rested on them came first to Ferin's grandfather, when in the days of the great sea kings he had come from across the water. The elder Connel landed on the island from a distant place of uncertain origins, but the tale is told of his great height, and extra digits on his hands and feet - and also about the strange encounter he had had with a god of light, who took him often to a beautiful kingdom, where there was no sadness, sorrow, pain, or death.

Connel committed his life to this god, the one who could protect from the "Evil Hand." Many believed, and followed The Way, encountering The Three in those days, enjoying wonderful times feasting in Tziyon, carried there in the spirit by the mighty gibborim. With the favor of Glaurius, Connel united the scattered tribes of the island, and reigned as high king for many days. With the protection of the gibborim, they remained safe from all their enemies, and none dared invade the island because of "The Great Power," which guarded the people of Eyre.

Still, there were those who rejected the truth, and worshipped the idols brought with them from beyond the sea, as well as the local spirits - of whom Cernunnos was chief. Known to some as "the goat god," he was the aggressive, riotous god of fields, fertility, and sorcery. The symbols of his power - the five-sided star, crescent moon, horns, and hazel staff - were drawn over the entrances to homes, carved from wood, and molded from every kind of metal, to decorate and protect their homes, or worn as amulets by the people. Bronze statues of goats, bulls or oxen guarded the tops of the hills, and people brought their animal sacrifices, silver and gold, and sometimes even their own children to serve as shrine prostitutes, in exchange for protection and blessing on their homes and livelihoods.

As belief in The Way increased, so did conflict with those who followed Cernunnos. Barbaric rituals polluted the land, and family members rose against one another, and family against family. Eventually, the followers of The Way succeeded in driving out the worshipers of Cernunnos by force and by war, but the result was sorrow and bitterness toward The Way. This enmity was deepened by the establishment of laws forbidding the worship of any but Glaurius.

But the people who did not know The Three were afraid of the spirits of the dead, of the forests, fields, waterways, mountains and hills - the nohedim who relentless tormented them. The laws forbidding them to worship these gods only succeeding in driving the cults into hiding, but with Connel's death, the worship of the "Glorious and Burning One" declined, supplanted once again by devotion to the local spirits.

And in the absence of protection from Glaurius, barbaric hordes invaded the island, and soon there was a new king, and The Way was lost and forgotten.

* * *

Lailah finished her preparations as Annalise, the young orphan they had taken in, ran out to her with their basket of food for the day, huffing and puffing, and laughing in the cold air. She accepted Lailah's help up, and settled in beside her on the seat. "We will see you this evening, daughters. The favor of Glaurius be with you today." The girls bent their heads, and received the blessing, with a warm hug from the handsome and strapping Ferin.

Lailah wondered again at her father's confusing religion, as the sound of Stitches hooves along the well-worn road, drummed a double-beat: *Glaurius/Cernunnos, Glaurius/Cernunnos - why does he waver between the two paths? If Glaurius is God, he should follow him. If not, he should follow Cernunnos.*

The October sun warmed them as they made their way to town, joined on the road by other merchants, who alike were all dreaming of good sales, and of the races planned for tomorrow. The ponies of Innisfallen were famous for their endurance and speed (as well as their meanness) and the weekends provided a time for the townsfolk to unwind, drink and gossip, and maybe make a few extra pence betting on the riders and their mounts.

Lailah's father and brothers had two ponies in the running, and would be finishing their work early this evening, to run them one last time. There was always a high atmosphere surrounding these "holidays," and today was no exception.

Lailah felt something stirring inside as soon as she and Annalise entered the town gates, where they were greeted by grinning watchmen who bowed and waved them on with with a flourish of their hats. "A wonderful good day to you, lovely Connel ladies!" The girls smiled back, and nodded, passing on to their location in the market.

Jumping down from the wagon, Annalise tied Stitches to an iron ring in the stone wall next to their booth, and then returned to help Lailah unload the clothing and other goods for sale. After arranging everything according to size and style, and the food in an attractive display, Annalise watched the stall while Lailah walked the mare and the wagon to the common pen outside the gates, and unhitched her to graze for the day.

Unseen in the roadway before her stood a gibbor, shining in the morning light, rainbow colors swirling and sparking from his supernal body. His sword flashed as he turned in every direction, scanning the territory for signs of nohedi, or Aruni himself. He observed the activities of those in the square; the winking of the eye in a shady deal, a nervous giggle revealing a lie, the secret passion of illicit lovers. He felt the brutish power of the strong who ruled over the weak, and the poor wretches who begged at the gates.

Masos thought about the solemn council weeks before, in the secret chambers of the King, when Prince Korban had stood to address Glaurius, Sofia, and the chiefs.

"The suffering of the people, and the evil that has destroyed the earth, is more than I can bear, Father. I must go now."

And as he stood now surveying the village, thoughts passed through his head. *Master Korban, I cannot understand your heart for these foul and ignorant creatures. Couldn't you just destroy them, put the innocent out of their despair, and make more of them? It has been such a long time, and they grow more depraved by the year.*

The thoughts reached his master.

No, Masos, we must follow the plan. For the sake of those who will believe, I will bring hope, healing and the courage to persevere until the end. Yes, for these, I will give my very life.

His conversation was interrupted by the sound of wheezing behind him. Masos shuddered, and then bristled, wheeling around to face his enemy.

"Chag, so soon? Your rebel band hasn't lost its edge, apparently."

"Perhaps you haven't heard, but I no longer go by that contemptible name." Ba'al Aruni raised himself to his full height and splendor, and indeed he was magnificent - an angel of light. His beautiful face appeared so innocent and inviting; colored light and song burst from within, but Masos stood unmoved by the glory.

Aruni, offended by the lack of respect, spat on the sandals of the mighty gibbor, and leaned menacingly toward him, with his finely sculpted hands on Masos's chest. Masos shoved his hands aside and in a split second, had the tip of his sword at the throat of the nohedi.

"I am aware, Ba'al Aruni of the great height from which you have fallen, and how deep is the fiery pit where you will soon be tormented for eternity. I will call you by no other name except Betrayer."

Aruni pulled away, disdainfully straightening his robe, and arranging the pure white hood over his long, golden curls.

"Oh Masos, you are so boring with your rules and protocol, so limited in your possibilities, confined as you are by your overlord. Real freedom is in pursuing what feels right to *you*, not in obeying the dictates of Glaurius. No, my friend, you are powerful! More powerful than you know, but you will never realize your potential chained to the throne of your master."

The comparison to a dog pierced like an arrow, but Masos rejected the insult. Aruni looked him over, like a piece of choice meat, reaching out his hand to stroke Masos's strong arms, and sighing wistfully, "Such a waste..."

Masos shoved his hand away. "You are the one who is abased, Betrayer. You have traded your glory for shame and contempt. I pity you. Now, leave this region - you are outnumbered."

Suddenly, thousands of serafs and gibborim appeared on the ground, filling the lower atmosphere. Some rode on horses, and others flew, but great power and authority emanated from them. Aruni looked dismayed, but Masos smiled with great satisfaction.

"Wonderful, aren't they? Majestic light-bearers...so strong and loyal. Completely trustworthy, and destined for victory."

Aruni cringed. Masos continued pressing his advantage.

"Yes, I will never forget that day, my brother. Do you remember? Oh, you were so certain you were right, and that we, too, would see and follow your cause - yet in the end, only a third of the serafs and gibborim followed you. And though that was a large number at the time, Glaurius has created more of them - something you can never do."

Seized with a sudden pang of loss, Masos rubbed his cleft chin, and turned to study the nohedi. "Do you ever regret your decision, Chag? When you are alone, and it is quiet, do you ever wish you could return? Do you miss the peace and joy that we have?"

As Aruni stared at the great and dazzling army surrounding him, the tiniest sting of remorse seized him. He thought of the abundant fields and azure skies of Tziyon, and remembered the bliss of his life there. And he thought of The Three, and inquired gently, his voice trembling ever so slightly, "How is Mother?"

"She misses you every day. We all do." Masos clenched his jaw, and waited to see what the fallen gibbor would say.

Just then, a buzzing and roaring sound came from the east, diverting Aruni's attention. As it came closer, a nohedi battalion appeared from the swirling, black cloud. Circling overhead like vultures, a foul odor of death preceded them; upon closer inspection, their bodies were black and filthy, but they had the most beautiful faces. Etched in their lovely features were sorrow, rage, pride, lust, and fear creating a confusing image to the onlooker.

Shrieking, howling, cackling and mocking jeers swelled from their boasting and jeering mouths, and in an instant, the tender moment had passed. Ba'al Aruni, now transformed into a great serpent roused himself, and his eyes returned to their reptilian coldness, carried away as he was by the intoxicating adulation of his army. He turned menacingly toward Masos. "Brother, there is nothing at all I regret - except that I did not lead my people from their captivity sooner!"

A thunderous roar escaped from the evil throng, as the nohedim banged on their armor, and brandished weapons, chanting the name of their leader. "Aruni, Aruni!"

Trained for war, the serafs and gibborim had already drawn their gleaming swords and poised their arrows, watching every move the nohedim made. Aruni appeared in the midst of the nohedim, and gave a parting shot.

"Masos, you know full well that this earth and all who are

in it are mine; all authority was given to me when Mogen and Cheva ate of the fruit. You have come with a larger force today, but we will meet again when you are not prepared, and make sure you are unable to ever return. I have had enough of your trespassing on my realm. I am the king of earth, and no one can withstand me!"

The bilious cloud roiled, and churned, and the screams rose to a fever-pitch. Aruni swelled to a great size, rose far up into the sky, a terrible dragon, with many horns, and covered in fearsome armor plates. Frogs, flies, hornets, and bats spewed from his mouth as he roared at Masos, and the seraphic army. He threw hail like fire to the ground, and then suddenly, the dragon and his horde disappeared.

"You are wrong, my brother, so very wrong. Your legal right to this world and to all the people is coming to an end."

Korban smiled and nodded through the veil. They spoke heart to heart. *Yes, Masos, I will come and do what must be done, and we will fulfill the mission.*

Chapter Fourteen

Nothing out of the ordinary here - one day was pretty much the same as the next in Innisfallen; the buzz of flies in the growing warmth of the sun, the odor of human sweat, hay and animal dung mixed with dust pervading the air. The feel of her woolen cloak around her, the warm fleece and leather boots on her feet gave a sense of comfort and normalcy, and Lailah sighed with contentment. Yet the restlessness that was her constant companion blew in with the shifting winds of fall, and a fleeting thought caused her to lift up her eyes from the commotion of the market place and the busy street, to the quiet hills beyond the confines of the village.

It was there that she saw him. Just a day like every other day that had ever been - the sun came up as usual, and Lailah had followed her routine. But today, unexpectedly, everything Lailah knew about life was about to change. In fact, the history of the whole world would be defined by things they all would experience on the tiny island in the months to come, but the real impact would only happen to those "with eyes to see."

In recalling that day, ever after, Lailah would describe it like this, "Before, there was a cloud over everything, filling even our happy times with a certain dread, because of the "dark something" that was always present. But hope drove away the fear and darkness when he came, and I could never go back."

Her heart pounded within her, as her eyes remained riveted on the man in the grey, hooded cape, walking staff in hand along the tree line. His silhouette fell across the straw-colored landscape, and behind him, stopping at the border, followed a small parade of animals: a doe with her fawn, a large buck with enormous, spreading antlers, a tiny cloud of flittering birds, a raccoon, bob-cat, and a cinnamon-colored bear.

Lailah marveled at the sight of the animals around him, and brought momentarily to her senses, glanced around to see if anyone else took notice.

Oblivious, the marketplace hummed with talk, the sounds of horse's hooves and wagons rumbling on the partially cobbled streets, the shouting of the vendors and crying babies. But when she turned again to look at the hills, she stared in disbelief at the sight of the man now bounding, leaping, and whooping with delight, straight down the incline toward her.

Lailah stood immobile and small before the power that radiated from him in waves; all she could do was yield to it, as it washed over her. And a song filled her ears - no, there were many songs. For as she stood before him, long-forgotten memories and dreams rose up from within her, each with its unique music, now presented in a new light.

First, she saw the death of her baby brother Enosh, and how her mother had grieved, rocking him in her chair by the fire for two whole days: this memory flooded back with a sorrowful choir that she couldn't see; following that, a fearful image of a great, hissing beast burst before her eyes, a recurring dream that tormented her as a child: this was accompanied by crashing symbols and piercing trumpets; lastly, she saw herself on the day she had discovered the cave, and standing on tiptoe, had traced the mysterious story with her small fingers. With this memory, a love-song of passionate longing gripped her and she swooned, losing consciousness for a moment.

When she came to, she felt strong arms holding her: with her eyes still closed, she leaned back against soft wool, the deep drumming of a heartbeat resounding in her ears.

Suddenly, her heart stopped, and she gasped for breath; when it started again, she felt it now beat in time with the heart of the stranger. Instinctively, she placed her hand on her chest, and opening her eyes, gazed up into eyes that held vast depths of space, planets, and stars, the future, and the past. She found herself falling into them, journeying further until she saw a shining, jeweled city in the midst of a beautiful garden. Outside the pearled gates of the garden stood a tree full of glistening leaves, from which fell drops of crimson blood. On the ground beneath the blood, flowers of every kind sprang up.

As quickly as she had departed, she returned, and a strange, burning sensation filled her heart: there was no physical pain, but a feeling of increase, and pleasing, joyful warmth radiated through her, like the sun in spring after the long, cold winter.

She looked into the warm brown eyes, as the stranger smoothed back stray hairs from her face. She weakened again at his touch, but he smiled, filling her with strength as he set her back on her feet.

Towering at least a foot above her, Lailah studied every inch of his face: expressive eyes fringed with dark lashes, and strong cheekbones, soft lips, and teeth white as milk. Dark curls fell around his shoulders, provocative beneath the hood, and the hands that gripped the staff were muscular and brown.

He smiled, but in his eyes she read a sad, mysterious, longing. He turned away, and looked to the horizon, and when he turned back, hope poured out from him like a rushing river.

He took her arm, and they walked back to the stall - Lailah strolling with a perfect stranger - smiling and laughing as if with an old friend. She finally broke off the interaction as they approached the stall, seeing Annalise's surprise.

"Annalise, this is..." when suddenly she realized she did not even know his name. "Korban. My name is Korban."

"Korban - what an unusual name," Annalise remarked dryly. The girls were increasingly familiar with travelers from different regions since the king had opened up trade routes to the far reaches of the earth. But this was a strange name. "What does it mean among your people?"

"It is something of great value one gives to God."

"God, who is this god, and what do you think is valuable to him?"

Lailah never took her eyes from Korban as he patiently and confidently responded to Annalise's interrogation. *I have never met a man like this man.*

"The God I speak of created everything, and rules over all; he is exceedingly powerful and very great, yet he desires to know and be known by people. He wants to talk to people, heal, advise, protect and comfort them. People are valuable to God."

Annalise disdainfully tossed her head. "Now *that* is something to laugh about! Where is this god of yours with all the evil of this world? Where was this god when my parents

97

were murdered before my eyes, and I was abused and thrown in the mud on the side of the road to die? No, sir, you are bewitched; you need to lay off the beer so you can see the way things truly are. No one cares about anyone but themselves."

At that, the twelve year old turned sharply on her heel, kicking a barley sack at the front of the stall, and wrestling it into place. Tears welled up in her eyes, but she defied them, streaking her cheeks red as she rubbed them angrily away. Lailah was stunned that she had so quickly revealed such a deep and private wound to the stranger. *But almost immediately, you feel that you want to be honest with him, and that he doesn't judge like other people do.*

Lailah looked at Korban and saw sadness - as if he felt Annalise's pain. Lailah reached out to touch the hurting girl, but Korban stopped her. *She needs to grieve, and I am not offended by her anger.* Again, the wordless speech. They watched as Annalise grabbed her staff, and headed off into the midst of the busy marketplace. Shrugging, Lailah turned her attention to her work, and Korban helped by grabbing the broom to sweep around the booth, smiling and nodding to passersby.

"Yes, ma'am! Why, look at those pumpkins! They're the finest in all of Innisfallen! And wouldn't this lavender sweater look lovely on you?" Lailah smiled at his gestures, impressed by his genuine interest in people.

Activity at their booth buzzed, and the morning flew by, with rapid sales. Annalise eventually returned, acting as though nothing had happened, and when it was time to stop for lunch, she cheerfully prepared the rustic table with the food they had brought.

Sitting on bales of hay in the sunshine, the three enjoyed tea with cream and honey - a new, rare delicacy, these leaves brought from beyond the sea - and munched on apple muffins and sharp cheese. Laliah removed her cloak, her long hair cascading in glorious strands of gold over her shoulders, a striking contrast to Korban's dark features. After swapping and sharing stories of the morning's transactions, the attention turned to their new friend.

"Mr. Korban, I deeply appreciate what you have done to help us today. Your kindness is very welcome. But surely, you are here for some other purpose or business - or perhaps you are merely passing through?"

At this, a lump formed in her throat, and she looked at him with a great ache in her heart, waiting in expectation for his answer. Her distress alarmed and surprised her. *He has somehow already become a part of me.* A surprising thought drifted in. *Could he be the one I have been waiting for?*

He smiled so tenderly at Lailah that Annalise noticed, but pretended to be unmoved. *I will never come under the power of this - or any man.* But suddenly, he turned to her also, as if responding to her thoughts.

"You can call me Korban." He paused and looked off into the distance, as if at something far away they could not see, and continued cryptically, "I have come to reveal truth, and to expose darkness." Lailah saw a smoldering anger pass across his eyes, but with no further explanation, the girls sat quietly for a few moments, afraid to ask more. Annalise finally stood, brushing out the crumbs of her meal from her long dress.

"So then you *are* some kind of holy man or priest - there are many of those around these days. I suppose there's money enough to be made in that business." Korban and Lailah couldn't help but chuckle at the sight of the small girl, griping like an old woman. She wagged her finger at them. "Watch and see if I'm not right! He will be here for awhile, do some of his tricks, and then disappear in the middle of the night."

Lailah retorted. "Annalise! Korban is not like that." "I'm so sorry, Korban, she is normally so sweet and no trouble at all. I don't know what's come over her." The younger girl whirled around to face her, defiant.

"Nothing has come over me, Lailah. You know nothing at all about this man, and have only just met him today. What would your parents think to see you making such close association with a total stranger?" She had worked herself almost into hysteria, and as Lailah moved toward her, to comfort her, the girl began to shriek. It was an unworldly sound, like a hungry wolf on a distant hill; she started to shake uncontrollably, and fell to the ground where she flailed about, beating her arms and legs on the cobbles.

Just then, another child - a boy of seven or eight - who stood with his mother by a fire in a nearby stall, began to have the same kind of manifestations. Lailah glanced in terrified helplessness at Korban, who had swept aside his cloak, and was bending down to Annalise. The tormented girl pulled away, and shrieked one last time, but as soon as he touched her hand and spoke strange words over her, the fit was over, and she lay as if in a deep sleep.

He gathered Annalise in his arms, and laid her on the table

at the back of the stall. "Give her a little water when she wakes up." He spoke reassuringly as he touched Lailah's hand, "I will be back soon, don't be afraid."

Lailah saw that the boy was squared off against two large men, and roaring like a lion, while everyone stopped their work to watch as the drama unfolded. Then, without warning, the boy suddenly leaped toward the brick fire pit.

But Korban was there in an instant, and caught him up in his strong arms. This time he spoke loudly enough for all to hear. "Be gone from him!" As soon as he uttered the words, the boy fell limp against Korban's chest. Returning him to his mother, he brushed his hand against the boy's cheek, and the child awoke, smiling.

The mother stared in gratitude and awe. "Thank you, sir." She hugged her son, and all stood silent as Korban passed through the crowd and returned to Lailah.

Everyone began to talk amongst themselves, marveling at the things they had seen, wondering what new power this was. The unpredictable behavior of violent or lunatic minds they recognized, but never had they seen someone overtaken by these fits return to their right minds. The exorcists and healers used secret and painful methods to treat the tormented, but often the rigors of their methods often resulted in death.

Most of the people seemed genuinely moved, but in a corner of the market a small group of three or four gathered.

"A powerful wizard, is he," offered a small man with a pointed nose and runny eyes.

"Telos, do not be hasty to draw conclusions about the man. After all, the gods have been known to come in human form." The one who spoke rubbed his well-trimmed chin, and turned to a tall, dark man who tapped a hazel cane on the cobbles, laughing quietly. "Well, Descartes?"

"There is much danger in superstition and religious ecstasy, Paracelsus. How do we know what really occurred here? Perhaps the boy was pulling a prank - as boys do?"

"But Master," said the young man next to the wall, holding the reins of a horse. "Thomas has had the fits for some time now - that was no mischief. Perhaps the man *is* a god?"

Descartes voice dripped condescension as he turned to him. "Boy, there are many things in life that are complex and hard to comprehend. But Philosophy is our guide out of the weeds of chaos." The child hung his head, confused now by the things he had seen and felt, and the educated reasoning of the older man. Turning his attention to his friends, the dark man went on.

"It is hard to lift the mind and soul from the pit of religious dogma, and millennia of venerating divine beings. No, once we were without excuse, but now is the time for man to come to the knowledge that he himself is the summa of existence." The others stood mute before the inveigling foreign scholar, gazing at the ground, wrestling their consciences into submission.

Across the square, Annalise had recovered, and the three returned to their work; Lailah and Annalise, too afraid to ask Korban anything, remained busy with buying and selling. The afternoon wore quickly on, and soon, they were packing up for the day. Lailah counted the money, while Annalise carefully folded and boxed up the remaining goods, and Korban retrieved Stitches. Lailah recorded everything in her book, pausing as she remembered the day's strange events. She wrote, *Saw Thomas Linnert cured of the fits,* in small print in the very back of the book.

Townsfolk nodded and waved with unabashed curiosity as the three drove toward home and the warm cottage. Korban, who drove the mare, smiled or nodded back, but still remained silent about what had happened. Finally, Annalise could stand it no longer.

"Korban, what happened to me today? I remember I was very angry at you, and I remember fainting and waking up, but that is all. Please, tell me."

Korban let the reins fall slack. Stitches knew the well-rutted road and the way by memory. He turned to Annalise who sat on a hay bale behind the bench. Lailah ached over his handsome, intelligent face that shone in the lantern light.

"Annalise, you were seized by a *nohedi* of anger. It is an evil spirit. It took control of you. Has that ever happened to you before?"

The girl hung her head in shame, but looking up, tentatively stammered, "I sometimes feel as though I am under a spell or hex of some sort. Is that what you mean?" She searched his face for reproach, and finding none, added, "I see things, too, that make me very afraid - and at night, my dreams are bad."

"You see creatures like men and they are doing very bad things, isn't that right, Annalise?" The poor girl nodded, and then began to cry in a stifled, choking way, her small frame shaking. Lailah covered her with a soft, wool blanket, and held her close. Big tears dropped onto the wool, and slid down onto the hay.

"It is okay, my child. You are safe now. " Korban reached over and placed his hand on her head. "Be free from this tormenting spirit, and receive peace." Annalise sighed deeply, exhaled, and soon her face brightened. Sitting up she looked ahead, as if remembering something, and began to sing softly.

Don't cry my child, the serafs are near
To keep you from fright,
And far from all fear
Here in the dark night
They surround you with love
Sent from Tziyon
Our home above...

Korban smiled. "Annalise, the terrible assault on your family has left a deep wound, and it is time to bring it to the light, so its power can be broken. All such violence comes from a very powerful but invisible being, who stalks the earth looking for lives he can destroy." He looked at her, and she returned his gaze.

"Then what happened to me and to my parents was because of him? What is his name?"

"Annalise, he goes by many names, and he has an army of nohedi who serve him. He lives outside of time, so he existed in the past, is now, and will be in the future. They are the so-called 'gods' of all the nations: Cernunnos, Istart, Zeus, Aprhrodite, to name just a few. There are thousands of these dark spirits with various names who wield control over the earth, and people serve them unknowingly. But there are some who willingly enter into covenants to serve Aruni and his followers."

Korban paused and gritted his teeth. The girls could feel anger and a power rise from him that was frightening. He stared into the darkness at this unseen foe. "But he will not always have such authority."

Annalise blurted out in fright. "But Korban, who can stop him if he is everywhere? What other force is greater?"

Korban lifted his eyes to the brilliantly sparkling stars and planets, and continued. "Annalise, do you see the sky and all the stars? Do you know what you are looking at? Stars are enormous spheres full of elements that cause them to blaze with fire. They are suns - just like the sun that lights up the day. And they are so far away, that if you could walk to them, it would take you many, many thousands of years."

He paused to let that sink in. "And one more thing - this sky overhead is known as a galaxy - kind of a village in a way - and there are many thousands upon thousands of them, filled with thousands upon thousands of stars. Stars as numerous as the sand on the beach." He smiled to himself, as if recalling something, then turned to the girls. They both stared open-mouthed at the sky, which they could never look at the same way again.

"The stars, the sun and moon, the galaxies, the earth, all the people, animals and all that you see was made by a power much greater than Aruni." He, too, was made by this One of whom I speak."

"This is the God you spoke of this morning?" Annalise dropped her eyes, feeling guilty now.

Korban looked at her with such love. "Little one - there is no need for shame. He knows your heart. He is very near to the brokenhearted and to those who need help. You spoke out of ignorance and pain. He understands, like a father who has pity on his children. You had a father like that, didn't you, Annalise?"

Memories of her father's tender love and protection, his sense of fun and laughter, and the way he worked to provide for his family, came flooding back. She cried out, "Papa! Oh, Papa! Why did you leave me?" She wailed for some time, like an orphaned child, and it seemed to Lailah that the grief would overwhelm her, but Korban spoke confidently, soft and low until she came slowly back to herself.

"Your father loves you very much, Sweetheart." He stroked her dark hair, and waited. When she lifted up her face, the peace was there again, but then she looked at Korban, puzzled.

"What do you mean, 'he *loves* me'? Don't you mean, 'he *loved* me?'"

"No, Annalise. I mean what I say. Your father is alive, and is with your mother. They are in the land of Tziyon, waiting for you."

"Is this where the God you speak of lives?"

"Yes, Annalise. He is the king of Tziyon, and all who die can dwell in his kingdom if they want to."

Lailah broke in. "So this God - what is his name?"

"The name of the king is Glaurius, though he, too, goes by

many names. He is the power behind all that is."

"Yes, I have heard that my great-grandfather served him, but my father wavers between the two - Cernunnos and Glaurius. Yet you say Cernunnos is evil. I think you will make many enemies here."

Korban clenched his jaw and released it. "That is probably true, Lailah."

Suddenly ablaze with questions, Lailah fired them off together. "Is Glaurius a man like you? Does he have a wife? Children? And what is this knowledge you have about the stars? Where did you get such power over evil spirits?"

Korban laughed. "Glaurius is not a man, but I am like him – so are you. And Glaurius has a wife and son, and together they rule over Tziyon, and intervene on earth."

She clearly could not begin to grasp this, and he laughed affectionately at the confused look on her face, continuing.

"The study of nature and the heavens is called 'science' in the universities, and men go there to learn ways to harness the power of the earth, which is a good thing. But increasingly, they leave out the One who created all things, so although they know facts and laws, the things I speak of will never be accessible to them, for I operate by the spirit of wisdom and revelation, which they do not know, nor can they comprehend it."

Lailah considered these things, as he continued. "And Glaurius, Sofia have power over evil spirits: the authority I have is from them, for I seek their guidance and protection."

"These are very great powers, Sir. Are you a priest of Glaurius, then, or have these gods given such powers to men?" She looked puzzled. "The gods of Innisfallen are jealous and vengeful, and give to no man." She thought of the small Glaurianist chapel, and studied his face in the lamplight."Why doesn't our priest have these powers, if he serves Glaurius?"

He returned her gaze. "I am a shepherd searching for lost sheep."

She spoke no more, as all her questions were answered in one glance from his eyes. *I am the One who is to come.* She knew in that moment, that the crude drawings in her hiding place indeed prophesied about him, and that the long years of dreaming, believing, looking and waiting, were finally over. She didn't know how it could be, but she believed what her heart told her.

Such a strange but wonderful thing - as though I am in a story written by an unseen hand - like a wave of the ocean moved by the power of the vast sea, or a small tree blown by the wind...

Pondering all that they had seen and heard, the girls sat quietly until Stitches turned off the main road, and pulled into the front yard of the Connel manor.

Chapter Fifteen

The Connel brood tumbled out of the front door of the large cottage, with Ferin in the midst of five of his children, carrying the tiniest - Megan - up on his shoulders. In and out of the tangle of legs the dogs darted, anxiously herding everything in the yard. Stitches whinnied in irritation as the boys whooped and hollered, and the dogs sharply barked.

Through the open door, in the warm glow of the fire and lantern light Miriam Connel stood, hands on hips, surveying the table, and the wild antics of her large family.

A satisfied smile passed across the face of the dark stranger. Lailah leaned over to him and whispered. "Father will be more than pleased when he hears about today's sales, and Mother will want to thank you by stuffing you like a sausage!" Korban laughed, and jumped down to greet Ferin and the boys.

"Well, now, who is this? I heard of some goings-on in the market today and of a handsome stranger who is in our midst - and here he is at my humble home! What may I call you, friend?" Ferin helped the girls down while directing the boys to their chores, and the unloading of the wagon-bed. Korban smiled, and firmly shook Ferin's hand, matching his confident welcome.

"I am Korban, Ferin, son of Brian, son of Connel." Ferin paused and cocked his head, continuing to shake the stranger's hand, and staring at him as if pondering a riddle.

"Mr. Korban, have we never met before? I could swear that I know you!"

"Where I come from, we believe that all of humanity comes from the same tribe, and that those who are enlightened will be joined back to it one day."

"Those who are enlightened? Enlightened to what, sir? That is a word I hear the philosophers using quite a bit these days." Ferin smiled derisively. "These 'thinkers' are rather idle, in my opinion, and seem to take advantage of many of the weak-willed folks around - getting hard-gained bread and meat in exchange for their lofty words." He peered a little reservedly now at Korban. "Are you a philosopher, then?"

Korban remained unoffended. "It is true, there is a rising tide of seemingly new ideas, but as for answers, it seems that the song remains the same: most of these thinkers seek to understand and control, but not all seek truth. Still, while many of them certainly are vagrants, perhaps taking time to consider and discuss the meaning of life is a good thing?"

He looked at Ferin's children. "For many people follow what they do not know, and stumble around in the dark, plagued by trouble all the days of their lives. If we could learn things that would lift the burdens of life - that would be good - would it not?"

Ferin tossed a stick for the dogs and clapped his beefy hand on Korban's back, as they walked toward the house. "Indeed, my friend. That would be good. I think perhaps it *is* time for some new ideas - a 'renaissance' isn't that what they are calling it across the sea?"

"Yes, Ferin." He chuckled to himself, as he thought about those who pursued Chag's siren call of knowledge so they could increase their power, and control the world. "A renaissance is definitely what we need."

"So Miriam, here is the man that all of Innisfallen is proclaiming as a great sorcerer, or a god - here at our very home! But I find him quite normal."

Ferin ushered Korban into the great room, and took his cloak and staff, hanging them in the corner. Miriam curtseyed and blushed.

"It is an honor, sir, to have you at our table. We did hear some great things today; welcome to our home."

"Thank you, Miriam, I am delighted to be here." Korban took her hand, and looked into her eyes. She felt power surge into her - like a cool wind - and heard the wordless speech. *You are my beloved child, in whom I am well-pleased.* She drew back her hand, transfixed in the middle of the room. "What did you say?"

He just smiled at her. Connel pursed his lips in a question, posed to Miriam and Lailah. Miriam shrugged it off, as Korban took the cup of wine offered to him by one of the boys. Laughing heartily, he raised it to his hosts. "Here's to the house of Connel! Long may it live!"

"Here, here!" Ferin tipped his cup, while Miriam turned to serving, and everyone noisily took their seats at the thick oak table. Ferin asked Korban to speak a word over the meal, and with the family chatter paused, his sonorous voice filled the room.

"Good Father, you have given us a safe place to gather, nourishing food to strengthen us, wine to gladden our hearts, and love to fill our souls. For this, and for our very lives, we give you thanks. Fill this home and this land with hope, and protect it by the might of your invisible power."

As he spoke, the room filled with the presence of an unseen force, and in awed amazement, the boys looked at each other, and at their parents, and finally at Lailah and Annalise who smiled knowingly. Smiles spread across all their faces, and Korban played with his cup in obvious amusement as he watched the reactions.

"What is it?" An inexplicable joy flowed like a river into the room, and from the top of their heads to the soles of their feet, it washed over them, flooding the room. A faint, shimmering, golden mist danced and swirled around the candelabra, ascending and descending as they watched openmouthed.

Suddenly, Korban began to giggle, and then one by one the others joined, until everyone was holding their sides in pain. Soon, the boys were rolling on the floor, and though no one understood why, eventually, the girls, Ferin, Miriam, and Korban were all collapsed with them, shrieking with delight.

The mist remained, and they discovered they could play with it, as it covered their faces, clothes, hands, and even dusted the furnishings in the room. They tossed it at each other, and waved their hands through it, mesmerized as if with some marvelous and fascinating toy. Lost in play and complete peace, they did not even realize they were in another realm. And they did not question it, nor did it frighten them.

Meanwhile, unobserved in the fire's glow, Glaurius and

Sofia looked on the happy gathering and Korban's first night on earth. "Soon, my dear, we will be one with them again."

Sofia's countenance clouded as she looked with longing at her son. "Yes, my love. For the joy set before him, he will endure the shame that is to come."

In the cozy room, the mist began to dissipate, and one by one, the weary revelers discovered they were ravenously hungry, and began to take their seats. But to the shock of all, the food remained steaming in the dishes. Soon, they were busy passing plates and eating in contented silence, recalling the bliss they had just experienced.

Eventually, Ferin spoke. "Well, friend Korban. How do you explain what happened here?" Everyone turned, grinning to their guest.

"Well, where I am from, joy is a very serious thing." He dipped a soft roll into the remaining gravy on his nearly empty plate of hot, buttered potatoes and herbs, cabbage, carrots and squash, and corned beef.

Savoring the flavors of the farm-fresh food, he raised his cup, complimenting Miriam on her cooking and Ferin for his hard work.

"Mm mm mm! In return for your hospitality and generosity, it is my pleasure to share what I have to give. And in my country, joy is the air we breathe." He looked around at their happy but puzzled expressions. "It's best not to think too much about it, really. Turn off your head, and keep open the door of your heart - that's the pathway to God."

He motioned with his fingers near his head, as if turning a key in a lock, and over his heart, as if opening a door. He gently poked the little boy next to him, and the child blushed with delight at the attention.

One of the older sons - a tall, intelligent boy of fifteen - questioned him. "But, sir, the old priest tells us we must learn and study the words of the fathers of Glaurianism, and keep all the laws. It is all very serious business – there is no laughter in our religion. And the ideas of the traveling sages are very tempting, as they regale us with their new ideas, and foreign experiences. They talk of the wisdom of the Buddha, the Mohammedans, the Greek and Latin scholars in Romu, and teach the glory of mathematics, physics, and the supremacy of science. They certainly appeal to the intellect of man."

"Chief among them is a Professor Descartes, who gathers people in homes to discuss all of these things. He and the other teachers seem very wise, and disdain the stories about The Way that have been passed down, calling them 'myths' and 'fables.' Also, many of the most powerful merchants, and the kings of the nations keep the people in thrall by the power of seers and astrologers. What is Truth, then? And by what power do you perform miracles, sir?"

Korban glanced at Lailah, who was gathering the younger ones off to bed, then answered the earnest boy. "There is a great mystery behind what you see - as you have heard in the story of The Creation, and The Rebellion. But there are many who reject the truth - as they have since the beginning. The one called Ba'al Aruni and his followers cloak themselves in ever-changing lies that appeal to the pride of man, and in religious practices that control people and assuage guilt. Finally, he entices them into the use of drugs, drink, and sex, or the lust for riches and fame. So it must be, for man was made to worship."

The young man sat a little taller, as Korban listened respectfully to him as a man, and not a child. "Friends, there are times in history where Glaurius breaks in, and stirs a restlessness in the hearts of men for freedom from oppression by the rich and powerful, and gives hope that the future for one's children will be better. That is a noble quest, and one which I heartily embrace, for as a follower of Glaurius, these represent the very essence of his plans for mankind."

Korban paused and took a handful of walnuts, thoughtfully munching as he gazed into the fire. He continued. "From the unseen realm, Glaurius is even now releasing wisdom and strategies to lift humanity from the grinding toil of bringing forth food and goods for survival, and to find cures for sickness and disease. Even to those who oppose him, he gives insight, that all might benefit. In all this, he longs to spark the dream and hunger in the heart of every person for something more, for friendship with the One who created all things, and who alone can satisfy the deepest cries of the heart, and break the curse that holds the whole earth in its grip."

He looked around the table. The two older sons, along with Annalise, Lailah, Ferin and Miriam stood or sat drinking fragrant tea, eating hot apple cobbler with cream and slices of sharp cheese, listening intently to Korban's words.

"What about each of you? Do you follow Glaurius, or something else?"

Goyim, the oldest, responded. "I am a believer in Glaurius, yet I do not follow the Glaurianists, for as you pointed out what good is a teaching or philosophy, or religion, if there is no life in it?

And looking directly at Korban, he added, "And the teacher himself provides the animus - the life - and the best hope of success, if he is present with his followers, in my opinion."

Korban returned the challenging comment with a smile. "You are absolutely correct in this, Goyim. Well said. But then again, perhaps the evidence of a successful teacher is the authority and influence of his students even in his absence?"

Ferin jumped in. "Korban, my grandfather swore that Glaurius appeared to him, but we have not had such an appearance since that time. Do we continue to believe without any evidence, and have hope despite the growing chaos and corruption in the world?"

Korban replied. "If there are remnants of the truth, and you believe, is that not a strong indicator of the power of your faith?"

"But what of their strong sorceries?" he blurted out, showing more fear than he intended.

At this, Korban turned and gazed straight into the troubled heart. There was silence in the room, except for the bells of the mechanical clock, and the snapping and hissing of the large log on the fire. Sofia and Glaurius stood invisible, looking upon the scene in the homey cottage, while slithering below in the darkness roiled a tangle of nohedim, writhing and cursing. Aruni appeared in the midst, and seethed at Glaurius, cold-blooded contempt evident in his sardonic laughter.

"I don't know why you are here, but perhaps you have forgotten this is *my* planet, and *my* people? Surely you heard the conversation from the child - the whole world is running after my science, because *you* have abandoned the world!"

He turned a jealous eye on the Connel clan. "Yes, they will always be tempted to believe in you because of that cursed 'image of God' in their DNA, but I am the one they make idols for, the one they *fear!*"

Glaurius remained calm, gazing with pity at the creature before him. "It is true, Chag, by the power of hate and dread, you cause many to serve you, but they were made to seek love and wonder. We are satisfied that love will never fail." Standing next to him, Sofia's spirit pulsated into the darkness, where it exploded into blinding light, causing the nohedi to scatter.

As they fled, she spoke, her voice a lilting flute. "You may deceive them, for a time, Ba'al Aruni, but love and mercy will triumph and bring total freedom to all who choose life." At this, the chief nohedi, blinded by the light, screamed like a strangled animal. "I will never give up!" he shrieked, and disappeared into the abyss.

Chapter Sixteen

Ferin pressed him. "Please explain to us how we are to combat the power of the Glaurianists, and the diviners." Korban's bemused gaze fell on each of the happy Connel's. "By the joy and peace that you just experienced, and that lingers still; this is the very atmosphere that surrounds Glaurius, and the force which no evil can withstand."

"And how can we fight arguments this way?" Ferin struggled to comprehend.

"Love and joy, peace and truth are gifts to you from Glaurius. These free you from fear, and are bold witnesses against the power of the sorcerers, the philosophers, and the Glaurianists."

Everyone looked around in amazement and wonder, and Korban began to laugh again, "So shall we practice some more?" He reached over to poke Ferin, who erupted with laughter, and soon they were wrestling like boys on the floor, tickling and yelping with delight. After a few minutes, they sat leaning against each other, gasping for breath and beaming from ear to ear.

As his behavior dawned on him, a look of concern began to creep across Ferin's brow, but Korban noticed, and intercepted the whispers of the hidden nohedi. "Now Ferin, there are places your heart can go, but your head cannot follow - best not to try and figure it out - just enjoy. You're perfectly safe here." He put his arm around Ferin, as though he were a little brother.

Ferin slid down until his head was in Korban's lap. Korban stroked his hair. "Ferin, the day is coming when you will always be able to see and know Glaurius. I am here to announce that his coming to earth is very near."

Ferin sat up, stunned, with tears filling his eyes.

"In the meantime, proofs of his love are everywhere you look! Here around this warm fire, and under this sturdy roof, there is evidence of God In the comforting arms of Miriam, in the beauty of your daughters, and in the joyous laughter of your sons. The bounty of your fields and herds every year attests to his kindness, and that he watches over you. The sun, moon, and stars all whisper his name if you can hear."

Ferin listened thoughtfully, then suddenly stood and exclaimed, "I believe *you* are the One who was foretold!" He glanced wildly around the room. "Yes, I feel it inside, that this is the time of which the prophets spoke. Something great is going to take place, isn't it?"

Lailah had been curled up on a fluffy sheepskin, pondering the words of Korban and her father; there was indeed a bigger story unfolding. Remembering the miracles of the morning, and marveling at the wonderful Presence now filling the room, she thought of the cave, and its mysterious drawings. *Yes, Lailah, you were right.* She turned to Korban, who was smiling at her.

"Yes, Ferin, something is coming - it is the end to Ba'al Aruni's kingdom, and the beginning of a new race of men and women who are free from his evil power, and who have authority in the earth. They will have the power over weather, to raise the dead, heal the sick, and bring freedom to those who are under the spell of Aruni."

"You mean like you have?" The earnest and innocent question from Padraigh, reverberated through the room. Korban smiled, delightedly.

"Yes, my son, and you will do even greater things than these: you will walk side by side with people through the difficult seasons of life, helping them stay strong. In all these things love is manifest - the greatest power of all."

"And how will this be? What will be the sign of this great thing?" Lailah asked.

"Glaurius will send his son to announce and demonstrate his kingdom, but they will reject, mistreat, and kill him. He will die as a sacrifice to Cernunnose. They will do it to cover their guilt, and to appease their gods. Nonetheless, he will come to life again, and will defeat all the gods, and bring peace and healing to the earth."

Ferin erupted. "How can this be? If Glaurius is the god of gods, how can he allow anyone to murder his son? And if Glaurius is immortal, how can his son be mortal? Perhaps this story is after all, like the myths of the Romans and Greeks? There have always been stories..." His voice trailed off as he shook his head, sighing with disappointment.

Korban rose and walked over to the clock on the mantle, observing the time. "There are many things you cannot understand now, but you will know all, at the right time." As he turned to face them, Lailah suddenly saw a vision of him impaled on a tree, with blood flowing from his wounds. *The man in the drawing!* He did not say a word, but Lailah's heart broke as she struggled to understand all that she had seen and heard.

"It is enough for now; there will be time to talk more in the coming days."

No one asked him why he was in Innisfallen, or how long he would stay, but Miriam had already sent Annalise and one of the boys to the guest house to prepare the fire and bed for Korban.

"Here is a bit more wine, and some water. Merle will go along with you to keep you company." The shepherd pricked up his ears and nuzzled against him.

"Thank you Miriam - and Ferin - for your hospitality." He looked over at Lailah and nodded. "I will be coming and going, for there is much to do."

Miriam squeezed Ferin's hand and responded. "Our home is your home whenever you require it."

Chapter Seventeen

The last leaves of harvest blew across the wet fields, as Lailah drove with her father to town. Foggy and grey was the day; she felt grateful to be dry under the wagon cover, surrounded by crocks of cream, butter, honey, and baskets of wheat, hazelnuts, hawthorn berries, dried lentils, barley and apples. The smell of warm bread in her lap lulled her back to sleep, and she dozed while her father chatted with Korban about the stock they drove before them - two fine dairy heifers, and three ewe sheep.

In the weeks and months since Korban had come, Innisfallen and the whole countryside was turned upside-down. Daily, Korban visited with anyone who was sick, infirm, or mentally ill. Lailah marvelled at the way he knew where to be exactly when help was needed. He taught with great authority, and everywhere he went, blessing followed. Being with him felt like floating down the Fargus on her father's barge - that great waterway which teemed with fish of various kinds, while abundant wildlife and waterfowl inhabited its shores - always flowing to the sea.

She stole a peek at Korban.

So much boundless but restrained power - like a war horse prepared for battle. Full of contradiction: he is intense, deep as the night sky, and like a man possessed. Yet he is never hurried, anxious or rushed, always hopeful and full of wisdom for every situation. He laughs like the joyous rushing waters in the creeks when spring has fully come, but his face is lined with compassion as he listens patiently to the stories of the old widows, and to the mothers who have buried their children. Overflowing with counsel, like an ancient one, but he makes others feel they are witty, important and loved.

Lailah recalled the strange confrontation in town yesterday morning. The gaggle of philosophers and occult healers now followed Korban from place to place as he visited people, waiting outside houses to see what had transpired, and then questioning him. But the people were delighted; they followed him, and and in gratitude, gave gifts and support to Korban. Praise followed him wherever he went, and a showdown was inevitable.

Mounted brazenly on the tops of the verdant hills surrounding Innisfallen, stood the altars to the gods of the pagan priests. The blood sacrifices and sexual rites still were performed either in the groves and grottoes, or under dark of night, but the conjuring ceremonies, incantations and possession rituals were conducted in full view of all the people, and the smoke from the sickly-sweet incense often hung over the town, bringing with it a sense of foulness and dark despair.

Wives and mothers fought in vain to keep their husbands and sons from the seductive enchantments of the ritual prostitutes, and their daughters from being stolen and drugged, and recruited into the ranks of those who's lives were broken and enslaved to the religion of the necromancers and Druids.

As the family wagon rolled into Innisfallen yesterday, Lailah noticed fierceness in the set jaw of Korban. He looked warily around, every sense on alert; there was not a trace of fear, but only the ever-present undercurrent of explosive power. Suddenly, a disturbance caught her attention at the gates.

A rail-thin girl stood on a stump, calling out loudly for the attention of those in the market place. "There he is!" She pointed a bony finger at Korban. He had jumped down from the cart, and stood calmly, his hands crossed in front of him.

"He is The One who is to come - the hope of us all!" Dressed only in an old woolen shawl covering a soiled satin dress, she shook like a leaf in the wind, and her voice sounded other-wordly, sending chills down Lailah's spine. Manto - a cruel, druid diviner with dark, sinister eyes - walked around assessing his property, and surveying the crowd to see the effect of her powers. Everyone stopped and stared.

If she lived for a thousand years, Lailah would never forget what happened next. Korban strode toward the girl and the man, and the small group of acolytes standing with them. He spoke just three words, "Leave her now!" but with the force and speed of a lion striking the neck of an unwary deer, they broke the spell over the poor girl, who shrieked, convulsed and collapsed into Korban's strong arms. A sense of awe settled on the crowd, along with a deep peace - like the sky after a storm.

The mediums and diviners gaped in momentary fear at Korban, whose unflinching gaze challenged any to respond. The ubiquitous Descartes inquired wryly of the augurers. "You know I disbelieve all your claims of spiritual power, but without invoking any god, this man has just undone your great sorcery. What explanation do you have for this?"

They shook their heads in stunned silence.

Korban gently stroked the matted hair of the young girl. Not more than twelve years old, she had clearly been neglected and abused perhaps by many more than this man. "Rianna? Darling, you can wake up now." She woke, a beatific smile on her face, as she gazed into the eyes of the stranger who knew her name. He kissed her on the forehead, and set her on her feet, holding her close to his side. Glancing down into her grateful face, he continued to speak reassuringly, his words caressing her like a warm, perfumed breeze.

"You are free." He lifted up his face to his detractors.

Paracelsus, the chief physician, sniffed in the direction of the slave-master. "Your mistreatment of this pathetic creature was destined for judgment in the scales of Fate: here, now, is your nemesis."

The renowned teacher gathered up his flowing white robe, and strode off to his stall at the other end of the market, followed by his students. Descartes, too motioned to his companions, and they headed off in the direction of the prophet's knoll, a flat, grassy outcropping just outside the gates, where they would practice their debates and long-winded speeches on all who walked the road. Only Manto and his votaries of the dark arts remained; in their black and gold robes, they flanked the priest, like nine pins.

"That girl is mine," he wheezed in anger. "I have paid for her, and I will decide when - if ever - to free her." The people looked at Korban to see if he would challenge the claim.

"Though you people practice slavery, it is not the will of Glaurius, who has created all men, women, boys and girls to be free."

At the name, Manto and his minions burst into mocking

laughter.

"Glaurius? And what has this false god to do with any of us? Look around, can anyone give us a sign of his existence? No, join with us, for you are indeed a mighty mystic, and use your powers! Together, we can rule the world!"

Manto grew manic, and his eyes shone with the effects of the herbs and plants used in his practices. Hoping his flattery had worked, he moved toward the girl. "And sir, take no thought for these poor unfortunates. Better that they are useful in our service, than abandoned along the roadside."

As he reached out to grab Rianna's skinny arm, an unmistakeable growl sent tremors through the crowd; Korban pointed his finger toward the gates, and sternly commanded,

"Go!" At the word, Manto flew backwards onto the muddy ground. Terror filled the sorcerer's eyes, and without turning around, he scampered away up the hill, his followers tripping along behind him like cockroaches exposed to the light.

Korban cried out to the onlookers who remained. "Do not fear the magic powers of the soothsayers, or become enthralled by the pompous words of the theosophists. And do not be deceived by the medical arts of the doctors, or any longer be bound by the laws of the priests of Glaurius. There are many voices, and many kinds of power - but I tell you again, do not be impressed by them, for all of these people are merely human, and cannot even keep themselves alive. One day, they, like you, will lie in the cold of death. And for all who follow their ways, death comes sooner and by means more terrible than you can imagine."

He paused, and looked around to see the effect of his words. All were silent, intent to hear. "Indeed, the myths and stories of Innisfallen echo the tales told around the world, and are true encounters people have had with the invisible world. The fairies, and little men, the gnomes, and dwarves, the mermaids, and fauns, gods and goddesses are all spirits from this dark world."

A woman from the crowd spoke up.

"But what of Glaurius, and the serafs who some have seen? Are they also of this world of which you speak? How do we know what is true, and who we should believe and follow?"

Korban turned to her. "You have heard the story of human history from the followers of Glaurius, and the priest; you know about the war between Glaurius and Ba'al Aruni, but you have not believed because of the weakness of those who preach and worship Glaurius. And you have grown weary of the many voices claiming your allegiance. This is why I have come - to free you from the futility of your thinking, from your own tendency to evil, and from the tyrannies of men who seek to control you. I have come to restore all things to you - all that Glaurius placed in humanity from the beginning."

"We have seen your power, Korban, and it is great, and when you teach and care for us, we see that what you say is true. You are kind, and speak with authority that no one else can match. Truly, if there is a Great King like you say, we would like him to be like you. But we are so small compared to King Henry. How then shall we be free from his control?" The woman looked around at her neighbors, who shook their heads in agreement.

Korban responded. "It is because of the lust for power that men rule over one another, but it was not so in the beginning. Though men lord it over you, I teach you a way of being that makes you *free* - free to love, to forgive, to hope, to believe in spite of all circumstances, and to see beyond the limitations of time and matter into the world to come, where there is no pain, no sorrow, no evil of any kind."

"You can each live in a new way if you will believe; you can know Glaurius, and walk in power and authority here and now - each man, woman, and child will be a king and priest."

At this, every mouth dropped open, and the tongues wagged. "Kings and priests? What are you saying - who are you, really?"

An old man, bent with age came near, and gazed up at him in awe. He whispered in sudden boldness, "Are you The Promised One that the prophets of The Way foretold?"

The crowd stirred nervously.

"I am."

Just then, a young father, followed by his distraught wife came running from the other end of the village. Carried in his arms was a lifeless boy of around eight or nine, wrapped in a blanket.

"Doctor, Doctor!" the father cried out, scanning the crowd for Korban. He roughly pushed people out of his way, calling out, "Let us pass!" Korban waited quietly as the man and his wife made their way through the mob. When at last they stood before him, Korban reached out to uncover the child.

"He has had a fever and a terrible cough for many days. The other doctors could do nothing for him, and it cost us all we had, and now our son is dead! Is there nothing you can do?" Korban looked at them and sighed with deep compassion, briefly examining the dead boy.

He tenderly touched the face of the weeping mother. "Just believe." Then he closed his eyes, and murmured the strange words; soon Laliah felt a shift in the atmosphere. When she looked again at Korban, she saw the power had come upon him. He turned to the hysterical and grief-stricken parents, and to the waiting crowd. With unmistakeable authority, he cried out:

"All things are possible to those who believe - even the power over death itself!" With that, he breathed deeply, and exhaled over the boy. "Child, I say to you, live!" To the shock of the parents, Lailah, Ferin, and all in the crowd that saw it, the child's eyes popped open, and he came to life.

One by one, many of the people dropped to their knees, bowing their heads.

"Truly, you are a god, Sir, and I did not know it!" Ferin, along with Lailah and Annalise also knelt on the ground before Korban.

But as awe descended over those gathered in the market, a movement caught Korban's eye. A young disciple of Descartes had lingered behind, watching from the hillside, just beyond the gate. Gathering up his scholarly robes, he ran quickly in the direction of the philosophers' camp; an inky black cloud surrounded him, from which echoed shrieks of indignation.

Chapter Eighteen

Korban continued to heal the sick, and raise the dead, traveling to the surrounding towns and cities, teaching the people, and stirring up his rival religionists. A group of young men followed him, many with their wives and children. He taught them about the ways of Tziyon, and as they believed, they, too, began to do the same works as Korban.

The crowds began to increase, and many left the ranks of the doctors, sorcerers, and philosophers. The grottoes and high places grew quiet, as the common people broke free of their oppression. Simple farmers, uneducated women, and all the children began to demonstrate powers of healing, prophecy, and to interpret dreams and visions. As the people ventured to more distant regions, droughts were broken as refreshing rains came, and the poor were set free from generations of poverty. Hundreds left behind addictions to drink and lust.

Some of the magicians and followers of Parcelsus and Descartes began to follow Korban, but Aruni and the nohedi stirred up the jealousy and pride in others. In all of this, the king was not absent, but as Lucan was a man of the State, and military strength was his religion, he maintained a distance, hoping the various groups would sort it all out. However, the enemies of Korban, impelled by the invisible realm, began to devise a plan to put an end to The Way.

One day, as Korban, his followers, and a crowd returned to

Innisfallen, representatives from Paracelsus, Manto, and Descartes met them at the western gate. "Sir, you and your 'Way' are causing unrest among the people. Since you have come, you have turned our way of life upside-down, and the people are running wild. How can we maintain order and peace, when you and your followers are causing such trouble?"

Korban answered him. "Bogs are formed when rain collects in depressions in the ground. Grass and other plants that grow beneath the water and along the banks decay, and the water becomes brackish and unsafe to drink. On the other hand, the river drinks up the rain, and snow from the distant mountains, and as it flows along, it gives life to fish, animals, plants and man. There is only death in things remaining as they have always been, but in the refreshing presence of truth, there is abundant life."

"So you are here to form a new government, then?"

The people in the crowd looked at Korban, and nodded their heads. "Yes, Teacher, this is what we need - we want you for our king!"

Korban remained silent as the crowd began to chant, "Korban is king!"

Incensed, the diviners and professors balled their fists and seethed at him. "Sir, silence your followers! They speak treason, and will have us all killed!"

But Korban responded, "You are not afraid for your lives, but only your livelihoods, and your lofty positions. You are all deceived, and are hypocrites, basking in your own glory and wealth, while all your followers are falling into the same pit."

The grumblers raged at him, but the crowd following Korban began to mock them, and chased them away. Korban watched them leave, knowing they would report to Lucan what had happened. The voice of Sofia came to him.

Son, take heart, for what is to take place, must happen soon. He saw her face, so full of love and concern; strength from her filled him, and he turned to face the crowd.

He dismissed them, calling only those who had been with him from the beginning: Ferin, Miriam, Lailah, and all the Connel clan who believed and labored with him day after day, and many other families who gave of their time and goods to support the work of healing and encouraging the people. In their eyes, he saw uncertainty mixed with hope and determination; knowing their greatest test would soon be upon them, he spoke.

"I have told you that the time would come when I would leave you. Now the time is upon us, and I want to spend the day with you, and share a final meal."

Ferin and Lailah's faces were crestfallen. "Korban, what will they do, and what is to become of you?"

"Be strong, and do not fear. Come." He led everyone out through the eastern gate, and had the people spread out on the rolling hillside in the warm, morning sun. Taking a basket of bread, one of cheese, nuts and fruit, and a skin of wine, he gave thanks to Glaurius, blessed the food, and with volunteers, began walking through the crowds passing it out.

Everyone ate and drank their fill; the children played, and laughter filled the air. The sound of flutes and tambours, dancing and merriment resounded across the hills, until the middle of the afternoon. As the sun passed overhead, many dozed in the shade. After their rest, Korban climbed a little ways up the hill, and began to speak.

"I came to free you from the bondage of Aruni; for my Father - King Glaurius - and for his kingdom you have been summoned. You are awake now, but soon I will leave you, and when I do, I will send you a special power so that I will be with you and in you forever."

Thane, a young fisherman spoke up. "Korban, where are you going? Can we not go with you?" His anxious questions echoed the sentiments of the rest.

Korban reached out and pulled him to his side, holding him close. "Thane, my son, you can not go where I am going yet, because I am going to The Land of Promise, to finish the homes I am preparing for you all. And you must remain, for there are many who do not yet know about my kingdom, and about my Father, and your father. As for me, the sons of Aruni will kill me, but in so doing, they will destroy their works by their own hands, for I will rise from death."

He looked over the old, the young, men, women, and children. "Love each other; and as I have healed you, heal one another. Do not be afraid, because I am with you, and will come back for you. I am Mysterion, closer than your very breath, ever attentive to your faintest cry."

Korban spent the next two hours wandering among the people, praying, laughing, embracing, and encouraging them. As the day faded, and evening approached, one by one, they left - hearts full, but with a pang of sorrow, and uncertainty - to return to their homes.

Only the Connel clan remained. Ferin's eyes searched the teacher's face, but saw only inscrutable love and majesty, and unmistakeable authority. Korban caught his arm, and held him close, savoring the scent of the fields, and the strength of his muscled body.

"I am so very proud of you, my friend." Big tears dropped onto the grey robe, as Ferin's body shook with gratitude and a sense of belonging that he had never felt before. Korban lifted his head, to look into his eyes. "You are an orphan no longer." Each of the family members drew close to Korban, and shared a long moment with him.

He spoke words of destiny and hope, and when he came at last to Lailah, he pulled her to him. Taking her hand, they walked away from the rest. The full moon rose over the deep blue hills, and stars began to twinkle overhead. He stopped, and took her face in his hands.

"Lailah, I know that you have faithfully waited and watched for me. You found the cave; and now you have found the answer to your questions."

With him, her thoughts traced the drawings on the wall - she knew them all by name - Glaurius, the burning man; Mogen and Cheva, the man and woman; and Korban, the man on the tree, with the great drops of blood sprinkling the ground.

"Lailah, I am yours, but we cannot be together now. I must return to Tziyon to complete all that must be done. In the future, there will be Connel women who come from you, carrying the seed of truth, and one day, a daughter will take the key which you will pass along, and then I will return for you all. For truly, you are a daughter of Cheva, and my promise to her must come to pass; I will restore all. Before that, my darling, there will be pain, but I have shown you how to access realms of joy."

Tears filled Lailah's eyes as she kissed his hands, her heart aching, knowing a dark and ominous cloud approached. He drew her close, and kissed her hair. Suddenly, the breeze stirred the trees, and he sang in a voice like a waterfall; caught up, she flew with him into the night sky, past the clouds and beyond the slowly spinning planets and the blazing stars. Together they slipped effortlessly beyond space, and always the song remained and surrounded her.

Soon they stopped moving, and she saw beneath her a rainbow-enshrouded sphere. In the midst was a colossal mountain covered with trees, and a crystal river flowed from the mountainside. At the base of the mountain, she saw a multitude of animals and birds and in the middle of these was a golden throne; on the throne sat a man shimmering with colored fire, and thousands of children surrounded him. There were also griffons - creatures that had the body of a lion, the head of an eagle, and were covered with many eyes; these flew around the throne.

A beautiful, black and silver-haired woman stood beside the fiery man, as music of violins, trumpets, great drums, all kinds of wind instruments, and harps drifted up to where Korban and Lailah stood. Lailah recognized the melody as the one which Korban sang.

> *"Down the mountain, the river flows,*
> *into the valleys, and over the hills,*
> *rushing, healing, we all jump in*
> *Leaping, dancing, free at last*
> *Jump in and become one -*
> *One in the river."*

"Such a strange song, Korban. What does it mean? She marveled at the intensity of emotion that pulsed from inside the orb, and watched in amazement as the joy-sound travelled in colored waves of sound and light into the far-off depths of space, enveloped the planets, and shook distant stars, causing the whole universe to tremble and shiver with delight.

"Glaurius and the power which we Three possess is the energy force holding everything together - is personified as a river. Love is the central element of our nature, and of our kingdom, and it flows from us into those who possess the same spirit - those who are of our family. Lailah, love must move and create, and heal and animate all within its path, or it is not love. It is love, flowing like a river from my followers, which will give life and hope to this barren planet now, and in the Day that is coming - the Day when I return for my bride."

He gently took her face in his hands again, and stared deeply into her eyes. "There is no power that can withstand love; love transforms and transcends even death itself." She looked trustingly into his shining face. "And in the river is where you can find me, and where we are one. In the flow of my spirit, I am with you, though you cannot always see."

He looked around at the trees, the darkened hills, at the moon and stars. "Nature speaks of me, and you can write me songs, and poetry; music is also the language of the heart. In the comfort of family and friends, and around the table, you can call me, and I will come; you will feel my presence."

He reached into his cloak, and pulled something out. "And there is this." He placed a leather-bound book into her hands. Opening the pages, a rush of fragrant perfume escaped. At the scent, she was taken back to days of listening to him teach on the hillsides, and near the ocean, and saw in her mind again the miracles, felt the nearness and security of his presence, heard his laughter, and enjoyed the merriment of the people as they celebrated and walked together in freedom.

She looked at him in wonder, and he smiled and explained. "The wizards and magicians have their books of spells, and secret charms, their logic and science - endless words. But these are *my* thoughts, *my* ways, *my* poetry, and *my* wisdom, and they are far above anything they will ever think or imagine. It's for you, and for all who love me. Pass along what I have told you, Lailah: muse, and absorb my words, and they will be life to you. They are the same as having me near, for I am in my words."

She cocked her head, not grasping all he said. "Soon you will receive power to comprehend all that I have told you. Remember me, and teach your children."

Suddenly the sound of horses and riders was heard, and torches lit up the road. Korban kissed her quickly on the forehead. "My time has come. Do not fear, my darling. But be brave and of good courage."

He led her back to the others, speaking last to Miriam. "You have been faithful in the presence of much opposition, and believed because of the words in the scroll. For this, you will be richly rewarded. Your daughters will have a special work for Glaurius in the future."

Miriam hugged him in gratitude, tears welling up in her eyes; then she looked down at her feet. "It was a woman, after all, who brought this great curse upon us, and it is only fitting that it should be so."

"No, Miriam, it was the love of a man, for a woman that he could not live without."

Just then, Ferin ran up the hill, and stopped, breathless, eyes wild with fear. Korban spoke to him, as he began to descend the hill. "Take Lailah, and all of you go home."

"But Korban, surely you can call upon Glaurius, and he will rescue you with many powerful gibborim!"

He reached out and gripped Ferin's arm one last time. "Do not fear, Ferin. Only believe, and wait until I come to you." He kissed Ferin on the cheek, and walked down the hill to face the soldiers, and the crowd of acolytes and teachers, and curious on-lookers, who were all eager for a spectacle.

"There he is, Captain. The one they call 'Master,' and 'Teacher,' who is calling for revolution." He turned to the crowd to elicit their support. "But we recognize no other ruler but Lucan, and no other 'way' besides what we have always known - isn't that right? He is dangerous, and must be stopped."

The people shook their heads in agreement, and nodded to one another. "That's right! He is nothing but trouble!"

Emboldened by this, Manto stepped up to pull aside Korban's hood, but the accused met their hateful stares with pity, and unruffled calm.

Stolus, the captain of Lucan's local guard turned on Manto.

"Are you kidding, witch?" He spoke to Korban. "What is it that you are guilty of? I have heard of many things attributed to you: of miracles of healing, multiplying of food, clothing the naked, and even raising the dead. These sound like religious concerns. For which of these things are you accused of treason?" He brought a torch closer, and studied Korban's face. "Are you planning an insurrection? You don't look very dangerous to me."

Korban raised his face to look into the eyes of the grizzled, battle-worn captain. Unconditional love, waves of peace, and an invitation to rest flowed from within the young man, out to the soldier. The crowd of detractors shifted nervously, as unseen, a band of light-bearing serafs surrounded the camp. Black figures slithered around like vipers at the feet of the professors, doctors, and others jumped like fidgety rats amongst the sorcerers and Druid priests.

Aruni perched overhead in a dead tree, watching the scene below. "Victory is within my grasp," he wheezed to a bloated nohedi that hovered nearby. "Soon, I will end this little movement that he has begun, and they will again be in my control. This earth is mine - won fair and square. Glaurius will never take it back. For I will put an end to *him*!"

He shrieked into the darkness, at his unseen foe. "You failed to convince the most important ones! Hahahahahaha! You cannot have power when the powerful will not follow you, and now they will kill your heir - your 'secret weapon.' No, you wagered on that infernal spark of faith to come alive in them, but they have rejected you."

At that moment, Korban glanced up into the tree, and saw Aruni there, his wizened body, hunched over like a vulture. A chill of terror swept through the ancient serpent, at the smoldering fire that blazed from the eternal eyes, and the nohedi chief trembled like a leaf.

"I have come to free slaves." He spoke directly to the captain.

"And what exactly are you setting them free from?" The man asked.

Descartes spoke up. "You see, he speaks crimes against the realm! Everyone knows we are the servants of King Lucan, yet you yourself heard him say he has come to set us free! We have no allegiance to this unseen God, but are our own rulers, committed only to the virtues of reason, and the common good. This schism between us is because of this man, and it is clearly not in our best interests to abandon what has worked so well."

The puzzled captain looked around, and back again at Korban who remained silent. Descartes took advantage of the confusion, and turned to the crowd, to stir them up again.

"Do any of you doubt what will happen next if we continue down the path with this man? The whole world is following after this stranger with his sorceries and talk of invisible gods. He is leading us all off a cliff! No, we have no king, no leader but Lucan, and no gods but science and reason!"

In the crowd were those who had followed Korban for the food, and for the wonder of the miracles, but their hearts had remained untouched. They refused to embrace him and his words, and now they raised their voices against him. "We have no king but Lucan. Lucan, Lucan, Lucan!"

Manto rubbed his hands together, in manic bloodlust. "I have news: the king has recently come from the mainland where he met with the leaders of the growing Church of Glaurius. Lucan has agreed with them to build an abbey, and promote worship there only. I myself have decided to submit to the superior teachings of the Church, and look forward to the unity we will all enjoy."

He smiled beatifically, until someone in the crowd yelled.

"You're a liar, priest! Why, you will never leave your incantations and devil worship. Korban follows Glaurius, and is a good man!" Others, confused by the priest's claims, listened as he continued.

"No man can claim to be a priest of Glaurius, but must receive the teachings of the Holy Mother Church! It is even as the saying goes, 'Like priest, like prophet, and the people love it!' We all must follow our fathers, our leaders, and our king. No one is free to hear from Glaurius on his own - we all know that is the role of a true priest - he is the go-between, the mediator!"

But someone cried out in protest, "Korban has taught us that we can know Glaurius for *ourselves*, that he loves us, and wants to speak to each one of us - we don't need a priest at all!" As the various camps began to go after one another; Stolus tried to quiet them down and gain control, but many were drunk, and the nohedi had stirred up the more violent among them, who began to curse, and fight with one another. Women began to scream, and mayhem ensued.

Ferin, seeing things devolve so rapidly, ran back up the hill from where he had hidden. He gathered the children and Miriam, and they began to retreat down the back side of the hill, while Lailah lagged behind, watching until the torches were no longer visible, grief overwhelming her. Ferin came to her, and wrapped her in his big arms, as she sobbed her pain into his chest, but there was no comfort there. He gently tilted her face up to look into her eyes. "Lailah, do you remember what Korban promised us?

She gulped big breaths, and nodded miserably. "Yes, Father."

"He promised to return. Let us be patient and believe."

Beautiful even in disarray, her loyal heart revived for a moment. "Where will they take him, Father?"

"To Lucan."

She shuddered at the thought of the man who ruled the island, the foreign monarch who cared about two things only: political maneuvering, and life at court. He would do anything to prevent a disturbance to his orderly rule. He cared nothing for the lives of those who could not gain him a social or strategic advantage.

"I imagine execution will follow swiftly." He carried Megan in his arms, and she lay against his shoulder, fast asleep.

"Perhaps he will be merciful, and exile Korban instead?" The agony of wishing for another outcome, but knowing the answer, melted his heart.

They had come to the wagon, and when all the children were asleep in the back, Ferin took her aside, whispering between clenched teeth, "Lailah, Korban is the required sacrifice to restore us back to Glaurius. He is the Curse-Breaker. I do not understand how it works, or why his blood is needed, but whatever happened way back in the beginning, it is the Creator himself who must give his life to restore what was lost." He spoke a wisdom she had never before heard from his lips.

"Lailah, I believe Korban is the son of Glaurius, which makes him God."

Stunned by the revelation, they looked at one another with awe.

"We have seen great things that we did not fully understand; Glaurius must be with us even now, so we must trust him." He directed the older boys. "Go on now, take everyone home."

He kissed Miriam. "I will go to the Great House to see what will be done. Try to eat something, and get some sleep." He took Lailah's hand for a moment, and disappeared in the dark, heading in the direction of the torches.

Lailah laid down between her sisters and brothers, hugging her arms to herself. Recalling the words of Korban, peace came as the exhausted girl listened to the rhythmic sound of the wheels, and the clip-clop of the horse's hooves. *I will not leave you as orphans, for you are mine. No, I will never leave you, nor forsake you.*

Miriam turned around at that moment, and their eyes met. *It will be okay, Lailah. Only trust.* She snuggled down next to Meghan, and drifted off to sleep.

Chapter Nineteen

Ferin caught up to within earshot of the crowd that followed the soldiers and their prisoner, but in the dark, he was undetectable as he walked along the roadside. Snatches of conversation mixed with the clomping of boots, shuffling of feet, and the howling of a wolf in the distance. Dust swirled and the wind whipped up, as the unseen nohedi shoved and pressed in on each other to see Korban in chains, walking beside a mounted soldier.

Hissing and cackling, giddy with victory, they sneered. "Son of Glaurius? Where is your help now, Super Man? You're going to squawk like a chicken when we're done with you!!" Their laughter echoed off the hills, but Korban walked quietly, unmoved in the midst of the tumult. As they came to a halt at the castle gate, the keeper appeared from the gabled upper story. He spoke briefly to the captain, and disappeared again over the battlements, to alert the guards on the other side. Soon, the heavy oak and iron doors creaked slowly open, and the party made its way into the cobbled courtyard.

The uninvited and noisy crowd was shut out, but Ferin spoke to the captain, who permitted him to accompany Korban. "That poor bastard is going to need a friend," he answered grimly. Hurrying well behind the soldiers, Ferin kept to the back of the large room in the stockade where Lucan would soon appear to hear the charges. Descartes and a Druid priest joked with two prostitutes that lounged like house cats on the dirty sofa. A rush of air ushered in the lieutenant, followed by the diminutive and perturbed Lucan, his black mop of hair framing a battle-worn face.

The work of ordering the barbaric malcontents on the island showed in his carriage; that the people resisted law, and the piety of the Church caused a continual grating, like the steady drip, drip, drip of a faucet. He longed to return to Engleland, to his mistress, to hunting, and to the peaceful exercises of his army. *Such a superstitious, rebellious rabble, will I never conquer them?* He muttered to himself, as a prayer to the Unseen One.

He turned to the business at hand, quickly surveying the group assembled there. *That greedy and pompous Descartes would have us all turn to the godlessness of his Gaulish sycophants - so contemptuous in their self-glorification. It's a pity, really, because he has some very good ideas.* Turning to the Druid, he seethed. *We will put an end to your blood-letting, and secret rituals. The beauty of Glaurius's sacraments and masses will purge even the memory of you from the minds of all. Not one of you - nor any of your writings - will survive the month.*

As his eyes roamed over the whores and soldiers, he saw boredom and foolishness, the careless servitude of the vassals that gave the rulers their purpose for existence. *How we love your worshipful attention, and need your work to build our empires. Poor, simple children, always clamoring for a king.* Finally, he stopped at the grey-robed man who stood shackled, beneath the circular lamp in the center of the room.

His heart stopped as he felt the drawing of quiet majesty; it flowed in gentle streams out to him, beckoning him into its embrace. Lucan began to feel light-headed, then afraid of what he did not understand. It seemed like many moments passed, and finally Korban raised his face to look at him. Lucan's life passed before him in an instant - his wars, acquisitions, palaces, mistresses, enemies, and vast wealth - all that he had fought for and believed in - and suddenly, it burned up like ashes before his eyes.

He gasped, and looked around, but no one seemed to notice - it was as if he was invisible, or in another place. But he quickly composed himself, not knowing what else to do. *Am I mad? Maybe it's the presence of the Druid - his sorceries are powerful. But, no, it is this man. I fear I must not harm him.* Korban registered no emotion, nor spoke a word, but Lucan felt his soul lay bare before the man.

He turned to Stolus. "Well, what have we here, that you

must rouse me in the midst of my evening rest?"

Stolus cleared his throat, "Sire, the leaders have brought charges that he is a sorcerer fomenting rebellion. They claim the people worship him, and want to make him king."

He turned to look squarely at Manto. "I find the first charge ridiculous coming from you, Druid. " Manto swallowed reflexively, but the sneer never left his face. Lucan turned the knife. "Yes, we will soon find out who the true witches and wizards are."

He looked at Korban. "Is it true? Are you a necromancer?"

Korban answered calmly, confidently. "I do not consort with, but rather raise the dead." It felt like the air was sucked from the room, as one and all considered the claim.

"Extraordinary! Have any of you witnessed these dead-raising miracles? For surely, this would be a very great power, enough to cause the admiration of all?"

Lucan stared down the philosopher and the priest, and looked around for corroboration from the rest. "Well?"

Several admitted to seeing the raising of the dead boy, and of knowing about another half-dozen people who were similarly restored to life. They also told of the healings, deliverances from evil spirits, and the multiplication of food. Lucan glanced around, and then at Korban. "So by what power do you do these miracles, my friend?"

"They are done by the power of Glaurius."

A window banged open in the wind that thrust its way into the room; the storm seemed to have gained teeth. Barely containing his disdain, he inquired further. "So then, you worship Glaurius? I worship him myself, and have installed my own priest here in Innisfallen. How is it that you have come here? From where did you receive your seminary instruction?"

"I come from Glaurius, and will go back to Glaurius."

Lucan, fresh from consultations with the head of the church in Engleland, became indignant. "Indeed? Well, young man, there is no precedent for any such a thing! There is order and strict protocol for priests of Glaurius, for far too many seek the riches that can be had." He shook his head. "It is important to carefully screen those who go about his altars. One must be known, and approved by one's elders - and by the Church. No, it is a weighty thing, and there are a great many rules to follow, one must have the correct theology."

He fumed and sputtered, blustering his way out of his discomfort. He patted his vest, and the scroll of orders that he carried. "Emissaries and young priests are preparing even now to sail to the island, to import the faith, raising the generations to come, in the fear and admonition of Glaurius."

The king had the plans and money to repair and enlarge the abbey in Innisfallen. "No, this charge alone is problem enough, for I am zealous for the purity of worship to Glaurius. Miracles or no, this will never do."

Korban stood silent as a lamb before its butchers. Lucan shoved back his chair, and slammed his fist on the table. "I will rid this land of all who would taint devotion to the One who is above all, who has given us his laws, and clearly shown us his ways." He turned and pointed his finger at Descartes. "Even you, philosopher! You will not corrupt the faithful with your 'humanism.'" He muttered to Stolus. "Take him away, he is deserving of death - the penalty for all sorcerers!"

Ferin could not believe his ears. Rushing to Korban's side, he searched the love-filled eyes, for answers. *Do not let your heart be troubled, only believe.* A callous soldier pulled them apart away, and Ferin dropped to his knees. One of the prostitutes had seen the exchange between them, and went to him. "Surely, he is a great man." Ferin responded to the skies above, pounding his fist into his hand. Between gritted teeth, he fiercely whispered. "He will rise again, the grave cannot hold him!"

* * *

In the meadow behind Lucan's castlestood a spreading tree, the most renown of all the Druid oaks, the last of the great oaks of the Kimber grove. But its leaves seemed to rustle in protest at the drama unfolding at its feet, and the branches clacked together in the ghostly breeze. Hordes of nohedi swirled in the treetops, as the executioner towered above the group of soldiers, his hood concealing his identity; he sharpened his arrows, as Korban was led out, and tied to the tree.

He stood mute and unresisting as they wrapped the ropes around him, with not a hair on his head ruffled; he made no attempt to escape, or to fight, and remained as compliant as a child, never opening his mouth. The moon suddenly appeared from behind the thick bank of clouds, illuminating the murderous scene, while the evening star and Jupiter twinkled beneath the clear outline of Regulus, conjoined in an arc around the moon.

Korban looked up, into the full face of the moon, and a smile crossed his lips. Glaurius took the hand of Sofia in his, and they nodded as they glanced down, hearts full of love and blessing.

Korban looked once more at each of the players in this final act. Each had their role. The king had judged, the captain carried out the orders, the soldiers waited, and the executioner slowly cocked the bow. He pulled back hard, it strained with the tension, and he hesitated. Korban closed his eyes. Finally, the fffttt of the arrow pierced the now-still air, and found its mark.

And darkness hid the moon, and the stars, and the face of Glaurius and Sofia.

Chapter Twenty

Stolus sighed deeply, and shook his head at the wanton slaughter. More of a philosopher than a soldier, he had become an officer to defend his family's lands, and because he deeply believed in the then-younger Lucan's devotion to reform and justice. But over time, Lucan's zeal for law and control, and his need for approval and peace had led him to lose his way.

The pool of blood became a stream, mixing now with the falling rain. A soldier removed the arrow, and the captain stood over the slumped body that was regal even in death. He gently brushed back the hair, and caressed his skin. *Barely older than my son - may he become a man just like you.*

Grief gripped his heart. *Oh, the innocence and courage of a just cause! You loved us, and gave us the hope of a better life. In you we witnessed the beauty of true freedom, and the possibilities of man aligned with the Unseen. You gave answers to our questions, and demonstrated real power over disease, and evil. But here you lie, defeated by the greatest enemy of all.*

He pulled himself away. "May you rest in peace."

He motioned to one of the soldiers to place him on the cart. "See that you are gentle."

Ferin stepped into the circle of light from the torches. "May I have the body, Sir?"

The battle-weary eyes met his, and Stolus nodded. Ferin reached impulsively for his hand, as the captain turned to walk away. "Do not grieve, Captain, for there is hope, and do not doubt, but believe, for he told us he will arise from death."

Stolus smiled at the simple fool. "Then perhaps he will, Master Ferin, perhaps he will." He spoke gently. "Now, see to it that you get home and off the road quickly, for it is a devilish night."

"Thank you, Sir." Ferin hitched his horse to the cart, and walked around to make sure the leather canopy protected Korban's body from the rain. He paused and studied the face.

Such a mystery, you are, dear friend. Master, Teacher, Prophet, Friend, Brother - and dare I say it - God? Mighty in power, yet you restrained yourself against those who sought to destroy you. Surely there is a judgment, a punishment for evil, but you showed love. And in the very midst of life's sorrows, you prepared a feast for us, showing us the future hope we have in your glorious Promised Land. We have seen much that is strange, much we do not understand.

He rolled up a piece of linen cloth, placing it under Korban's head, and climbed up onto the wagon bench, then clucking to the mare, he headed down the dark road for home.

* * *

Ferin pulled into the flooding yard, where the rain flowed in every direction. Miriam stood in the doorway holding the lamp, as the dogs bolted from the house. "Send the boys out!" Ferin shouted over the howling wind, and the creaking oaks. She shut up the house, and soon the two older sons appeared, running out to help their father. Worry showed on their faces when they saw the body in the back of the wagon. "It is the Master. Quickly, lads, for the storm is fierce - we will put him in the guest house!"

The three labored at their task, but soon they were inside, safe from the roar of the storm. Lighting the lamps, they placed Korban's body on the bed. A wonderful peace engulfed them, as Ferin led in prayer, squeezing their hands reassuringly.

"We must try to get some sleep - we will prepare the body in the morning, and place him in our tomb. Come, now."

* * *

All night long, the heavens rocked, and the earth reeled in an invisible war. It felt to Ferin as though the sky would be torn in two, or the great trees uprooted, and the stone manor itself might pitch upwards into the shrieking blackness. But inside

138

the house it was still as a limpid pool, and Ferin fell fast asleep, as soon as he hit the pillow.

The sun was well up by the time he awoke, smiling with deep satisfaction, still connected to a wonderful dream.

In his dream, Glaurius stood at the outer gates of a magnificent house. Ferin instinctively recognized the radiant face, wreathed with curly white hair and beard. As the king stretched out his arms, he rushed into their embrace, hiding himself within the great strength of the king, as though sheltered in the heart of an impenetrable fortress.

Glaurius murmured his name, with his head face buried in Ferin's thick hair. "My son, my son, how dear you are to me." Ferin stayed for some time, absorbing the feeling of safety and belonging.

Finally, Glaurius took Ferin's hand, and placed it on his chest. Beneath the linen robe, Ferin felt the strong, steady beating of the king's heart. Next, he placed Ferin's hand over his own, as Ferin looked at him in wonder; the hearts beat as one. "And so it is with all my children - our hearts are entwined." Lost in wonder over the things he saw and felt, he slowly turned to the sound of a lullaby that drifted in on a perfumed breeze behind him.

He then met the endless depths of Sofia's blue-green eyes; she seemed so familiar to him, and then he realized the feminine presence that had also been in his mother. "Ferin, I am Sofia."

Weariness he did not know he carried, fell away as she reached out her hands and drew him to her. Such comfort, such softness, peace, and deep stillness enveloped him, while warm waves of mother-love washed over him. He drifted on the buoyant atmosphere, aware of neither weight nor time, void of anxiety and pain. He stayed in her embrace for some time, but slowly began to rise from the profound bliss, as Sofia kissed his forehead. She smiled at him, and pointed in the direction of the interior of the house.

"Go on, now, have fun. Go see what we have prepared for you!"

Suddenly curious about his surroundings, he pulled away, gazing in awe at what his eyes beheld: each of the doors to the interior of the house were crafted of a single, iridescent pearl, trimmed out with hinges and handles of shining gold. Jewels studded the hardware, and intricate carvings of birds, flowers and other strange symbols pulsed on the pearled surface, as if alive. A misty atmosphere of swirling colors led him into a foyer, and then to the library and art gallery.

As he passed through these rooms, he marveled at statuary cast in bronze, silver and gold, and adorned with gems, and carvings from all kinds of multi-hued wood: there were replicas of exotic animals and birds, things Ferin had never imagined; agile and powerful tigers, fleet-footed zebras, brilliantly-colored flamingoes and toucans, and a perfect image of an elephant. Paintings of pastoral scenes lined the mauve walls, and shelves filled with books, rose to the second floor. In various places were comfortable couches, lamps, tables, and plates of food.

Enormous gems studded the walls and outlined the stairs and ceiling, sparkling in rainbow-hued splendor as light flooded into the open windows. Twining on the outside walls, and around the windows, grew flowers and foliage of every kind, and an intoxicating perfume of flowers and fruit filled Ferin's nose; strains of orchestral music drifted in from an open door across the enormous vestibule. He turned to look back at the king and Sofia, who motioned to him to continue in the direction of the music.

Crossing the marble and jeweled tile floor, Ferin noticed clear water running underneath, and saw fishes leaping and darting in the river. Marvelling at the joy and peace surrounding him, he seemed to float to the open door.

Weightless! What a wonderful feeling. Carried on the air, he drifted into the lighted entrance, and out into the yard.

Hundreds of children, teenagers, young men and women, middle-aged, and old people covered the grassy lawn, playing every kind of game: croquet, tennis, bocce, tag - and running, tumbling into heaps, and laughing. Platters of food, and pitchers of colorful drinks burdened wooden tables, and he recognized serafs scattered in the midst. One fat seraf gathered a group together for a dance, organizing everyone into a line that snaked around the yard. The musicians - people and serafs - had dozens of instruments, and played songs Ferin could not even describe for their complexity and beauty.

The music became increasingly fast, and soon everyone - young and old - were in a pile on the ground, laughing and playing. Ferin longed to join in the fun, and started to walk out though the door, when he felt a hand on his shoulder. He turned to look into the face of an enormous man-like creature.

He felt that he knew this being, but before he could ask, the seraf explained. "We are your servants, and constant companions, watching over you for the Master. I have been with you all your life; my name is Jabel."

His mouth hung open at the thought, and gazing at the massive presence, he began to laugh. "Thank you, sir! How confident I will be from now on!" Jabel bowed modestly, but with an impish grin. "I am at your service, Master Ferin."

"Then please tell me, sir, is my mother here?" Jabel motioned with his eyes for him to turn around, and as he did, he saw Lily, her raven hair cascading around her shoulders, as beautiful as ever he could recall, her face, beatific in the morning light.

"Mother!" She was larger than him here, as was everything, and she easily enfolded him in her arms, like a child. He swooned from the emotion, but the strength of her love sustained him. She stroked his forehead.

"My son, how proud I am of who you have become! You are standing strong in the midst of difficult times; continue on in faith, and patience, leading your children, and whoever will believe." She added softly, "I often watch you."

"Watch me? How can you see me from here, Mother?" She kissed him, and set him on his feet. "My son, we can see into the world in which you live."

As Ferin considered all these things, Jabel reached out to take his hand. "It is time to return, Master Ferin. Are you ready?"

He looked with sadness at his mother, but suddenly, Glaurius coming from behind, scooped Ferin up into his arms, while leaping, and dancing and singing a silly song; Ferin laughed, as Glaurius squeezed him tight one last time, before setting him down in the middle of the small crowd. He was passed from one person to the next, and hugged, kissed and spun around until he fell on the ground in blissful contentment. "We will see you again very soon, my love," Lily crooned.

Jabel stood grinning, looking down at the burly man sprawled out on the cool grass. Reaching down, he pulled him up with two fingers.

Ferin waved goodbye with no sense of regret, as Jabel led him to the edge of the garden. On the way, he inquired of the mighty seraf.

"Jabel, why do you call me 'Master'? For you are a very great prince, and I am only a man."

"Ferin, there are no sons of Glaurius who are 'only men,' for those who have awakened to life are his true sons, and we

141

are your servants. A royal son or daughter, is heir to all that is his - especially the earth, which was created for man; yes, you are lords of creation, broken as it now is, and we help you in your war against Aruni."

Ferin cast a quizzical glance at him. "Yes, Ferin, it is a war against mankind, and especially against you, and all followers of The Way. Aruni will never give up his rule, until he is finally destroyed. In the meantime, he battles for the hearts and minds of men."

Ferin sighed, wondering at the profound joys he had experienced since first meeting Korban, and the reality of the dangers and sorrows of life that still remained. The seraf smiled. "Master Ferin, you now have access to peace and strength, that will help you in your journey through life, and you have me." He flexed his enormous bicep, and pointed at the bulging muscles, beaming with pride.

"But on a more serious note, there is nothing that can happen to you without the permission of Glaurius - and you will be the better man for the struggle."

They walked to the edge of the mown field, and stood before a shaft of light that descended through the clouds below. "This is the portal where you will return." Ferin peered down into the swirling light, and waited.

"Ferin, tell others what you have seen and heard, and take heart; be strong, and remember the promises of the King."

With that, Jabel bowed low, and Ferin dropped down through the shimmering portal.

Chapter Twenty-One

Ferin dressed, and descended to the kitchen, where the Connel children sat at breakfast, Miriam having prepared a feast of sausages and eggs, warm hot-cakes, fruit and tea with cream. Lailah appeared surprisingly contented.

"Well, everyone seems quite alright today, my love," he whispered to Miriam as he grabbed a kiss and passed a platter, serving the younger children.

"We have all had very beautiful dreams," she said, with a happy smile.

"As have I!" He joined his excited family, who for the next half-hour recounted their stories of their nocturnal visits to Tziyon, and the sights and people they saw there.

"Grandmother was there," said Padraigh.

"And my little kitty!" piped in Meghan.

"And Glaurius bounced me on his knee!" said another.

"I beat a seraf at nine pins," boasted William.

"Such a wondrous place..." Miriam gazed dreamily at her tea, and Ferin marveled at the experience: that they had all crossed over to the other side. Delighting in the tales for some time, he finally rose to clear the table, speaking quietly to Miriam in the kitchen.

"We should attend to the body, and bury him today."

She met Lailah's eyes, as she entered with dishes for the wash water. "Yes, we must prepare the herbs and spices, and wrap the body, burying him today at sunset, as is our custom."

After breakfast, they gathered the aromatic herbs and spices: chamomile, balsam, lavender, marjoram, thyme, cinnamon, and cedar oil they mixed with salt, and carried it across the courtyard to the guesthouse. Cautiously opening the door, they stepped into the dark room, and stood before the empty bed, where Korban had lain.

"Where is he, mother?" Lailah cried out, her hand going instinctively to the key around her neck. It was warm beneath her fingers.

"Oh mother, he is *alive* – just as he said!" And suddenly, he appeared before them, in the center of the hearth. They ran to him. "Korban, how can this be?"

"Miriam, I have the power over death, and all the powers of darkness."

He went with them to the house, and ate a meal, sharing his heart, and the things to come. "There is much to do, for Lucan will bring his priests and monks, and set up false worship, only remain faithful, and many will come to know the real power of my father. For it is not in empty rituals, or dusty books full of words, or in droning prayers and endless rules that you attain to this higher life, nor is it a reward for your good works, or something you receive only after you die. No, you can come into my presence anytime, by simply calling out to me, and believing. I am going to Tziyon to prepare the house for your arrival - there is much to do."

He smiled at each one. "Keep this truth always in your heart, and do not be deceived by what you see, for this world of darkness is passing away. And do not believe everything you hear, for the enemy has endless words, and many voices. Do not be swayed by fine-sounding arguments, or wealth and position, for I am not in those things."

"Korban, will we see you again?" William, the middle boy sat on his lap, and gazed into his face with deep concern.

"William, you are a conqueror, and I will be with you to make you strong. Do not fear anything, because I will rescue you in any trouble."

He prayed for, and kissed them, blessing each one. Coming at last to Lailah, he took her hands in his. The thought of losing him again was a heavy burden, and great tears fell from her eyes. He gently brushed them aside.

"Lailah, I am giving you greater understanding for dreams and prophecy; with this power you can predict the future, understand the times, and avert droughts and other disasters. This wisdom will help many people, and will be passed along to your daughters. Also, the key you guard must be given to your first-born daughter, who will pass it to her daughter and so on. Pass along the truth you have heard, and the truths you will learn."

With that, he kissed her one last time, and exhaling over them, released a swirling, colored mist that filled the room.

Lailah suddenly saw the King and Sofia standing before their armies, the banners with the three golden lions on the scarlet background, snapping above them in the breeze. Behind them, the snow-covered peaks of Glaury rose majestically into blue skies that went on forever, and the thunderous song of thousands of thousands of serafs crescendoed and sent shock waves into the room, where everyone fell under the power. For some time the music and visions continued, and all shook with the vibrations of Heaven.

And when they returned, the sun was setting in Innisfallen, and Korban was gone. But his unmistakeable presence remained long into the night, and for many days their hearts were full of wonder.

Chapter Twenty-Two

Down through the centuries, the Glaurianists, built up their system of false worship, exporting it to the whole earth. At the same time - in large measure as a reaction to the angry god, and the loveless religion they presented - humanism, philosophy and scientific reason became a hybridized religion, while among the deeply ignorant, pure animism and witchcraft continued to enslave millions.

But with the advances in travel and writing, followers of The Way multiplied as well; there were increasing numbers of reformers and believers who carried true power, and possessed the light, love, peace, and freedom that Glaurius gave by his presence with them, and many people longed to know an all-powerful God who created and loved them. Though they were often hunted and persecuted, the message spread.

And Lailah's key was passed from generation to generation of Connel women, though few knew its meaning. It was nothing more than a superstitious family relic, until it came to the One to whom it was destined.

* * *

Perched on the arm of the sofa, Maura surveyed the twinkling city below. Taking a long drag off the tightly rolled joint, she dug her toes into the hand-woven, Oriental rug beneath her feet, and held her breath a long time. In her hands, a Lennox plate painted with wildflowers balanced delicately; she glanced at the picked-over take-out, and exhaled a cloud of smoke across it. Glazed broccoli, noodles, baby corn, pea pods and bean sprouts transformed into insects - a dark, furry spider with tiny, beaded eyes scurried away, and shiny-winged locusts hummed, and took flight. She recoiled at the sight, and shivered, then burst into uncontrollable laughter. "That is some crazy weed!"

Dancing lightly across the wide oak floor, she stopped before the large black and white lithograph of Dore's, *Dante in the Dusky Wood*. She had purchased this piece as a tribute to Virgil, the Roman epic poet, who was, for her, the gatekeeper of prophetic secrets. And Dante represented the classical Glaurianist belief in Hell, the place of eternal damnation and suffering, that was passing away, making way for reason, and the glory of human achievement without god.

However, as she looked closely, Dante's anxious face and haunting eyes gaped at something Maura could not see. The reluctant pilgrim's every nerve seemed on edge, as he resignedly shadowed Virgil down, down, down into the underworld, the last rays of light illuminating the ancient script above the door, *Abandon hope, all ye who enter here.*

Suddenly, without warning, Maura found she had entered the picture, and was in the shadows of the Italian hillside, crouching behind the leafless trees, trembling as the skeleton-like branches clacked and shook in the ghostly breeze.

She screamed in terror at the excruciating pain of claws piercing her skin, and the sight of hideous black creatures that dragged her mercilessly backwards by her legs and hair, toward the infernal door. The profound darkness and machine-like brutality in the eyes of the beings sent ice into her soul; glancing upwards at the sign, bilious plumes of sulfur roiled from beneath the door, and in the distance, a bell mournfully pealed. She remembered Donne's familiar line, *Ask not for whom the bell tolls, it tolls for thee.* As if reading her thoughts, maniacal laughter echoed from the regions below, and Maura immediately jerked back to reality, gasping and gripping the floor with the wild panic of a drowning victim.

She found herself a few feet from the Dante painting, staring into the puckish grin of Grateful Dead guitar virtuoso Jerry Garcia. Holding her arms about her body, she shook involuntarily, teeth chattering.

Grabbing the fiery-colored afghan from the back of the

leather sofa, she wrapped herself in the soft llama wool, rocking and moaning. She slowly connected with the sensation of her heartbeat, and breathed deeply, breathed, repeating her mantra until relief slowly flooded over her. For a brief moment, she was back in reality.

She peeped cautiously out of her cocoon, but the psychedelic compounds in the marijuana heightened all her senses.

Objects morphed randomly as she looked around the apartment, with sounds rushing into and out of her ears, like the tide.

She surveyed the decorating scheme of her apartment. She had spent a small fortune on a designer in an attempt to replicate her father's home in Santa Fe, mining the worlds of architecture and fashion to create a living space with peace and balance. But in the gathering night, it seemed to take on a life of its own, exposing her narcissism and greed, and tearing down her confidence. *Who decorates like this in San Francisco anymore?* The usually comfortable, familiar apartment whispered accusations; the heavy southwestern furniture, and stuccoed walls cried, *Look at me!*

Unable to escape the taunting, she began to listen to the lies. *Look out the window - people are down there right now in those darkened alleys, with no place to even lay their heads. You don't care about the poor, or anyone but yourself.* She shuddered. *Is that true?* Adrenaline rushed through her veins, and fear flooded her heart. Then the unseen nohedi twisted the knife. *You are a disgrace!*

But suddenly the terrible thoughts disappeared, redirected by an unseen hand, and new thoughts came to her. *Home. Where is my home?* She began to cry softly, hugging her knees and moaning, again rocking back and forth, sitting now on the foyer rug. She recalled herself as a little girl swinging in the yard, saw her father smiling and laughing.

Her mother sat in the floral-cushioned rocker, cranking the handle on her grandmother's vintage ice cream machine, long, dark curls cascading over her tanned shoulders. There she was with her brothers catching lightning bugs in the dark, the sound of crickets loud in the cool air. Another snapshot – with herself the center of attention at her 10th birthday party, her handsome father beaming as she posed for pictures. *Seems so long ago.* The ache of the memories gripped her.

In the misty, grey-blue light of late November, a figure

hovered and whispered into her ear; she leaned against the wall, smiling, her eyes closed. Then long finger-like tentacles reached into her skull, and images of her barren life again appeared again.

Maura, you can never go back, never go back. And then again, the countering whispers, *Surely, somewhere there has to be goodness, hope, and love?* Back and forth it went, with Maura as the ball. *No, forget about that utopian fantasy, it's dog eat dog, survival of the fittest, kiddo!* Thoughts came rapid-fire.

She thought about Nathan, the love of her life. *No, Maura, he isn't your answer – as if you'd be happy at home taking care of a bunch of kids, baking cookies! You're thirty years old, with no husband, and no kids. And your work and friends? Think about it, Maura, your friends have their own mountains they're climbing, and there are plenty of journalists out there trying to save the world, and they care far more than you do.*

She walked toward the wall of windows, high above Montgomery Street. The artificial lighting in the boardrooms of the world's power brokers pulsed across Jackson Square in the Financial District; the deep darkness of the Bay stretched to the horizon, and lights in the high-rises around hers began to peep on in the growing night.

Far below, she watched the movement of tiny cars and trucks. A thundering silence now replaced the voices, as Maura stared into the growing gloom before her. *How strange to be in this box of metal and glass so far up in the sky.* The ocean looked like a mass grave, covering the immeasurable sins of humanity, but the thought pierced her heart, *the hidden things will be revealed - there is a day of reckoning.*

Fear and despair washed over her, as the nohedi mocked and played her like a puppet on a string. But then a beloved melody flowed into her ears, *Somewhere, there is a place, there's a home, for you and me...* The battle raged, as she gazed down into the shadows between the massive buildings, the looming steel canyon beckoning like a mother.

Lay down, lay down and rest, my Darling. Forget everything and sleep; I am here. You are so tired, so weary. Hypnotized by the soothing voice, she imagined herself breaking free of the weight of her body, and soaring up into the darkness of space to the stars.

Then the thought came. *Just do it – open the door, stand on a chair, and fall into the velvet darkness! There is peace here, and rest for your soul.* She moved obediently toward the sliding glass door, pausing before the marble bust of Plato, his vacant eyes straining to see into the unseen realm. He spoke to her. *For souls are ever hastening into the upper world, where they desire to dwell.*

The wind howled and rushed maddeningly in, as she slid open the heavy glass door. She pulled a chair over to the railing, and stood on it, her back to the railing. *Breathe.*

Maura closed her eyes and imagined falling, as she leaned over backward. But at that moment, she was yanked back to reality, by strong arms that held her firmly against a massive chest. Looking up into the eyes of her man-like rescuer, she saw the swirling blue of the summer sky, and caught the aroma of myrrh and cassia that seeped from his clothing. Though his brow was furrowed with concern, there was no judgment or accusation; the gibbor smiled, touched her face, and set her back inside the apartment on the sofa.

With a fleeting sensation of feathery softness brushing her face, a glimmering mist swirled around him, and he was lost from her sight.

A lingering lightness remained, as Maura sat on the couch a very long time. The candles on the low table in front of her held her gaze, and she stared into the flames. Thoughts whirled like leaves in an early winter storm, but one word echoed repeatedly down the corridors of her mind. *Saved.* The word was heavy with awe, and she struggled to comprehend what had transpired - a powerful, invisible *Someone* had rescued her from death, crashing into her world from another realm.

Chapter Twenty-Three

I almost killed myself because of those voices.

The massive crowd watched the gigantic video screens. As Maura spoke these words, a lusty roar of approval swelled from the floor of the colossal amphitheater, reverberated to the moorings of the mountains, and rocketed back again, shaking loose great boulders from the sides and roof of the pit. Here it is that any who love The Lord of Darkness, are taken at the hour of their death by his evil hordes, to pass their miserable eternity in endless torment. For all who choose the ways of darkness, and love the king of the underworld, will be forever united with him, their desires and deeds fulfilled at last.

The nohedim danced spasmodically, erupting in animal roars, grunts and screams, in the red-black haze of smoke that belched from various flumes in the floor and walls. Red eyes turned from the screen and stared dumbly in delight at the sound of cracking whips, screams, and *drag, drop, drag, drop, the* unceasing tune of the Inferno. Several giants shook people like ragdolls and slammed them on the stone floor, picking them up, and petting them tenderly, only to slam them down again as they screamed. They dragged them by their torn arms or legs, then dropped them, bending down to kiss them like small babies, and crushing their heads with rocks, over and over again.

A wheezing calliope stood floor to ceiling in a quarter of the monstrous hall, its rusted poles and garish, painted ponies with their dead eyes rose and fell to the music of an enormous pipe organ, on which a nohedi frenetically cranked out a gothic funeral mass. The giants threw their people onto the ponies, and stomped their feet to the music, laughing and grunting as the calliope whirled and shook non-stop for an hour, two, or more at a time.

A pall-draped booth was erected in the middle of the cavern, where nohedim and their slaves came and went through a hole in the floor, ascending and descending steps to the lower circles of Hell. A bank of computers covered the walls, where condemned men, women, and nohedim observed everyday activities of people in the world above. A half-man, half-rat creature wheezed to a tall, distinguished looking man.

"This girl is displaying disturbing resistance to our pharmacopeia. I'm not sure what to do." The man glanced at the screen displaying Maura again, and then at a mogen of the nohedim, who stood nearby; his pus-filled face encircled in a wreath of smoke.

Mogen Oni spoke. "Frederick, this family has a secret calling from The Evil One, extending back to the Middle Ages. Unpredictably, their women awaken; it was a McConnell female that married the 'miracle worker,' Martin of Tours. Together with a small band of followers, they spread the knowledge of The Way all over France." Under his breath he added, "Their power was very great, and neither did they betray Glaurius when their time of testing came. I do not know what our Enemy's plans are, but this girl is an integral part of it, and must be stopped."

Frederick cleared his throat, and rubbed his chin. Not to be bested by a nohedi, he added with a conceited air, "Is it not also true that a later ancestor - Mary Chevalin - led a revival among the Huguenots before we killed her?" To illustrate, Frederick tapped the screen, and with his finger, traced the meandering red line that appeared on the diagram of Maura's family tree. "Yes, this is a dangerous line indeed."

The rat-faced nohedi clambered up the rock wall to peer over his shoulder, its eyesight diminished from the darkness of the pit, but Frederick shoved him back. "Get the hell away from me! Don't ever touch me, or breathe on me, you foul thing!"

Scathed by the rebuke, Minmar leaned back his beak-like head, and howled. At the signal, a hundred nohedim ran to him, and leaping on Frederick, tore pieces of skin from his body, hair from his head, gouging out his eyes, and ripping out his heart and intestines.

The parts flew through the air, and attempted to reunite. The hands screamed and trembled and bled, and scampered to the eyeballs rolling away on the floor, and the teeth chattered to the bits of ear and spleen, and the valves of his heart cried to the feet and to the spine. The nohedim chased and played with the fragments of Frederick, as the organ pipes shrieked, the ponies pranced, the whips cracked, and *drag, drop, drag, drop* echoed off the walls.

Frederick began to come together piece by piece, and finally, he stood, somewhat chastened in front of Mogen Oni.

"Bring him to me." The low growl from the speakers overhead, caused a tremor in the room, and every creature fell on its face to the ground. Nothing stirred except the frantically spinning calliope.

Chapter Twenty-Four

So she had been rescued, but she was still high, and still alone in her apartment. Maura got up from the couch and wandered around the living room, not sure what to do, as her thoughts again began to bounce from one thing to the next. As she began to think of who to blame, Maura suddenly remembered: *Andrew!* Andrew Rush, one of her boyfriends, and purveyor of all things psychedelic, had left weed for her on his way out of town on a buying trip for his import business. But he *had* warned her, laughing. "It's pretty potent – don't smoke alone!"

She paid no attention, having smoked weed every day since high school. She had never had such a bad trip before, and even after five hours, it felt like a jet engine roared inside her chest, as the still-active compounds showed little sign of fading. *Please, help me through this.* Hands shaking violently, she reached for her phone.

Stop! She willed the buttons to stay in one place as Nathan's face appeared on the display, but they refused, and transformed into line-drawing figures that leaped off and ran away across the coffee table. Miraculously, his voicemail came on, but the message boomed like Darth Vader. *Unavailable, unavailable…* Then she remembered. *Oh, crap, no help there – and what would he think anyway? Probably take me to the emergency room - or more likely, the psych ward at Sierra Linda.*

Carefully making her way across the living room, Maura

caught a glimpse of herself in the antique mirror in the foyer. She paused, captivated, as though looking at someone else, and reached up to touch the white satin folds of her blouse. A long, dark curl lay provocatively across her open throat, the reproachful voices forgotten for the moment. Transfixed, and temporarily forgetting the fear, she smiled, *who is the fairest of them all?*

Her eyes roamed approvingly over the length of her image. She admired the black, split skirt and its perfectly proportioned fit to her curves. But the pleasure was short-lived, as the unsolicited lyrics of a song suddenly stabbed through her musings.

Lord made a lady out of Adam's rib, next thing you know you got your women's lib.
Lovely to look upon, heaven to touch. It's a real shame they've got to cost so much. She wants money…

Her delight crashed. *Is that what I am - nothing more than an expensive toy?* In her mind she saw it - her high-octane career – the gorgeous women and powerful men, luxury hotels, private jets, corporate moguls, heads of nations – paraded before her, their faces sneering, fingers pointing at her, heads shaking.

Maura grew more perplexed by the moment. *But I'm one of the chosen!* She had never questioned her position in society, yet now, under the scrutiny of the nohedi, her life and dreams seemed like a lie.

The truth was, all Maura knew was the kind of affluence and influence that opens doors everywhere: her place in the world was determined at birth, and she had happily maintained the course marked out for her. Famous and influential friends, private schools, exclusive vacations, domestic servants and country clubs – she was perfectly at home with her privileges. And her father's motto, "*We* are the world," encapsulated her duties as an Enlightened One, ushering in the age of the global community.

We must free all people from the constraints of marriage and reproduction, and tear down the dividing walls between the nations; we will heal this good earth, and make it a safe, peaceful, tolerant, loving, and clean place - with plenty for all.

Many practices and teachings of Korban had became woven into the tapestry of collective beliefs that she and her peers advocated, and formed the foundation of her religion.

"Yes, my job is to expose and bring down the lies of fanaticism and superstition, until every last trace of ignorance, and intolerance is gone."

Her pulse raced as she spoke aloud, her heart drumming at the thought of the future, free world. Breathing shallowly, with narrowed eyes, she gripped the cold marble of the hall table and leaned in, confronting the invisible enemies of Progress. A voice spoke to her, *One day very soon, you will have the power to begin removing them - you will see it with your own eyes.* She stared into her brown eyes, vowing to annihilate every…last…one.

Filled with rage, she slowly, backed away, and then began to laugh hysterically. Morphing into yet another persona, she stopped, distracted again by her image in the mirror.

Drawling seductively, she channeled Scarlett O'Hara, "Oh, but I can't think about that right now - I'll think about it tomorrow!"

She wandered to the kitchen, managed to find the corkscrew after some trouble, and opened a bottle of petite syrah from the wrought iron rack on the countertop. As she carefully poured, the crimson fluid mixed with smoke, and swirled and splashed into the goblet. Holding it to the light, she smiled, sniffed and took a long, savoring drink.

Mmm, mm, mmm. A witch's brew, hahahaha. And added, *a good witch, of course.* The comment brought to mind a friend from college, a white witch. In her memory, Jessica rose, tall, blonde, and beautiful. She had taken Maura under her wing during freshmen year, as Jessica was interning in the English department at Stanford, while working on her PhD. In addition to being incredibly promiscuous and bisexual, she wrote mother-goddess poetry, studied Tarot, Kabbalah and raised medicinal plants, her small apartment overflowed with vegetation like a wizard's bower.

Recalling those days, Maura remembered how she had savored the attention, teasing Jessica, and stringing her along. Partying, comparing epochs of writing and art, and experimenting with the occult was a fun pastime, but Maura had no time for Jessica's jealous fits. She had bigger ambitions, and finally escaped relatively unscathed, except for a few angry phone calls.

Funny to think of her again after so long. She drummed her fingers on the granite countertop, and recalled the images of skeletons and other mystical figures on the tarot cards, and how deliciously scary it was to get the Death card. She chuckled, remembering. They had laughed whenever it was turned over, but though she would never admit to it, she remembered being nervous at times, and wondering "what if."

Hell. There it was again - the threat of eternal damnation and torment that the Glaurianists used to control the unquestioning millions. She slammed her fist into her hand.

Soon that lie will be forever extinguished from the minds of future generations. No, men and women are not innately evil, unable to handle personal freedom, and needing laws and punishment to control our wild impulses; it is because of these lies that our evolution to the glorious freedom of god-likeness has not advanced. But when we have destroyed belief in this lower-level, homicidal god, we will soar!

Maura shook her head in disbelief. *Glaurius - illogical, inconsistent, invisible - impossible for thinking, rational people to accept. And yet, the cult continues to declare, "Thou shalt not, thou shalt not, ad nauseum..."*

* * *

Growing up in The City by the Bay, the McConnell clan proudly made its mark on history - a history forever altered by the iconic artists, thinkers, and music of the late 20th century. Their religion and worldview were a synthesis of the ancient sorceries, and philosophies of the past, dusted off, and repackaged for a new generation.

Aruni knew how to entice through big ideas, and alluring faces and voices, just as he had done from the beginning; the proud heart of man despised the reality of The Way, and as always, the great men and women of the earth craved attention, notoriety, uniqueness, adulation, and power.

And down through the millenia, Aruni used these tendencies to steadily and secretly craft his plan, weaving a consistent narrative whose genius would appeal to the pride and sensuality of man, and one day bring all of humanity into a single belief, where he would finally unmask himself, and rule the earth in plain sight of all his adoring worshipers.

She took another sip of wine. *But what does happen to us after we die?* She thought about her new interest in Gnosticism, and what she'd learned at a recent retreat, how she had to come to a *knowing* of how things worked, or keep cycling through incarnations until she became One with the ineffable god. She thought of her old friends the English poets, and remembered reading Shelley in a meadow full of summer flowers, as the sun went down in pink and gold. *When I die, I want to wake up in such a world of eternal love, peace, beauty and glory...*

The seraf who guarded her, whispered, *Heaven.*

But the word made her feel confused and troubled. She thought of the classic Glaurianist teaching, and then about John Lennon's song lyrics. *Imagine there's no Heaven.* She shook her head. *So do we become light energy - part of the cosmos? There are so many ideas, and they all seem to make some sense. But I'm driving myself crazy looking for the answer.*

Maura noticed the wine had slowed her senses down; she closed her eyes as it hit her stomach, and saw heat surge like a thermal scan down her arms and into her fingers, fan across her breasts, rush down her legs, finally pulsing through her feet. She smiled and stretched out her toes as if in front of a roaring hearth. But then she recalled again, the ordeal with the nohedi. *Why were they dragging me down to Hell?*

She saw movement on the periphery of her vision, and turned to see what looked like black lightning, zigzag across the threshold, and pass through the door to the living room. Her gaze never wavered; no clear form was visible, but she could feel an impish presence.

Is that a Poltergeist? She had learned from Jessica, the German word for a mischievous spirit which misplaced, stole or ruined belongings, and harassed people, making them doubt their sanity as they appeared, then disappeared. As much as she hated to admit it, Maura was no stranger to the nohedi.

When she was a little girl, their presence plagued her. The vaulted ceilings and tall windows of the sprawling Victorian mansion she grew up in, its polished wood and marble floors, massive paintings, chandeliers, and furniture, many entrances, closets, and built-in cabinets - as well as a terrifying fourth floor attic above the house – created anxiety for Maura as the sun began to set, and night came on.

Across from her bed, was a tiny locked door by which to access the walkway and storage between the eaves and the outer walls of the house, on which the little latch often jiggled in the dead of night, leaving the terrified child voiceless and quaking, until exhaustion closed her eyes. The ancient oaks guarding the mansion dropped small, dead branches throughout the starless, windy nights of rain that blanket the Pacific Northwest in winter, and Maura waited with every nerve strained, for the inevitable assault of vampires, ghosts, mummies, and kidnappers.

The nocturnal battle began to threaten her health and schoolwork, and her frustrated parents took her to the best child psychologist in the city, who subjected her to a line of questioning that made Maura feel ashamed, and even more isolated. The therapist concluded the problem was "an overactive imagination."

As she got older, she became nearly obsessed with vampire romances, horror movies, séances, Ouija boards, astrology and horoscopes, palm reading, and spell-casting. And no one ever guessed there was a connection between these activities and Maura's fears - they were just fun games. But for Maura, who could see into the spirit realm, they were very real indeed.

Chapter Twenty-Five

A preparer-nohedi clamped iron manacles with two-inch spikes into the flesh of Frederick's wrists and ankles, and enclosed his waist with a larger one. With Frederick dangled like a puppet from the chains connected to each manacle, a guard-nohedi carried him into the booth, and descended the slimy granite steps to the lowest circle of the pit. Blood gushed from the screaming and moaning man, and the nohedi slapped him every few seconds. Along the walls, living men and women were impaled on oily sticks and set aflame to light the way; the smell of burning hair and skin hung in the air, and Frederick vomited continuously.

Around and around, they wound their way ever lower, past massive iron doors stood marked with signs describing the heart of those incarcerated there. "Liars," "Cowards," "Traitors," "Greedy," "Lovers of Self," "Unforgiving," "Pretenders," and finally, at the lowest level, was a wall of iron with an immense sign overhead - "The Merciless." In this twisted world, people were labeled by the character they had developed on Earth.

The nohedi spoke to the door, and it disappeared into the floor, the weight of it sending shock waves through the underworld. Frederick cast a pitiful, pleading look upwards toward his captor, who squeezed his head with one hand, crushing his skull. He dragged the lifeless man across the threshold, and stopped for a moment to adjust his eyes to the sudden illumination.

Large numbers on the ground counted out the distance: six hundred and sixty-six yards into the cavern, the nohedi moved from inky blackness to fiery white, orange and red light that rose from the side of the stone ledge. He stopped, and shading his eyes, surveyed the lake of fire.

Here the temperature rose to 1,500 degrees; having come from the colder upper regions, steam now issued from Frederick's cracked skull. Sulfur, and the odor of the rotting dead and their burning flesh assaulted them, and in the roar of the flames from the flowing molten rock, the screams of multitudes of tormented people, and the hysterical laughter of their demented oppressors, ricocheted off the walls.

The nohedi left Frederick on the ground, and stood on the rim of the walkway, peering over. According to the numbers on the far wall of the cauldron, the very center of the inferno was six thousand six hundred and sixty-six miles below.

Passing before him in the bubbling lava were people, shrieking as they were carried along in the flotsam of twisted sky scrapers and airplanes, oil wells, cars, trucks, concrete buildings, great ships, power plants and weapons; asphalt pavement, giant stores of every kind, plastic containers and bags, computers and televisions, schools and university buildings, cosmetics, pills, bottles of wine and liquor, shampoos, lotions, animal carcasses, furniture, houses, apparel and shoes; cargo trains wrapped with railroad tracks, castles, palaces and restaurants, an endless ocean of books and cd's, cell phones, cathedrals and churches, movie theaters and hospitals that floated, disappeared and reappeared in the blazing sea. And interwoven through it all were twined telephone wires, cables and every kind of fence.

Along the sidewalls of the cauldron were outcroppings of granite, and in the fiery sea, peaks rose from the flames. Nohedim with hooks and long, spiked poles cast about for people, stabbing and dragging them up on the rocks where they flopped around like fish. Once on the rocks, the creatures flung them from ledge to ledge in a game they had contrived, purely for entertainment. When they had finished their amusement, they flipped the captives back into the lake.

The nohedi kicked Frederick in the head, and he came to, his cranium intact once again. A giant sucking noise began, like the ocean receding from the shore, and the lake of fire opened up in the middle. Lurching and straining, a massive throne emerged from the depths of the fire, lava dripping off its sides. At the level of the nohedi and Frederick, it came to a standstill. A granite walkway appeared and connected the rim of the walkway to the rocky outcropping on which the throne stood. Steam and smoke rose and hissed. The image on the throne turned to look at Frederick and the nohedi.

On the iron throne sat the transmogrified Aruni – who now, after centuries, had become an enormous lizard with the head and tail of a dragon. His reptilian eyes snapped rhythmically open-shut, as he turned his attention to the nohedi. Fear gripped the creature, and he shook so violently, that he dropped Frederick again and again. A dissonant banging and clanging occurred as Aruni shifted on the throne, trying to conform it to his growing girth. A noxious cloud of rotting flesh and burning garbage billowed from the depths below.

"Hail, Ba'al Aruni!" The Lord of Darkness waved his claw peremptorily, annoyed and bored with the trifling troubles of his rule.

"Vile human, what is going on with this girl?" The nohedi grabbed Frederick's remaining tuft of hair and yanked him to his feet. The poor wretch trembled on the narrow bridge, as the nohedi kicked him toward the throne. "Bow before the Emperor!" Frederick teetered and fell on his face before the massive and imposing power on the throne. The nohedi prostrated next to him, answered in Frederick's stead.

"Exalted One, she is of the seed of Ferin Connel."

He shifted his weight and turned a withering gaze at the nohedi. "I see. Let me ask you - what is your name?" The nohedi trembled uncontrollably at the contemptuous tone of Aruni's voice. "Oh, that's right. You do not have a name, *do you?*"

The dragon swished his tail, sweeping rocks like dust, from the walls behind him. "No, you are one of the heartless vermin that scurry around here for my pleasure, aren't you? Let me ask another question, if I may."

Poisonous with sarcasm, he leaned in closer, "Is there any way that *I* do not know exactly who this girl is - and everything about my world, for that matter? How *dare* you insult me?"

The nohedi jumped and screamed in terror, this once joy-filled seraf who had beheld the glories of Tziyon, now forever destroyed by pride and greed. "I beg you for mercy, Master. I despise myself, and am not worthy to serve such an exalted

One. Forgive me!"

But Aruni was the cleverest of all the creatures of Glaurius; since he lacked omniscience, he was as dependent as any general on his spies, but the nohedi were not aware of this, and lived in dread of his power.

"Tell me, what is happening up there?"

The nohedi continued on in anxious chatter. "Sire, as you know, Maura McConnell is a descendent of Ferin, son of Connel." The creature nearly stumbled into the story of Korban being raised from the dead, but caught himself. This was never spoken of to the master, under any cirsumstance. Aruni's eye-slits narrowed, daring him to go there. "Yes, well, you know the prophecy, Sire, and her maternal grandmother has passed away, leaving her a safe-deposit box."

Wincing, he added. "She met, and believed in Glaurius at the end of her life. I fear she was the keeper of the key, and it will come to the granddaughter."

Aruni roared and shook the bowels of the earth at the sound of the hated name. Great boulders dislodged from the ceiling, and chaos ensued, as nohedi scrambled about to escape the wrath of the dragon.

When the dust settled, there was silence for several minutes as Aruni considered his strategy. Turning to Frederick, he asked, "Is there any reason to suppose that this creature will accept the preposterous stories about our enemy? Has she had the proper education?" The pathetic man responded.

"Your majesty, she has had the most scrupulous attention that money can buy. Reason and revolution are in her blood, and she loathes the religion of that imposter. Still, she has a gift of seeing, and that sets her apart from others. In her growing isolation, she could turn to him and his tricks for solace."

He lowered his head, and mumbled. "In a recent attempt at self-murder, she was rescued in the act by a gibbor. She was heavily medicated, and within our grasp, but she is now looking for answers."

Aruni tapped his talons on the arm of the throne, the clack, clack, clack echoing off the chamber walls. He slid off the dais and raised his horned head to the roof, then snaked back down to within inches of Frederick and the nohedi. "Make sure she *never* finds out that her name is *already* written in his book!"

In response to the violence of his command, the fire blazed up in the lake behind them, roaring like a hungry beast. With an impulsive wave of his claws, Aruni nodded to the nohedi,

"Toss him in there – and be quick about it!" Frederick screamed in terror, as the clawed foot of the nohedi kicked him, manacles and all, into the suffocating air, and he landed with a "plop" in the middle of the roiling soup. Aruni sipped a goblet of wine, offered to him by a servant, and wiped his brow with a pristine white cloth, sighing, as if the exertion had worn him out.

He purred in a soothing voice to the nohedi. "Don't worry about him, you will find a replacement - there are thousands more just like him – rebellious, proud, and eager to do my will. The fire needs their blood, and I do so love to hear their screams." He gestured with his claw, taking in the dimensions of his realm, and smiling dreamily. "The music of my kingdom…it completes me!"

"Hahahahahahahahahahahahahahaha! The great emperor beat the arm of the throne with his tiny claw, and a rumble responded below. The device clattered and staggered, and disappeared into the pitch black hole, as Aruni's crazy laughter echoed off the walls.

Chapter Twenty-Six

M aura threw out a curse, and finished the rest of the wine. *Food is next – I have to get this under control.* As she opened the fridge, a burst of light spun her backward several feet, and she erupted in hysterical laughter. *Okay, we need music.*

Cherisse, her white exotic cat, sauntered by, apparently oblivious to all the activity. Maura heard the purring even at her height as the animal rubbed against her ankles, and glancing up at Maura, it grinned, and spoke to her. *What shall we listen to?* But when she looked again, the cat was perfectly composed. *She looks like the Cheshire Cat.* Maura imagined the cat was a conspirator in this strange land, and looking for evidence, she timidly lifted and held the creature before her at arm's length, gazing transfixed as the green eyes morphed into the open-shut slits of a reptile. The cat smiled enormously, ominously; Maura gasped and dropped it to the tile floor.

In the living room, she tried to focus and select music, and was eventually successful, despite the titles and psychedelic artwork springing to life on the album covers. Her shaking hand pressed the button, and the needle swung across and floated gently to the edge of the record. The familiar, whining guitar coursed from the speakers, each longing and plaintive note plucking her heart.

Gonna leave this broke down palace, on my hands and my knees,

I will roll, roll, roll. Make myself a bed, by the waterside, listen to the river and sing sweet songs to rock my soul.

Maura swayed like a willow, caressing Cherisse who had returned for a second attempt at love. Maura held her close this time, though still slightly wary. They drifted along on the melody for a few minutes, until jarred by a demonic roaring from the speakers. In desperation, Maura cried, "Please, please, please stop!!!"

She forced herself to try the refrigerator again, and this time there was no explosion of light, but instead, a chorus line of dancing raspberries leaped from the top of the cheesecake. *Aaaggghhh!*

Maura grabbed the Styrofoam box that held the remains of her lunch, and slammed the door, then managed to eat several bites of the cheese and avocado sandwich, with some potato salad.

For a half hour, the music weaved its magic, and eventually, after the food and wine, Maura began to come down. She yawned deeply several times, and laid her weary head on the sofa, closing her eyes. But as the grandfather clock in the foyer sounded, she was alert again. *Dong, dong, dong.* Fear rose up in her again, as she thought about the warnings of judgment promised by the Glaurianists.

She had first learned about their beliefs from her maternal grandmother. As a child, Maura accompanied her on weekly visits to her church - St. Lucia – to drop off food and clothes for struggling families in the parish. Though her daughter, Ellen, had deserted religion for the handsome junior senator from California, she was determined to expose her granddaughter to it.

During those rides in the spacious Town Car, Maura saw a lot of things - the lure of divine security in exchange for good works - and that church events were a great place to make connections in business and politics. Giving generously also lowered taxes, but very few people actually followed the "thou shall nots." All the statues, formalities and teachings did was instill fear in her, and after a decade and a half of school and Progressive indoctrination, she politely rejected her grandmother's religion. She and the others like her were after all, men and women forging a new society, deconstructing the moral codes and gods of the past into their own image reflecting liberty, equality, brotherhood, reason, and science.

Maura once asked her father if Glaurius was real, and he sat her on his lap, pointing into the vast summer sky. She looked admiringly at his hazel eyes and the handsome, tanned face she so dearly loved. "No, Maura, there is no one out there watching over us. Divine power is in you, in me, in the sky, the trees and birds; we are all part of God, and earth is where we must create Paradise. When we listen to our hearts, we will do what is right every time."

She saw a flicker of vulnerability – a glimpse of regret – as he spoke. He stared, as though looking into the nations. "Maura, people are suffering all over the world because of companies that ruin their land, and do not pay them enough to eat, working them until they are old and sick. Many children like you have no parents, and cry themselves to sleep from hunger; they have no voice. But above all, it is religion that keeps the poor quiet and obedient, and it must be eradicated."

Then he drew her close, so she could feel his warm body, and smell his familiar cologne. He held her protectively for a long moment, as if she were one of the orphans he described.

It was the last time he would ever hold her.

* * *

When we listen to our hearts, we will do what is right every time. She glanced at the clock, hoping for some answers. Nine o'clock. She sighed in frustration and threw off the afghan. She spoke aloud to break the gloominess, and silence the ticking off of minutes. "I have an early day tomorrow – goodnight!"

Just do the next thing, Maura, it'll be all right. Her thoughts began to focus as she tried to put the living room and kitchen in order. She left a few lights on, and her favorite jazz station playing quietly. *Everything will be back to normal soon. Go take a bath.*

The bathroom décor transported her to the tropics, with its sanctuary of hibiscus, ferns, and red and white poinsettias that grew up the stone walls. A statue of a snowy egret stood next to the brass tub, as if peering into the depths for a catch.

Turning the fixtures, Maura released a cascade of water, and soon steam rose and filled the room, like fog on a lake at dawn. Maura broadcast two handfuls of Dead Sea salt infused with neroli and lavender across the surface of the water, and watched, mesmerized, as individual grains drifted like snowflakes to the bottom. As the water level rose, she plunged her arm in, whirling the salts into a mini blizzard. She dried her hands, and lit the standing candles.

As her hands passed by the flame, the ruby ring on her left hand reflected the candlelight. Her heart swelled with a pain that surprised her. *Nathan, where are you?*

She would never have made herself so vulnerable to him in person, but here, now, her heart knew the truth. *Lonely.* She placed the blame on the scapegoat, Sheila - his wife. *Another holiday season coming, and he is still with her.* The exquisite, blood-red stone pulsed like a miniature heart, enthroned but held captive in the fine, gold setting.

She pulled her gaze away and yanked angrily at her clothes, throwing everything in a heap on the floor. After testing the water, she slipped into the steaming bath and turned on the jets, settling back against the jade tiles that ran along the top of the tub, as the strains of Samson and Delilah drifted in.

Delilah was a woman, she was fine and fair. She had good looks, God knows and coal black hair. Delilah she gained old Samson's mind, when first he saw this woman he couldn't believe his mind.

Behind her closed eyes, a vision slowly appeared of a seedy hotel room in the Tenderloin – San Francisco's red-light district - along with the raucous laughter of a man and woman, and the sound of creaking bedsprings. Then she was back in the tub with the music. Again, the vision appeared, and she was in a stare-down with an overweight woman with disheveled orange hair, smeared lipstick, and a ripped camisole who mocked her.

She wiped the back of her dirty hand across her red lips. *You think you're all that with your fine looks, education, friends and money? You're no different than me – at least I make money giving myself away!* The man's face was in shadows, and they roared together with laughter, grunting like mating farm animals.

Maura sunk lower in the water, her thoughts jumpy, then furious.

* * *

A mist covered Maura's nakedness from the eyes of those who kept watch over her. "I'm going to speak to Glaurius. He will tell us what we should do – He understands their make-up better than we." Encircled in blinding light and colors, the other gibbor nodded.

"Peace, my brother. I will watch until you return."

As Michael turned his thoughts to the King, he instantly manifested in the Garden of the Lilies, at the edge of the Fountain of Tears. He tried to stand, but melted with an intoxicated smile, at the feet of his master.

"Hahahahahahahaha!" Glaurius scooped him up effortlessly, and spun him around. "Oh, you are my great joy and delight, Michael! But stand up on your feet, my son!" The king set him down on wobbly legs, but held him by one shoulder, just in case. "Come, now – how can I help you?"

Michael shook his head, and laughed, "Oh, Father, you tease me! You know I cannot withstand the power of your love."

Glaurius grabbed him again, hugging him, kissing both cheeks, and the top of his head. "Michael, you must try harder! Hahahaha!"

The gibbor replied with a beaming, yet still dopey grin. Glaurius cupped his face and smiled. "That face! I love that face! Now, what do you want to know about Maura?"

"Okay, well, we know that you know everything that's happening down there right now, but frankly, we're a bit nervous. After all, they are a higher order than we are – even before they awaken. She smoked that weed, and the nohedim are tormenting her much more than usual. And there was the dramatic near-dive off the balcony. I am afraid of losing her. Is it almost time?"

The Eternal One thoughtfully stroked his beard, and stared into the pool, gazing at the reflection of the lilies. He reached down, plucking one of the white flowers, and closed his eyes, musing on something Michael could not see.

Known by many names – Jehovah, Yahweh, El Shaddai – he pondered the bloody centuries since the exile of Mogen and Cheva from the Garden. The gibbor waited respectfully, awed at the emotion coming from his master, toward this unremarkable human.

"She is so close, my son, so close. But there are a few more things she must go through before she is really ready – before she will choose me over all the other things the world offers – before she knows that I am - and this is - what her heart longs for."

His arm gestured from one end of the massive garden to the other, encompassing the grassy knolls, ponds, cabins, flowers, fruit and shade trees, birds, bees, smiling men, women and children, and every kind of animal under puffy, white clouds in an azure sky, that floated peacefully above the kingdom of Tziyon. Glaurius sighed contentedly.

"Ahhhh, the music of my kingdom - peace, and laughter."

He looked at the gibbor again. "I am so eager for the moment she awakens, and sees for the first time!" Michael gazed contentedly up at his master, from the warm grass beside the fountain. "Then she and all of her descendants after her will finally be free."

"My son, do you know what this fountain is?"

"Yes, Father, I do."

Glaurius raised his eyebrows in a question. "Well?"

Michael giggled drunkenly. "Um, I wasn't sure if that was a rhetorical question." The gibbor rolled over onto his stomach and kicked his feet back and forth, his chin on his hands, anticipating the story. Glaurius gently stirred the water in the bowl of the fountain, and dreamed again.

"These are the tears of the children of men, Michael. Although their pathway is tortuous at times, I feel the pain with them, and I see when they shed a tear. All of them have tasted sorrow, and when they cry, I cry with them. Soon, I will bring them here, and they will see, and know how much I have loved them, and that all of their suffering has made them victorious; Maura still has trials to overcome, and tears to shed."

Glaurius cocked his head at a sound Michael could not hear, but he smiled knowingly, as he often saw the king in such moments, when Glaurius would hear the faint, final breaths and beating heart of a child who was coming home.

"Sire?" He waited, until suddenly he could see through the vaporous veil separating the two worlds.

From beyond, blew a chilly wind, then the figure of an old woman, her hunched-over body wrapped in a threadbare jacket. She winced in pain as she made her way slowly, suffering etched on her thin face; she stopped amidst the people rushing past, and leaned her fevered cheek against the cold stone wall of the Ferry Building.

Unfolding an ancient and grimy flyer, she smiled, and stroked the picture of the man impaled on a tree, his body bleeding out. Comforted, she sighed and clutched it tenderly to her breast, as tears fell down her wrinkled face. She glanced up above the noise and hardness of the city streets to the blue sky, where seagulls wheeled and sparrows soared. Suddenly, pain seized her, and as it did, she surrendered, sliding slowly down the wall, crumpling unnoticed into a heap on the sidewalk. Her fingers stiffened around the picture of the man, as life left her.

A shadow passed across Glaurius' eyes. "Please go get Sarah Anne from the Embarcadero." Then, with joy spreading across his face, he declared, "This is her Getting-off Place – she's coming home."

Chapter Twenty-Seven

Despite her fears, Maura's eagerness to please, genius IQ, and natural beauty won her father's attention. The theme of societal evolution crouched in every conversation: every action and reaction, every person, every thought was calculated and weighed in an unseen balance - compared and contrasted, sifted and judged - according to its usefulness to the movement, and he treasured his smart daughter, because relationships were practical: family, friends and colleagues all had to fulfill a purpose, or they wound up as profanities. Senator Jim McConnell's charismatic personality and cult-like following led even his opponents to make great sacrifices, if only to have his approval, and a place at the coveted table.

As his career exploded, and his wife, Ellen, remained busy with social outreaches, and a brood of little ones, she became increasingly resentful, often criticizing and nagging him when he was around. As a result, his normally fun-loving and charismatic personality began to erupt with rage, which he took out on Maura and her siblings.

In a tool room that connected the kitchen to the garage, he hid a two-inch wide oak stick, where he marched them in a terrified, whimpering group to dole out beatings, and vent his fury. But far removed from the rest of the house, the screams went no further than the shiny varnished panelling of the old walls, the secret hidden from the world.

Still, Maura loved her father, and was a frequent observer in the music room where he and his friends hammered out strategies for elections and business deals, and when asked, she warbled the blues, or precociously recited the poetry of Thoreau and Whitman. Sometimes she played a jazz piece she was working on, and her long, thin fingers were supple and strong as they flew over the immaculate keys of the Steinway.

There was a small stage with soft lighting that illuminated her innocent, beautiful, and intelligent face, framed by luxuriant dark hair. Her body was on the cusp of change, and as she performed with emotion and passion, the possessive desire of the gathered wolves, pulsed like a fever in the close air.

As she got older, Maura wrote her first poetry, articles, and essays at the oak desk, surrounded by the conversations of her father and his friends, as they plotted mergers, proposed candidates, and compared notes on the progress of the movement. Although much of his time was spent in Washington, when he was home, her presence never failed to amuse, and in the haze of cigars, strong coffee and Chivas, he intermittently roared his approval with such comparisons as, "That's the next Gloria Steinem right there, " giving her the clear impression of what pleased him, and a target at which to aim her soul.

This unconscious embracing of her father's creed affected her ability to exercise control over even her own body, as the power of sex crashed into her world. The heat and lust of adolescence had spun her into unsolicited encounters with hairless boys who groped her, and bruised her soul. Overnights with her girlfriends brought more confusing feelings, as under the sheets in the dark, she satisfied their unmet needs. She would learn over time to wield her wounds as weapons, but the shame and secrecy embedded themselves into her growing identity, as she fell for the deception of settling for less.

Maura leaned forward and absently lathered up the loofah, methodically scrubbing her tired body. Her thoughts returned to her parents.

Living large in every way, the senior senator from California had an appetite for heirs and mistresses.

And Ellen, to manage her own frantic life, returned to the habit she began in college - pilfering her doctor-father's medicine cabinet of pharmaceutical samples of barbiturates and sleeping pills. Later, armed with a perpetual prescription, this became her refuge, until she essentially became a recluse, leaving her career, her charitable activities, and coming out of the house only for required events, looking beautiful as always, but bone-pale.

As the life of her children went on without her, Ellen spent her days reading in her room, or watching biographies and the History Channel, cocooned on the divan, the din and animated light of the television her sole companion. In the morning, she would still be there, tranquil as a corpse.

Maura's father was tremendously busy with his career, and she only saw him a couple of times a month. She and her siblings were raised by surrogates and 'servants;' he made promises to his children that he sincerely intended to keep, but inevitably, "something came up." But how often she had longed just to sit with him one more time, put her head on his shoulder, and have him stroke her hair as he had when she was a very young child.

Father. The cry came from somewhere deep within, unearthed and sharp.

She had poured out her heart in a diary during this brief time of introspection in her early teens, on long walks in the open fields near her house. Often, during those days, she felt a peaceful presence - some invisible power that comforted and protected - in contrast to the stark and lonely atmosphere at home.

"Home" was a black scar, especially at night, when she was tormented by nohedim. Eventually, she began to drink secretly from the ample liquor supply in the house, and then moved on to smoking pot with friends. During high school, she smoked pot every day just to control the fear and pain, but it wasn't long before she had tried a number of other drugs, and used them regularly.

* * *

When we listen to our hearts, we will do what is right every time.

As Maura lay in the steaming bath, she noticed the affects of the marijuana was wearing off, a quieter buzz now replacing the jet engine sensation. Remembering what happened on the balcony, she trembled; the idea had come from inside her head, but it wasn't her, she was sure of that. *No one has ever committed suicide in our family.*

She thought of her mother, *No, our lives are living deaths...*

She couldn't refrain herself from the comment as she thought about the McConnell drama. Yes, their dysfunction was iconic, tabloid news, but she had never contemplated suicide. No matter what came her way - childhood disappointments, her mother's death – she had always pressed on. True, she was a little apprehensive about the holidays and spending time with her messed-up family - and feeling blue because Nathan was going to Tahoe with Sheila and their kids - *but that came from left field.*

Managing to avoid the bonds of marriage, Maura had filled her life with a steady stream of handsome and powerful men, and her writing career. The closest she had come to it was with Paul Sutton, son of Governor Hal Sutton, and while Maura's passion for Paul lasted a year, when he wanted a commitment, she broke it off.

Maura drifted back from reminiscing, and realized the music had stopped.

Why all the guilt – like I've done something wrong? Maybe I'll call Aaron Feinberg, but better not mention the imps and voices...

Chapter Twenty-Eight

Glaurius sat on his gold-trimmed couch, leaning comfortably against the cushions, gazing into the shimmering stones, gently passing his hand over the deep purple amethyst. "The endless river of crimson blood and the purifying red of fire, meets the unfathomable depths of our power and love, deep blue as the ocean - where all their mistakes are buried."

The minstrels paused and nodded, then continued on their harps, guitars, drums, clarinets and flutes, playing now in a minor chord, as they adjusted to Glaurius' mood.

The king reached over and took Sofia's hand. Gazing into her eyes, he put her fingers to his lips and kissed them. "My Sofia, you are indeed beautiful beyond words."

From the purple coverings of her seat, she pressed her hand against his chest, and the diaphanous sleeve of her gown slid down, exposing her strong, tanned arms and jeweled hands. She seemed timeless: her body was fit, her face very beautiful, and only a few, slight wrinkles accented her blue-green eyes.

"My Dear, I have a riddle for you. What is the hardest thing to tame?" Glaurius asked, as he leaned toward her, and set the ephod in her lap. Sofia smiled broadly, revealing perfection in her bow-shaped mouth. Her eyes flashed with anger for a moment, and then she answered in a voice that sounded like a bubbling spring of fresh water on a hot day.

"My Lord and Husband, it is the tongue of man. This tiny part of the body is the most destructive force on earth, but in the mouth of the wise, it is a fountain of life!"

She held his chin in her hand, and gazed adoringly into his eyes, amethyst, diamond, ruby and topaz gems twinkling on her long, shapely fingers. Then she stood and removed her soft lavender outer robe, the white silk lining shimmering like water. After kissing him, the queen smiled coyly, and skipped lightly down the few steps to the marble dance floor.

As the musicians plucked a tune evoking sunlight and rainbows, wind and starlight, Sofia danced; every step and movement seemed choreographed, the clear notes of the instruments synchronizing perfectly with her twirling and jumping, as if she and the musicians were one.

Glaurius, enraptured by the athleticism and beauty of his wife, watched delightedly, until he was interrupted by the riotous laughter of the chevar Korbanim as they jostled and wrestled their way into the room. These young trainees in prophecy and healing, came forward together in happy conversation, filling the air with the scent of cedarwood and myrrh,. They hugged and kissed Sofia and the King, apologizing for the intrusion.

But there was no sense of breaking protocol, and no correction or shame, but rather total acceptance and love. The warmth of the large hearth fire, drew them into the room that was filled with a sense of belonging, purpose, family, and lives lived well and happily; the walls were lined with thousands of pictures of people of every age, and from every nation. The men found places to rest in the cushioned wall nooks, on the numerous overstuffed chaises and couches, and on large pillows on the floor, as light poured in golden, shimmering, rainbow colors through the open windows, accompanied by the scent of lilacs, hyacinth and roses, and a joyous melody that floated in from the meadows.

Soon, the scent of fresh bread wafted into the room, and gibborim, serafs, and men, women and children from every nation, who had already died on earth, and were now present in Tziyon, entered, carrying platters and bowls piled high with food.

A large seraf gestured with his hand, and the dance floor expanded in circumference, while overhead, a long, fully furnished table with floral-cushioned benches descended, and stopped in the center of the room. The ceiling opened to the outdoors, where the overhanging trees spread their leafy branches like a canopy, and birds twittered, and doves cooed.

The hardwood table exuded an aroma of spices and cedar, and when anyone sat on the bench cushions, a scent of violets and roses escaped from the fabric.

The setting of the table was artful, and by design, the variety of plates, flatware and glasses reflecting the taste of each person seated. Some things were wooden, others colored glass, fine china, pottery, silver or gold. The one constant item at each place setting was a rounded crystal goblet that reflected the light within each person who sat before it.

Those who carried the food arranged it on the table, amidst bowls of pale yellow butter, saucers of fresh-picked rosemary, lemon-thyme, oregano and basil, cruets of olive oil, creamy dressings for the salad, and piquant sauces for pastas and vegetables. Cutting boards with an array of cheeses were placed near every grouping of eight. Bottles of new wine from the vintners' cellars aired as all gathered to eat.

Each one who had carried the food took their seats first. "To your cups, Beloved! Glaurius began by pouring and savoring the aroma of the wine in his goblet. Raising it, he invited the others to join him. "Our brothers and sisters, who create the food and wines we eat, are honored today in our sight. Your service and artistry delight and sustain us, and make us glad. Thank you."

The gardeners, cheesemakers, vintners, chefs, and their helpers beamed with pride, as around the table, the rest of the family expressed their love and appreciation for them through loud cheering, clapping and whistling.

The musicians and Korbanim sat next, followed by the queen, with Glaurius sitting last of all. As everyone took their places, each looked carefully about, sliding the benches to make sure the person to their side could sit easily. Conversation occurred in groups of eight or ten, and no one spoke too much, though some were more boisterous and passionate, while others spoke quietly, taking their time with details.

The children received the most careful attention, as their words were considered of the utmost necessity, and deeply insightful. Every need for attention was met, and there was no competition, rivalry, hidden jealousy or ambition that marred the atmosphere.

Polite attention was given to serving, and the meal conversations were interspersed with pauses: "Would you like some more wine? More butter for your bread?" Requests to "Please pass the potatoes," (or other food or drink) were kind and patient. The meal lasted for a very long time compared to meals on earth, and there was no hurry, because in Tziyon, there is always time enough.

Topics of discussion varied from the fermenting of the latest grapes, to the new-born goats, softball teams, surfing, weaving, and of course, as always, the "after party."

"I still think that a warm sun shower would be a riot! Imagine billions of people all over the earth dancing, rejoicing, and splashing in puddles together for hours – no, *days* - while the music plays, and the birds fly, and the animals play all around." The little girl who shared this dream, rested her chin on her hand, as she stared out the window, imagining it all.

A seraf with a slight belly asked, "But how will we feed all those people?" Glaurius chuckled, and chimed in.

"Dragon-slayer, for this occasion – and until everyone finds their vocation and establishes a routine – like this." He snapped his fingers, and suddenly, over their heads, a sheet appeared, filled with all kinds of food and wine. After the oohh's and aahh's, he snapped his fingers again, and the sheet vanished from their sight.

"Hahahahah! Well, done, Father." Korban raised his wine glass. "To that Day - when our enemies are vanquished, and the children all come home - and I wed my bride!"

"Here, here!"

"So be it!"

"Come quickly!"

"Hahahahahahahaha!" Much laughter and pounding on the table erupted, and then, raising their goblets, all joined in merry song, shared jokes and riddles, while some gave speeches, and everyone drank more wine, and toasted loudly. After some time, the fruit, desserts, coffee and teas arrived.

Sofia and Glaurius – great bakers, coffee and tea crafters in their own right – served the pastries they had baked in the morning, while the Korbanim removed the dinner plates to a cart that had appeared from the kitchens. When it was filled, a short seraf with bright eyes spoke to it.

"Go now, and wash the dishes." Off it raced to the kitchen, where it entered a washing closet, and water and soap performed their magic. Afterwards, the dishes were returned to their cupboards by the serafs who served in the kitchen.

Other carts came with delicately painted teacups, saucers

and mugs, along with warm spice-and-carrot cakes and chocolate chip cookies, chocolate mousse, brownies, blondies made from brown sugar, honey and butter, warm apple pie, and fresh peach and strawberry ice cream, bursting with fruit. The scent of cinnamon, nutmeg and vanilla wafted through the room.

Throughout the meal, people would take up an instrument and play, whether solo, or in groups. All were skilled with every kind of string, woodwind, or percussion instrument, and the children of the different countries, played many styles and tempos of music.

There were artist's easels set up in various locations of the room, and outside in the yard, for painting scenes of nature, portraits of each other, or whatever came to mind. Glaurius and Sofia delighted in each one, drawing the small children onto their laps to admire their work, or share a long hug.

Alongside each dessert plate, lay a card with a unique, personalized blessing written by the card makers – a beautifully scripted encouragement along with a small painting of an animal or a scene, that depicted a wish for the individual receiving the card.

After the meal, Glaurius turned to Korban. "Ben'i, my son, come." Glaurius' words poured like liquid love, as he patted the seat next to him. Korban rose from strumming a guitar on a seat at the window, and came to Glaurius. They embraced, and touched - face to face, forehead to forehead, and nose to nose. Korban joined him on the bench cushion where he saw his father holding the ephod. "The stones of prophecy, Father. The amethyst is glowing."

"Yes, Korban, the bloodline of those who bring justice, and care for the poor. It has remained intact, but still, justice is not done, and it has been a long time."

As Korban looked into the large, smooth stone, the image of a woman became clear, as Maura appeared, on the phone, typing on her computer, and giving directions to people in her office. She looked very intent, and anxious. Glaurius turned to his son, "She could never imagine that all she now builds for is a wicked counterfeit, and doomed to destruction."

"Yes, Father, her 'dream' is a twisted shadow of the real thing." His face darkened. "She and others like her have pursued Chag's agenda with such passion, giving their very lives to his global agenda. And this beastly system - which is bloating ever larger – continues to captivate multitudes.

Blindness and greed sweep more and more into its grip, where Aruni controls their every move and thought."

Glaurius shifted in agitation on the bench, and suddenly pounded his fist on the table. "Meanwhile, the Glaurianists count their money, sleep, and eat, denouncing the sins of their nations, and angrily cursing those who threaten their peace and safety. They meet once a week to sing songs in my name - songs that do not rise past the ceilings of their meeting places."

Sofia took his hand, and guided it over the other stones of the ephod, closing her eyes and praying. Soon, the stones began to glow, and within each one, images of a man, woman or child would appear. Each person was full of light and a quiet power, as they prayed for a diseased, dead, or crippled person, or gave food to the hungry, or spent time with those who were lonely and hurting. Others spoke words of blessing over their leaders, and prayed they would have wisdom to rule, or spoke words of truth, and encouraged the hearts of the fearful. And some just did their daily work and chores with excellence and integrity. But all had the same focus: remaining connected to the vision and agenda of the invisible kingdom, and bringing its value system to earth.

"These who carry The Message continue to increase: they are rejecting independence, ambition, pride, and earthly fame and power, choosing the road that leads straight to our hearts, our power, and our presence. They are preparing the earth for our return; these are the true heroes."

"Yes, my son. They are becoming a powerful army who can cut through hearts of stone, to free the captives of men. As Chag's kingdom snowballs in size and scope through deception and tyranny, ours is burning away his lies, by the power of love."

"And my bride is soon to awaken?" Korban removed his gaze from the stones to look at his father.

"It is time, my son. I have seen that she will choose very soon."

In the the amethyst, Korban saw Maura through the mist, tears streaming down her cheeks, as she stepped out to towel off, stumbling and crying, and throwing herself onto her bed. She curled up in the towel, pulling the snowy white comforter around her. Korban touched his forefinger to the stone, speaking with authority in a strange language; she fell mercifully asleep.

"That is all for now." Glaurius met his eyes, and Sofia rose to take both their hands in hers. "Tomorrow is another day," Father and son nodded in agreement. Glaurius rolled up the ephod and slipped it in its velvet cover, handing it to a seraf who was standing by.

"The training that Aruni has given her will not be lost; it will be her bread, and soon she will help to destroy his house. Yes, she will tear it down with her own hands."

Glaurius caressed his son's hand, and they intertwined fingers. "It is all because of you, and your sacrifice, Ben'i." He smiled warmly, affectionately. "Now she will awaken, and bring other children to freedom; for though she is serving the enemy at present, she is a forerunner. "

Glaurius imagined the day, and everyone picked up on his thoughts, as thoughts can be perceived at the same time in that place. A cry of unrestrained joy erupted.

Sofia and Glaurius bowed to Korban, while swaying to the rolling ballad, and together, everyone lifted their cups and sang, in honor of the One who had made the way:

> Here is love, vast as the ocean, loving-kindness as the flood
> When the Prince of Life, our ransom, shed for us his precious
>   blood
> Who his love will not remember, who can cease to sing his
>   praise?
> He will never be forgotten, throughout Tziyon's eternal days.

The Korbanim danced with all their might, joined by the serafs, gibborim, and all the people. The musicians played with abandon and passion, and all cried out, shouting the victory of the One who had won The Great Battle. On and on it continued, for a long, long time, till everyone fell to laughing and wrestling on the floor, or spilled outside onto the grass.

Chapter Twenty-Nine

Maura slept fitfully, waking suddenly in the middle of the night, her mind and body exhausted from the hours on the drug trip, with the cry of sirens from the street far below drifting in from the slightly opened window. She was less jittery, but a lingering sadness drew her attention.

How lonely the world is. As she lay in the dark, holding the blankets close, she thought about Nathan again, her thoughts drifting back to when they first met - at a writer's workshop in Mendocino. Hoping for a much-needed rest after finishing her Master's degree, she'd planned the getaway, but also because she needed to decide what to do about Paul.

She was sitting on a wrought iron bench, playing around with some ideas on her laptop, and finishing off a half a joint, when Nathan Rivers strolled up the hill. She choked, and coughed, red-faced on the roach between her lips, and he turned - surprised, delighted, and roguish - an unruly brown curl falling across his forehead. With the sun at his back illuminating him, he was the irresistible image of the Greek god, Adonis.

He stopped and smiled, seemingly amused at her coughing fit; he continued, unselfconsciously clapping his hands together, while whistling to a nuthatch in the oak tree overhead, where her nohedi hovered unseen, in the branches.

The creature craftily directed her attention to the song that wafted from the speakers on her laptop, and she caught the sense of serendipity - that this was a moment that was meant to be.

Just outside this lazy summer home, ain't got time to call your soul a critic, no...wake up to find out that you are the eyes of the world. The heart has its beaches, its homeland and thoughts of its own.

She stared at the dazzling man, across the unfinished letter she was typing. Nathan spoke first, while pointing at the roach. "I believe that kind of thing is still illegal here in California, isn't it?"

She froze for a second. "Are you a cop?"

"No, lovely lady, I am but a humble poet and carpenter – Nathan Rivers, at your service." He bowed dramatically, as Maura rolled her eyes and grinned in relief.

"Nice to meet you. I'm Maura McConnell." Around them, the setting sun blazed on the sycamores, as boats began to pull up for dinner at the vineyard's dock. And in the last warmth of an exceptional fall day, the cool of evening descended quickly; in the quiet air, the sound of the ducks at the water's edge – finishing their last meal of the day - muttered at the crumbs tossed to them by the kitchen staff.

The handsome stranger smiled charmingly, taking the initiative, "Mind if I sit down?"

After some small talk, Maura offered him some of the roach, and now it was Nathan who coughed, and Maura, who laughed. Easy and absurd conversation followed, till the sun set behind the mountains. They sat for a while in the peace, until the sound of her rumbling stomach broke the spell.

"I sure am hungry - join me for dinner?" Nathan asked. "I think it's grilled salmon tonight, with salad, and that great bread from Aunschutz' bakery." Maura salivated involuntarily, hoping he hadn't noticed.

And the nohedi also licked its lips.

Comparing notes over writers ancient and modern stole away the hours, as they discussed Nietzsche's "Superman," and the ideals of the perfect society. After dinner, they danced, the wine and jazz raising the tide of romance. They lingered long into the night, their shared passions joining them together, as Maura's invisible companion set the trap.

As Nathan held her close on the small dance floor, the

conversation became more personal. "Tell me about you, Nathan. You've heard my story."

He paused thoughtfully. "I grew up outside Rutland, Vermont - a farm boy. My dad inherited a Holstein dairy business from his father, and 115 acres of prime, New England, granite-laced dirt."

"So you made big rocks into little rocks?"

He chuckled. "Exactly – but I did get to drive a tractor!"

"There must be tons of work on a farm."

He brushed a stray hair from her face.

She reached up and undid the gold clip in her hair, he dark locks falling across her shoulders. He smiled admiringly, involuntarily touching her hair. Maura smiled and closed her eyes, enjoying his touch.

"There sure is a lot of work," he continued, "from cleaning and inspecting the cows, caring for the calves, shoveling and spreading manure, mowing, baling and stacking hay, growing and storing the grain and corn for their feed, milking twice a day, processing the milk, cleaning the barns and sheds, repairing stone walls and fences, and all the paperwork: inventory, buying, selling, permits, finances - I've done it all. We also produce maple syrup - another industry all its own."

She let out a whistle, and smiled. "What did you do for fun?"

"Well, when I could sneak off, I spent time roaming the hillsides, hunting small game and fishing the streams. I looked like a "Lost Boy" all summer in my cut-off shorts, with my fishing pole, and a lunch tied up in a red bandana, pretending I had endless free time. And of course, I always had a book."

His nostalgic recollections created a picturesque world for Maura, who could see the hot, summer day, and long-legged boys with cowlicks leaping from a frayed rope swing, as hornets droned in the dusty raspberry bushes on the riverbank.

"Did you have any pets?"

"We always had German shepherds, and lots of cats to control the mice population. A couple of them were pet-quality." He stroked her bare forearm and chuckled. "I had an Arab mare that hated snow. She'd only ride in the summer, but when she took off, I felt like Aragorn racing Brego across the plains of Rohan. She was a fine runner, and started out in life winning endurance trials in New Mexico; my dad won her in a poker game."

"Nice, a horse with a story. Have any brothers and

sisters?"

"It's just me and my sister, Kim. We had a younger brother that died as a baby…"

"I'm sorry. What happened?"

"Yeah, that was pretty rough. We were at a family reunion at my grandfather's place in Montpelier, and my aunt Nora was supposed to be watching Colin – he was two at the time. She got distracted talking, and when she finally looked around, he was gone. For two hours, everyone searched, until finally they remembered: he loved Grandpa's boat. My dad made a beeline for the boathouse, and dove under the dock. Nathan shook his head. "He tried to resuscitate him for two hours; nothing was ever the same after that."

Maura buried her face in his shoulder, envisioning the scene.

Nathan lifted her chin, "I'm sorry, Maura. That's a pretty heavy story. Let's sit down." He led her to a sofa by the fire. "I'll go grab our drinks – be right back. You all right?"

"Sure, I'll be fine. I just can't imagine the pain for your family…"

Nathan returned with a full glass of Cabernet, and urged her to sip some. His concern touched her. *Paul never worries about me like that. He comes from a line of one-dimensional women: strong.* She had always had to fight and compete, but Nathan seemed to have *sympathy.*

They talked some more, their hearts twining together over their common interests, and his man-of-the-earth storyline was evocative of another era. *Or maybe it's just the romantic lure of the unfamiliar? But isn't it peculiar timing – just as I'm breaking up with Paul?*

With a pang of conscience, her thoughts drifted back, and she saw Paul in a different light. *It seemed like only yesterday. He was so handsome, so strong and warm.* She was drowsy from the wine and food, and lost in her own thoughts as Nathan talked, but suddenly she was all ears.

"I only stay because of the kids."

The nohedi held its breath, waiting to see what Maura would do. She blinked uncomprehendingly at his words, but as the nohedi played her heart-strings; she fought bravely to resist, but was seduced, finally, by the strong fingers absently stroking the long-stemmed glass in front of him. She went willingly –

down, down, down, with her lovely neck on the block: like a lamb to the slaughter, like a cliff diver, leaning over and free-falling into the swirling waters below.

Flitting over to the bartender, the nohedi sunk his talons into the man's skull, and he obediently turned up the volume on the bar stereo:

In brazen support of the conspiracy, the lyrics broke in:

Sweet Annie Blythe - such a trusting young thing,
sang like a bird upon the wing
Though exiled from her family
she somehow seemed to find her way -
wandering here, and wandering there,
Till she finally found her knight so fair...

Rattled by the penetrating words, Maura nervously excused herself to find the rest room, and in her haste, she stumbled. Nathan stood, caught her around the waist, and she melted against him. He smiled and righted her, stroking her cheek, but in his eyes, she saw the unsettling confidence of a conqueror. Maura forced a smile as she walked unsteadily across the dance floor, past the tables of fellow conferees, her face blazing with shame, and vulnerability – unwelcome feelings for a woman who went through men like magazines.

She recovered quickly, however, anger steadying her as she imagined the internal dialogue of those who watched her pass. *Hmmm! I already have the job lined up that all these people want. Someday they will be begging ME to look at their stuff!*

But another voice chimed in, as the nohedi whispered accusations. *But how many are committing adultery tonight, and giving themselves away?*

Adultery? Hawthorne's scathing "Scarlet Letter" maintained top honors in her ivy-draped world as a classic example of the hypocritical, cruel religious fanaticism which the country was founded on. There was no middle ground in this debate; no one had the right to have an opinion about the choices of consenting adults – regarding anything! Philosophically, she believed marriage to be a partnership with blurred lines, but now her heart rebelled, though she could not account for the confusion.

In a circle of light in the bathroom, a hidden seraf released thoughts of love's cherishing, faithful, and selfless qualities, while the nohedi who had followed her, whispered its own ideas. Maura's thoughts collided, as she considered her university professors, parents, friends, colleagues and all who shaped the culture: those who were most admired in politics, academia, science, literature and art were free thinkers, *and* free lovers.

Adultery? She thought of her father, who even before divorcing her mother, had simply set up a new house with his girlfriend. *No, marriage - like everything else - is in a process of evolution.*

But the thoughts wouldn't stop. *What – or who - am I violating?* It was a scary feeling, as her thoughts kept stubbornly returning to the ancient codes of the Glaurianists. *Thou shalt not...* The nohedi alternated between this, and releasing thoughts of sexual desire and pleasure, and the dream of finding her soul mate – the one who would make her dreams come true - while the seraf patiently repeated the power of honor and respect. But finally, the nohedi whispered, *Follow your heart and you will never be wrong.*

The familiar line was a subconscious trigger; immediately, her confidence returned, and she came back to herself. *Everything will turn out just fine – I've got this!*

Of the many men who had pursued her over the years, she had so far managed to avert this complication, and had never been attracted to a married man, preferring the adventure of capturing an unconquered one. However, there was never a man – married or not - who made her feel like Nathan Rivers did.

With her mind made up, and armed with new strength, she sighed with relief, the pesky demands of her conscience now silenced. *I'm gonna ride this train wherever it goes,*

She dried her hands and playfully tossed the paper in the trash like a lay-up.

The nohedi snorted with glee, and turned its smoldering gaze on the seraf, who threatened, "You may have won this skirmish, but you have already lost the war!" With that, he vanished in an explosion of light and color, as the nohedi disappeared into the darkness.

Maura returned to the table, smiling and happy: she and Nathan left the restaurant hand in hand, stopping many times to kiss on the way to her room. Any lingering concerns she felt about his attraction to her, dissolved when he leaned her against an oak tree, and sought her mouth with his own hungry one. She smiled contentedly at his weakness. *Oh, how the mighty have fallen.*

After making love, she lay awake for some time, watching his beautiful, sleeping face as the melody on the laptop spun its tale.

Cherise was brushing her long hair gently down
It was the afternoon of carnival
as she brushed it gently down
Ruben was strumming his painted mandolin
It was inlaid with a pretty face in jade
as he played "The Carnival Parade."

Cherise was dressing as Pirouette in white
When a fatal vision gripped her tight:
Cherise beware tonight!
"Ruben, Ruben tell me truly true;
I feel afraid and I don't know why I do,
Is there another girl for you?"

"If you could see my heart you would know it's true
There's none Cherise, except for you, except for you
I'd swear to it on my very soul,
If I lie, may I fall down cold..."

When Ruben played on his painted mandolin
The breeze would pause to listen in
before going on its way again

Masquerade began when nightfall finally woke
Like waves against the bandstand dancers broke
to the painted mandolin

Looking out to the crowd, who is standing there?
Sweet Ruby Claire at Ruben stared, at Ruben stared
She was dressed as Pirouette in red
And her hair hung gently down

The crowd pressed round, Ruby stood as though alone
Ruben's song took on a different tone
and he played it just for her
The song he played was "The Carnival Parade"

Each note cut a thread of Cherise's fate
it cut through like a blade

Ruben was playing his painted mandolin

When Ruby froze and turned to stone
for the strings played all alone
The voice of Cherise from the face of the mandolin
Sang, "Ruben, Ruben tell me true
for I have no one but you."

"If you could see my heart, you would know it's true
There's none Cherise, except for you, except for you
I'd swear to it on my very soul, If I lie, may I fall down cold…"

The truth of love an unsung song must tell
The course of love must follow blind
Without a look behind
Ruben walked the streets of New Orleans till dawn
Cherise so lightly in his arms
and her hair hung gently down…

As the song ended, Maura felt a sudden stab of fear, but clinging to Nathan's arm, she fell asleep to the haunting strains of the guitar.

Chapter Thirty

Still awake, Maura propped the pillows up behind her, and leaned against the knotty pine frame, continuing to review her life with Nathan. After the writer's weekend, Nathan had stayed at her place whenever he could, with the excuse to his wife that he had to stay late in the city. With Maura at the paper, they eventually rented and decorated this apartment in Jackson Square, and for six and a half years, created their own world in the city, with friends and business associates that never crossed paths with his other life.

But as Maura passed thirty, she began to grow restless, and regularly fantasized about Nathan divorcing Sheila to marry her.

He would propose like this: it is sunset at the fountain at the Palace of Fine Arts. He takes her hands in his, and looks into her eyes, "I'm so sorry for the waiting, the loneliness." He shows her the envelope with the final papers, and pulls her close, kissing her hair. Then down on one knee, he pulls out and opens a ring box. Against the dark velvet background shines a 2-karat diamond from Tiffany's. "Maura, I love you and want to spend my life with you. Will you marry me?" She pulls him up, and cries, "Yes!"

Thinking about it again, her heart stood still as she saw the tear-streaked and despondent faces of Nathan's children in her mind's eye. She shook her head, biting the edge of the comforter, pain flooding her heart. *I could never be the cause of their broken hearts...*

She was transported back to the day she had arrived home

after school to find her father directing the movers to take his things from the house. She saw her little brother Tommy sitting on a landscape rock, with tears streaming down his face. Finally, Senator McConnell came over and patted him awkwardly on the shoulder.

Maura watched in anguish from behind the curtains in the dining room, as her father mouthed words, and Tommy screamed and grabbed his father's leg, his little chest heaving in grief. He would not let go, though Jim tried to shake him off like a large bug. But a nanny came and held him, while he sobbed on her breast.

As the dark blue Lincoln drove away, Tommy ran down the long driveway, and sat staring down the road through exhausted eyes, unyielding in his 8-year-old devotion.

Maura had gone to bring him up for supper, taking his hand in hers, as they walked back to the mansion.

"Will Daddy come to do my homework with me?"

An adult at 14, she steeled herself against the heartbreak and fear in his young eyes. "No, I don't think Daddy is coming tonight, Tommy, but I'll help you." She led him through the enormous front doors, across the marble foyer, and down the hall, the sound of their shoes hammering the oak floors, and echoing off the cheerless walls.

A cry rose from deep within, *He was so young and trusting!* But just as quickly as her compassion rose, she turned angry at him, and threw off the comforter, enraged that the scab that hid that wound had torn open again. *Tommy, why are you so weak?*

With little Tommy's face etched in her thoughts, she thought of how he had struggled all of his adult life with drug addiction, broken relationships, and prison, and her emotions careened off in another direction: this time, the nohedi was ready, and deftly turned her rage against her father. *How could anyone do that to such a lovable little boy? Oh, but it was really easy for you, wasn't it? After all, you had your ambitions, money, and glamorous life and friends - you didn't need us, I get it.*

In her mind, she saw her father's haughty face, as he was standing beside Monica, his gorgeous, trophy wife. Then the face of little Tommy returned, along with a deep sense of helplessness. She screamed at her father. "I couldn't protect him. That was YOUR job! Didn't your vows mean anything?"

Her chest heaved in anger, and her thoughts grew murderous. She calmed herself, and continued her inner dialogue.

Vows - who thinks like that anymore? She remembered her parent's wedding picture, and thought about the promises they'd made before the priest, and their friends and family. Of course they'd only done the church ceremony thing for the sake of her grandparents, but it still nagged at her.

So strange that the Glaurianists have these laws and rituals that no one follows, but I can't seem to escape them.

Maura thought about her mother's stories of growing up in the church of Glaurius, with the droning of Latin phrases, smoky incense that made her cough, the private vestibule where her family had gathered on their knees, and the soft-handed men in white robes that bowed and kissed altars and statues.

All perverts and hypocrites...

She hit the remote for the fireplace, watching the artificial flames ignite, and mesmerized by the dancing figures within. *But if all those laws and rules don't matter, why do I keep feeling this way?*

Turning her thoughts aside, the nohedi found its mark. Addressing the god of her grandmother, Maura exploded. "Glaurius, the great and powerful - where were *you* to protect my brother?"

Suddenly, the sterile silence of the apartment was shattered by the jarring ring of her cell phone. It was Nathan. *Why is he calling?*

"Hello?" She knew she sounded like a six year old.

Nathan's voice erupted. "Sweetheart! I saw you had called! I miss you."

He is so perfect. She cleared her throat. "Nathan, it's the middle of the night."

"I know, I know. I couldn't sleep. And I figured you might be up toiling away at one of your brilliant, world-changing articles. What are you doing?"

I guess I can tell him a little bit of the truth. "Well, I smoked some pretty strong weed earlier, and I'm just getting sleepy now."

He laughed. "Maura, Maura, you do love the stuff, don't you?"

She nodded somewhat ambivalently. "I guess I do."

Her thoughts drifted, as she pictured him walking the kids to school in the morning, eating dinner together, and tucking Aaron and Abigail into bed.

"Listen, I'll be in around one o'clock tomorrow. Got a

couple of people I need to see, but I want to see you before I leave for the holiday. I'll be at the apartment around six, to take you to dinner - I made reservations at La Jardiniere."

Really? Why? The exquisite and romantic restaurant was usually reserved for very special occasions.

She stammered a response.

"That sounds wonderful. What's the occasion?"

"Well, you'll just have to wait to find out..." *Something in his voice. What is it? Triumph? Elation?*

"Maura I have some great news, and can't wait to tell you."

"Awesome, I'll be ready at six, see you then."

"I love you - can't wait to see you - goodnight."

"Goodnight, Nathan, I love you, too."

As she hung up the phone, a feeling of dread stole over her.

* * *

She lay back against the pillows. *Good news.* What was in his voice, resolve? *No, determination.* It dawned on her. *He's divorcing Sheila!*

Her uncertainty over their future as a couple had led her on her side affair with Andrew. She struggled with it at first because she loved Nathan, but she was chafing in her role as mistress, and needed to do something. She wasn't in love with Andrew, but for months now, the tables had turned as she had secretly hoped, and Nathan was hard at the chase. He hated that her attention was divided. But in the midst of the drama, Maura discovered the truth: she was terrified of commitment, and of giving her heart away. *You can't trust any man...*

She had met Andrew at the coffee shop on the corner, one late afternoon when Nathan was in Baltimore on business. The memory of Nathan's kiss as he teasingly pulled on her lower lip in parting was making her angry at the moment as she sipped a steaming latte on that cold spring afternoon.

She was staring at the flames in the gas fireplace, cursing to herself, as she realized that up till now, that was all she had with Nathan - artificial fire. *They never leave their wives if they can have a mistress for free...*

The noisy scraping of a table interrupted her thoughts. She turned to find a somewhat disheveled, Gerard Butler look-alike, rearranging chairs in a circle. Glancing at the cat wall clock, she realized it was nearly six. Poets, professors and musicians used the room for informal gatherings, and she guessed he was making preparations for such an event. *A Bohemian-hipster,* she smirked, also noticing his knitted scarf and easy manner.

Probably a Russian language student - everyone is a Marxist these days... He saw her glaring at him. "Sorry for bothering you. I didn't know it would make so much noise. We are meeting with my Russian teacher. The poet, Mirislav Odonev? He also teaches at the university. We meet here once a week."

Maura smiled weakly and rubbed her temples. "No, you're fine. I just have a lot on my mind. Bad day." *Was I right or what?*

He bent down to retrieve her glove that had fallen on the floor. When he stood, he was smiling with a big dopey grin, and she found herself laughing, in spite of herself. "What on earth are you so happy about?" she asked.

"About meeting such a pretty girl," he answered, looking into her eyes.

"I don't know that I am all that attractive right now, but thanks for the compliment." She had tried to camouflage her itchy red eyes with makeup, but to no avail.

Not much fun, these spring colds. She gathered up her coat, willing herself to leave the warm impress her body had made in the leather sofa.

She pulled on her gloves and beret, and walked over to say goodbye to Heidi and Toni, and leave a tip. "See you tomorrow," she said drumming the counter before she turned for the door.

Gerard beat her there. "Madame," he offered with flamboyant gallantry as he held the door for her.

"Um, thanks."

"I'm new to the neighborhood. Do you want to have dinner together sometime and show me around?"

"Drop dead," somehow translated into "Well, maybe," as it made its way out of her mouth.

"Great. Is tomorrow at six okay – meet you here? Oh, I'm sorry. My name is Andrew. Andrew Rush. What's yours?"

"Maura McConnell."

He reached out to shake her hand as she replied, "Dinner sounds great. See you then."

Into the moment between Andrew-Gerard asking her name and her answer, popped the image of Nathan after making love – conquering her – again. He was the only man who had ever brought her to complete abandonment – death as Donne had observed. But right now she didn't care; she was feeling frustrated with Nathan, and needed a change.

She was a little apprehensive about going out with a total stranger, but considered herself good at reading people. *Right - then how did I get into this mess with Nathan?* Most of her life - like Diana the huntress - she had been careful to avoid capture, but Nathan had been a persistent hunter, and she needed to get free.

Andrew's a graduate student – intellectuals are pretty safe. Except for the Unabomber, of course, she added wryly.

She met him for dinner. They walked through the warming night air of late April to her favorite Italian eatery. A second generation of Cinanni's labored over handmade, cooked-to-order pasta and an exquisite array of sauces. There were just three wines on the list, two desserts, and plenty of crusty, whole grain bread that came with a fresh table-side salad, and homemade minestrone.

They ordered a large plate of grilled eggplant and mushrooms served with artichoke capellini, and a smoky provolone and tomato cream sauce. Sharing a half bottle of Chianti, they talked about their lives and families.

Andrew's father was a diplomat, and died before Andrew was two. His mother, according to Andrew, was a fanatical follower of The Way, and off-shoot of Glaurianism. When he spoke of his father, it was with a look of adoration, but he shot arrows of undisguised hostility toward his mother. Her conscience warned her, *it's not a good sign when a man treats his mother with such contempt.* But after dinner, he walked her home, chastely kissing her hand before opening the door and saying goodnight.

He was friendly and easy to be around, and they slipped into a routine of meeting for dinner at Andrew's apartment twice a week. They read Dostoevsky and shared tumblers of icy Stolichnaya and fruit juice all summer, and slept on the balcony. Making love was pleasant, although not deeply satisfying. Andrew was fun and undemanding, a welcome relief from Nathan's tumultuous passion and restless intellect. Andrew was a fan of the Grateful Dead, Bob Dylan, Eric Clapton and the other rockers of the previous generation, and loved to go to concerts and clubs that covered their music.

Maura was also in love with the music of the Dead; the hypnotic melodies, and the mysterious and seductive lyrics were the basis of a shared language and experience – a brotherhood – that felt like family – the only one she'd ever known.

Andrew had money and time to kill, so they had a whirlwind summer before she decided to tell Nathan. It made Maura feel empowered to have two lovers, and she could forget about Nathan's wife. *Never be dependant on a man.* If she kept herself from caring too much - from believing for too much - she could never be hurt.

Nathan's first reaction was shock, when she told him about Andrew. He stared at her, furrowing his brow as if trying to comprehend, which made her mad. Men and women came and went in each other's lives so easily nowadays; it seemed archaic to deal with feelings of jealousy and betrayal.

He didn't say anything as he searched her face and paced, willing his emotions to obey. Yet, she had hoped for just this response. Well-schooled in the ways of men, she fully anticipated his simple and characteristic behavior. *No matter how advanced we become as a species, they always react the same way when a woman takes a lover.*

Nathan asked the usual questions; "How did you meet him, where was I, what does he do?" She assured him that of course she still loved him and wanted him, but that she just found herself falling for Andrew also. She explained that some women have a capacity to love more than one man, and that she was in love with Nathan and Andrew both. No, she was not thinking of marrying Andrew or moving in with him, but Nathan was often unavailable because of family commitments and work, and she enjoyed Andrew's company during those times.

Given his circumstances – married with children - he couldn't protest very much. They eventually settled into a comfortable arrangement. Andrew was not exclusively hers, either, but was pursuing a French exchange student. Whether or not it had yet led to his bed, she didn't know, since Adrianna was several years younger, and didn't seem to share the same interest in Andrew that he clearly had for her.

At any rate, Maura had an assignment that was going to take her overseas for several weeks that fall; she need some time and distance from her intrigues. Her vlog involved Afghan families that had survived the Taliban and the American liberation - how were they moving forward, what was life like?

What she encountered there left her changed. Because of the limits placed on her interactions with the men, she spent a great deal of time with the women and children. While disappointed with the slow change there during American occupation, she couldn't deny things were a little better. Among other things, some girls and women were able to go to school. It was wonderful to see them as they chatted, heads close over their books while they walked the dirt roads to their classes. Young mothers sat and passed the days weaving, with looms purchased through micro business loans, while their laughing young children played nearby.

There was a sense of security in the air that was absent on her last trip, before the war. School-age children sat attentively in clean classrooms, built by church volunteers from around the world. Despite Maura's dislike of the church, she couldn't deny the gratitude displayed by the people for the missionaries and American soldiers.

Living among mothers from the Third World was very different from watching her friends in the States who had children. More and more of them were staying home, but still had a career, while others worked full-time, and had nannies and housekeepers. The Afghan women, in contrast, played with their children and were always holding them, listening to their stories. They were together all the time, working, playing, and laughing.

Maura began to return to her hotel room in the evenings with a growing emptiness. She was 29 years old and unmarried with no prospects for the future. She had been faithfully using the Pill for years, but began to reconsider her position of postponing children. *I don't need to be married to raise a child.*

As a very young girl, she had loved to play "house" with her dolls. But her brothers made it impossible to express this joy. "That is so stupid!" they would taunt. And seeing how her father spent more time with the boys, she realized that if she wanted his attention and affection, she would have to give up these activities. So after her 8th birthday, she gave away all of her dolls to the housekeeper's granddaughter, and made a vow never to display this weakness again.

Returning from Kabul's hovels, however, she began to think about having a baby, as she settled back into her life with Andrew and Nathan, and finding herself increasingly unhappy. She decided not to tell Nathan or Andrew about her plan to go off birth control. *It's none of their business anyway.*

Maura grabbed the sleeping pills that her brother Evan, the doctor, had prescribed for her, and popped two. She fluffed up the pillows, and snuggled down into the softness of the comforter, and repeating her mantra, fell asleep.

She dreamed she was on a beach in Manzanillo, surrounded by turquoise waters and brilliant white sand. The sound of the surf was tranquilizing. Nathan walked towards her, tanned and gorgeous in his cut-off shorts, his shock of curls had a blonde streak that made his hazel eyes leap from his face. They made love behind a sand dune, under a full moon.

As she lay unsuspecting, a dark spirit now loomed over her, and Maura dreamed of Omar, the reporter she had met in Kabul. He also walked toward her, his white cotton shirt open to the waist, his dark eyes drinking in her form, as he touched her breasts. He held her neck and pulled her to himself, unbuttoning the gown that fell to the floor. He picked her up in one motion and laid her on the bed. As the nohedi lay on top of her, she opened herself to Omar in her dream.

Over and over the nohedi took her to heights of ecstasy and abandon, as she gave in to the wave of seduction. She woke suddenly, her body soaked with sweat. Stumbling to the bathroom, she turned on the light and looked at her reflection; her hair was disheveled, and the mascara she had forgotten to remove was streaked across her face.

What was that? In the kitchen, she fumbled for a glass. The cold water soothed her burning throat. Disoriented, she made a cup of tea, and sat in the living room until the sun broke over the misty ocean.

Chapter Thirty-One

Maura dressed in black exercise capris and a pink and black tank, and applied cover stick to the dark circles under her eyes. As she put on her watch, she glanced at the time – 6 a.m. *Two hours to kill before the interview.* She straightened up her apartment, thankful for the small rituals of life; her mind was still a little disengaged and she was jumpy, but the Praxil was working, and she knew what to do next.

She never left her apartment without meditating, so as usual, she sat on the big floor pillow, her back firm and straight against the wall, with her knees in the lotus position, and her eyes closed. Inhaling the fragrant incense that burned in its censer, she began to chant, descending rapidly into a meditative trance. The nohedi attached to her spirit, as she swayed gently, her mind envisioning a fiery glow; she began to gather strength. Her feelings of disassociation disappeared, and fear and loss were replaced by confidence and peace. She smiled. *Here is one place I can always find rest.*

After a half hour, Maura took a deep breath and relaxed her neck. She stretched for a few minutes before getting up, and then bent down to touch her palms to the floor, chuckling. *I've still got it!*

She made a light breakfast, and watched a few minutes of the morning news, and then gathering up her things, she double-checked the lights and heat, and then slid into a lined raincoat on her way out the door.

She pressed the button, and when the nearly-full elevator arrived, squeezed into the remaining spot in front of the doors. She smiled at the man to her left, and greeted Phyllis, the floor manager's wife who occupied the most space with her vacuum. "Have a good day," Maura offered, as moments later, the door opened and she flowed into the garage with the sea of fellow riders.

"You, too," Phyllis said as she pressed the button for the upper floor and the doors closed again.

The yellow glow of the security lights cast an eerie light at any hour, and the smell of oil and asphalt was a gloomy reminder of the prison this part of the Bay had become, encased, as it was in concrete and steel. Despite the benefits, she felt increasingly like a rat in a cage. Like in the Matrix, sometimes the idea haunted her that she had far less control over life than she believed.

What if this is all a lie? Sometimes she felt eyes staring at her behind the surface of the visible world; maybe the freedom she imagined was just that - imaginary.

She opened the trunk and threw in her gear, careful to lay her raincoat and work suit across the top of the bags. She slid onto the smooth leather and shut the door. The sound of solid steel closing into a well-designed latch was comforting.

Thank Glaurius for the Germans! She turned the key in the Mercedes' ignition and briefly warmed the engine, checking the gas gauge.

Popping in a John Coltrane CD, she turned the heater on high and pulled into the exit lane, zipping around the corner and up the ramp into the grey daylight. Drizzling rain fell on the windshield, which was always a questionable blessing. *It cleans the street and leaves acid rain spots on my car.* She turned left onto Columbus Avenue, and made a mental note to call her neighbor in Lewiston. *Sabra can open the cabin and have a fire waiting Saturday night.*

Twenty minutes later Maura turned into the publishing plaza and slid her card through the scanner. The bar cheerfully rose to let her pass, then fell treacherously behind her. *No escape.* She turned right down the ramp, around the corner and into her parking space. The private gym and spa was on the first floor overlooking the street and park, and Maura listened to music as she pedaled, watching people on their way to work.

After her workout and shower, she dressed, put on

makeup and dried her hair with the dryers provided. She checked her trim body in the full-length mirror and approved of the black skirt, and winter-white silk blouse. Her legs looked fabulous in black-patterned stockings and red heels. She knew she'd be turning heads all day, and added a spray of perfume before checking her lipstick to leave. She felt calm with all the endorphins flowing into her body from 40 minutes of strenuous exercise. She forgot the events of the last couple of days, and put on her work face.

Swaggering into the lobby, Maura pushed the "Up" arrow on the elevator. *Open sesame.* As the door opened, she entered and walked to the back. *Yes, the world is my oyster.* She hummed cheerily and tapped out time until the elevator stopped. The doors opened before a glass-fronted lobby with the name of the paper in gold letters over several sets of gleaming white French doors. It was the Nordstrom's of media, presenting the kind of trendy professionalism and prestige that Thomas Harrison Granger wanted to display to the world. Nohedi swarmed in every corner, orchestrating the work, in accordance with Aruni's master plan.

The paper was king of the hill, the last and best of its kind, its reporters still embedded around the world in various theaters of war, and pushing the elitist agenda forward, against a sea of rising conservatism.

She marched through the doors, greeting secretaries and office help, pausing once or twice to inquire about some personal matter. She was a bright light of humanity in an ocean of intolerance, and hate that lurked in the towns and hamlets outside the glass doors, beyond the reach of the concrete bunkers of the City.

She delivered more than "news" - she was a mother to orphans, a rescuer of the poor, and she knew it, priding herself on the sage counsel she offered and a shoulder to lean on in need. She was The Lady Maura, and she passed by her subjects with a compassionate word for every hungry heart.

She headed for her office and Tom waved to her. "Here she is! Good morning, Dona – are you ready?" he whispered when she reached him. He had been calling her that since she started working for him. It was a reference to the notion that the ruling class should provide for the common people – 'noblesse oblige.' "It's our bread and butter," he had smiled beatifically, without the slightest hint of irony.

He hired her after reading the article in Groundswell

magazine that featured her and other talented graduates, forecasting political trends for the 21st century. "25 Future Leaders Predict." In the article, she envisioned a new movement of talented young people invading the dark world of welfare and want, using their family influence, wealth and skills to help the less fortunate. She drew on the work of 60's activists, calling on a new generation to take up the charge. He already knew her family, and had been waiting patiently for her to "come of age;" she was everything she was supposed to be. "Hire her," he told Dick Haynes, his editor in chief.

It was to be expected; there would always be open doors, and great opportunities, because this was her destiny. But today as she approached Tom's office, self-doubts whispered. *Something feels wrong, like I'm sleepwalking through life – or maybe the proverbial frog in the pot?*

This last thought made her shudder, and she pushed it aside. It was probably just her job. As a now-seasoned journalist, Maura saw the tragic side of life as well as the glamor: innocent children caught in the crossfire of war around the globe, the rape and defilement of women in American homes, families devastated by cancer and AIDS, and natural disasters that seemed anything but natural.

She had experienced pain and disappointment up close, and sometimes wondered if there was any good left in the world. *It used to seem simple - putting the right people in the right positions of power would change everything.* But even with a cooperative president, and increasingly unified world leaders, it wasn't happening fast enough. In fact, it seemed like things were getting worse. *It's all because of the religious right!*

She brushed away the thought about how they might ultimately have to be dealt with. *We're not there yet...*

Tom Grainger was a lion in winter, his thick, snowy hair, and tall frame were still strong after all these decades. Like a fine old ship, his face was lined with the stresses and strain of navigating the globalist journey, fighting the wars for tolerance and human independence, and preparing the way for the "super man." Nietzsche's vision burned within the publisher's very soul, and the mad genius sprang forth in every conversation. Maura was in awe of him; he was the sage of San Francisco, and none of his flaws dimmed her worship. His heart was nearly perfect - Zarathustra for a new age.

"Good morning!" Tom treated her like a comrade, like a daughter, but he also sometimes flirted with her; she was always in a splendid confusion, but no matter, he always knew what to do, and wherever she might be around the world, or whatever trouble she faced, he had resources and people to help.

Too bad he can't tell me what to do about Nathan. She tried to keep some semblance of a professional relationship with him, and didn't confide with anyone at work about her private life. She had an uneasy feeling, though, because while Tom acted like they were equals, and as though he respected her, there was sometimes an unexpected comment, look, or questioning tone of voice, that kept her off-balance, and made her wonder what he *really* thought - if at the end of the day, he believed she was maybe a little bit of an outsider.

Today, Maura was going to discuss her book, *Veiled Faces, Veiled Hearts*. It had been two weeks on the top 10 and was opening new doors for her – this time in the United States Senate. A press secretary had called to set up an address to the Committee on Foreign Relations next month, to discuss reproductive rights in Afghanistan, because the battle for choice there had a serious enemy - fundamentalist Muslims.

From her early days on the reporter's beat – covering city council and Women's Health Services meetings – she had progressed under Tom's watchful eye. Growing in her knowledge of politics and women's issues - especially abortion - she was an eloquent and passionate voice in the battle to ensure the right of women to control their own bodies.

She smiled to herself when she saw Germaine Parkson. *This will be easy.* She would thoroughly enjoy this interview, playing with the visiting anchor from KQBC who had been in love with her for years. She was articulate and comfortable in front of the camera, and the substance of the interview was the familiar territory of the feminist manifesto.

Home turf - reproductive rights, oppressive patriarchy, progress, choice, empowerment. She would get a good hunk of change for her time, and her smile would flash around the world - what more could anyone ask?

Tom moved away from her, and she shook hands and greeted the camera crew. She never forgot a face or a name, and people loved her. *Every planet has its moons.* The interview was in Tom's office; the gas fireplace displayed a comforting artificial radiance that put Maura into an almost nostalgic mood. She sat on the leather sofa, and sipped tea, feeling as confident as ever.

The makeup guy fussed with her hair, and gave her some fresh color and cover-up, while the camera people waited patiently. With her makeup done and every hair in place, Maura settled back in her chair and took a cleansing breath. She made a mental note of her afternoon to do list: *Compose an outline and begin my research, doctor's appointment at 3:30, go home, and get ready for Nathan.* She pressed Andrew's speed dial number to discuss their plans for the weekend.

As the phone rang, Maura sighed and thought about Nathan. What was she going to say when he popped the question? Somehow, she felt she would know when she saw him, although she had no answers now. She felt a pang of regret. *If only there was no Sheila.* If only she could trust Nathan, if only he could take charge of everything, tell her what to do and make decisions for her. If only she wasn't a grownup. She thought of Ty, her best friend in all the world. *He understands, but he's always in trouble with his own boyfriends!*

She left a message on the machine.

Chapter Thirty-Two

"3-2-1!" the director whispered, and pointed at Germaine Parkson, with two thumbs up. Parkson smiled broadly into the camera lens. "Good morning. Today we are talking to one of the most devoted representatives of the women's movement – beautiful, successful and compassionate – Maura McConnell. Many of you know Ms. McConnell from her articles in Modern Feminist. She is articulate, visionary, and today is promoting her new book, which she completed after several weeks in Kabul, Afghanistan. Thanks for joining us Maura."

"Good morning, Germaine. Thanks for having me on the show." Maura smiled radiantly, drawing him into her orbit.

"Your book gives a disturbing account of life in Kabul – particularly for women. Can you tell us what your observations are about the radical religious traditions there, and what correlation you see with the rising tide of fundamentalist Glaurianism here in the US? In your expert opinion, how do these beliefs impact freedom for women – particularly as it relates to that most basic of all rights, the right over one's own body?"

Maura looked into the camera eye and began to speak as if by rote, the nohedi dictating every word. She folded her hands and at times looked pensive, considering the weight of her words, while at the same time playing for the audience around her. As her words heated up, she could feel power flow out from her, but unexpectedly an image of the children of Kabul at the feet of their mothers appeared in her mind as well. Like the ghost of Tiny Tim, she saw individual faces and heard their laughter.

But she dug her nails into the bottom of the chair and pressed on, "Life for women is very hard in the Middle East." She saw the bright joy on the faces of the women as they sat gossiping in the sun, and braced herself against the confusion that rose inside her.

The focus of the interview was the current president's blunders in Afghanistan, and Germaine wasn't interested in any good news her book detailed; she would screw up the interview if she mentioned the other side of the story, so she fought the invading thoughts.

She intoned for several minutes about the need for a comprehensive medical plan to help the poor, which must include abortion-as-birth-control. "Women cannot be burdened with caring for numerous children, when the nation lacks basic necessities - like food - to feed them. The religious beliefs in Afghanistan continue to be a grave threat."

At that moment, a seraf released another memory to her: Maura remembered the funeral of little Alishama, who had died from typhus. His family followed Glaurius, and she had met them by accident, when she noticed they were always by themselves, and took an interest in them. They were always very kind, and shared the little food they had with her. She could never forget how, despite the difficulties, his mother had thanked Glaurius for the privilege of having him those five short years. *And she was incredibly brave in her faith, in the face of terrible ostracism.*

She finished her discussion with Parkson, disturbed by the conversation in her head. Parkson finished up with her accolades, and recommended the book. Off-camera, she hurriedly thanked him, feeling like she was underwater, trying to get to the surface for air. Jumping up, she fled to the ladies' room.

"Wait a second," Tom said and grabbed her elbow gently. "That was great. You were serious and related your observations well. You presented the people of Kabul in a tangible way, made their struggle personal. You did a fine job; your book and ideas will have far-reaching impact for years to come."

Maura blinked and stuttered, "Thanks, Tom." She was grateful that no one seemed to notice her abrupt exit.

They probably think I'm feeling the pain of the people. The interview had been like an out-of-body experience; she was saying "abortion, reproductive rights, blah, blah, blah" but couldn't stop thinking of the fierce love the Afghan women had for all of their children. Though their lives were unbelievably hard, the dream of a better life for their children strengthened them to go on. *And I know that Tom isn't that one-dimensional either.*

This is all so complicated! Islam is such a repressive, heartless religion, and women in these nations have no voice, no power – they need our help! But without their children, what joy do they have left – or what reason to live?

In the private bathroom, Maura suddenly thought about last winter in Anchorage. On the last night there, she had been alone under the vast Alaskan sky, when the aurora borealis appeared, glowing like fire from another world. She remembered the mysterious, dancing lights, and how a strange but familiar Presence had filled the atmosphere around her. In this moment - as then - reality fled away, and that "Otherness" filled the room, the unmistakeable but evanescent Someone or Something, that moved like the wind that stirs the trees.

Who are you? What do you want? she whispered, but the throbbing silence answered her in a language she didn't understand. And like a wave of the sea, as suddenly as the presence had come, it receded, and was gone.

She stood alone again before the mirror, her frightened, dark eyes gaunt in the pale beauty of her face. *I am so thin...*

Willing herself to forget all that had happened, she washed her hands, avoiding the reflection in the mirror, and on the way out the door, she missed the trash as she tossed the paper and hurried to her office.

Nohedi and seraf stood behind the veil, one in the dark, one in the light.

* * *

Maura sat back with a contented sigh, pushing away from the desk. *Good job.* She hit the print button. After writing without interruption for a couple of hours, she felt better. And talking to Nancy, her assistant, had helped her sort out her thoughts about Nathan; she was thankful she could trust her to never repeat it.

Nancy had taken her order for lunch, and brought back a

salad. Maura munched the bread sticks, and sipped iced green tea as she read the news online. Glancing at the clock, she was relieved to see she had another hour before her appointment with Dr. Plank.

She ate the last bite of salad and cleaned the remains of lunch from her desk, when the phone rang.

"Hi Maura, it's Nathan," her assistant stated simply. It irritated her that whenever Nancy announced his or Andrew's calls she felt a stab of conscience. "Great – thanks, Nancy."

"Hi, Nathan. What are you doing? I was just thinking about you."

"I'm downstairs. Can I take you to lunch? I'm going to Jonas's bookstore opening and left myself a little extra time."

"Sorry, I wish I could, but I have a doctor's appointment in an hour. She paused. "It was sweet of you to come by."

Nathan tried to sound more cheerful than he felt. "No problem, I understand. It's hard to dash off at the spur of the moment – everybody's busy." He chuckled, and added a jab. "I'll just have to make an appointment next time."

"Well you *will* see me tonight." In the early days of their relationship, the thought of scheduling would have been absurd. She was always running off to see him, her coworkers jealous of their affair. *How things have changed.*

"I know, I just couldn't wait!" She smiled at this, pleased that he still wanted her. "Why are you going to the doctor, are you all right?"

"Oh, yes, I'm fine. It's my OB-GYN, you know, my yearly exam."

"Are you sure that's all? You'd let me know if there was anything else, wouldn't you?" Nathan asked in a quiet voice.

She was touched by his concern, and how hard he was trying to connect with her, and she suddenly felt vulnerable, wishing she could pour out all her heart longed to say. But she fought the urge to open up to him. "No, Nathan everything's fine. I'll see you tonight."

"Ok, great! I love you – see you then." He hung up the phone.

For Pete's sake! Why didn't I take 20 minutes and go see him? I could do the editing at Susan's office while I'm waiting. But she knew the answer - it was a part of her protective strategy to be the one calling the shots. Self-restraint was key if she was to navigate this relationship with Nathan, and make it out with the least hurt possible.

She pushed away from the desk and walked to the window overlooking Golden Gate Park. She saw families playing together, now that the sun had burned away the fog. *That's Nathan and Sheila and their kids…*

"But he doesn't love her, he loves me!" But then the seraf redirected her thoughts. *Sheila and the kids are real people and any man who would leave one woman will leave another. I need to be careful.* Fear began to wash over her. *How could I do that to her, and to their children? No, I couldn't live with myself.*

She began to form a plan, and imagined moving forward without Nathan. *I could go back to school and get my PhD – that won't take long – and when I'm ready, I can be artificially inseminated. People do that!*

And for now, I think it just needs to be over with Nathan - he needs to get his head straight, and do the right thing. There will be someone else…

A baby with Andrew was out of the question, orf course. *He would make a terrible father.* And as she thought more about it, she finally warmed to the idea of breaking things off with Nathan. Just last week over coffee, her friend Kathy had assured, "Maura, you're making a big deal out of this husband thing. You have money, a great job, and you're *hot*. There are lots of guys out there – why are you wasting your time on married men and little boys? You need to start over and find someone who loves you and is single. Use an internet dating site - they have a high rate of people falling in love and getting married. I say ditch these two and get serious - you're not getting any younger."

But is that even possible? Could I commit to anyone for the rest of my life? And does my secret dream even exist - the storybook life where Dad goes to work and Mom stays contentedly at home with the kids, cooking, car-pooling, writing, and baking chocolate chip cookies? Can two people actually stay together until the kids are grown, and live happily ever after - two old people holding hands on the porch swing as the sun goes down?

She shook her head. That certainly wasn't the world in which she lived. Most of her friends were already into second marriages or in the process of divorcing over "irreconcilable differences." *Nancy is the only person I know who is like that and is happy, and her church thing is a big part of that, which is definitely not me.*

She walked back to her desk, and snatched the story copy from the printer.

Chapter Thirty-Three

Maura shut down the computer and cleared her desk, stopping by Nancy's desk to give her some final directions.

"Sorry for the meltdown before, I think I'm PMS," she laughed, avoiding eye contact as she pulled out a short list for her assistant. But when Maura handed it to Nancy, their eyes met. *What? Don't judge me!* It was another surreal moment, and it freaked her out. Pretending to take a call, she quickly left the office, all but running to the main doors and the elevator.

The elevator doors were already open when Maura approached, and they snapped shut like her conversation with Nancy. *Why do I feel surrounded?* She couldn't shake the unease that had begun with the bad trip, a sense of trouble that approached like a winter storm.

As she descended to the parking garage, song lyrics intruded into her thoughts:

Just then the wind came a-squallin' through the dark,
but who can the weather command?

The doors mercifully opened, but gone was the flippant confidence she had felt this morning. She walked to her car and slid inside. As it warmed up, she suddenly felt a pang of guilt because her shiny Mercedes cost more than the GNP of some small nations.

Shut up! Maura's anxiety was growing over the unwelcome interruptions of her long-quiet conscience. She had spent many late nights in college in a haze of marijuana smoke, and over lines of cocaine and bottles of expensive liquor, arguing philosophy and religion, and in those hours, she had settled her beliefs.

So what gives? Her moral compass was going haywire, and guilt started to flood in, as her terrified ego screamed, *I am master here!* She pulled into the street, observing the gathering dark clouds as a foul omen. She turned on music, and drove, trying to clear her head.

Arriving at Dr. Plank's, Maura found a parking spot in the tiny lot, and walked around to the front of the old building.Situated on a side street in a residential neighborhood, Susan Plank's office was in a beautifully remodeled Old Dutch home. The mature sycamore maples on the front lawn were bare of leaves except for a few stragglers holding on against the wind, like old men fearful of death. *They'll all be gone tomorrow,* Maura noted with an edge of bitterness.

The potted chrysanthemums on the top steps were brown and dry, and Maura sighed at the thought of another long winter. The doorbell jingled as she entered the warm reception area, where she hung up her coat. She walked to the front desk to sign in.

"Hi Maura," a cheery voice greeted her, and she looked down to see Susan Plank, smiling as she knelt near a file drawer, her glasses at the edge of her nose. Susan's halo of soft white curls framed her face, and at a chubby fifty-something she looked like Snow White's fairy godmother.

"Hi Susan. How are you?" sounding more pleasant than she felt.

"I'm just fine. Give me 5 minutes, and I'll have you right in, okay?" Stephanie, the receptionist offered her some hot cider.

"Thanks, that's great,"

Choosing the loveseat by the gas fireplace in what was once the formal living room, Maura sat and took her printed story out of her bag. Calming classical music on NPR's afternoon program floated from tiny speakers on the oak wall shelves, and watercolor paintings of meadows and flowers decorated the pale yellow walls. The flameless, scented candles on the mantle completed the atmosphere of peace, designed to comfort nervous patients.

Just as Maura finished the first paragraph mark-ups, Theresa, Dr. Plank's PA, slid open the pocket doors. "You can come in now, M. McConnell." She followed Theresa past portraits and photographs of smiling families. *I'd love to see my picture up there.*

In the bathroom, she changed into the colorful cotton gown, peed into the cup and left it on the specimen tray in the bathroom.

Maura opened the door to the exam room, and closed it behind her. Susan sat on the round stool, making notes in Maura's file, but stood and gave her a hug when she came in. Pointing to the table, she ordered, "Now sit on up there like a good girl."

Maura fake-groaned, and climbed onto the exam table, positioning her bare bottom on the paper cover. "Susan, how do you do it? There is not a woman alive who looks forward to these exams."

"Maybe not, but a lot of women are alive because they have them."

"That is a true statement, right there." *My mother might be alive today if she'd had hers regularly.*

Susan pulled on gloves, and warmed her hands under the lights. "So what's new with you?" she asked with interest and a warm smile. "How is the life of the global journalist? And what about your love life?" she asked, with a mischievous smile.

"Work is fine – a little crazy this week. As for my love life, well, it's a little complicated." She laughed weakly.

Susan Plank had graduated first in her class from Sarah Laurence and attended medical school during the turbulent years of the women's movement. Her beliefs were completely in line with Betty Freidan and Gloria Steinem, with her long-time lover, Amy completing the feminist picture of rejecting marriage as a construct of male domination. But she had been a wise friend and mentor to Maura for many years.

Maura shivered.

"Oh, you're cold. Here, let me turn up the heat a bit. You'll be nice and warm in a minute." Susan put the stethoscope in her ears and warmed the bell before putting it on Maura's back. "Anything you want to tell me? Problems with your period?"

"Well, my periods have always been a little erratic - but I think it's stress."

Dr. Plank grinned. "That's probably true, my dear. Our bodies are damned sensitive."

"Take a deep breath." She placed her hand on Maura's shoulder. They had met while serving on the Run for the Cure committee a few years back. When Maura's mother was diagnosed with cancer, Susan walked with them through the maze of exams, biopsies, and treatment options. Maura was thankful for their history, which made her visit today a little easier.

"Have you been doing your monthly breast check?" Susan asked as she slid her hands through the opening in the side of Maura's gown. Her hands were warm and firm, as she moved them over Maura's breasts and armpits.

"Yes, I'm pretty good about that."

Susan nodded happily as she finished the other side and confirmed there was nothing out of the ordinary, adding "But I would like to see you begin regular mammograms starting this year, given your history – just to be safe."

"Alright, go ahead and lie back now, you know the routine," she laughed as Maura frowned.

"Yes, Ma'am, I do. Spread 'em wide, feet in the stirrups, aaaggghhh!" She obeyed, and Dr. Plank laid a cotton sheet over her knees. The examining light was warm. *Relax, if you tense up it'll only make things worse.*

The door opened, and Theresa came in and stood beside the table.

"Are you okay?"

"Yeah, I'm great!" Maura lied.

Susan grinned under her headlamp.

Each time Maura came in for her Pap smear and cervical exam, the apprehension grew, as with each passing year the odds increased against her. Difficult periods, endometriosis, miscarriage, fibroid tumors, cervical abnormalities, hysterectomy, early menopause, breast cancer had all become seemingly part of the package of modern womanhood.

Spread out on the exam table, Maura was side-swiped again by the nohedi, as a scene suddenly flashed before her eyes. She was lying on an operating table, hooked up to monitors and under anesthesia. Susan was working between Maura's spread legs, reaching deep inside her body, desperately trying to remove something. She barked orders to the assistants who stood nearby, laughing and talking. The heart monitor suddenly flattened out, and there was silence. In panic, she jumped.

"Maura, are you all right?" Dr. Plank asked with concern,

as she looked over the top of the sheet that covered Maura's bent knees.

"Oh, I'm sorry. I guess the speculum pinched a little," she lied again. "I'm fine now."

"Well that was it, my girl – we're all done." Dr. Plank removed her surgical gloves and reached up to shut off the exam light. She stood up from the round swivel stool and stroked Maura's leg outside the sheet, smiling down at her. "Everything looks fine. You can get dressed now, and I'll see you in my office."

"Great. Thanks, Susan." She pulled one leg at a time from the stirrups, and sat up. Stepping down onto the wide oak floor, she padded softly across the hall into the dressing room. Despite the pleasant atmosphere of the office, Maura felt strange and ill at ease. *I've got to get that Praxil prescription refilled.* She dressed slowly, murmuring her mantra in an attempt to restore her taut nerves.

Finally, her mind rested. *I'm going to tell her I want to have a child, and get her advice.* She gathered up her things and headed to Susan's office, tapping gently on the closed door.

"C'mon in!" Susan finished filling in Maura's chart, adding her initials to the end of the notes, and set it to the side of her desk. She sat back in her chair, removed her glasses, and folded her arms across her chest. "I'll send the samples to the lab today, and get back to you next week with the results." She paused, and Maura jumped in.

"Susan, I have to talk to you about something, but oh, I'm sorry – was there anything else?"

Susan shook her head. "It can wait. Go ahead."

Maura explained the situation with Nathan and Andrew, then, biting her lip, added, "But I'm thinking of having a baby anyway. Am I nuts? Ever since my trip to Afghanistan, I've been thinking about it. I know I'm almost thirty, but it's more than that. Andrew isn't my soul-mate. We have a good time together, we're friends, but that's it. I believed Nathan was the one, but I've begun to doubt whether there is such a thing."

She finally took a breath. "He's going to ask me to marry him tonight, but I just can't. He's going to divorce his wife. But what about his children, Susan? I can't be responsible for him leaving his family."

She stood up and began to pace. "Why do I hang onto this dream of a husband, children, growing old together, grandchildren?"

Susan waited, a little stunned at the uncharacteristic outburst and exposure of herfriend's heart. "Wow, there's a lot going on in there. I guess I don't know how good I have it, with just Amy and me." She chuckled, softly, and then continued. "You know, Maura, there are perfectly fine alternatives to the traditional family model, and other ways of getting pregnant." She paused and smiled. "But in your case, those other options are a moot point."

Maura stopped pacing. "What do you mean?"

"Well, I hope this is good news; Theresa tested your urine sample, and the results are positive. You're going to be a mother."

Maura's mouth dropped open.

"So this is a surprise. Are you *sure* you haven't had any symptoms? Nausea, tiredness? Do you know the date of your last period?"

Maura sat down again, supported by the arms of the chair, and suddenly feeling small and afraid. "Symptoms, hmm. No nausea. Maybe I'm a little more tired than normal. My last period was in September, and it was spotty."

"Well that puts it around eight weeks then. Baby's fully formed, and just needs time and good food." Susan smiled again. "So, this *is* good news?"

"I'm in shock," Maura said, clearing her throat. Her mouth was dry and she began to sweat. "I don't know what to think, it's so unexpected."

Susan thought for a moment. "Well, Maura, despite our best attempts to plan our lives, sometimes the unexpected happens. Taxes, car accidents, Republicans in the White House, death – and pregnancy – all can happen without warning."

She continued. "The question is, what do we do when the unexpected happens?" She looked at Maura and volleyed the question across the desk.

Maura glanced at the clock on the wall behind Dr. Plank and suddenly heard the second hand ticking sharply, her conscience at attention. *There's a baby growing inside me!*

Susan swiveled in her chair and stood up. "I used to have those same dreams, Maura, but then I grew up, got busy with work, and Amy came into my life. It wasn't really accepted for a lesbian couple to raise kids, so we didn't pursue it. I often wish things had been different, but the world is not like in fairy tales. My father left when I was a little girl, and my mother had to struggle just to feed us. And I was sexually, physically, and emotionally abused by most of the males in my life, so I don't have much to offer you in the way of advice about men. But I do know that you have to know your own heart, and what it is you want out of life, and then make it happen."

Know my own heart? I don't know the first thing about my heart...

Seeing the struggle on Maura's face, she added, "Maura, it's possible you are looking to motherhood to complete you. Many women do, but that's not a reason to have a child. Maybe you need to do some more soul-searching before you make such a life-changing decision. Having children is a big responsibility."

Maura shrugged. "I keep hoping my dream will come true; I haven't been willing to accept that my life might turn out differently than I'd expected. Now the two things I've wished for are staring me in the face, and I'm scared to death! And if I end things with Nathan, how would I manage being pregnant, with the demands of my job? I had hoped to come here and discuss it rationally with you, and make plans. But surprise – I'm already pregnant!"

"Maura, you're in great health, with a great job - you could take a leave of absence from work. I know it's a shock, but you're going to be fine. I suggest you take a few days and think it through. After Thanksgiving, give me a call. If you feel like you're just not ready, we can schedule a termination of this pregnancy. Maybe this isn't the best time for you to have a baby."

Maura stopped breathing for a moment and looked at Dr. Plank. "You mean an abortion?" she asked in a whisper. Suddenly, Susan's face seemed menacing and unfamiliar, far away across the big oak desk that separated them.

"Yes, that's an option. It is a simple, painless and inexpensive procedure. I can schedule you for a morning appointment, and you'll be back to work the next day. I perform terminations right here every week."

Maura's mind raced. Relief flooded her at the possibility of a way out, but the idea terrified her.

Susan stood up. "Think about it. You've got some time. Don't let this spoil the holidays."

Maura stood, too, and Dr. Plank hugged her.

"Is there anything else I need to know?"

"You're around eight weeks pregnant, so avoid alcohol, prescription drugs – even Tylenol or Advil can affect the baby.

You'll want to get a little extra sleep. I do recommend if you decide to terminate this pregnancy, that you do it within the next few weeks. It will be safer for you and easier since the fetus is so small."

Susan waited while Maura picked up her things.

"I'll be in touch, Susan – thank you." Maura walked to the front desk.

"Great, I'll talk to you soon. Take care, Maura – and Happy Thanksgiving."

* * *

Maura slipped the receipt into her purse as the bell clanged on the way out the door. She walked slowly down the steps. *I can't believe I'm pregnant. Why don't I feel anything?* As she pressed the car remote, her phone rang. Glancing at the ID, she saw it was Andrew. She had also missed call from Nathan.

"Hello?" She answered without thinking.

"Hello, brown-eyed girl, how are you?" he growled temptingly.

In the background, she could hear Mick Jagger crying out, "Oooh, Baby, why you wait so long?" and felt the bass pounding through the phone, calling to her. That was the great thing about Andrew – carefree and ready to party, he didn't let the pressures of life get to him. Although she had plans to spend the night with Nathan, she wished she could go over to Andrew's and get high, and make mad, passionate love. The pull was strong to escape from this crisis - it was all she could do to say no.

"Hi Andrew. I'd love to come over, but I have plans with Nathan. No, I don't think he's interested in a threesome. Yes, I'll call you. Miss you, too, bye." Checking voice mail, Nathan had left a message that he was running late, and would be by around seven.

She leaned against the car for support. *Andrew was pretty high.* The wind on the back of her neck brought her to reality, and she got in the car. *I feel like my life is spinning out of control.* It took all her will-power to move ahead to the next task on her to do list.

Stop by the cleaners, pick up bread...

Traffic was slow as usual, but after her errands, she made it home by 6:20. Gathering her things, she walked across the garage into the open elevator. A tabby cat with a missing eye jumped down from the trash can by the door. Sand ran across her path. It screamed as she accidentally caught its tail under the toe of her shoe. Cursing as she tripped into the empty elevator, she relaxed against the paneled wall, lost in thought as the elevator soared up the belly of the building. *Hush, little baby, don't you cry.*

What on earth was I thinking? She tried to recall any time when she had forgotten to use birth control in the past two months. She was always careful now since going off the Pill. Then it hit her. *The Greenwich Village street party!* She was out with some friends and had run into Andrew. Normally, she planned her times with both Andrew and Nathan because of her work schedule, but this was an unexpected rendezvous. After a few drinks and several lines of coke, they spent the night at his apartment. Maura remembered it was more intense than usual, the drugs giving them unbounded energy. She dismissed her normal precautions in the urgency of the moment, and was a little worried afterward, but within a few days, she had a slight period and assumed everything was fine.

But it's not fine. She panicked. *This is Andrew's baby!* She turned the key in the lock and opened her apartment door. *I can't believe it! What is Nathan going to think? He wouldn't even want to marry me now!*

She wondered if one of the appeals she held for him was that she was childless, and they could start fresh with a family of their own. The idea of starting out with a pregnant wife – pregnant by his rival – might be enough to change his mind. *Nathan's not like that. He loves me.*

What do I care? I'm breaking up with him anyway! Maura set her bags on the polished marble tile in the foyer, and hung up her coat. In her mind, she saw herself fully pregnant and coming home late from work to an empty apartment. The despair of the scene was thick, as she envisioned unlocking the door, shifting grocery bags from hip to hip, dropping them to the floor, and then pushing them into the foyer with her foot.

What am I going to do? Overcome by a wave of exhaustion, she fell onto the soft pillows in the corner of the couch. *When I was little, I'd just read the 8 Ball and get answers.* Her thoughts whirled unchecked, and in her mind she imagined Nathan standing outside her apartment, knocking. As she opened the door, distraught, he demanded to know what was wrong. "What's the matter, Maura?" He took her hand and pulled her over to the couch. "Come sit down and tell me, please!"

She sat staring at her hands, struggling to speak. "I had a pregnancy test at Dr. Plank's this afternoon and it came back positive." She pictured the look of surprise on his face before he responded.

"Well, sweetheart, I wasn't expecting this, but it's wonderful news. I was going to wait, but I think now would be the right time to ask you." Moving the coffee table away from the couch, he dropped to one knee, taking her right hand tenderly in his. "Maura, you know I have loved you since we first met. You touch me in a way that no one ever has; we were meant for each other." His eyes grew misty as he held back his emotions. He shook his head trying to take it all in. "And now we have a baby! I know it's taken a while to work things out so we could be together, but I told Sheila last week I want a divorce. And you won't believe this – she's in love with someone else, and wants to marry him!"

Maura continued to stare at the floor, until Nathan gently reached up and lifted her chin, turning her to face him. She looked at him blankly while he spoke. "Maura, did you hear me? I want to marry you, and be with you forever. I want to wake up with you, grow old with you, and play with our grandchildren together, and there's nothing stopping us now." He swallowed hard, looked down at her hands, and back again at her face.

"Will you marry me?"

She slowly took back her hand and looked sadly into his eyes, shaking her head. The words fell like hammering blows. "I'm sorry, Nathan, but I just can't. I've waited and dreamed for this moment, but I'm just not ready. It doesn't feel right – your family breaking up, me being step-mom to your children. I love you, too, but there's something else I need to do. I have no clue what it is, but I know there's something more – something I was born to do and I have to find out what it is." She took a long pause before adding, "Nathan, I'm pretty sure this baby isn't yours."

The scene dissolved as Nathan's tortured gaze stared back at her from a distance. The seraf stood nearby.

As she sat alone in the dark, she made her decision. I'm going to tell Nathan the truth, and that it's over between us. I'll call Dr. Plank tomorrow and make an appointment – hopefully for next week. And finally, I'm going to register at Columbia to start my PhD. I've been dreaming about it for years, and this is the perfect timing – a fresh start for a new year.

She fixed her makeup, and turned on some lights, checking her watch. *Nathan will be here any minute!* She finished pouring two glasses of Chardonnay as the doorbell rang.

Chapter Thirty-Four

Nathan was greeted at the door by a pleasant but aloof Maura. "Hi Nathan," she said and gave him a peck on the cheek. He decided against scooping her up in his arms. Maura turned around abruptly, and he followed her into the apartment, setting his bags down at the door, and from habit, slipping off his shoes.

"It's okay; you don't have to take them off."

"Maura, what's going on? Did I do something wrong?" He towered over her, his brow furrowed, the curls she loved, falling over his dark eyes. She started to reach up and smooth them back, but caught herself.

"Nathan, we have to talk. Come sit down." Maura handed Nathan his wine glass, and sat about a foot away from him on the couch. She wanted to see his reactions, but not feel him too close. She wasn't sure she could go through with it if she could smell him, and feel the heat of his body next to her.

"So, what is it? What's going on?"

"Nathan, I have something to tell you, and it isn't good news."

He stared at her, trying to read what was coming next. "Did something show up at your doctor visit? I was afraid something was wrong. You have been so secretive lately." Nathan squeezed the stem of his glass and waited for her to continue.

"No, there is nothing wrong with me. What do you mean,

'secretive'?"

"Well, you haven't seemed all that interested in me for the past couple of months; you're distracted when we're together – it seems like you're just going through the motions."

"You're right, Nathan. You're right." Maura paused briefly to gather her thoughts. "I have been doing a lot of thinking since I came back from Afghanistan. Something happened to me there that has been hard to forget - the needs, the lives of the people – I've been thinking a lot about how I'm living my own life. I don't have all the answers yet, but I feel like I need a change. I want to look at everything I'm doing and know why. "She paused. "I thought that being married to you is what I wanted, but I'm not sure anymore."

He started to interrupt, but she put up her hand.

"I'm almost done, I need to finish while I can – this is really, really hard."

She took a deep breath. "Nathan, I know you say that you don't love Sheila and she doesn't love you, but what about your children? Maybe you could get into counseling and save your marriage. When I was in Afghanistan, I saw a love that didn't fade despite terrible circumstances. In the face of a woman-hating religious system and gut-wrenching poverty, I saw a love that defied these things, and it changed me forever. I also saw the pain of daughters who were abandoned or neglected by their fathers, and I can't be responsible for doing that to your daughter. I know that's where we are headed, and I just can't go there."

Nathan had been staring at the photograph of him and Maura at Yellowstone a couple of summers ago. Maura's words hit him, and he could feel that the furtive pursuit which had charged him all these months and years was ending. He had always known it would end this way; there was a tragic quality about their relationship like Paolo and Francesca - the doomed lovers of Dante's Inferno - who pursued each other in Hell, but throughout the long ages of eternity would never unite.

Nathan cleared his throat. "Have you and Andrew gotten more serious?"

"No, Nathan, this isn't about Andrew. The feelings I have had for you are much deeper than what I could ever feel for Andrew. This really isn't about you, it's about me. Haven't you ever felt like there is something you were meant to do, and you just have to find out what you were born for? I've felt like this since I was a little girl, but I haven't discovered it yet - and I'm not getting any younger; I'm afraid of missing my purpose. I've decided to go back to school and get my PhD, and teach."

Nathan looked at her, his eyes filled with hurt and anger. "Did you know that I planned to ask you to marry me tonight?"

She nodded her head. "I suspected."

He took a deep breath. "You asked if I've ever felt like there is something more to life, and there is: it's you. You are my muse, and my dream of the future - that's as metaphysical as it gets for me. And while I appreciate your concern, I must confess that I don't share your hopes for my marriage. It's over."

What am I thinking? I could close this space between us in a moment. In her fantasy, Nathan could make all the darkness go away.

"Maura, you can have your dream with me. I *want* you to pursue your dreams."

He looked at her with longing, and Maura hesitated as she thought about what she was leaving behind, her heart weakening as she re-hashed the day's crazy events.

For a fleet second, she saw Nathan pushing a stroller, happy and smiling, as he stopped and pulled her close to kiss her. But then she saw Nathan's children seated on the edge of the fountain, tears streaming down little Abigail's face. Maura careened back to the present.

She shook herself free of the vision. "I had a pregnancy test today and the results were positive - I'm pregnant."

Nathan stared vacantly for a few seconds, then looked at Maura questioningly. "So, how do you feel?" He asked, groping for direction.

"It seems like it's happening to somebody else; like it's not real."

Nathan ran his hand through his hair, and sat back into the sofa, swilling his wine in one gulp.

She went on. "There's something else, Nathan. I'm pretty sure this is Andrew's baby, not yours. I calculated the time – you know I'm pretty careful to keep track of my cycle and birth control. I remember being with Andrew one night about a month ago and we didn't use any contraception. It was a spur of the moment thing."

Like we used to have. Nathan brooded over the thought of Maura and Andrew enjoying a spontaneous, passionate night together. He looked at her, and their eyes met. Maura's dark hair fell cascaded over her shoulders, and in the candle glow, she had never looked more beautiful. But where he had always seen desire and familiarity, he now saw something new. There was a faraway look in her eyes, and he realized, sadly that she was lost to him. The connection between them had broken, and a suffocating pain squeezed his heart.

But there was also something else – now *he* felt troubled by thoughts of destiny and responsibility.

He knew he had to graciously accept Maura's decision. He looked at her one last time. "Are you sure this is what you want? I know you are a strong woman, but I need to know you're going to be all right."

"Yes, I think so, Nathan. I'd be lying if I didn't say that I'm scared. I'm not sure I'll find what I'm looking for, or if it even exists, but I know I have to try."

He stood. "Well I guess that's it, then?"

She nodded and stood to hug him, misery flooding her heart.

"If there's ever anything I can do, please don't hesitate to call me." Tears welled up in his eyes as he looked down at her. "Let me know when I can pick up my things."

"I'll call you after Thanksgiving."

He put on his shoes and coat, and she reached up to kiss him on the cheek. He tried to pull her to him, but she gently resisted. "Go try to put your family back together – no kid should have a broken family."

He smiled bravely, and without turning around, walked through the open door and down the hall.

Maura waved at his back, and closed the door.

* * *

When she woke up the next morning, the sun was streaming across her bed. She glanced at the clock, shocked to find that it was past seven. For a moment, she laid there, clutching the comforter to her chest, suddenly recalling a dream she'd had when she was sixteen years old.

The alarm read 6:30, as she floated to consciousness, with a a word written in ancient script written on a banner, stretched over head. "Metamorphosis." She had repeated it over and over as she awoke, and driven by curiosity, she had looked it up in the dictionary at the school library.

Met-a-mor-pho-sis *1. A complete change of form, structure, or substance, as transformation by magic or witchcraft. 2. Any complete change in appearance, character, circumstances, etc. 3. A form resulting from any such change.*

After that, the word seemed to have taken up residence in her soul, fueling an insatiable hunger. Throughout her college years, she read everything she could about religion, literature, poetry, and philosophy, and tried many different avenues of spirituality. But though she gained knowledge, she never seemed to break through to a sustained wholeness or transcendence, which was her goal.

But as she thought about it again, she wondered. *Maybe the word is not a message for me at all, and I'm really just going around in circles. Or maybe I'm following the siren's song and will end up like Odysseus, in a really bad place. Maybe it's not personal, but what I'm already doing – changing culture…*

She climbed reluctantly out of bed, and padded to the bathroom, inspecting her face in the mirror. Under the bright track lights, it hit her. *I'm pregnant, I broke up with Nathan and I'm going to get an abortion.* Nohedi and seraf were at their posts, battling for her thoughts, but it seemed to Michael that she was completely deaf.

Think of something else - do the next thing - take a shower. She reached into the stall to turn on the controls. As the cold water ran through the pipes and gave way to warm, she undressed and stepped under the running stream. She closed her eyes and repeated her mantra, as the water fell like drops of fire. She began to cry, and didn't hold back.

She cried for her family, the world, and herself. She cried because she was pregnant, and was going to have an abortion, and she cried because there was no hope. There seemed to be no end to the grief, but finally, she stopped. *I just have to move on. Susan said it's not that big of a deal - I can have an abortion, and get back to normal.*

Armed with this tentative assurance, she cleaned up the bathroom and got dressed. As she dried her hair and put on makeup, she suddenly saw herself as an old woman, applying heavy makeup to cover her ancient face.

Her normally slight wrinkles appeared deep and tired, and her rouged cheeks reminded her of Shakespeare's whore – a woman way past her prime who continued to try and sell the one thing she still possessed. The image shocked her, and her hand trembled as she tried to apply mascara. Taking a breath, she steadied herself, closed her eyes, and her normal face returned. *I have to call Andrew and tell him I need to spend Thanksgiving alone.*

After making her bed, she packed for her trip to Napa,

where her family spent Thanksgiving, and then for the mountains, where she planned to spend the weekend working at her cabin. She wheeled her bag to the front door, and realizing she hadn't eaten since lunch the day, she went to the kitchen for some breakfast. Taking several long drinks from a bottle of grapefruit juice, she perused the contents of the fridge, and made an omelet.

She flipped on the Boze CD-radio on the windowsill to get the news and weather, and as the sound filled the room, she relaxed a little, listening in on the conversation of a favorite morning show. For a moment, things seemed almost normal as she chopped vegetables, whisked eggs and milk, and shredded cheese.

As she watched the butter sputter and sizzle in the pan, she began to think about last night. *I would be making breakfast with Nathan right now if I had made a different choice.* Pouring the eggs into the hot pan, she turned down the flame and made coffee, measuring enough for two cups. *Both for me.*

She folded up and covered the eggs, then made an English muffin, and went and ate in the living room.

She shut off the radio that was still announcing the traffic report and cracking commuter jokes, and turned on the tv. She was not a fan of the morning shows and was normally already at work by now, but she watched with detached amusement as a group of her peers tore into some right-wing zealot. *A dependable voice in a changing world.* Maura knew the show's slogan.

The moderator probed for answers from the conservative senator minority leader who stated he would not vote to raise the debt limit. "Let me see if I understand this correctly, you think it would be better to shut down the government than to keep things moving forward?" She shook her head and mocked him with her smile. "I guess I just don't get it."

Her prey struggled to explain how the country was moving to an irreversible collapse because of reckless spending, and the pathetic – or purposeful - makeup job made him look like a dead fish.

"But this is *America*, the greatest nation on earth," exulted Mother-goddess anchorwoman. "We have some problems, but I can't share your gloom and doom opinion." She smiled beatifically, thanked the humiliated man, and broke for a hemorrhoid commercial.

Maura shook her head at the unfathomable resistance of

these conservatives and other so-called "patriots," and took her finished tray to the kitchen. *They've ruined this country – WE are the true patriots.* She ran the dishwasher and cleaned out a few things in the fridge that were on the verge of spoiling. Throwing a couple bottles of green tea into the padded cooler, she cut up cheese, veggies, and added a box of crackers.

After brushing her teeth, she grabbed her makeup bag, checked the windows, and turned off the thermostat. Finally, she hit the on switch for the answering machine, pulled her barn coat from the closet, grabbed her bags, and locked the door.

Exiting the elevator, Maura opened the car trunk and tossed in her bag and cooler. She slid onto the cold leather driver's seat, and fired up the engine, rubbing her hands together as she waited for the car to warm up. She slipped on her driving gloves, checked the mirrors and turned on NPR's morning classical program. Pulling out of the garage, her car purred into the southbound traffic, and as she sipped latte from her travel mug, she started to feel better

Maura drove through the back streets in rare, brilliant sunshine, feeling a range of emotions. *Maybe I should call The Philosopher.* Aaron Feinberg wrote a trendy Dear Abby column for the paper. He had a reputation as a wise counselor for post-moderns trying to make moral decisions, helping them sort out their dysfunctional pasts; Maura read him every weekend.

Maybe he'll meet me for coffee. She had talked briefly with him a couple of times at various events, and he always projected an aura of compassion and wisdom, standing with folded hands, like a priest.

Maura punched in speed dial 2 for her sister, Peg. "Hey. What's up?"

"Hey yourself – not much." From the screams in the background, Maura knew she had called at a bad time. "What is the matter with them?" she asked, envisioning Peg's 2 year-old twins hitting each other as they fought over a toy.

"I'm feeding them breakfast," Peg said. Maura heard the edge in her voice.

"Bad night?"

"Yeah, Roger didn't get home till after two." Maura knew her brother-in-law was working overtime at the power company, as the city was upgrading its emergency system.

Maura - who normally could sleep through a train wreck – never understood why her sister was restless when her husband worked late. "Let me guess – you stayed up for him again?"

"You know I did; I can't help it. I just can't sleep until he's home." Maura also knew Peggy waited with a pistol under the sofa cushion, and that she knew how to use it. Mama Lion instincts, Peg said.

"You'll find out someday, Maura. So why'd ya call?"

"I know this isn't the best time for this bombshell, but I wanted to tell you before we get to Dad's."

"Hang on, then, I'll put on my headset - be right back."

Maura waited a few minutes, listening to her nephews bawl and talk in their adorable baby voices. She hummed and eavesdropped, till Peg's voice came back on the line.

"Okay, done. Sorry it took so long - go ahead."

"No problem." She took a deep breath and went for it. "I went to Dr. Plank's yesterday for my yearly exam, and the urine test was positive. I'm pregnant."

She could imagine her sister's shocked expression, and waited a couple of seconds longer before she spoke. Peg let out a low whistle.

"I'm pretty sure it's Andrew's baby, and I'm thinking of getting an abortion."

Peg sighed, exasperated. There was no love lost between her and Andrew. "He's irresponsible and spoiled – a big kid." She frequently told Maura. "Nothing like Roger."

Peg was fifteen years older than Maura, but of another era, and lived an ordinary life with her husband, toddlers, and tv talk shows. She thrived on security, and her main adventures came in the form of gossip and family intrigue. In contrast, Maura *lived* a life-style of the rich and famous, and though Peg often chided her for her "loose morals," she was extremely devoted to her, acting in many respects as the mother Maura never had.

Poor Peggy. With a slew of unmet- needs, she was high-strung and nervous, and particularly obsessed with the fear that she might go to Hell. She attended services at her church every morning, lit candles, and prayed to the statues. She couldn't seem to shake her fear of death, or find answers to her questions about the afterlife.

Peg was home again after years of working for the city; a mid-life pregnancy came concurrently with the wedding plans of her youngest child. An additional surprise was that the ultrasound photo revealed twins!

For Maura, her sister's marriage and family were her only contact with Middle America. Here she saw concrete evidence that an intact home with dad, mom and children was still a possibility, but she also knew they had lots of problems.

"An abortion?" The tone of Peg's voice revealed a mixture of terror tinged with deep sadness. Maura heard the struggle, but Peg knew better than to try to manipulate her with guilt. "And you think it's Andrew's?"

"Yeah, I've gone over it in my head, and I'm pretty sure when it happened."

"I'm so sorry it's not Nathan's."

As Peg's grief washed across the phone lines, Maura became defensive. "C'mon, Peg. You've always known that wasn't going to happen. Even if he left his wife – which, by the way he told me last night he was ready to do - it's just way too complicated. Anyway, you're Miss Morals – what about his kids?"

She could see the drama unfolding in her sister's mind, the one where Maura and Nathan walked arm in arm out of the church as husband and wife. Still, Peg's feelings were all over the map about her relationship with Nathan, because along with her Glaurianism, she cherished the New Age soul-mate fantasy that everything should be sacrificed to bring a fated couple together.

And, she's always had a thing for Nathan. Maura's real-life romance provided Peg with vicarious excitement and passion, and she was deeply implicated in the story line. Nothing would have pleased her more than to have Nathan as a brother-in-law; she could continue to enjoy him in fantasy without actually having an affair, whenever she chose.

"What did Dr. Plank recommend?" Peg asked, praying for another option.

"Well, of course she asked me what *I* wanted to do – that was her main concern."

"What did you tell Nathan? Doesn't this fit into your plans after all – you've waited years to marry him. I would have thought you'd be thrilled!"

Maura recalled the previous evening. *She's right, what am I doing? I can't believe it's over.*

"Peg, I just couldn't go through with it. Lately, every time I've thought about marrying Nathan, I see the faces of his kids."

Peg was quiet, as she searched in vain for comforting words, but the words on her tongue were barbed and selfish, as she thought about Maura's future without Nathan.

Maura wasn't prepared for the arrow that shot through the phone, as the nohedi thrust in a jab.

"Well, it doesn't look like you have much of a choice, now, does it – getting an abortion, I mean?"

Maura was now in a mild rage. "Actually, I have a lot of choices. I just called to let you know, and was hoping for a little sympathy. My mistake. Look, I need to go. I'll see you tomorrow. And please don't tell anyone in the family." Maura clicked out of the call before Peg could respond.

I'll show her. She's just mad that she can't ogle him anymore. I'm going to have this abortion and get my life back. She picked up speed in front of the paper, and whipped into the parking garage, screeching to a halt in front of her nameplate. She grabbed her laptop and bags from the seat beside her and stomped off to the elevator, punching the "Up" arrow, as she fumed and waited for the doors to open.

One thing's for sure, I'm not going to wallow in this. Nobody cares anyway. I'll handle this like I handle everything else - by myself. I have never needed anyone's help, and I don't intend to start now.

* * *

Maura swept into the front doors and headed straight for Tom's office. She sat heavily in the red leather wingback and opened her laptop. Tom was on a call, with his back to her.

"You, know, Jack you've been a real saint all these years; Marie's illness has taken its toll in missed opportunities, and its been a huge burden emotionally, and financially. I don't think anyone would fault you if you pursued a divorce. You're only living half a life anyway. Kristen has been patient, too. Heck, even the kids want to see you get on with your life and have a second chance. It's not like you're fudging on your responsibilities – you're still footing the bill – but you and Kristen can get married and have a normal life. It's a real noble sentiment, Jack, but for God's sake think about yourself for a change! She could go on like this for years, and you will have wasted the rest of your life."

Maura wished she wasn't hearing this conversation.

"I know, I know. Everything's gonna be fine. Let me know what your attorney says. There'll be paperwork and then the financial arrangements, but a few weeks from now, you'll be a free man - just keep that in mind. I'll talk to you tomorrow. Say hi to Kristen." He hung up the phone.

She thought of the sad story of Jack and Marie St. Claire. After 25 years of marriage, Marie had developed multiple sclerosis, which left her bound to a wheelchair. Once a vibrant, East Bay socialite, she now lived in a nursing home. Her husband, Jack, an investment banker, hired a live-in nurse for the first three years, and then began his affair with a beautiful widowed associate, eventually putting Marie in a nursing home.

Maura recalled sailing with Jack and Marie in Sausalito, often meeting Marie for lunch, and attending several Thanksgiving dinners at their gorgeous home - before the illness. Marie was a fabulous hostess, always tanned and trim; she had been a buyer for Neiman-Marcus, and was a former model. She and Jack seemed truly satisfied and happy together, and had successfully raised two children, but just a few years later, the whole picture was fractured. Maura shook her head as Tom spoke. *Another proof that there is no God...*

Tom spun away from the window. "Hey – good morning - what's the matter?"

Maura had been staring into space, with a frown on her face. "Oh, mmm, nothing. I was just thinking about Jack and Marie - you know, remembering the great times we had – before."

"I know - it's so hard to accept, but there's just no hope for Marie. I was out to visit her over the weekend – Cissy and I went to Stanford on Saturday afternoon. She still has that beautiful smile, but her mouth is getting more and more crooked. But she was so peaceful and happy – like a little girl. Anyway, I think Jack's making the right choice - she doesn't seem to understand much of what's going on; the attendants wheel her into the common area for meals and activities, then back to her room to take a nap. Jessie and James see her twice a month – they take turns every week – and that's her life. The doctors say she has five years tops."

"It's sad, anyway." She didn't dare to say that she thought Jack should have stuck with her. *But why should Jack suffer? Oh, why is everything so complicated?* Maura sighed and pointed to her laptop, "Well, Boss, I'm ready. What do you have?" She knew the only way to make it through the day was to focus on work. She still had to call Dr. Plank, and she wanted to call Aaron Feinberg to see if she could meet with him before she left for the weekend.

Thoughts of the upcoming holiday loomed, and she made a silent plea that it would pass quickly and without her breaking down in front of her family. *I better lay off the booze.* She imagined the weepy scene that might ensue if she was under the influence of too much holiday cheer.

A half hour later, Maura closed her laptop and made her way to her office, stopping along the way to chat briefly with a couple of the other writers. As she passed by Nancy's desk, she saw her in the copy room, her brow furrowed. "Good morning, Nancy, you ok?"

"Hi, Maura. How are you? Yes, I'm looking for something I misplaced, but it's nothing critical – I'll find it."

Maura suddenly felt as if her pregnant condition and her plans were emblazoned on her forehead. She wished she could take Nancy into her confidence, but despair crept up and whispered, *No one understands, no one can help.*

Nancy reached out, "Are you all right Maura? You look pale."

Maura roused herself and responded. "Mmmm – yes, I'm fine. Just need some time off. Nancy, can you hold my calls? I'm trying to get some work done before I leave, and I don't want to be disturbed."

"What about Nathan?"

"No one, please."

The plea tugged at Nancy's heart, but she just nodded. Maura steeled herself against the kindness in Nancy's eyes, as she escaped into her office and closed the door.

She got right to work making tea, checking emails, and her voice mail. *A strong cup of mate is what I need – and an early lunch.* She realized she was ravenous, though it was only a couple of hours after breakfast. She wondered, *is it because I'm eating for two?* She pulled food from her refrigerator, and heated up leftover dumplings and rice in the microwave. While the carousel turned around, the scent of Chinese spices and sesame oil made her mouth water.

She took her meal to her desk and punched the number to Susan Plank's office, clenching her teeth. The phone rang and a receptionist picked it up.

"Dr. Plank's office, may I help you?"

"Hi, yes, this is Maura McConnell. Is Dr. Plank available for a phone consult? I need to speak with her."

While she waited, she remembered Aaron Feinberg and made a note. She forked a dumpling and swirled it in plum sauce.

"Ms. McConnell?"

"Yes?"

"Dr. Plank is free – hold on."

"Okay, thanks."

"Hi Maura, how are you?" Susan sounded a bit distracted, and Maura pictured her studying a patient chart or x-ray while on speakerphone. *My life is critical here and she's too busy to even pay attention. Whatever - just get it over with.*

"I'm fine, Susan, thanks. Hey, I just wanted to make an appointment with you to take care of this, umm pregnancy," as if she were calling in stock selections to her broker. *There, that wasn't so hard.*

"I think this is probably a good choice for you right now, Maura, but I know it's not easy."

What could you know about it, Susan?

She heard Susan flip through her calendar. "How about Tuesday morning bright and early – is 8:30 all right? I try to get these out of the way before I see my prenatal patients."

"Sure, that'll be perfect." *Get it out of the way.*

"Okay, I'll get Stephanie back on the line to give you some instructions and we'll see you Tuesday. Oh, I almost forgot - no alcohol."

There was an awkward pause as Maura thought about that advice.

"Scratch that. No instructions, except that you need to fast breakfast. See you then. Happy Thanksgiving."

Click.

Yeah, alcohol would only be an issue if I was gonna keep it. Timing's a funny thing.

Stephanie came on the line. "Hi Ms. McConnell, I've made your appointment for 8:30 Tuesday morning. Please don't eat anything after 9 p.m. the night before, and if you could get here around 8:15 to fill out paperwork that'd be great. Do you have any questions?"

"No questions, thanks – I'll be there Tuesday morning at 8:15. Goodbye." She flipped through her Rolodex for Aaron Feinberg's number, and took a breath.

"Dr. Feinberg's office."

"Hi, this is Maura McConnell. I'd like to speak to Dr. Feinberg if he's available."

"Sure, Ms. McConnell. Let me check." Maura was thankful for her name recognition - it opened doors, and saved her from explaining her business.

The secretary returned to the line. "He's free and will be on the line as soon as I hang up."

"Thank you."

"My pleasure. Here he is."

Aaron Feinberg's Brooklyn accent broke her reverie. "Hi Ms. McConnell, how are you today?"

"Fine, Dr. Feinberg," she said, enviously choking on his title. Even so, she hated the title-and-name game.

"How can I help you?" *Right down to business.*

"Well, I have a situation I'd like to discuss with you. I'm leaving this afternoon for several days, and wondered if I could see you before I go."

"Well, I can make some time as a matter of fact. My 11:30 appointment cancelled. Will that work for you? Do you know where my office is?

"Yes, I do."

"If you haven't had lunch I could order us something."

Her radar went off. He seems kind of giddy – what's up with that? Oh, yeah, he recently divorced his wife... She rolled her eyes.

"You know, Aaron, on second thought, I just realized I have something else going on at noon. I think I'll wait till after Thanksgiving, and give you a call."

"Ok, but I have a couple of other spots this afternoon, too."

"You're amazing, thanks so much, but I think I'm trying to cram in too much. I'll call you next week."

"That'll work. I'm looking forward to it."

Of course you are. She hung up the phone. *Why can't men and women just be friends??*

Her boss was the only man she'd ever met who managed to keep his head around her. *But there was the night that he almost kissed me.*

They were waiting in his Cadillac in front of a club, while his wife Cecilia - Cissy - ran in to discuss dinner plans with a group of friends. The night was bitter cold, and the heater was comforting as they traded thoughts on their latest project, a UN compassion summit on women in the developing world. They had worked late every night for a week; Tom admired the stamina and spark of his newest reporter. Her sharp mind and dogged determination to understand the world they were shaping energized Tom. Her vision and passion ignited his, and he found himself drawn out of the cloud-realm of ideas, into her earthly sphere.

Maura and Tom sat and talked quietly, while jazz played seductively on the radio, and a lull entered the conversation; their eyes met, and a strong wave of desire washed over them. Tom was the most powerful man she had ever met, and the feeling of wanting him to take her into his arms and kiss her, overwhelmed her. Maura teetered inside, as on the edge of a cliff. *Will he kiss me?* She was dear friends with Cissy, but she was in love with Tom as a student to a mentor.

She wasn't sure how, but through all the temptations around him - and while others in their circle of friends were having affairs - he had stayed faithful to his wife. Cissy had been his muse since their days at Berkeley, and she imagined it would always be so.

Tom had closed his eyes, and took a deep breath, and when he looked at her again, he had regained his composure; the opening of the car door broke the spell.

Cissy climbed quickly inside, her teeth chattering. "Man it's cold out!" She coughed dryly from the frigid air. Demure and regal, she pressed her gloved hands to her rosy cheeks and smiled. Cissy was astonishingly beautiful in a confident, childlike way, and everyone adored her. She was wise and kind, and in all the years Maura had known her, she had never seen her flustered or angry.

She was also brilliant, with degrees from McGill University, an MA from Berkeley and, finally, a PhD in clinical psychology from Stanford. She was also slightly mysterious, with a smile like the Mona Lisa. No matter how well you thought you knew her, she possessed an aloofness that made her even more alluring. Her hair was long, thick, dark and always slightly unkempt, and her full, red lips looked like she had just made love to Tom. Everything about her was sensual, and Maura found herself desiring her at times. But while her past lesbian encounters had whetted her appetite, she hadn't yet expressed her desire to Cissy.

Flushed from the close encounter with Tom, Maura stared straight ahead and adjusted her scarf while she composed herself.

"Are they coming to dinner?" Tom asked, turning to smile at his wife.

"They're leaving in five minutes," she replied as she buckled her seatbelt, unaware of the drama that had just occurred. It was doubtful, however, that Cissy would have been terribly concerned about their near miss – she was close to Maura, and encouraged her in her friendship with Tom, knowing the wisdom he had gleaned in his many years as a journalist was important to share with the young writers on staff. And she knew he would never stray.

So when she needed her, Maura knew Cissy would be there for her. She dialed Cissy's cell phone.

"Hello?" The familiar voice was comforting.

"Hi Cissy, it's me."

"Hi Maura." Maura could hear the clatter of pans in the background.

"Are you baking?"

"I am – therapy. What's up?" The banging stopped.

"I have some news, and I really need to talk to you." Maura felt like she was in a bad dream.

"What's wrong?" Cissy sounded concerned.

"Well, there's no other way than to just say it – I'm pregnant."

There was silence for a couple of seconds. "Oh, wow. Maura, let me put this in the oven, and wash my hands. Hang on a minute."

The oven door opened and shut, and Maura heard her setting the timer. Footsteps crossed the kitchen floor, followed by the noise of running water.

"Maura, what are you going to do?"

She pictured Cissy on the leather love seat in front of the kitchen fireplace, twisting her hair as she always did when she talked.

"I'm going to take care of it on Tuesday."

There was silence on the other end. "Wow, that's really heavy. Are you sure?"

The hackles rose on the back of her neck. *Can anyone tell me what the big deal is here? Abortion has been safe, legal and common for decades! Isn't this MY choice?*

"I don't think I have much of a choice, Cis. This baby is Andrew's, and I'm not in love with him. And I told Nathan it's over between us. He asked me to marry him last night and I said no. I've decided to go back to school, so it's not exactly the best time to have a child."

"Hmmm. You've had a busy week. Do you want me to go with you?"

"Yeah, if you can that'd be great. I might be a little spacey afterward, so if you could drive…"

"It's no problem. Does Tom know?"

"No, and I was hoping you wouldn't tell him." Maura suddenly felt ashamed, and knew that although he would never say so, Tom would be very disappointed at her mistake. An untimely pregnancy was a thorny nuisance that could mar her career, and made her appear careless and weak. She could not afford for anyone to think of her that way.

Maura felt so vulnerable. *This whole thing is a real mess. But it'll be over in a few days.*

"When is your appointment?"

"It's Tuesday morning at 8:30."

"Are you going to come get me, or do you want me to drive my car?"

"I'll be at your house at 7:15 Tuesday."

"Ok. I'll tell Tom we're going to breakfast." Cissy hesitated, and then asked her. "Maura, are you going to tell Andrew?"

"No, absolutely not - that would be the ultimate humiliation. He's got the hots for some eighteen year old in his Russian class. I'm not going to tell him." Pain rose up in her heart. *He's not going to rescue me, either.*

"Sure, I understand. It'll be okay, Maura. Try to have a Happy Thanksgiving, and I'll see you Tuesday."

"Thanks, Cissy, Happy Thanksgiving." Maura hung up and dialed Andrew's number.

"Hello?"

"Hi Andrew." She skipped the foreplay and jumped right in. "I'm finishing up at the office and plan to leave in about an hour. Yeah, I'm all ready – I packed this morning. But, Andrew, I really need to go by myself. I hope you understand. Sorry it's last minute."

She imagined him grinning, and pulling on his goatee. "Oh, sure, okay. But I'll miss you."

Her face flushed with rage. *You're such a liar.* He wasn't disappointed at all; now he could have the weekend with his French girlfriend. He had met her at a party one night last summer. Petite with long dark hair and freckles, and agate-green eyes, Andrew was immediately fascinated with her accent and tinkling laughter. He had become less available, and his phone machine picked up more often.

Then the thought struck her. *He's in love with her! Well, it would complicate things if he knew about this baby – and what would little Adrianna think about him then?*

"Well, I hope you find something to do – I wouldn't want you to be alone." Her voice dripped with scorn, but he was oblivious.

"Thanks for thinking of me. Have a nice time."

"Thanks – see you later." She slammed the off button with her thumb. *This relationship is so superficial, and is so over!*

As she thought of the appointment Tuesday morning, she tried to be hopeful, but it seemed like forever. *Please, help me make it through the weekend.* She hurriedly left the office, glancing around to make sure the place gave no evidence of her scattered mind. As she turned off the lights and shut the door, Nancy looked up from her desk, the ever-present gaze of concern lighting on Maura.

"I'm going to get a jump on the traffic," Maura said, attempting to smile. *Why does she look at me like that?* Her assistant's sixth sense was annoying, and she resented being the unsolicited object of those sympathetic eyes.

She knew how it worked – as a follower of The Way, she considered it her vocation in life to convert her boss and coworkers. But truthfully, she couldn't accuse Nancy of that; she was outstanding in her work, and mysteriously silent about spiritual things.

Maura again feigned a call, putting her phone to her ear, gushing a quick "Hello? Maura speaking." She mimed "I'll call you, and Happy Thanksgiving," to Nancy, while heading down the hall.

Chapter Thirty-Five

Maura crossed the Bay Bridge, and joined the serpentine line of vehicles heading north. She glanced at her clock and sighed. *I'll bet it'll take an hour to get to I-5.* She drummed her fingers on the steering wheel. *I can't get no…satisfaction. Hey, hey, hey – that's what I say.*

Playing with the stereo settings, Maura found a talk radio station. A lullaby played behind the sounds of a baby laughing. "Know that you're not alone," said a woman's comforting voice. "If you are pregnant and afraid, call us. Give your baby life."

Maura stiffened and punched the off button hard with the palm of her hand. She had been able to forget for a half hour, and resented these troubling reminders.

How am I going to make it through this holiday? She hit the steering wheel and tears welled up in her eyes; the stress and sleepless nights were beginning to take their toll. And the more she thought about spending the holiday and her father, sister and brothers, the more she wanted to run.

Maybe I can call and explain that I have a big story that just came up, and I need to work. Damn, forget it - everyone's expecting me, and Dad will be disappointed. No, I need to put on a good show.

During a stall in the traffic, Maura remembered the new Praxil prescription Dr. Plank gave her. She downed two pills, and fished through her CD's for some quiet music.

The gentle strains washed over her bruised heart as the medication kicked in. Soon she was at peace, humming along to the music, and edged onto I-5. An hour up the highway, she stopped at a Starbuck's and used the restroom, calling her father to find out the plans for the evening.

"Hello there! How close are you? Everyone's here – we're just waiting for you. How's the traffic?"

Maura answered his questions, and he added, "Meet us at Bill's for drinks before dinner - Lillian's, of course – reservations are for 6 o'clock." The famous restaurant was where they celebrated most events.

"Okay, Dad. See you in an hour or so." She ordered a mocha latte, and headed west, to Napa. The traffic was crowded on the narrow road, and at points just crawled along, as people flocked from the city to relax for a few days.

The anti-depressant had performed its magic, and all was right again with the world. Gone were thoughts of Nathan, Andrew, and the baby. Only this moment existed, and the anticipation of joining her family for Thanksgiving.

After an hour and a half, she followed the exit for St. Helena, and after several miles, turned off into a gated neighborhood. At the end of a street, she drove down a short road, where her brother's house was hidden on several acres, and parked in front of the garage.

Her brother Bill was a leading prosecutor in the Bay Area, and carried the legacy of Uncle Leon McConnell and the Rose and McConnell law firm into the new century. *He's done us proud.*

As she approached the door, she hummed a tune.

Now what's to be found by racing around,
you carry your pain wherever you go,
Full of the blues you're tryin' to lose,
You ain't gonna learn what you don't wanna know.

But Maura reminded herself that she would soon be nursing a glass of wine and engaging in superficial conversation.

Just then, the door opened and Ty Benson bowed with a flourish.

"Bon nuit, Mademoiselle le writer. Comment ca va?" He came to her, kissing the air near both cheeks.

"Thanks for bringing?" He looked behind her for a present

bag, but seeing none, made a face. "Well, then, any good gossip?" He whispered confidentially, "Any cute boys for me? I'm afraid this little hamlet is quite played out…"

She smiled, and pulled out a card from her purse.

"Mais bien sur!" He clapped his hands joyfully and whisked her into the spacious living room.

Poor Ty. He's almost as pathetic as me. She floated across the hard wood floors to her waiting family.

Her father sat at the grand piano, his strong tenor voice crooning above the crowd.

"Starlight and roses, you bring to me…" He marked her approach with a big grin. His avocation as a lyricist had produced several notable jazz singles, and this was Maura's favorite. Remarkably handsome at 70, the slate blue turtleneck under a black wool blazer drew out his azure eyes. He held everyone's attention. *The patriarch surrounded by his adoring family.* Her heart soared for a moment, then crashed cruelly back to earth. *It's just a show – an image – like Shakespeare's old whore, fatefully flawed.*

Please! Do these voices go everywhere? She swore under her breath, and forced a smile as she embraced her brothers, sisters-in-law, nieces and nephews. *I need a drink!*

In mid-kiss with baby Amalia – Bill and Katie's newest – Ty rescued her with champagne.

"You're a lifesaver," she whispered.

"Yeah – what's eating you?" he asked, as usual seeing right through her.

"I've just got a lot on my mind," she lied, and he went after it.

"Well, when you want to talk, you come get me." He kissed her lightly on the lips, and pinched her cheek too hard.

"Later."

Why does he have to be gay? She thought sadly of their many heart-to-hearts, and how well he knew her.

Ty had met her father while waiting tables in DC at Glavin's Grill, her dad's favorite lunch spot. Ty served his table every day for a year, and eventually they became friends. Jim needed someone to help with events, lobbyists, and business clients, and Ty's meticulous attention to detail - as well as his ability to keep a cool head when important people were around - were just what the senator needed. He proved to be an excellent choice, and Jim never had to worry again about social events. Ty was thrifty enough, shrewd, and knew how to pull together all the right ingredients and people to make any occasion a success.

Ty now served as Mr. McConnell's personal assistant, accompanying Jim on trips, and was involved in every aspect of his daily life. So far, Ty was discreet, and his personal life hadn't affected Jim McConnell in a negative way: he was bright, handsome and trustworthy, and had become like family. Whenever there was a McConnell occasion, Ty ran the show, and he and Maura had become close friends over the years, as they shared a love for jazz, drama and city life, and during Senate recesses, he often hung out with her in the city.

But the last time he had stayed over, Maura discovered she was having conflicting feelings about him. Arriving back at her place pretty drunk after a night clubbing, they were in the kitchen eating bruschetta and laughing. At one point, Ty walked over to where she stood next to the sink, and inadvertently brushed up against her, as he reached over to wash his hands. Surprised, she felt passion ignite, and when she looked into his hazel eyes, his full lips pursed in surprise, she moved in to kiss him, closing her eyes. When they met, he touched her face and smiled sadly, breaking the spell. "I'm sorry, Maura. I just can't."

She knew about his past - how his father had left when he was very young, and though his mother did her best, there was a gaping hole that made him a target for pedophiles. Eventually, it became a way of life to weaken under the spell of the men that pursued him.

"I almost wanted to kiss you, Maura." Confusion clouded his face. But it seems like I've always been gay, maybe even born that way. I just know it feels weird with you."

"It's okay, Ty. I'm just glad you're my friend." They hadn't really talked about it since.

Maura mingled with the relatives, and a couple of hours later, everyone piled into cars to drive to dinner. Ty caught her arm as she put on her coat.

"Ride with me?" For a fleeting moment, she saw them driving off together, leaving the world behind.

"Of course."

As the last to leave, he set the alarm system. They walked through the cool night to the garages, where he opened the door and helped her into the Lexus.

Maybe I shouldn't tell him. She bit her lip. Just keep it light. But there's no way he's leaving me alone until he finds out what's going on.

"Hey," he said, as he turned the key. "Want some music, or do you want to talk?" It wasn't a choice, but his eyes were genuinely concerned. Their common bond was the sharing of doubts and failures; where they had to keep up the pretense with others, together they were like survivors on their own private island.

"We can talk."

She told him everything – how she had broken up with Nathan, her pregnancy, and her plans for Tuesday morning, Aaron Feinberg, Andrew, her sister, school, and the accusations in her head, and the Praxil.

He was quiet as she talked. Though he could be amazingly superficial sometimes - like a fifteen year old girl in his romantic life - there was a depth to him that gave Maura something to lean on. When they parked in the crowded restaurant parking lot, he reached over and took her hand.

"Maura, I can't say I know exactly how you feel, but I do know about losing a dream. It's so painful. It's selfish of me, but I am depressed about what you just told me; I always think of you as the one person in my world that is going to make it – you're the wind beneath my wings – how corny is that? And now your life's a mess – sorry. I want to help you; sometimes I think of moving to the City to live with you because we get along so great, and now I've got this feeling like I want to take care of you. I would love to see you pregnant and a mother – I know how much you want that. But then I'd be your gay friend helping you raise a baby as a single mom, which is kind of weird."

Maura, stared at him for a few seconds, and then burst into laughter. But then, remembering Nathan, and noticing that her ring finger was still bare, she felt sad again.

"Ty, I know I've always been able to rise above whatever life throws my way, but I have to admit I am afraid this time. I'm taking Praxil and drinking more – what if I never stop and I end up like my mother? I'm tired, Ty, and I don't know what to do. I'm beginning to feel like nothing I do matters."

He smiled. "I don't have a good answer for all your troubles, Maura, but I do know there's plenty of booze inside this restaurant, and after a good meal things will look better. C'mon, we'll talk more later."

She was thankful for his inability to stay depressed, and held his hand as they walked into Lillian's. Her family was in a private room, still working out seating arrangements when they came in. She and Ty sat closer to the kids, where they could avoid the conversations of the other adults.

Lucky break. She opened the napkin on her lap and sipped a glass of wine. Dinner was pleasant and uneventful as she picked at her food and drank too much. Ty was a comforting presence, but the bright spot of the evening was laughing and talking with her nieces and nephews.

After dessert and coffee, everyone returned to their various homes and hotels, and Maura and Ty drove back to Bill's, where she would stay in the guesthouse. On the drive, they laughed and reminisced. Along the way, Ty pulled into a gas station for gum, and clove cigarettes, while Maura used the restroom.

As she washed her hands, she glimpsed a small booklet on the floor and picked it up. On the front in big red letters, was the question, "WHERE ARE YOU GOING?" As she read further, there were cartoon scenes of a man dressed in a robe performing miracles, and confronting sorcerers and religious leaders, and hanging out with common people. In another scene, he was impaled on a tree and blood flowed from his wounds. Finally, there was a picture of him, smiling as he sat on a white horse, surrounded by animals and people in a beautiful, sunny meadow.

Turning it over Maura read the prayer: "If you do not know where you are going in life, talk to Korban. He understands and is the answer you are looking for. He loves you, and died so you could know the meaning of life. Call on him today; he will set you free." She saw it was a publication of followers of The Way.

The words began to resound in her head, and she struggled against the fear that rose up inside her. But there was an equally terrifying thought that in this chance reading lay the answer to her questions about life. She hurriedly stuffed the pamphlet in the pocket of her leather jacket, and walked out to the car.

Ty had the driver's seat reclined, and lay back with his eyes closed. The sight of him caught her breath. *He is so gorgeous!*

At the sound of her open door, he sat up and smiled, turning the key. "Let's go home," he yawned sleepily.

She closed her eyes and settled back, the music lulling her to sleep. For a moment, she dreamed she was making love to Ty, and waking contentedly in his arms.

When they arrived back at Bill's, Ty took her right to the

guesthouse, gently nudging her awake.

"We're here." He opened the door and carried her things to the bedroom. Maura took off her shoes and sat on the oversized floral couch, poured a glass of water from the pitcher on the coffee table, and downed another Praxil from the bottle in her purse. Ty walked out from the bedroom, and stood over her, pushing the hair back from her forehead to kiss her goodnight. She looked up at him and smiled sadly.

"Thanks, Ty."

"Goodnight, Maura. I'll see you tomorrow." He exited, gently closing the door.

* * *

Maura slept until mid-morning and woke to the sound of rain on the roof. She had dreamed of high-mountain meadows, and walking hand in hand with Ty. She shook her head. *So much for fantasies, although, maybe I could change his mind. Oh my God, did I really just think that? But what if our friendship got weird? Nah, better keep the status quo for now, because what I really need is his friendship.*

She showered and dressed, took a Praxil and walked with her umbrella through the rain to the main house. Thanksgiving dinner would be around one o'clock, after Mimosas and a light breakfast. As she walked across the driveway, leaves from the big oaks were torn away, and carried high up into the air over her head, as the wind played tug-of-war, and then dashed them to the ground. Thankful for the big, warm house, Maura pulled off her boots in the foyer. She sifted through the moccasins in the cedar box, and found a pair in her size.

The sounds of laughter and conversation joined with the scent of fresh-roasted coffee and cinnamon rolls, greeting her from the big kitchen where the family was gathered. *I'm going to just relax, forget everything and enjoy myself today.*

A long, white-pine table with seating for 20 was the centerpiece of the spacious room, and a gleaming array of appliances, a big island, and banks of pine cabinets filled the space. A stone fireplace and a sitting area with a leather sectional completed the room, surrounded by windows that overlooked the patio, pool, and garden.

The foul weather seemed a world away, as soft music floated from the recessed overhead speakers. Ty came to her bearing a tray of Mimosas, stunning in black skinny jeans, and a winter-white v-neck sweater. As he kissed her cheek, she caught the scent of his cologne and gulped.

"How did you sleep?" he asked cheerily. She was thankful that he shared her approach to the day - enjoy, no worries.

She got to talk to everyone, catching up on their lives, and was intoxicated and happy, as she snacked on banana-pecan muffins, fruit and juice, the kids played board games on the floor, her brothers and sisters and their wives one-upped each other, and she and her father discussed some of her investments, and new stocks he was considering.

They ate dinner, and afterwards, she and her younger sister, Anne wandered off to the corner couch in the solarium with their coffee. After some small talk, Anne opened up. "Maura, I have something to tell you." Her younger sister was born when Maura was 10, and it wasn't until Anne was in high school, that her older sister took an interest in her. Anne left for New York right after graduation, becoming successful in the fashion world. She had married a much older man, and had two kids, but their lives were pretty rocky.

Maura stirred her cappuccino with a Pirouette and nibbled off the end. She was feeling safe curled up on the oversized sofa, wrapped in afghan, as the cold rain beat against the windows, and wasn't really in the mood for someone else's problems. *I hope this isn't bad news...*

"Maura, Joe and I started going to church a few weeks ago – a little community church near our house. His drinking problem came to a head on Labor Day weekend, and I told him to straighten up, or I was filing for divorce."

She paused. "I guess my threat got through, because he found an AA group and started going every day. Sometime in mid-October our neighbors, who also go to the church, invited us to their home for a weekly group study and hang-out time, and after that we started going to church every Saturday night or Sunday."

"Joe would come home talking a mile a minute about the things he was learning, and I attended Al-Anon meetings so I could understand about our family dynamic, how addiction works and all that. Long story short, our lives are changing; the kids are learning tons, and I've been looking at how dysfunctional our family was – Mom and Dad, the boys, us girls - it's been a real eye-opener. They tell us at the Al-Anon meetings that the first step to freedom is to admit to having a problem."

Well, well, well, there it is.

Maura was in no mood for Anne's confession, and patronizingly patted her hand.

"That's great, Anne. I'm glad things are going well for you guys. You all seem really happy."

She sipped her Bailey's and coffee, and stared at the rivulets running down the glass. She drifted far away from Anne, wanting to sleep, and not think about anything. *I wonder what it would be like to lie in a white dress in death - safe under the dark earth.*

Anne's voice called her back. "Maura?"

"Oh, sorry, Anne. I was just thinking."

"That's okay." Anne leaned toward her sister, a look of concern furrowing her brow. "But I hope you don't mind my asking – are you all right? I've been watching you since you arrived, and you don't seem like yourself."

Maura shrugged and laughed, annoyed by Anne's new persona.

What could she possibly know about what I am going through? No, there would be no shared confidences today. *First my assistant, and now my sister, I feel like I am being surrounded by these fanatics.*

"I've just had a lot more to do than usual – I need a little rest and I'll be brand new in a couple of days. Don't worry about me."

Anne took her rebuff gracefully.

"Okay, well. Maybe you can get in a nap this afternoon. We're going to visit Grand Kate in a little while – I'd better go get ready."

Grand Kate was their mother's aunt, and a favorite relative of the family. She had lived most of her adult life, with her husband, ranching in Montana. Jim and Ellen had taken the family a few times for summer visits that included wonderful parties with ponies, clowns, homemade ice cream and lemonade. In the winter, there were skating parties and bonfire sing-alongs. Grand Kate never forgot a birthday or Christmas, and gave expensive gifts to her great nieces and nephews, who took the place of the children she never had.

Maura felt a sting of shame that she neither remembered nor wanted to visit this now-elderly lady, who spent her days alone in a private nursing home, and she was thankful that Anne would represent them all.

"That's great – I wish I could go," she lied. "I have some

work to do, unfortunately. Please give her my love." Maura smiled condescendingly from the couch, and Anne, suddenly bold, looked down at her sister before turning from the room.

"Maura, I know you think I'm weak and foolish, but I am not going to live in denial about my life or our family. I refuse to leave my kids the McConnell legacy of addiction to pills, alcohol or pornography, and I want a real relationship with them. Our money and privilege have been a curse; no one in this family is really happy. But I want something different for Joe and I, and I'm willing to do whatever it takes to break the cycle."

This unexpected outburst silenced Maura, every word piercing her heart.

"I know you think I've really gone over the edge, but the change in my life and the direction I'm taking is all about the One who has already come to heal and to save broken humanity. He has opened my eyes, and I'm never going back to what I was before. He is real – Glaurius is real – I've experienced him for myself!"

Maura considered several possible responses, and finally mumbled, "Mmmm, wow." She remembered the pamphlet she'd found in the convenience store bathroom, and its probing question, and looked at Anne.

"What do you believe about Heaven and Hell?"

Anne, surprised at the question, thought for a couple of seconds.

"The Book of the Way says that everyone pursues their own desire, and will murder and fight, steal, kill, and lie to get their needs met. You know the story of Creation, and the failure of the first couple - how Ba'al Aruni deceived them, and how they gave up their authority." She paused, as Maura took a mock-weary breath; she steeled herself against the supercilious reaction she had grown accustomed to, yet she was resolute in the certainty of what she knew.

"Yes, Anne, I know the fable of how humanity was cursed because of simple curiosity after eating a harmless piece of fruit - every culture has their pre-scientific legends that explain their origins. But we are living in the 21st century, and no educated person could ever believe - no offense. Honestly, Anne, what's wrong with you just believing in you? Plain old determination, healthy life practices, and therapy can cure anything. I know life feels crazy sometimes, and having solid answers is tempting, but turning off your brain to follow baseless myths is not the way to be successful and happy."

Anne cringed, and Maura felt a stab of remorse. "I'm sorry, Anne, I just meant that I don't believe religion is the answer to our problems, in fact, I think it's the reason we are going over the cliff! People are frozen with fear over possibly breaking the rules of their sundry religions, and they kill and enslave each other to enforce their religious systems. Anne, "God" is the problem, not the solution, and religion - and all their so-called gods – are the only things standing in the way of us building a united, free, and peaceful world."

"So I guess that makes me an enemy, Maura?"

"What are you talking about, Anne? I never said that."

"Well, what's the logical conclusion, Maura? Look at the marketplace of ideas and the divisiveness in our country. Those who follow Glaurius - whatever their persuasion - are becoming increasingly vilified."

"Well, it's not like you all don't ask for it. I mean is there nothing our president does that you can find agreement with? I get sick and tired of hearing the endless complaining and accusations about everything we do - I will say "we" since the progressive movement is in charge politically at the moment. Don't you guys have something productive to do like feed the poor or heal the sick? Why do you need a god – can't we find common ground in making this world a better place?"

"Of course. Those are all good things we should do."

Maura interrupted. "Well, maybe if you did them instead of fighting about all the things you don't agree with, you might not find yourself so oppressed and marginalized. No one is going to fault you for doing the right thing."

"That's not really what we do - point the finger at other people, Maura. But there are a lot of legitimate violations of our constitution, and of what is decent and right, and the moral law on which this country was founded. These laws have been the basis of western civilization for thousands of years, and now they're being utterly abandoned and replaced by mob rule, and whatever feels right. What kind of world vision is that?"

Maura jumped in. "The laws you're talking about are universal laws that intelligent people all agree on - like murder and stealing. They were around long before Glaurius supposedly gave them to mankind. Frankly, most of his other so-called commandments can be done away with! When we learn to just all get along and love each other, and not judge others - like your prophet Korban said - the world would be an awesome place. I mean is it so hard to understand that two people of the same sex really love each other, and want to get married and have a family? Why is that anyone else's business? And abortion - why are we still fighting about this? It's safe and legal - just get over it! It's a woman's basic human right, and nothing will ever change that."

Anne clenched her fists, digging her nails in her palms to control herself.

"You have an excellent point, Maura about what we should be focusing on. It's hard sometimes, because I see the country we grew up in sinking like the Titanic, and I worry what the future holds for my children. Part of me wants to fight to save what was, but then I look to the mess our nation is in, and I want to save what is."

"Save it? Honestly, Anne, look at the rate of divorce among the Glaurianists and other church-going people. It's as bad as among us "non-believers"! *And* there's a lot of gay love, church splits, abortion, stealing - who are you guys kidding? Maybe the self-centered, angry, rule-loving god you all follow is the product of your own hearts, your own thinking - have you ever thought of that? Most of you seem to look just like him."

Anne shot back. "Well, I am new to all this, but I do know that I have had a very powerful experience with Glaurius, and I know he's real. I actually visited Heaven in a vision, and saw him. And I am definitely being changed from the inside out. And yes, even in the Church, there are conflicting opinions about what he really is like, and how we should live."

"*Even* in the Church? You mean, *especially* in the Church, don't you? I just know there are a lot of you that are always telling other people how they should live, when they're so messed up themselves; I don't get that. I mean, if Glaurius is a spirit, and all-knowing as you say he is, and if I am made in his image, isn't he able to show *me* where I'm falling short? I mean that's just common courtesy, isn't it? Why would he have angry, hateful people wasting valuable time and resources to tell me? Seems like he's probably powerful enough to get my attention."

She went on. "And what about all the end-of-the-worlders, and the conspiracy theories about FEMA camps in Montana? Where do thinking people come up with this stuff? It makes it very difficult to take your mental health seriously."

Anne thought about this for a second.

"Well, I'm not sure about that, but Korban said our

enemies would even include those of our own family, and that we would be hunted down by a global government that would be in power in the future. It seems like we're very close to that."

Her anxiety was evident. "Maura, I'm deeply concerned about your prideful assumptions of your superiority, and claim to lead the world. You have no idea what's really going on. Think about it, Maura - how seriously do you take your beliefs, and your work? And how do people like me who believe in Glaurius fit into your worldview? Are you just hoping we will stop believing when we are somehow 'enlightened,' or is there something more that would need to be done to keep us silent? I know a thing or two about how dangerous people like us are to your agenda, and how stupid you think we are. I went to college, you know."

Maura ignored the question, and turned it right back on her sister. "Really, Anne? Is that how it is - everyone who doesn't buy into your fairy tale is out to get you, including your family, and are you and Joe building an underground bunker, stocking up on food and ammunition - filling the minds of your precious children with fear? You seem very confused." She was flush with rage.

Anne gulped, big tears popping from her eyes; she brushed them away angrily as Maura continued.

"And your narrative of a god in Heaven who threw the human race out of Paradise, cursed them, and who continues to condemn their every move is actually the foundation of all evil. And these useless, antiquated ideas, and lack of vision and concern for *this* world will be your downfall!"

Anne quickly gathered her things and rushed from the room. Maura sighed and shook her head.

The nohedi grinned wickedly.

"Created all things, the earth is his, Heaven when you die? No, dear sister, this world is all there is, and *we* are the world!" Maura punched the pillow next to her.

Well, that was fun.

She stood up and cracked her neck. *Great, now I have a headache.* Confusion filled the room, as the nohedi spun a web of lies and dark thoughts about her sister, and about Glaurius, and his followers. But hidden in a shaft of light, her seraf, Michael, received instructions straight from Glaurius.

Those people cannot agree on anything, and yet there is something pure about both my sister, and Nancy, something appealing about their unshakable confidence; I don't have that kind of

252

unwavering faith in anything or anyone, and have more questions than answers. But one thing is for sure - I could never believe in fables, like they do.

She reached for her purse, and took a Praxil, and laid her head on a pillow, clutching another close to her chest, under the afghan. In a few moments, she fell asleep to the sound of the rain beating on the roof.

* * *

Maura dreamed she was walking along a strip of desolate beach. The sky – overcast, ominous – felt ready to explode, and a sense of disaster filled the air. Lightning, terrifying in its intensity, torched the ground, and she could see cities on fire, far, far away. It felt like the literal end of the world.

Ahead of her in the distance, she saw a figure – a man in a white robe. As she approached, she saw him writing with a stick in the wet sand, his back to her. Undisturbed, he rose and slowly turned to face her. His eyes – like a raging fire – burned right to her heart. She clutched her throbbing chest that suddenly ached with longing, and when she reached out to touch him, he disappeared, but through the screaming wind, she heard his whisper all around her.

I am Korban, the One you seek.

Maura clenched her fists, and screamed at the heavens. "Where are you, and why do you hide from me?"

She staggered backward and looked down at the writing, which the surf raced to obliterate. The words changed from an ancient script, to modern letters, and she made out the word, outlined in pulsing gold and purple – *MARIPOSA.*

Suddenly, the sky opened up, and a shaft of sunlight pierced the brooding heavens. The end of the light ray appeared at her feet, and hundreds of butterflies fluttered in the radiant beam. The wing colors were brilliant tones of azure, rose, violet, red-orange and gold – flashing with a life of their own.

As she gazed in awe, the creatures vanished one by one, until a solitary butterfly flew onto her outstretched hand, opening and closing its wings. It spoke to her in a language she didn't understand, but in her thoughts, she heard so clearly. *Paradise is more real than you know.* She saw Korban standing in the shaft of light, and then he rose up and disappeared into the clouds.

She looked out over the ocean. It was no strain to see to the

253

far horizon; her eyes possessed telescopic power, and she could easily make out the towers and walls of a massive city. The foundation was a thousand feet high and composed of ten layers of precious stones: sapphires, diamonds, rubies and emeralds, amethyst, topaz, turquoise as well as other stones she had never seen – every color of the rainbow flashed with fire.

Her eyes moved upward and examined the gates, set at quarter-mile intervals, of mother-of-pearl, glistening with a changing palette of subtler colors. Suddenly, her eyes returned to their normal state, and Maura stood on the shore again, the clouds frightening. She was alone.

She awoke, startled by a crashing sound, and heard the cry of her nephew Alec who had tripped over a stool. Maura's brother, Tim ran in and scooped him up, apologizing when he saw her sleepy look.

"Sorry, Sis." Maura sat up and rubbed her eyes.

"Hey, don't worry. I needed to wake up – I've been asleep for a while." She glanced at the grandfather clock and noticed the time. She had only slept for 15 minutes.

The pill had made her dopey, and Maura struggled to return to her surroundings. *Maybe I'll go to the guesthouse and sleep, I'm more tired than I realized.* She stood up and arranged the pillows on her way to the bathroom.

Ty walked down the stairs at that moment. "Hey, Sleepyhead. Want to get out for a while?"

No! I want to find Korban, and see the city again!

"Sure, Ty. How soon are you leaving?"

"How about a half hour? You look like you'll need it." He laughed, but then paused in mid-step when he got a good look at her.

"Are you all right? You look like you just saw a ghost."

"Thanks, Ty, you look awesome, too. I just dozed off and had a weird dream, that's all. I'll go get ready."

"Okay, call me when you're ready." Ty sauntered into the den.

Maura could not get the dream out of her mind, or the face and eyes of the man. *I am Korban, the One you seek.* She walked out of the house, into a burst of sunshine that pierced the clouds, and cupping her hand over her eyes she looked up to see a magnificent double rainbow overhead. Sparrows and finches darted above her in the branches of the oak trees, and the wind was unusually soft and fresh.

Entering the guest house, she paused before the mirror.

The voice in her head sounded familiar. *Korban is the Savior of the followers of The Way.* She put her hand over her mouth. *Korban is the son of Glaurius, and the city is Tziyon, the capitol of his kingdom.*

She questioned in her mind. But there was no fanfare, no entourage, and no royal robes?

She shivered, despite the warm fire, and brushed it off, quickly changing into grey flannel slacks and a cashmere turtleneck. As she touched up her makeup and dabbed on perfume, she struggled with the dream. *It was like he knew everything about me...*

Ty had already pulled up, and sat waiting in the car with the window down.

"I didn't call you yet." She zipped up her leather coat.

"I know, but I've had enough of screaming kids."

He jumped out, and helped her into the passenger seat, smiling warmly as he closed her in. He pointed out the sky before shutting the door. "Beautiful, isn't it?" He buckled the seat belt and asked the usual. "Do you want to talk, listen to something, or be quiet?"

Maura didn't miss a beat. "Ty, I had the most amazing dream!"

"Go for it," he said, and began the drive.

They drove out of St. Helena, into the country, past hillsides of brown and barren grape vines, and the close-built homes of the local workforce, their small farms a nostalgic glimpse into a simpler way of life. Geese flew overhead on their destination south, and an occasional raven was scavenging in the pastureland, or wheeling up to the sky, the large, ebony wings silhouetted against the leaden backdrop of the clouds. Maura leaned back and closed her eyes, then recounted the sequence of events in her dream.

Ty listened, spellbound at the narrative, and imagined the shining city, the shimmering butterflies, and the mysterious stranger. Finally, Maura broke the enchantment and sat up, looking at him.

"He said, 'I am Korban, the One you are seeking.'"

Ty didn't answer right away, as the thick presence of the seraf filled the car.

"Wow, Maura, I don't know what to say. It sounds like 'a message from beyond.'"

"Yeah, I guess. It was really crazy, I can't stop thinking about it." She told him about the conversation she had had with her sister, just before she fell asleep.

"Well, then the conversation probably triggered the dream. I can't believe she's falling for all that."

"Yeah, but it definitely seems to be making a difference in some areas of her life. I think it's 'The Way' that she follows. Kind of confusing – who is who, and what they believe. She seems to share that apocalyptic view of the near future that some of them have. Pretty paranoid."

"Like?"

"You know, the right-wingnuts' pro-second amendment, survivalist rhetoric."

Maura sat back, twisting her hair as her thoughts wandered back to the strange dream.

"So if it was nothing, what about all the cities on fire, and the dark clouds? That felt like divine judgment." She shuddered. "It felt so *real*, not like a dream at all!"

"Well, we all had religious instruction as kids – probably just came to the surface talking to Anne. Nothing to worry about, I'm sure."

She sighed, and stared out the window. "You're probably right, best just forget about it." But she couldn't forget about it. She thought about the word Korban had written on the beach.

"Ty, you speak Spanish - what does Mariposa mean?"

"It means butterfly, why?"

"That's the word he wrote on the beach - in my dream."

He smiled at her. "Can't get it out of your head, huh? Tell me, was this guy good-looking?"

"Why?" She looked at him coyly.

"Well, you seem pretty stuck on him."

"He was, actually - it felt like he was my soul mate."

"Oh, *that* kind of dream."

"What do you mean, 'that' kind of dream?"

"Part of the subconscious, like you mentioned – unspoken needs expressing themselves in other states of consciousness, like dreams. Social scientists don't exactly understand how it works. But I don't believe there's such a thing as 'The One.'"

I am the One you seek. She remembered the little pamphlet she'd found in the convenience store the night before, and reached into her pocket, pulling it out. Leafing through it, she read aloud, running a finger over the picture of Korban. He looked just as she had seen him in her dream – the same simple robe, the penetrating eyes.

"Where did you get that?"

"I found it on the floor of the bathroom when we stopped for gas last night."

"Why do you still have it?"

"I don't know, just thinking about stuff lately I guess."

"What kind of 'stuff?'" His eyes narrowed, and he pursed his lips.

"I had a pretty crazy time the other night, after smoking some psychedelic weed I got from Andrew." *There is no way I'm telling him about anything specific.* "Yeah, I saw Hell and all these evil creatures. Really freaked me out."

Ty shook his head. "Well, I'm sorry that happened. But you know, these are just vestiges of religious baggage; it takes time to cycle these ideas out of the gene pool. Nothing to worry about." He took the pamphlet from her. "This is good for nothing but the trash - and scaring annoying children."

He smiled at her, and she felt safe for the moment. As they drove on, Maura noticed empty milkweed pods beating out a staccato rhythm in the driving wind, next to a stretch of marshland.

She suddenly realized where they were headed. "You're taking me to see Mom, aren't you?"

"Well, you always go, but you haven't mentioned it yet - I know you have an awful lot on your mind?"

He glanced at her to see if she was upset. "Would you rather not go?"

"No, Ty, thanks for remembering. I'm just tired."

Her mother had been dead for 5 years on November 22nd, which was also her wedding anniversary. Maura never could forget the irony; Mrs. McConnell had pined away in bitterness for over twenty years after Jim left, her life revolving around that one great betrayal. Even in death, she drew attention to the broken covenant, and her singular claim to James Edward McConnell.

Despite the years of emotional distance between them, Maura had been involved during her mother's battle with cancer, in a way that brought some healing to them both. Although her mother was weak and frail, and very pessimistic most of the time, Maura saw herself on a mission as she cared for her in the last days and weeks of her life.

Maura knew the turns of this country road by heart; the years of visits to the Abbey for special occasions washed up from her memory. Although the previous generation's religious practices were purely ritualistic to her, they were still part of the social fabric into which she was born, and in contradiction to her avowed atheism, the Abbey was a religious place that didn't creep her out, but gave her a vague sense of connection and heritage.

At the bottom of a hill, Ty turned right, and drove about a mile off the road, until St. Francis Abbey appeared. A short jog along a gravel road brought them to the front of the chapel. Ty parked, and came around to open her door, offering his hand to help her from the car. She glanced quickly away from his disarming grin, and wrapped her coat around her body to keep out the chill wind. They walked the field-stone path to the massive oak doors; Ty pushed one open and they heard the air as it rushed in.

Maura instinctively reached for the porcelain basin of holy water, and blessed herself. Ty also stuck his fingers in the water, but shook them off with a disdainful flick of his wrist. Past the rows of pews, they approached the altar, and heard a cough from the hall.

"Hello!" Ty called out.

"Yes, hello," came the reply, as a young man about their age appeared through the side doors. He walked forward with his hand outstretched, and a copy of Augustine's 'City of God' in the other.

"Gabriel O'Brien," he said warmly. I'm overseeing things while the brothers are at a conference. May I help you?"

He looked more like a jazz musician than a cleric, with his goatee, short red hair, and hipster glasses.

"I'm Maura McConnell - we're here to visit my mother's grave." She was slightly embarrassed as she explained this to him, realizing, of course that in general, the Abbey cemetery was for those who served at the Abbey. But because of her uncle's position as monsignor, and her grandparents' generous patronage, the McConnell's enjoyed certain privileges.

"Ah, yes. I believe I have met your sisters, and one or two brothers – and of course, I know Monsignor McConnell." He wasn't effusive like most people who knew her family, and although he wasn't judgmental, she also sensed he wasn't impressed.

"And you are?" Gabriel turned to Ty.

"Ty Benson," he said. "I work for the McConnell's."

Patronage, nepotism, privilege. She could almost see the wheels turning in Gabriel O'Brien's head, accusing her. But he wasn't scornful at all. Still, it felt like he was in her head. *Who is this guy?*

Ty looked around, and breathed in the peaceful atmosphere, oblivious to the thoughts that began to bombard her. He toed the Persian rug at his feet, and checked out the artwork on the stone walls.

Maura tried to appear calm. *Calm down, he's just a guy, and he's not communicating telepathically to you – get a grip!*

"I hope we're not disturbing you, we usually come out at Thanksgiving, but have never met you. You're reading Augustine, I see?"

"Oh, yes. Most Glaurianists consider him our greatest theologian, for all the wrong reasons, in my opinion. Followers of The Way best remember him as the author of infant baptism, which I agree undermines personal accountability. Also, he did feel that the Glaurianists represent the only true church, which is of course, nonsense. Still, I read this for the vision of the new heaven and earth, and the city of God."

"But enough of that, I guess I can't help but preach." He turned to Maura "I recognize you - you're the writer. I saw you last week on a morning show, talking about your experiences in Afghanistan."

She smiled, and nodded, pleased that he had watched her.

"I thought what you had to say about the women and children there was very insightful," he added, as he rubbed his goatee. She thought back about her diatribe on abortion and reproductive rights, and suddenly felt guilty. He said nothing, but the accusations flew from the nohedi. *You are missing something here, pushing this agenda; does it make you feel powerful?* She had to pry her eyes loose from his penetrating stare.

She waited for him to say more, but he just smiled kindly, oblivious to her inner turmoil. *He is totally messing with my head!*

Ty tugged at her elbow, motioning with his head toward the back door.

"Well, it was nice to meet you, Father O'Brien. We'll just pay our respects, and not be too long. Happy Thanksgiving." She quickly added, "Did you have dinner here with, um, your people – I mean your friends?" Even though he scared her, she never liked to see people alone over the holidays.

He chuckled. "Thank you – it's just Gabriel. I like to follow Korban's teaching to call no one 'Father' but Glaurius himself. Yes, one of our families who live nearby invited me over; I spent the late morning and early afternoon with them. I enjoy their company a lot, and we always have a wonderful time – I especially love their children – all nine of them!"

Dear God, did he really say "all nine of them?" She gulped involuntarily at the thought.

Gaabriel reached out to shake Ty's hand, and held it for a long moment, then clasped his other hand over it as well, and looked into Ty's face, studying it.

"Mr. Benson, you have a very special call on your life, did you know that?"

Ty looked astonished, trapped like a fly under a microscope. Gabriel continued in his gentle, authoritative voice.

"From the time you were a little boy, Glaurius has had his hand on you. But it looks like life has taken its toll – and through some very key people." He let that sink in for a moment, before continuing. Ty's eyes met his, and tears welled up. His body slumped, and he swayed as though he'd been moved by a strong wind. Gabriel caught him, and held him in an embrace. Ty fell on his shoulder and moaned softly, as the priest stroked his head, comforting him as a father would. Gabriel whispered something into his ear.

Maura stood captivated by the power in the room, and the tenderness of the scene. *If there is a God, could he be like this?*

Then the moment passed, and Ty moved away; Gabriel steadied him and clapped his biceps. "You're going to be all right," the priest said with feeling. "Please give me a call after you've had a chance to think about what I said. I'd like to see you again."

Ty wiped his eyes, and blew his nose with a handkerchief. *What was that? The priest wasn't propositioning him – the encounter was so pure, so holy.*

Sunshine streamed through the stained glass, piercing the cold grey of the sanctuary. An enormous stag grazed in a bed of lilies, and the three stood bathed in a rosy light.

Ty looked at her, and she squeezed his hand. The priest glanced at Maura, and she saw a lion lifting his shaggy head, preparing to roar. She breathed in sharply and held her throat. Gabriel O'Brien looked away and the vision abruptly ceased.

"I must let you go," he said, gesturing toward the back of the abbey. "Please be careful driving home," he warned as he led them to the door and squinted with concern at the leaden skies overhead.

"Yes, well thank you."

"Come back for a visit anytime."

"Definitely."

Ty followed Maura into the garden tomb area. The priest shut the heavy door behind them, and they were alone in the bleak courtyard. The wind and rain blew from the east, and black clouds formed on the horizon. The temperature had dropped dramatically, and two large crows beat their wings furiously overhead, cawing as they flew into the storm.

At their feet, asters and chrysanthemums curled their brown leaves, strands of foliage drooped like the wet tresses of a forest nymph, and long stalks of gladiolas lay slashed in piles along the walkway. Maura pulled her coat tightly, and Ty put his long arm around her. She relaxed into his body, relieved that he was there; like shipwrecked souls, they provided strength for each other in life's hard times.

They walked to Mrs. McConnell's grave. The headstone was a simple marble slab, engraved with four lines of script.

Ellen Kathryn McConnell
Born: February 8
Died: November 22
Beloved Daughter and Mother

A flourish in each corner was the sole decoration.

Maura recalled the funeral, and how empty all the words had seemed. The ocean of sympathy cards and flowers could not erase the truth; hers was a life of unfulfilled longings, and deep disappointments. *What dreams did she have as a girl, a young woman? I loved her, but never really knew her.*

She and Ty stayed for a few minutes, and then she kissed her palm and placed it on the head stone. Maura looked up at Ty, and pressed her gloved hand to his face. "Let's go."

They walked quickly out of the garden and onto the gravel drive, as sleet began to fall like arrows from the sky. Safely in the car, Ty looked out the windshield and shuddered. "Sure is ugly out there now."

They crunched along the abbey road until they came to the country highway. As soon as they pulled onto the paved road, the car skidded slightly across the wet surface, but Ty quickly gained control.

"Take it slow, let's just get home in one piece!" Maura leaned back in the seat, thinking about Gabriel O'Brien. "What was with the priest? What did he say to you?"

Ty waited, thinking about how to explain it to her. As the car climbed the hill, he turned his face away from the road to look at her, and in that split-second, Maura cried out in terror, pointing out the windshield. Snapping his head back, he saw the blinding headlights of a tractor-trailer crest the hill, and come straight at them. They both braced for the impact, but suddenly everything slowed down.

In the glare of the headlights, they saw what appeared to be an enormous granite wheel, filled with swirling rainbow colors that flickered like flames of fire. Standing next to the wheel, they saw a man with light brown hair, in jeans and a leather jacket. He looked right at Maura and Ty, then reached up and pushed the truck into the air over the car. They watched as in horrifying slow motion, the semi snaked sideways like a living creature, twisted back again, lurched upwards, and rolled end over end, towering over them in the growing twilight.

Like a great hissing dragon, fire spit out from the engine, and sparks from the skidding tires lit up the sky. The headlights spun rays of light that cut through the rain, and finally the beast landed with a deafening crash and shriek, behind them.

Maura and Ty stared in disbelief at each other.

"What the hell was that?"

"Oh my God, Ty, how are we still alive?" She hesitated and then blurted it out. "Did you..."

He finished the question. "See the wheel and the man?"

She nodded, afraid.

"I did."

They sat for a minute, processing, each remembering their last words, as the truck bore down on them.

"I love you, Maura."

"I love you, too!"

Chapter Thirty-Six

Maura and Ty replayed the nightmare in their minds -
twenty thousand pounds of steel racing at them,
then caught up and tossed over their heads like a
toy.

The car had glided gently off the road, and the
transmission was in park, as they sat in stunned silence. But
suddenly, Maura screamed again, pointing out the back
window. Down in the shallow ravine, a shower of sparks had
begun to escape from under the mangled hood of the truck, and
Maura saw a man struggling to get out of the driver's broken
window. He staggered out of the rig, and stumbled up the
bank, clutching his leg. He dove over the embankment just as
the truck blew. The blinding fireball sent them diving for cover,
too.

Huddled together on the seat, Ty covered her with his
body.

"Are you all right?" he asked protectively. Maura had
never seen him display such strength, and she found herself
gratefully surrendering to his direction.

"I can't think very clearly, but physically I think I'm okay -
it feels like we're in a dream." *She's probably in shock.* He leaned
over to hold her close. "Everything's gonna be all right," he
stroked her hair like a frightened child.

Within minutes, the sounds of sirens pierced the night, and
soon police cars, fire trucks and an ambulance surrounded

them.

They heard shouts, and the light from a flashlight flooded the car, as a firefighter's distressed face appeared at Ty's window.

"They're alive, and look okay!" He shouted above the sound of the driving rain, to the emergency personnel standing behind him, and opened the door.

"You two all right? Anyone else with you?"

"We're fine – no, it's just us."

Maura pointed down the hill, "I saw the driver of the truck escape - he dove over the embankment there."

"Thank you, we'll take care of him."

He asked a few more questions about the accident, and began to shake his head in disbelief, letting out a low whistle.

Ty didn't mention the man in the headlights.

"You two sure are lucky. Some might say it was a miracle - if you believe in things like that." He looked at both of them like he knew more than he was letting on.

They both laughed nervously.

"Yeah, I guess you could say that." They looked at each other, and then at their shoes.

"Well, let's get you into an ambulance - we'll take you to St. Helena to make sure you're alright, and have someone drive your car."

Ty looked at Maura, who nodded in agreement. "Just to be on the safe side."

"Get me a couple of ponchos, and help them to the ambulance!" he bellowed to his assistant who had run up.

The EMTs returned with rain gear, and a tall blonde technician appeared at Maura's door.

"I'm Michael – I'll be taking you to the hospital." He spoke gently, his voice sounding like water in a stream. Suddenly, Maura felt a deep peace, and slipped out of the car, and into the refuge of the poncho, under Michael's protective arm.

She climbed into the brightly lit ambulance, anxious to see Ty, who stepped up behind her. She breathed again when she saw his roguish smile.

The attendants secured them both for the trip to the hospital, but they had one last glimpse of the infernal scene before driving off. Maura shuddered, observing the compressed body of the truck, reflected in the orange and blue flames the firefighters worked to contain. Ty shook his head in disbelief and reached for her hand across the narrow aisle. "We are so lucky to be alive."

As they rode the fifteen miles to the hospital, the lights of the ambulance flashed out their warning across the dark, sodden fields. Maura wondered who the truck driver was, and marveled that he, too had survived. She imagined a different scene, one where their twisted bodies were pulled from the wreckage, or even worse, incinerated in the blast. *How fragile life is - or is it? Why were we all rescued? Rescued...*

The second time in as many weeks.

But as usual, she had no answers, only questions that echoed across the silent night. She began thinking about her baby, Nathan, and her family. *If only I had died, then my problems would be over.*

She glanced over at Ty, the light from the street-lamps illuminating his features, and saw his expressive face, too, in turmoil. *He looks so young, so lost – like a little boy.* Shaken at the sight of his vulnerability, she realized that she really knew very little about him. *Who is he really? Can any of us truly be known by another?*

The familiar tidal wave of loneliness hit her again; there was no one who identified with how she felt about her unborn child, the terror concerning the abortion, the loss of her dream with Nathan, the humiliation she felt in her bond with Andrew, or the emptiness that haunted her in her relationship with her family. *I am alone. Not even Ty understands – and when the weekend is over, I'll be going back to my life, alone.*

The ache struck a deep place; embarrassed, she turned her head toward the wall of the ambulance. Great, sorrowful tears soaked the pillow. Michael sat at the foot of the gurney, head bowed in prayer. Unseen, he swept each tear into a bottle, nodding in agreement at instructions only he could hear.

* * *

They drove down the wide, glistening, main street of St. Helena under the haze of orange streetlights, and turned quietly into the emergency entrance of the hospital. This was the birthplace of all the McConnell children, and her maternal grandparents Etienne and Theresa Martin had both trained here. Her grandfather's reputation as a surgeon was legendary, and his wife served many years as a beloved and well-respected nurse. Maura felt relieved to be somewhere familiar.

Ty squeezed her hand and smiled weakly as they pulled

her bed from the ambulance. "Do you want to call your Dad or should I?" He sounded strangely distant.

"Um, if you feel up to it, that'd be great."

"Sure."

They were wheeled in, and parked in a hallway. After a brief exam, the PA on-call let them get off the beds.

The lobby and emergency area were empty except for a mom and dad and their two kids. From the look of it, their visit wasn't too serious, as they all sat unperturbed reading, playing with toys, or watching tv. *Probably just a minor holiday accident.* Maura was thankful that she didn't have to endure another shock to her already frayed nerves.

Michael got her off the gurney, and drove her in a wheel chair past the nurse's station, and into a curtained exam area. She sat on the exam table, and soon, a doctor appeared. She immediately recognized the slightly matured face. "Alan Solomon. Are you practicing here?" Maura asked, amazed to see her former neighbor, and childhood friend.

"Well, Maura! It has been a few years. I guess we haven't seen each other since when, graduation?" Dr. Solomon thought back, pursing his lips in concentration. He had a cleft chin and handsome, chiseled face, and looked strong from working out. "Can you sit up?" he asked, with a concerned look.

Maura forgot her trauma, and her instincts went on high alert. *There's something different about him – what is it?* There was an unmistakable peace, and he seemed indifferent to her charms. Before forcing her thoughts away from him, she glanced at his left ring finger, searching for a wedding band. It was bare.

"Deborah will get some info on you, while I make sure everything's all right." He gestured toward the black woman who entered at that moment with a clipboard.

"Hi, I'm Deborah Howard. I'm going to ask you a few questions - personal information and medical history, ok?"

"Sure, I'm fine, really – considering."

"She can remain in her clothes." Alan turned to the accident report on the counter.

"The police lieutenant on the accident scene called us, and explained that you and your friend appeared unharmed. I recognized your last name, of course, and wondered if it was any of the family. What happened out there?"

Maura replayed the disaster, while providing information to the PA. Alan listened to her description of the truck sailing overhead in slow motion, and how they were saved from death. He stood in silence for a moment, and then turned from the counter where he was writing, to look into her eyes. "Maura, do you believe in miracles?"

Surprised at his intensity, she balked. "Well, sure. There are all kinds of unexplained events in life - I guess we call things that turn out well for no logical reason, miracles, right?" She looked at him, quizzically, sensing that he was talking about something else.

"Yessir, that's how most people look at it." He said nothing else, but walked over to the bed, took her wrist and timed her pulse; it fluttered under his touch. She blushed and turned away. He checked her eyes and listened to her lungs. "Everything looks okay so far, but we need to get some pictures of your neck and spine, to make sure there's no damage there. Often the pain won't start till a day or so after an accident. It's better to be on the safe side."

Dr. Solomon handed the chart to Ms. Howard. "Let's get her up to x-ray." The PA exited the drape to retrieve the wheelchair, and Alan turned his attention to Maura, folding his arms across his chest. "Maura, I have seen my share of devastating car wrecks - when human beings race around in metal boxes there are bound to be accidents. Almost every week, I have to break the tragic news of the death of a loved one to bereaved friends and family. Yet on rare occasions, there is a break in the battle, and something extraordinary happens. Natural law is suspended."

"From your own description, the semi that was headed for a direct collision with your vehicle, inexplicably flew overhead and missed you. You and your friend are safe and alive. Looking at this from a purely statistical standpoint, the odds against your surviving such a wreck are overwhelming. Yet, here you are."

He paused as the words sunk in.

Alan leaned toward her. "Maura, this wasn't a 'lucky break' - your life was spared."

Straightening up, he added soberly, "I don't know what you believe about God, or what's going on in your life, but it looks like you've been given a second chance at life; I recommend you use it wisely."

Maura shifted uneasily on the bed, and looked down at her hands. When she lifted her eyes, Alan placed his hand on her shoulder, and met her glance. "It was good to see you again,

Maura. Take care." Before she could respond, he whisked behind the curtain. She heard him giving directions to Ms. Howard, who had reappeared with the wheelchair.

"Let's get you upstairs for those x-rays so you can head home to your family. After all, it's Thanksgiving!"

Chapter Thirty-Seven

Your rain falls like crazy fingers
Peals of fragile thunder, keeping time
Recall the days that still are to come, some sing blue.
Hang your heart on laughing willow
Stray down to the water, deep sea of love
Beneath the sweet calm face of the sea, swift undertow.

Cloud hands reaching from a rainbow
tapping at the window, touch your hair
So swift and bright strange figures of light float in air.
Who can stop what must arrive now?
Something new is waiting to be born
Dark as the night you're still by my side, shine inside.

Gone are the days we stopped to decide where we should go, now we
just ride.
Gone are the broken eyes we saw through in dreams gone, both dream
and lie.

Life may be sweeter for this, I don't know,
Feels like it might be all right,
While Lady Lullaby sings plainly through you
Love still rings true.
Never could reach it, just slips away but I try.

Make the most of my life. She endured the chilly x-ray

department, and her bare skin against the steel and plastic. Afterward, Ms. Howard returned her to the reception area, where Ty stood in front of the tall windows, lost in thought.

"Hey." She said quietly, positioning herself close, and gazing up into his eyes. He put his arm around her.

"Did you call my father?"

"Yeah, I called before I went into the exam room. I assured him we were fine, and that we'd return to Bill's as soon as they were done with us." Ty cleared his throat and glanced in the direction of the café. "How about a latte? I sure could use some caffeine."

"Good idea," Maura nodded.

They bought their drinks. "Let's sit for a minute. I'd like to process what happened back there."

Maura nodded thoughtfully, as Ty sat, stiffly, strangely distant, avoiding her eyes as he gathered his thoughts.

"That encounter with Gabriel O'Brien touched me on a deep level, and I don't want to miss whatever message I'm supposed to get from this brush with death." He looked at her. "And I'm seriously confused about you and me. Everything in me wants to run; I want answers, but I'm not sure where to find them."

Maura listened intently. *He does have feelings for me.*

"I feel like I need to take some time and seriously think about my life, abot what I want, and stop playing around."

He looked at her with questioning eyes. *Do you get it? Are you all right?*

Maura reached over and patted his knee. "That's a really good idea. This has been quite a day - we should go home and get some rest. I know you'll find the answers you're looking for, and you know where to find me if you need me."

She stood up. "I'm sure everyone's anxious to see us."

On the drive back to Napa, they spoke very little. As they turned down her brother's road, Ty finally broke the silence.

"Maura, what are you going to do about the baby?" She had been matter-of-factly checking off her to-do list in her head, and was irritated at Ty's choice of words.

"Ty, at this point, there is no 'baby' – there is a mass of cells reproducing. The wonder of abortion is that if you take care of it early enough, there's no harm done. I am in no position to raise a child right now – I've decided to go back to school – but first I'm taking a nice, long vacation."

Ty parked in front of the door, turning to stare at her in

270

disbelief. "Maura, I can't believe what I'm hearing! You are an intelligent woman! What is this 'mass of cells reproducing'? What do you think is going to happen in a few weeks if they *keep* reproducing? Haven't you ever seen an ultrasound picture? You will get a big belly and be more beautiful than ever, as a human being is growing inside you! It doesn't matter if you and Nathan aren't together, or that you don't have your ducks all in a row to bring a child into the world. Yes, it wasn't planned, but no child is an accident..."

Maura listened in stunned disbelief, staring at him, open-mouthed.

"What on earth are you talking about? Did you hit your head in that accident?"

He stared straight ahead, fidgeting and tapping the steering wheel. "No, I didn't hit my head, it's just that I've been thinking for the last two hours about what happened, and why we were spared. Don't tell me you don't see how miraculous this all is? There is no reason on earth that we should be alive right now, and without a scratch."

Maura was speechless, his words stung.

"Well, I don't know exactly why I'm still alive, but if I had died, I wouldn't have to make any more decisions!" She began to tremble with rage, and turned it all on him. "This is *my* life, *my* body, and *my* future, and I'm not going to give up my dreams to take care of a kid. I cannot take care of a child and go to school by myself. So unless you intend to help, I suggest you keep your opinions to yourself!"

Maura pulled the handle to open the car door, as her father came out of the house with a golf umbrella. She slammed the door, without looking at Ty's reaction.

"Maura!" Jim's voice was edged with concern. "Let's get you inside." He shielded her from the rain, taking her elbow to guide her.

Ty leaned forward, his head on the steering wheel, alone with his thoughts. Anger and helplessness rose in him like a winter storm; he pounded his fist onto the back of her empty seat, then got out of the car and slammed the door.

His head bent slightly to avoid the cold rain, he walked down to the barn. The bright halogen light over the wide doors flooded the yard, and he walked to the side entrance, pushing open the door. Adjusting his eyes to the small nightlight in the office, he stood quietly, listening to the drowsy sounds of the horses as they shifted their weight and snuffled hay. The barn cats ran from their patrol to rub against his legs, and he shooed them away. *It's so peaceful here...*

Ty wasn't one for introspection; he had always just let life take its course. But tonight he felt the pull of eternity all around him. Here was a dry, secluded place where he could sort out the events of the last twenty-four hours.

He switched on the gas fireplace, watched from the cracked leather seat of an old rocker, as the flames burned away the gloom. Rocking slowly back and forth, his thoughts and feelings to flow, and impressions flooded over him, as he waded into the forbidden regions of the past.

Like a roulette wheel, his mind stopped on a crucial memory, and it flowed back as if it were yesterday. Gazing into the fire, Ty recalled the feelings of dread, and the sinister presence.

He had awakened in fright, rubbing his sleepy eyes; horror seized him again, as he felt the heat of the man's naked body still next to him in the hotel bed.

He whimpered involuntarily, crying out for his mother, but the hard crack of a hand against his head silenced him. For a few hours he had slept, exhausted by the abduction and the uncertainty that had invaded his world, but now he was wide-awake. Like a cornered animal, he curled up into a tight ball, but the stranger overpowered him, and forced himself again into the boy's tiny body.

Back in the present, Ty heard himself scream. He tried to stop the memory, and the pain. *No! I don't want to think about it – it hurts too much!*

Rage rose up from deep inside, a flaming fury toward the man, and the other men who had molested him as a child. *I wish I could kill them all!*

He wrung his hands, beating his fists on the arms of the chair, and soon, another scene appeared: a parade of faces - the men and boys who had been his lovers, or who he had used for sex. He buried his head in his hands and began to weep. Slowly at first, the tears came, choking and burning in his throat, as Ty re-lived the terrible victimiazation that had marked his young life, and the shame he carried for those he had violated. The tears became a flood, as he processed the pain and confusion. Finally, he stopped, and sat staring into the darkness.

Why, Glaurius? Why did you let it happen? The question burst from the prison of his broken heart, and he fell to his knees. It taunted and teased, the sound of his agonized voice echoing down the silent halls of eternity, as despair teased and flitted around him like a mad bird. Slowly he lifted himself from the dirty floor, and grabbing a saddle blanket from the stack, walked down the main aisle of the darkened barn. He threw the blanket on the ground, and sat with his back against the wall, staring into the darkness.

Another memory appeared: he was with his parents, sister and brother at the ocean. He smiled, recalling the hours they had passed together in the fascinating world of starfish, shells and sea birds. *That was before...*

Then he saw his fifth birthday party at the animal farm - complete with a pony ride, and the face of his beautiful mother, her laughter and kisses showering him on his special day.

His young father stood apart, observing the antics of the crowd of children. Suddenly, he swooped Ty into his arms, and led the procession to the bountiful table stacked with presents, food, and a four-layer cake.

Unseen in the darkness of the barn, Glaurius stood beside Ty, his face clouded with concern, and love. And as Ty sat on the dusty barn floor, another voice broke through his anguish and emptiness. *Yes, that was before. You were happy and safe. And you can be, again, my Son. It's your choice.*

The long-forgotten voice whispered in his ear, and then Ty saw a light gather around him. *Are my eyes dim from crying?* But few feet before him, a form of a man come slowly into view, and the mysterious Presence, waited, pulsing with life. Ty marveled, but wondered at his sanity. *Can it be, after all this time?*

The wordless voice spoke. What is it you want, my son?

Ty fell on his face, covering his head with his hands. "Glaurius, forgive me, I don't need to understand - please help me!" He didn't move or breathe.

My son, look at me. Broken people do terrible things...

Terrified, Ty slowly lifted his gaze to the man's face, where he met eyes brimming with a fierce and protective affection, and power and majesty radiated all around him in waves.

I forgive you; be free. Overcome, Ty again fell on his face, and began to shake. Building in intensity, what felt like an avalanche of pain, trauma, fear and memories, slid away from his heart, and suddenly disappeared, taking with it the weight of shame and despair that had been his constant secret.

As the familiar inner turmoil fled away, Ty felt for

something solid, taking inventory of what remained. He held his breath, afraid he'd gone mad. *What else do I have, but what I have always known?* He slowly raised his head again, searching the deep eyes of Glaurius.

From the shadows, Sofia appeared, pouring out the medicine of comfort, love and acceptance, while Glaurius held him. As life and power enter into the emptiness of his heart, he slowly connected with his earliest childhood feelings, in what he would later describe as "a divine therapy session." Conflict-free self-acceptance, innocence, hope, and belonging surged through him.

Ty remained still for a long while, looking up occasionally into the tender eyes, lost in wonder and love as the healing flowed.

Growing gloriously sleepy, he collapsed on the blanket, his thoughts drifting off into happy memories; he heard the words, "I love you; all is forgiven, and forgotten, and I am always with you, closer than your breath, and I know your heart and your needs, even before you speak." He watched in amazement as Glaurius and Sofia began to grow dim.

As Ty sat against the barn wall, the sounds of the dozing horses, the scampering cats and the crescendo of rain on the roof brought him back to this world, and he realized that though he couldn't see them, he could still feel the undeniable presence of Glaurius and Sofia. He peered into the darkness, looking and listening for danger, and rummaging through his heart. But there was no more fear, no uncertainty, no sense of doom, or waiting for the ax to fall. All he felt was peace: peace about his past, his present, and his future, and he felt peace about Maura. True, he didn't have any answers, but he felt an amazing confidence that all would be well.

Ty got up from the floor, and brushed himself off. "Man, am I hungry!" He laughed with delight, a grin spreading full and easy across his face, as he stretched his body with contentment. In the office, he switched off the heater, and put the blanket back. Opening the outside door, he jumped onto the wet grass, leaping and twirling around, his arms reaching to the sky. He lifted his face to catch the rain, and hoolered, "I'm alive, I'm alive, I'm alive! Hahahahahahaha!"

He felt such joy about what had happened to him, and like he wanted to tell the whole world. *But what now?* He wanted to celebrate, but couldn't think of anyone who would understand, or be awake. It was approaching midnight, and the house was dark, except for a dim light in the kitchen.

I have a great idea – let's go raid the fridge!

The voice resonated inside him, full of the personality of the King. With no hint of concern that he would be overheard and if anyone thought he was crazy, Ty responded affectionately, out loud, his heart full of awe and gratitude.

"Thanks, Glaurius, it's so wonderful to have you back in my life!" Visions of a turkey sandwich, with pumpkin pie for dessert sealed it, and he trotted off across the driveway.

A low-watt carriage light illuminated the back porch to the kitchen and pantry, and Ty slipped in quietly, shaking off the rain and removing his shoes. Maura sat with her back to him at the table, and turned, startled, when she heard the door open. Her face was hard, but his heart was filled with sympathy and compassion for her.

"Hi," he said affectionately. "I'm real sorry I upset you before. You're right, I don't know what you're going through, and it's not like I've offered to help. It wasn't my place. Please forgive me."

She looked up at him, puzzled. "Ty, where have you been? And what's going on? You look so different!"

He wanted to holler and yell, and tell her all that had transpired in the barn. *But how can I? How do you explain such a thing?*

"I've just been in the barn, thinking. Then I realized how hungry I was, and decided to come eat." He paused. "I'm glad you're here, so I could apologize. I don't like it when you're mad at me."

Maura could tell she wasn't going to get any more information out of him. "Yeah, well. We waited for you, and I rehashed the accident, and everyone went to bed. I fell asleep in the solarium, but I just woke up and decided to make some chamomile tea. And the desserts were calling." A tiny smile played on her lips.

She looks so small, like she's carrying the weight of the world...

She stood up, put her cup and plate in the sink, and brushed off the table. "Well, I'm going to bed. I'll see you in the morning." Heading for the door, he reached out, and put his hand on her shoulder.

She looked at him, freaked out by the tenderness in his eyes.

"Maura, I'm so glad you're alright. I mean, I'm so glad you didn't..." he hesitated, choking up. "I'm so glad you weren't badly injured in the crash, or killed. I-I I don't know what I would do if anything happened to you." He brushed his hand across his cheek, battling the strong and puzzling emotions.

She stared at him, completely at a loss. "Um, wow. Thanks, Ty. It was pretty scary, wasn't it?"

They looked at each other for a couple more seconds, but finally, Maura broke the spell. *Keep moving forward, Maura...* She reached out for the door knob.

"I decided to leave after dinner tomorrow - I've got a lot of work to do, and need to air out my head. Just wanted to let you know. And I'm sorry I yelled at you before. Goodnight."

"Goodnight, Maura. Sweet dreams."

Chapter Thirty-Eight

Almost ablaze still you don't feel the heat
It takes all you got just to stay on the beat.
You say it's a livin', we all gotta eat
But you're here alone, there's no one to compete.
If mercy's a business, I wish it for you
More than just ashes when your dreams come true.

Maura walked quickly through the drizzle, dodging
puddles of water. At the guesthouse, she removed her shoes
inside the door, and locked up. After brushing her teeth, she
popped her sleeping pills and crawled under the puffy down
comforter, falling quickly asleep.

She woke, and wasted no time packing and loading the car.
Around noon, she said her goodbyes, and threw a cooler of
leftovers and a thermos of tea on the passenger's seat and
coasted down the long driveway. The back roads were still
fairly empty of traffic, as she headed for the highway.

The sun shone weakly through the fog, as Maura settled in
for the four-hour drive to Lewiston. She turned on the news
and sipped tea.

The ride was uneventful, and she arrived late afternoon,
turning into the frosty lane leading up to the log cabin, and
parking in the small gravel lot next to the house. Taking the last

sip from her cup, she sat quietly, adjusting to the silence. *It's so peaceful here.* She relaxed, but as soon as she closed her eyes, the image of the semi truck bearing down on her, shattered the solitude. *I need a drink; this is going to be harder than I thought.*

Maura jumped out of the car, and ran up the porch steps. Finding the key under the mat, she stepped into the cozy great room, to a fire blazing in the wood stove, its doors opened to full effect. *Thank you, Sabra!* A bottle of petit Syrah aired next to a glass on the island, and she went right to it, pouring with shaking hands, taking a long drink.

There, that's better. Now to unpack. She returned from the car with her arms full, the freshly spread stone in the driveway, crunching under her feet.

The last of the sun's rays filtered weakly through the remaining foliage on the sycamore maples in the yard. Mist rose from the surface of the pond, and Maura thought of the Lady of the Lake, catching a vision of herself lying cold and wrapped in weeds, beneath its inky surface, as the never-predictable, and unwanted whispers of the nohedi invaded the quiet.

She saw shadowy figures from gothic stories: ghosts, vampires and suicides, men in mourning coats and women in high-collared black dresses float by, and disappear into the fog.

As the figure of Jimmy Palmer appeared from around the pond, a cry stuck in her throat; she clapped her hand over her mouth in relief. Jimmy was her neighbor, and the brother of her longtime friend, Sabra. He took care of all the repairs and landscaping on the property.

Fortunately, he hadn't seen her stricken appearance, absorbed as he was with the dog at his side - a fine-looking German shepherd. Maura quickly composed herself, cocked her head, and smiled.

"Jimmy, what a relief!"

"Hi, Maura - did I scare you? Sorry 'bout that." He grinned mischievously as he approached.

Maura rolled her eyes. "Yeah, sure you are! You're an overgrown boy!"

He charmed her with his "aw shucks" grin. "Yes ma'am, I cannot tell a lie. I still love to scare girls – 'cause you ladies are never more charming than when you're in distress, and we can ride in and rescue you."

"Oh brother!" Maura groaned and shook her head. *The woman that you rescue would be a lucky one indeed.*

"So let me rescue you from your luggage." He reached

over to grab her suitcase, and several other items, then bounded up the steps, holding open the door.

"Such a gentleman - thanks!"

He took a sweeping bow. "At your service."

She took a sack from him and set it on the counter.

"That's everything. Thanks for helping, Jimmy; I guess I'll see you around. Say hi to Kimberly." She thought he would leave, but instead, he stood there, waiting. He looked at the bottle of wine.

"Oh, would you like a glass?"

"Well, if you're not in a hurry to get rid of me." *That'll be the day.* She had had a thing for him for years, but he was obsessively married to a woman who totally used him, at least as far as all his friends and family was concerned. *I wonder why he's not running off to Kimberly.* She poured them both a glass, and handed it to him.

"Cheers, Happy Thanksgiving, Jim. How was your day?"

"Um, yeah, it was great. With the family, you know. How about you, Maura?"

"Great, things are great."

She turned to unload her cooler into the fridge. "I'm famished - time for a turkey sandwich. Are you hungry?"

"No thanks, I'll just finish this and let you get settled in."

"Ok, sure. Have a seat."

She motioned to the rocker, and he sat down, taking a long swallow of the wine.

Something's not right here.

A log popped in the stove. "I'll check the fire." He tossed in a new log, and poked his head out the front door. "Bella, what are you barking at?" He saw the intruder - a porcupine - ambling across the yard. He laughed and warned, "There's no reward there, Silly, you'll be sorry."

He finished off the wine, and returned the glass to Maura. "Thanks for the drink, I'll see you around." He turned away, quickly, awkwardly, but then stopped at the door. "Sabra asked me to see what you need in town - said to bring her your list."

"Sure, give me a minute to check. I can't remember what I left here last time."

"I'll wait on the porch and keep an eye on the killer porcupine."

Why is he acting so weird? He seems kind of lost. She inspected the pantry. *Peanut butter, crackers, raspberry jam, baked beans, green tea.*

The kitchen cupboards had some old cereal, brown sugar and spices, which she tossed in the trash. *Toilet paper, almond milk, oatmeal, butter, creamer, salad stuff and fruit, goat cheese, tomatoes, corn tortillas, beans, salsa, a roasting chicken. That's good for now.*

Maura ripped out the loose-leaf sheet, bringing it to Jimmy on the porch, his striking features accented by the rugged alpine setting. So hot in baseball cap, flannel shirt and boots, she sighed wistfully at what Kimberly took for granted every day.

"Here are a few things I can use, and thanks again for helping me unload."

Jimmy stuck the paper in his shirt pocket, and patted his thigh for Bella to follow him.

"Awesome, one of us will drop this off in the morning, see 'ya."

"Ok, say hello to Kimberly."

He looked at her and steeled his jaw. "She's gone, Maura, about 6 months now. Filed for divorce – I got the papers in the mail yesterday."

The news hit her hard, but was utterly predictable; handsome, hard-working, local boy swept off his feet by heiress, who tires of banal, small-town life, and leaves him for greener pastures. *At least they never had children.* Maura caught herself, realizing maybe Jimmy wouldn't see it that way. With a guilty pang, she thought of Nathan, wondering how he was picking up the pieces of his life.

"I'm sorry," Maura said softly, and with real feeling. She hated to see Jimmy torn up over someone like Kimberly. *At least I never played games with Nathan.* She sniffed, smugly assured that her own motives were above reproach.

He turned around to face her. "You're thinking I should have known better. Well, you're right. Everyone told me, and I refused to listen. I should have listened to cooler heads." He bent down, and threw a chunk of stray gravel into the driveway. "There's a lot of truth to the song, 'Black Magic Woman' - I fell right into her trap. It's pretty embarrassing. But worst of all, I really love her."

"Hey, don't be so hard on yourself, Jimmy. Kimberly is beautiful, and you're a trusting person – that's what people like about you. But maybe you just moved too fast – it takes time to get to really know people." She patted his arm. "You'll bounce back, you're a smart guy with a lot going for you."

He gave her a grateful smile. "Yes, I'll survive. Thanks for the vote of confidence."

Maura shrugged and suddenly blushed. "Anytime." *Please don't have seen that, Jimmy Palmer!*

He walked off the porch, tipping his hat, "See you later, Maura."

"Okay, have a good night." *I will definitely see you later.*

* * *

The next morning she was up early, a little hungover from the wine and sleeping pills, but after she showered and ate, she felt pretty good, and pulled out her laptop to work.

With the sounds of classical music filling the room, she researched and wrote steadily for a couple of hours, stopping when she heard a truck in the yard. Looking up, she saw Sabra shut the car door with one hip, groceries balanced in her arms.

She ran to the door. "Sabra, let me help you!" She grabbed a bag and gave her a quick hug.

"Hey, you, thanks. There's more in the car. I guess somebody's starving around here!"

Maura bit her lip as she thought about the baby inside her. "Yeah, this mountain air sure makes me hungry!"

Inside, Sabra raised an eyebrow as she placed the paper bags on the counter, next to the open bottle of wine. "You're imbibing a little early, aren't you? Still in the holiday spirit, eh?"

Maura set a bag on the table, her back to Sabra, and pretended to read the label of the chicken intently. She looked over the top of her glasses at Sabra and said, "I'm sorry, what did you say?"

"Nothing, Maura. How do you like the wine?"

"It's delicious. Would you like some?" She smiled confidently, refusing to give into guilt.

"Not right now, but thanks. So, what's new?"

"Not much. I had a nice Thanksgiving with my family, but I left early to work on this article. I'm planning to take a sabbatical from work, and go back to school in January. Actually, it won't be a full sabbatical, I'll still write, but not full-time. How about you? How's Chuck?"

"Everything's fine. I guess you heard about Jimmy and Kimberly?"

"Yeah, not much of a surprise, but it's a tough break."

Maura fidgeted, indicating the small talk was over. Sabra noticed.

"Well, it's good to see you. I can tell you're in work mode, so I won't bother you. Call me if you need anything. And remember what they say about all work and no play - the craft fair is this weekend if you want to come. Cider doughnuts, pumpkin pie – all your favorites." She turned briskly. "See 'ya!"

"I'll call you later."

They had met while taking writing classes together at Berkley, and became fast friends. Sabra's appetite for men was well-known, and they developed quite a reputation together. Sabra came from a journalistic dynasty in New York, and after her mother died, her busy father left her to the oversight of domestic handlers. She received a monthly installment from her trust fund, and could buy whatever she wanted.

They had kept in touch over the years, after Sabra discovered Lewiston, and settled down there. She married a contractor, and financed his construction company, which they managed together, and had served as mayor the last six years. Their two daughters, Regina and Arabel enjoyed small town life, and vacations to the Bay. Sabra still flirted with any male around: she and Chuck would fight over it, but at the end of the day, they were inseparable.

Maura unloaded the shopping bags, setting aside eggs, tortillas, cheese and veggies to make a breakfast burrito. She poured a tall glass of mango juice and downed half of it in one drink. She hummed along to the opening of "Scheherazade" as she prepared brunch, and ate in the living room.

"Back to work." Earlier in the week, she had bookmarked several sites with information about the extreme, right-wing political associations of Family magazine. *This is a movement, not an innocent publication designed to help families.* The more Maura read the blogs and comments, the more she raged over the dangerous and archaic ideas.

Narrow-minded bigots. They misinterpret the Founders, and exploit the free market and our electoral process to maintain power, and promote their agenda of misery all over the world...

"These intellectual Nazi's have no idea what Jefferson or Paine meant, nor do they understand Kant, Montesquieu, Hegel, or the evolution of philosophy, and the big ideas that form the basis of our advancement. They do not appear to have the intellectual capacity for the dialectic, but are deceived by superstition, dwarfed in their imaginations."

She smirked and highlighted, then deleted.

"I can't really call them intellectual Nazi's, now, can I?"

As she worked and reworked her article, the nohedi provoked her to anger, and her thoughts rushed in a furious stream; all the hours of lectures at her university, the stirring speeches by the leaders of the progressive revolution, and the books, art and music of the movement flowed from memory, as she crafted the article.

She quoted Abby Hoffman:

Revolution is not something fixed in ideology, nor is it something fashioned to a particular time period; it is a perpetual process, embedded in the human spirit.

Exhilarated, she continued on till dinnertime, stopping only to sip water and use the bathroom, until dinnertime. She had forgotten the fire, which had burned down to a thick layer of coals, and now, aware of the cold, she stuffed in some split logs, working the bellows until the dry wood roared into flame.

Grabbing an apple, and her fleece jacket from the peg behind the door, she stepped onto the porch for some fresh air. Lifting her face to the setting sun, three large ravens passed overhead. They cawed loudly, and Maura squinted her eyes, listening closely. In the sound, she heard the cries of people yearning to be free, *We are called to speak for those who have no voice! We are the ones to whom the future will pay homage, in the ages to come.*

She heard barking, and saw Bella at the bottom of the oak tree, nagged by a couple of squirrels. Jimmy skipped a rock onto the pond, and waved to her.

He shrugged over the dog.

"Guarding her turf!"

Maura laughed, and sauntered off the porch, heading his way. Jimmy called Bella, but she darted away toward the marsh. He let her go, and walked toward Maura.

"Well, tomorrow's another day for training, I guess. Good thing about small-town living, everybody knows whose dog is who's!" He watched her crash through the cat tails, and leap into the water. "Crazy dog. Acts more like a lab than a shepherd."

Maura smiled. "I guess I don't know much about that – dogs or small town life."

Jim picked up a stick and studied her.

"Yeah, you're a city girl. Well, it isn't for everyone, that's for sure. Some people can't take it all the time." He tossed the stick in the water.

"I'm sure sorry about Kimberly, Jimmy. Must be awfully painful."

"It sure is, it's hard being alone up here. Not a lot of options for meeting new people."

They walked around the pond, and Jimmy stopped at the bench he had made.

"Want to sit for a minute?"

"Sure, why not? I'm warm enough - for now."

Maura's thoughts ran on. *I wonder if the thing with the dog was a ploy to come by and see me.* She smiled at the idea. *We could spend the night together – it'd cheer us both up. On the other hand, he's pretty vulnerable right now, and not the type for a casual fling - and I don't need the drama.*

They sat next to each other under the darkening skies, drinking in the surroundings, as sparrows soared, and mallards glided along under the sliver of a rising moon. She rubbed her gloved hand over the smooth wood, and imagined Jimmy in his workshop, making the bench. She could see him as he selected just the right wood with lots of grain, and tooled and smoothed the curved arms. There he was spending hours assembling, staining and putting on layer upon layer of lacquer to protect it from the rain and snow. Then he'd placed it in this beautiful spot.

Everyone knew the months he had spent on the beautiful log home he'd built for Kimberly, working with such devotion and love. *I wish a man would love me like that...*

She thought sadly of the child growing inside her, and remembered the dream she'd had the other night about being married. *But it was just a dream.*

Jimmy cleared his throat and peered across the pond, and she snuck a peek at him. Her eyes wandered to his strong, expressive hands, and as he tossed bread to the ducks, they roved over the rest of his body.

Maura stroked her manicured nails along her thighs; he suddenly looked at her with a surprising hunger. She leaned toward him, and when they met, fire coursed through her like a drug. She surrendered to the swirling ocean of temporary madness and delight.

"Let's go back to the cabin," she said breathlessly, pulling him up. They crossed the lawn, crunching through leaves, and when they reached the porch, he picked her up and pushed open the door. He took her to the bedroom and laid her on the bed.

But as he began to fumble with her shirt, he suddenly stopped and looked down at her, his eyes full of shame.

"What is it?" she asked in stunned surprise. He struggled to compose himself, as he sat on the edge of the bed.

"Maura, I am really attracted to you, it's not that, but it just doesn't feel right. I don't want to demean either of us by a random act of mating, and I'm pretty sure that's all this would be; I'm kind of old-fashioned I guess."

He wiped his face with his hands, trying to clear his head.

"I'm sorry, I've got to go."

Maura lay staring at the ceiling, as his boots hammered across the kitchen, and out the door.

She pulled off her shoes, and climbed under the blankets. *That didn't go too well.* But after a few minutes of lying there, trying to figure it out, she fell asleep, and when she woke, it was pitch black outside.

Padding in her moccasins out to the main room, the only light came from the embers glowing in the wood stove. The space was warm, but a depressing darkness and apprehension tugged at her. In the kitchen, she gulped down a Praxil with some wine, and made a sandwich, returning to her writing for a few hours.

She went to bed at midnight, and slept fitfully, waking at dawn to a weird, yellow-grey light that struggled through the fog. She filled the woodstove, as the sounds of perking coffee cheered the kitchen, then showered and got dressed to go to the craft fair.

Her thoughts drifted to Jimmy as she stood under the steaming water, wondering what to make of their heated encounter. She certainly felt the sting of rejection, and was embarrassed that he had withstood her charms - that was certainly unwelcome and unfamiliar territory. She had been certain that the dog chasing drama was an excuse to see her, but what if she was wrong about him?

She toweled off and dressed in grey corduroys and a forest green turtleneck. Shaking her dark curls free, she tugged a wide-toothed comb through her hair, and put on make-up, smiling with satisfaction at her appearance. *He just needs time - probably just got scared.*

She headed to the kitchen for coffee, dreamily remembering the chemistry between them as she stirred in the creamer. *He's so different!* She was more than intrigued.

The sun burned off the fog, and she drove over to meet Sabra at the school. She saw Jimmy from a distance, at his furniture booth, but she was careful not to approach him. He glanced her way a couple of times, though, as she shopped and browsed the other stalls. Sabra picked up on it.

"What's going on with you and my brother?" she asked, as they sat together under a fiery red maple, sipping spiked cider.

Maura licked her lips and smiled contentedly, remembering their scorching encounter, but careful not to arouse Sabra's big-sister instincts.

"Well, we definitely connected, but then he backed out. I don't know if it's Kimberly, or what, but there we were in mid – you know – and he just stopped."

Sabra looked over at her brother as he brushed sawdust away from a chair he was working on. She sighed. "Jimmy's the epitome of loyalty and trust - and naiveté. I've never quite understood him. He has this noble view of women, marriage and family, but at least with Kimberly, his judgment sucks." She looked back at Maura and smiled viciously, "Now don't get mad at me, but I think he showed good discernment in your case. He's on the rebound, Maura, and far too tame for you. You'd mess him up bad!"

"Thanks for the vote of confidence, Sabra. Am I really that dangerous?" She laughed, but saw the concern on Sabra's face as she looked at her brother again.

"Okay, it was a bad idea – I admit it. But who could blame me? He's drop-dead gorgeous." She paused for a moment and continued, "I know you will find this hard to believe, but I did sort of think about what I was doing before I did it. I just decided that he was old enough to handle it, and thought it might cheer him up – you know, show him he's still 'got it.'"

"Maura, Maura. You are a piece of work." She looked at her phone, it was Chuck. "Chuck's ready over at the sheep pen." She shook her head. "Maura, seriously - don't you ever get sick of the chase? Like don't you ever want to settle down?"

They walked through the fallen leaves, toward the animal arena at the edge of the ball field.

"As a matter of fact, I do sometimes." Her tone turned more serious. "I broke up with Nathan, Sabra."

Sabra turned to read her face. "Looks like he got to you."

"Yeah, and I really do love him, but I just don't want the drama. He and Sheila are getting divorced."

"Because of you?"

"No, Nathan said she's been seeing someone, and wants to end the marriage. Not much point in keeping up the facade anymore I guess. She loves this other guy."

"So why isn't that your open door? Seems like your opportunity, Maura. What is the real issue here?" Sabra's question made her uncomfortable.

"I'm not sure, what do you mean?"

"Are you afraid of commitment, Maura? Or working on a relationship?"

Maura paused. "Maybe both." She kicked up a stone, and they both watched it roll off the side of the path, and down the embankment. "A rolling stone gathers no moss?" she smiled, and shrugged her shoulders.

"Therapy, girl, you need therapy!"

Sabra strolled up to Chuck, and grabbed him around the waist. He turned from tying up his horse, and kissed her on the mouth. A pang of jealousy shot through Maura.

They passed time with the locals, and Maura bought a purple Merino wool sweater, and a pair of matching gloves. As they walked back to the booths through the parking lot, she peeked at Jimmy from under the brim of her straw hat. His glance met hers, and suddenly, she felt she had somehow violated him, but quickly brushed away the thought like a cobweb from an old window. *What did I do wrong?*

Chuck and Sabra walked with her over to her car.

"Want to come over for dinner, and maybe catch some drinks and dancing tonight? We've got a great band lined up at the Mountaineer." Sabra grabbed Chuck's butt. "And we've got some hot guys around here."

Maura smiled. "Thanks, but I'm going to head back to the cabin and get to work. Deadline, you know."

"Alright then, guess I'll talk to you tomorrow."

Maura hopped into the Mercedes, and sped off, waving through the closed window.

"That is one stressed-out gal," Chuck said, shaking his head and pulling Sabra close. "Come here, woman." He looked into her eyes and kissed her hungrily. "Let's go home."

Chapter Thirty-Nine

Maura's phone rang as she drove into the yard. *Dad - wonder what he wants?* Aside from getting together briefly at holidays and special events, nothing had ever really changed between Maura, her brothers and sisters, and their dad. After Ellen died, there was some recognition with her siblings that maybe they should all try to get along (whatever that meant), but nothing was ever dealt with. All the problems, the abuse, neglect, abandonment, alcohol, adultery was just not talked about – ever. And her father just stayed busy as always.

She answered. "Hey Dad, what's up?"

"Hi Maura, I just wanted to call and let you know that Grandma Martin passed away this afternoon."

The news was no surprise, given her grandmother's advanced age and failing health, but she felt a stab of pain losing someone once dear to her. She didn't say anything for several seconds.

"Um, wow. Well, she lived a long time, and maybe it's for the best." She though about how her grandmother had languished for several years in a county nursing home, all the family's money having been squandered decades before. It hurt to see pictures of her in recent times, with her once sharp mind, strong body and beautiful features only a memory, replaced by images of her in a generic hospital gown, wild-eyed and incoherent, her hair an unruly mop on top of her head.

"The funeral will be next weekend." Just that. No mention of whether he would go or not. *Of course he's not going - she's no one to him.*

"Okay, thanks, for letting me know. Talk to you later."

"All right, Maura. Goodnight."

"Night." She sighed heavily, thinking about her dysfunctional family. There were some great memories of the early years of her life, with happy family gatherings of dozens of cousins, aunts and uncles, and her grandparents, but the bitter taste of the bad was always there.

She stepped into the yard, and felt the wind pick up, noticing a few dark clouds gathering in the northeast. *Better check the weather.* In the house, she flipped on the heater, and turned on the weather channel. Pulling on her new sweater, she shivered as she made a pot of coffee, and returned to watch the news.

The weatherman made the local announcement: "First snow of the season could surprise us tonight in the higher elevations." She had overheard a couple of the locals mentioning snow flurries earlier in the day, but she hadn't given it much thought. *Such a beautiful fall day.* But from the look of the sky, it certainly seemed like a possibility now.

"Eight to ten inches anticipated, beginning mid afternoon, tapering off Monday morning by noon. There will be heavy rains along I-5, and low-level flooding possible in the Bay Area."

"What in the world?" She thought of driving down the pass Monday afternoon.

Once it starts, they'll close the road, but if it's slippery heading down the hill, I'll have to use chains, and no way do I want to chance it. I'd love to wait till Tuesday for the roads to be okay...

"Crap! I can't miss my appointment, with Susan, that's for sure." She talked back to the weatherman.

"Dang, guess I'll have to leave early."

She began to clean up, and made food to take on the trip, leaving the rest for Sabra.

After finishing up the last of the dishes, she loaded the car, poured the rest of the coffee in her thermos, grabbed a wool blanket and checked her flashlight batteries. *I guess that's it...cell phone's charged, got snacks. I'll call Sabra from the highway.*

She locked the cabin and headed out of the driveway, as the thought hit her. *If there's flooding in the city, Susan may cancel my appointment anyway.* She crossed her fingers: she just wanted it over with.

Big snowflakes began to fall, as she wound to Highway 273, and the temperature was falling fast, but she made her way down Buckhorn Pass before any heavy accumulation fell. The switchbacks were slick, but she was careful. When she finally had cell service near Redding, she called Sabra who got on her for driving in the storm, wondering what the hurry was. "Big deadline," Maura lied.

"Yeah, whatever – did you ever hear of email?" Sabra asked sarcastically.

"I'll be fine, it's not raining too hard. I'll call you later." Maura hung up first.

Sipping coffee and listening to music, she drove cautiously down I-5, as semi's weaved in and out of the right lane. The rain was getting heavy, and her wipers barely kept up with the deluge. In Willows, she stopped to use the restroom and bought some cashews. Other drivers dashed into the small convenience store, soaking wet from the storm.

"Hell of a storm!" The guy greeted a state trooper at the checkout. "What are they saying further south?"

"Bout the same – if you don't have to drive it's best to stay off the roads tonight." The trooper nodded and ducked back out into the storm. Maura paid for the nuts and followed him out, driving behind him on the highway until he pulled over for a car that had hydroplaned wildly and landed in the median. His lights receded behind her, as she nervously continued. *That was close.*

Outside, two serafs sped alongside the vehicle, keeping watch with their dozens of eyes, fire blazing all around them.

She stopped again in Fairfield, then just before the Bay Bridge, sending up a prayer that there would be no flooding on the other side, in the low-lying areas. A lot of people seemed to have heeded the warnings to stay home, as there were relatively few cars on the road.

The traffic picked up as she hit down-town, and so far, it didn't seem that it had rained much yet.

It was after six when she pulled into her parking garage, and slumped over the steering wheel. She unloaded her stuff on a cart, and took the elevator up to the lobby.

The reception area was empty except for a young man at the front desk. She grabbed the mail from her box, and took the elevator to her floor. Throwing open the door to her apartment, she unloaded her stuff quickly, and sent the cart down the hall.

After grabbing a quick bite to eat, she watched tv for awhile, then took a hot shower and collapsed in bed. Her answering machine beeped; she hit the mute button and passed out.

She woke up at 8:30 to the sound of rain beating against the windows, groaned and rolled over.

With a pang of memory, she recalled mornings with Nathan: they would make love and shower together, then lounge in their robes drinking espresso. The paper would arrive, and they'd swap news stories or interesting gossip from the entertainment pages. They typically went to a favorite spot for brunch, and then walked in the park; kissing and watching people go by. *That's all over now.*

She pulled on her robe and slippers and walked to the big west windows in the living room, watching sadly as individual rain drops hit the glass and slid down, dissolving into the rest. *This is my life, just part of the collective; there is really nothing outstanding or unique about me...*

She looked out toward the ocean, and sighed, her heart aching. Remembering the dramatic rescue from her suicide attempt on this very spot, and the strange events of the last few days, she laid her face against the pane, and wept, whispering into the silence.

Glaurius, are you there? Are you real? Can you hear me? Her ever-present companion whispered back, *we are all ultimately alone, Maura: each one must do what the times require, and leave the world a better place for those who come after. Then you, too, will flow into the cosmic gathering of all those bright souls who have enlightened the world, to become part of the divine consciousness that impels mankind. Continue to follow your heart, for that is all there is.*

Unseen Michael reached his hand toward her, but Korban shook his head. "It is not yet time, my friend. She must come to the end of herself before she will believe - the power of Aruni's deception still captivates her." He looked at her and clenched his jaw, wiping away a tear.

The nohedi, stroked his thigh, suggestively eyeing the mighty seraf. But Michael merely touched the edge of his sword, and the creature screamed and vanished into black smoke.

"All right, Korban; I don't like your methods sometimes, but I honor your ways." Korban smiled and the two disappeared.

Maura spent the day writing, doing laundry, and cleaning

the apartment, since her housekeeper was on vacation for the week. She also went through and collected several boxes of clothes and items that belonged to Nathan, becoming slightly energized as she purged his presence. Late in the afternoon, as she sat reflecting, her eyes fell on the photo shelf. She grabbed the big leather album that held family pictures. Leafing through, Maura passed by baby pictures of her siblings, early shots of her parents in love, and family gatherings before she was born. Finally, she came upon her baby pictures. In one, her dark eyes twinkled with delight at the toy dancing off-camera, her face radiant with joy.

She studied the picture with intense curiosity, as if looking for answers. *What a happy baby.* She looked with wonder at the small fingers, each with their tiny nails, the gentle curve of the ears, the velvet skin and lash-less eyes. *She looks so trusting and eager, so excited about life.* But then her eyes fell on the next photo of her father, as he held her in rapt adoration. Then it hit her: *she looks like the favored object of a loving father's care...*

Maura closed the album and hugged it close, tears falling on the backs of her hands, as she rocked gently back and forth, *Hush, little baby, don't you cry, Mama's gonna sing you a lullabye.*

As the evening shadows closed around her, she continued to rock, and sing, and cry.

Chapter Forty

Monday arrived cold and steely, wrapped in Death. It swirled around the clawed feet of the nohedim, as Maura had dressed with resignation, and she and Cissy drove, unsure of what to say, their destination like Damocles' sword overhead. When they arrived at Dr. Plank's, Cissy squeezed Maura's arm, and Maura forced a weak smile. Her friend settled onto the couch in the waiting room, while Maura filled out the brief medical history, the various permissions, and the liability waiver.

By signing below, I release this medical group from any liability for side effects not directly related to the procedure, including emotional and psychological effects. I recognize that all outpatient and non-emergency, elective procedures carry some risk, and while termination of pregnancy is a routine procedure, complications could arise. Excessive bleeding should be considered serious, and be reported immediately to your medical provider.

Maura suddenly remembered the vision she had had on the examining table during her last visit. Her heart pounded, and her hand began to shake as she moved it down the page to sign at the bottom. *Like Faust, selling my soul to the devil.* The nohedi laughed hysterically, its presence causing a rising panic. As if observing a by-stander, she watched herself sign slowly, carefully, one stroke at a time.

The death warrant.

When she was done, she meekly set the pen down on the

clipboard, and brought it to the counter, where Stephanie and the old bookkeeper sat, their lips twisted, their eyes unseeing. Stephanie took the paperwork. "Thanks, Maura. Follow me and we'll get you out of here in no time."

When Maura had undressed, the girl knocked on the door and led her to the exam room. "Take this," she said efficiently, "and Dr. Plank will be with you in a little while. She has another patient ahead of you." Maura was left alone in the cold room, and turned over the little paper cup. A tiny white pill tumbled out, and she held it up to the light.

Etched into the harmless-looking pill was a large "A." *A - for abortion, adultery, abandonment, acquiescence.* Like a child, she obediently swallowed the drug, and stared out the window into the cold, grey eyes of the world.

After half an hour, Susan came in with an assistant she didn't know. Maura followed them mutely, dazedly observing the flurry of preparations, and hearing the explanations as if from underwater; she blinked hard at the blinding lights, and heard her own silent scream in the emptiness, as she lay down, down, down like a sheep to the slaughter.

The impressions came swiftly. To the left, she saw the clear glass centrifuge on its shiny stand, 18 inches high, and five inches in diameter. And she saw paper sheets and a surgical tray full of instruments; she heard Musak, and heard Susan say in a businesslike tone, "Are you okay, Maura? We're going to start. You may feel a slight tugging sensation, but it shouldn't hurt. It will only take a few minutes."

Then the whirring began, as the motor in the jar hummed to life.

Frightened, but too numb to respond, Maura fought back tears.

"Okay," she bleated.

She looked at the wrist bracelet, and the number on it. *470687, I'm a number, that's all.*

Wishing she was out cold, she willed herself to cooperate with Susan's directions and comments.

"Go ahead and put your feet in the stirrups, Maura. That's it." As she spread her legs apart, and felt the cold steel, she realized there was no turning back.

Dr. Plank placed her gloved hand on Maura's abdomen, and then sat down, hidden behind the sheet draped over Maura's knees. The light was warm on her upper thighs, and now mercifully out of her eyes. She felt fingers spread her vulva and insert the long, plastic, vacuum tube. Up, past her cervix, now soft from the laminaria. The machine whined gently, and Maura dozed for a moment.

But she was ripped out of her peace as the battle began inside her, and the strong suction pulled on her uterus; her mind struggled to imagine what was happening, as she laid there drugged, unable to respond. *The baby is fighting!*

Time made no sense, but it seemed that almost as soon as it had begun, it was over. In the now-quiet room, she turned to look into the blood-spattered jar.

What have I done? Helpless under the effects of the drug, the nohedi replayed the drama for her: the baby refusing to give up its life, and the doctor and the machine searching it out, pulling it apart, piece by piece, until they finally pinned it against the wall of her womb.

But around her, everything was perfectly normal – from the snap of Susan's latex gloves, to Barry Manilow on the radio.

As the doctor and her assistant cleaned up, Maura turned her dry eyes away from the jar, fighting waves of nausea and despair. *I'm so sorry, Baby, but we are all powerless against the machine.*

"I-I think I'm going to throw up." The assistant grabbed a plastic bowl and held it for her. Maura leaned weakly on an elbow, and retched.

* * *

In the recovery room, she slowly came off the drug, and dragged herself off the table, changing into her clothes, and mopping up blood from between her thighs. Standing before the mirror, she couldn't look at her eyes, but turned away and walked out to the front desk. Cissy looked up at her, concern etched on her face. *Why does she look so guilty?*

She leaned against the counter for support, and Stephanie asked her if she felt okay.

"I'm fine, thanks, just a little light-headed. I've got a friend to drive me home."

"Great, here are your follow-up instructions, but you should be fine. Dr. Plank will call you later this afterneoon." Stephanie smiled crisply, professionally, and handed Maura back her credit card.

"Okay, thanks." She walked over to Cissy and put on her coat.

They drove back to Maura's apartment in silence, and Cissy brought up some chicken soup she had made. Maura stared at the yellow ceramic pot.

Yup, chicken soup is just the thing...

"I'm going to call you later, to make sure you're all right."

"Thanks, Cissy. I just want to sleep for now."

The ride in the elevator had been surreal, and even now, she felt like a stranger. As she had turned the key and entered the icy apartment, it seemed full of warning. *But I have nowhere else to go.*

She drank some water and took the painkillers Susan had prescribed, and climbed into bed, her only comfort the little warm space her body created in the comforter. She turned on the electric blanket to stop the shivering, and finally fell into a dreamless sleep.

It was after 8 when she woke up; the drugs had completely worn off, and she felt pain deep inside her body, as if a giant scab had been torn away. She drank some wine and took a Praxil, and a couple of hits off a joint, then stared for a while out the windows. *Nothing is real.* She felt numb, and planned to stay that way.

Just then, across the plaza, the lights of the Holiday Tree came on, sparkling in the darkness of the damp night. Michael, unseen, stood next to her.

Get dressed and go for a drive. The thought surprised her, and she dismissed it, puttering around the apartment for a while, pretending she didn't hear. He said it again, then again. She felt a sense of anticipation, but there was also a heaviness she couldn't shake. The seraf placed his hand lightly on her head, and closed his eyes.

She responded at last. *Like I need this? I seriously just want to veg out.* He whispered again. *Get dressed and go for drive, it'll do you good.* She still took her time, and ate a sandwich, but finally she got dressed in a wool mini and boots, and zipped into her leather coat to head out the door. At the last minute, she grabbed the wine and put it in her bag, ignoring Michael's warning to leave it behind.

In the elevator, she asked aloud, "So, where is it I am going?" *To church,* came the surprising answer. "Is that so? Well, what church is open on a Tuesday night in San Francisco?" *Drive to Treasure Island. 401 Mill Creek Road.*

She was high, so it didn't strike her as overly weird that a voice in her head was telling her what to do, and in fact, it seemed vaguely familiar. *A church? What will I do when I get there?* Silence.

She drove through the insane traffic on the Bay Bridge, dodging construction cones and blinded by the lights, but eventually made it across to the island. After about 20 minutes, she slowed in front of a white, two-story building at the address she was given. The sign, in flowing red letters, read "The Promised Land," and a dozen kids were talking on the sidewalk, or riding skateboards.

Go ahead and park, you're safe. Michael walked ahead of her, and she followed the invisible path, past the skateboarders, and through the big, wide doors, where twenty-something's and parents, and old people sat at tables in the lobby drinking coffee or tea. There were little kids running around, and people walking out an exit with artist's easels, and musical equipment.

Some people smiled and nodded hello, but she continued past them all, through the doors, and into the main room, which was an old theater. It had new, comfortable seats, and she stood there in the shadows, watching the musicians on the stage. *What kind of a church is this?* The sweet melodies of the singers, soared up to the painted ceiling of the old theater, and the acoustic tiles, padded seats, and carpet, created a crystal-clear sound.

"My lover's eyes haunt me,
his passion pursues me
and I am overwhelmed,"

The young woman's voice was filled with emotion and vulnerability.

Maura sat in the corner, feeling drawn into the song.

"Surrendering to this wanting,
I cannot resist your desire."

She heard a sound of rushing and rustling in the darkness, and turning around, saw nothing unusual; but her eyes fell on the narrow stairs leading to the balcony, and a light that illuminated them from above.

Curious, she rose to her feet, and followed the seraf up the winding steps, taking a seat on the front row. She noticed the lyrics to the song were on the screens at the front of the room.

"You light up this darkness

and nothing else matters,
when you are here beside me
and I feel how much you love -
how much you love me."

Maura became attuned to the steady, driving beat of the
bass drum that felt like it was pounding inside her chest, and
the air around her suddenly seemed alive, and she began to
shake, struggling to hold back the tears that burned in her eyes,
falling like drops of fire on her face. The words resounded in
her skull, and she tried to cover her ears with her hands, but she
couldn't stop hearing. *How much you love me...*

It's some kind of magic, they're trying to put a spell on me. The
music had stopped, and Maura peered over the railing,
scanning the people on stage, but no one was even looking
toward the balcony. They stopped singing, and the girl on lead
guitar gathered them together in a circle to pray.

She watched them as they joined hands and bowed their
heads.

Afterward, someone turned on a CD while they finished
up, and Maura sat quietly.

My foolish dreams led me higher -
or so it seemed to be,
but in the end all that was left
was cast into the sea.
Why? Tell me, why?
Why? oh tell me,why?
When all I ever wanted
was a place to call my own
to be a part of something
and to never be alone
Alone, alone
For so long I looked for you
in every passing cloud,
but then today, you passed my way
and pulled the curtain down
Down, down
And I see you now
I see you now

Maura sat in rapt attention.

"Excuse me, Honey. Are you okay?" The small voice
inquired behind her, and she turned to look into the limpid eyes

298

of an elderly black woman.

"Um, well, I guess so." She hesitated.

"What's your name, chile?"

"Maura, it's Maura McConnell."

"Well it's mighty nice to meet you. My name is Maybell Carter."

The woman hobbled up beside her. "Mind if I sit down?"

"No, please do,"

"Thank you, darlin.'"

Maybell sat and sighed contentedly, humming along with the music.

"I jes love dat song."

Maura nodded, "Yes, it's nice."

Maybell looked at her. "I been dat foolish dreamer."

"Excuse me?"

"Lak dey's sayin in the song. Like a foolish dreamer, thinkin you goin higher and higher, gettin closer to love, but yo is jes plain *lost*!"

"Yeah."

"Shore - ain't you never felt lak dat?"

Maura just stared at her hands, folded in her lap.

Maybell continued. "Hmmm, I see yo is thinkin 'bout somethin mighty serious."

Maura glanced over to meet the wise and kind eyes. "Something told me I should come to this church, so here I am. I don't really know why - I don't go to church, or even believe in God; this is the strangest thing I've ever done."

The woman smiled, nodding her head in agreement as if in conversation with someone Maura couldn't see. *Is she crazy? Who's she talking to?*

The old lady looked at her again.

"What do you mean, 'something told you'?"

"Uh, I don't know, it was just a really strong impression in my mind."

"Well, Honey, it looks like Glaurius is speakin to you."

Maura looked at her and raised her eyebrows.

"Oookkaayy..."

"Let me explain. I have lived in this city all my life. My husband died when I was only 25 years old, and I raised my kids alone, kept 'em off the streets by the grace of God. They all workin and raisin' families and come to this church. Brother David - he's our pastor – is a good man. And Glaurius has been wid me all this time, and I'm gettin ole."

She paused, staring off into the past. "I come to know him when I was jes a little girl, about 6 years ole. It was in a little Glaurianist church on 11th Avenue, a beautiful spring morning. My mother, says to me, 'Now, Baby, you bin learning about Korban and Glaurius, and dey wants to come closer. You all pretty today in yo dress, but is yo heart free?"

"Yes, Mama, I know. Glaurius has been speakin to me, and I want him in my life and heart for always!"

"Okay, then. When the pastor asks all the children to come up, you kin go to de front. Then he's gon ask if anyone want to come and follow Glaurius. You jes kin say yes, and we will see what will happen. I be right there wid you."

She stopped and dabbed at her eyes with a flowered hanky.

"Oh, my dear. How I do go on! What's your name agin, chile?

"Maura. Maura McConnell."

"Thas good, a pritty name. Gaelic fo Mary. And McConnell, das an impo'tant name - go all de way back to the first followers of the Way."

A bit more educated than she appears. Maura looked at her, puzzled.

"You wonderin how I knew dat. Well, I worked fo many years as a housekeeper fo an Irish family. You know, you pick up things." She smiled mischievously at Maura, and continued.

"So I went up to the front, and we waited fo a few minutes, and soon a gentle Presence came into dat little church - felt like somebody big and strong, but kind and full o love. I felt peace and a joy come into mah heart dat I had neva knowed, and has never left me right up to this day. Now I had my problems, sure as anyone, but I always knowed dat he was wid me." She had been looking happily into the past where Maura could not see, but when she finished, she turned to face Maura, her eyes steady and alert.

"Do you want to have Glaurius in all yo tomorrows, chile? He shore does love you. I know it don make much sense in dis world, but trust me, dey is mo goin on 'round here than mos o us reconize - if you know what ah mean. There comes a time when you gots to believe by what your heart says. " She eyed her, kindly, "And yo lookin lahk somebody who kin use some help, if yo don mine ma sayin so."

Maura thought dismally on the trauma in the doctor's office, and about Nathan and Andrew. *Your heart knows*. But what a liar, and how confused her heart seemed at the moment. *Or maybe I'm just plain crazy...* Fear, despair and shame engulfed her, as she struggled against the narrative of the old woman, and Eternity seemed to loom around her.

Stammering, she stood on shaky legs to leave. "I want to have the peace you have, Maybelle, but I'm really confused right now. Thank you so much for sharing your story." As she tried to step past the old woman, Maybell gently took her hand.

"Chile, you gon be alright, I jes know it. Glaurius got a speshul plan fo *you*. You is a McConnell woman, after all! Lan sakes!" She shook her head, and smiled wide. "You be sure and come back to see us, ok Miss Maura?"

"Ok, Maybell, I promise. Goodnight." She wanted to hug the old lady, but decided against it. *That's just weird, hugging a stramger."*

She made her way down the narrow steps, through the lobby, and out to her car. The sky was clear, and a couple of stars peeked out. Driving home, she couldn't stop thinking about the peace and the powerful *something* in the church, but also the fear. *So much going on, I just need time to sort it all out.*

She stopped for coffee, and scratched out notes about all that had happened in the last week.

> the bad trip, and being rescued by???
> the interview w Germaine and the voices
> the panic attack at Dr. Plank's (a vision??)
> my sister Anne and her new-found religion
> beach dream/Korban/mariposa
> Gabriel O'Brien
> near-death experience w the semi
> Alan Solomon's warning
> the "operation"
> Promised Land church/songs/Maybell

She twirled her pen around and around in her fingers, but couldn't make any sense of it, and finally gave up. She folded up the paper and put it in her coat pocket, paying the barista on the way out.

Chapter Forty-One

The week flew by, as Maura registered for school, racing the clock to make up for lost time. By Friday, she was wiped out, but had the weekend free to spend with the family, and all the activities involved with her grandmother's funeral. Saturday morning dawned cool and sunny, as she dressed in black jersey, black heels, and her grandmother's pearls.

Arriving about an hour before the service at St. Lucia's, she mingled with family and friends, careful to avoid Peg and Anne. Her father was of course not there, but a huge number of cousins, aunts and uncles, and church and business friends were. And Ty was there. She saw his tall frame down on one knee, attentively engaged in conversation with an earnest, and adorable five-year-old girl. Her dark curls tumbled down her back, and her almost black eyes took Maura's breath away. *She looks just like me.*

She didn't realize she was staring, a stricken look on her face, but Ty gently excused himself from his little friend, and came quickly over to her, concern etched on his face.

He took her elbow. "Maura, are you all right?"

She shook it off.

"Yes, I'm okay. Just tired I guess."

"Well, I know these things are never pleasant - family gatherings and all. Lots of old stuff – and old people."

She laughed. "Yeah, it's all a little creepy."

He looked at her, trying to read her face.

"What?"She burst out in irritation.

"Um nothing, just wondering how your week went." He looked at his shoes, and then around the room, waiting for her to react.

But she didn't.

"Good, it was a productive week. I am officially registered at school – that was the big event. Now I can relax."

He was visibly annoyed. "Right, well, congratulations, and good luck with that."

She unloaded on him under breath, teeth clenched.

"What is your problem? Did I miss something here?"

He threw up his hands and leaned in to whisper, "No, Maura, you didn't miss anything at all. You're fine, everything is wonderful and life is awesome, all the time!"

He walked away, leaving her to fume alone. *What in the world was that about?*

Just then, Heather Flannery, the family attorney, walked up.

"Hi Maura, so good to see you."

"Hi Heather, thanks, it's nice to see you, too." *Either she didn't see what just happened, or she has the decency to keep quiet about it.* Maura sighed, and regained her composure. Heather held out an envelope with Maura's name written on it, in her grandmother's handwriting. Her heart began to pound. *I wonder what this is.*

Heather placed it into her hands. "There are a few other things for you from the house - a little jewelry, and books - we'll go over that in a couple of weeks. But I was supposed to give this to you right away."

Maura opened the envelope.

"A safe deposit key?"

"Yes, apparently there's something inside a box at the bank. I have no idea what it is, but honestly, Maura, your grandparents didn't have much left. I wouldn't expect any big surprises - no hidden treasure."

"Yes, I know. Well, thanks, Heather."

"Sure thing. I'm sorry for your loss; she lived a good life. Let me know if there's anything else you need. Good to talk to you."

"You, too."

The funeral was typical of the dry, lifeless Glaurianist ceremonies she was accustomed to, no surprises, and everything was in order. *Ashes to ashes, dust to dust, no expectations, no promises, just the ephemeral and infinitesimal possibility of Paradise, someday...*

Ty didn't talk to her after the service, at the cemetery, or at Hardin's Inn, where the reception was held. After a long, difficult day, she could finally leave.

She made it to First Commerce Bank the following Tuesday after work, slipping in through the revolving door. It was cool inside, and quiet; she remembered coming with her grandmother years ago as a little girl, and how she enjoyed the exterior granite walls, high ceilings, marble floors, and hanging brass lamps. It was a marvel of depression-era architecture. *Of course banks had the money for such buildings...*

She looked around. Little remained of those childhood days except the building, and no one she knew worked there anymore. Everything was digital, efficient, and sterile, and the warm incandescent lights were of course replaced with corporate-standard ICF bulbs, emitting the ubiquitous, grayish-blue institutional light that she hated.

She sat on a couch in the lobby, until someone came by to help. After checking Maura's ID, an assistant manager led her back to a room of safe deposit boxes that smelled of dirty metal and Clorox. The manager pointed out the correct box to her, and left her alone.

Maura opened the box, and found another box inside. She carried it to one of the metal tables, and sat down.

As she took the top off the smaller, brass box, she saw a plain wooden box inside. There were hinges on the back, and as she lifted up the lid, an aroma of cedar, and citrus flowers escaped, teasing her nose, and making her feel slightly buzzed. Inside the box was a simple, ancient-looking, key. She picked it up, and turned it over and over in her hand. It was clearly not cast on a machine of any kind, and although it was badly tarnished, appeared to be made of silver.

*Look more closely at the key...*She pretended not to hear. *Rub along the shaft with your thumb.*

She looked around to make sure no one was watching, and began to wipe the key with the inside of her black tee-shirt. After half a minute, she looked at it again.

She had scraped off enough dirt to make out some letters, and with her heart pounding, she wrote them down on her notepad. "They're so beautiful! And all capitals: T-Z-I-Y-O-N. What on earth does that mean?"

She thoroughly inspected the boxes for markings or any directions, but there were none. Frustrated, she put the safe deposit box away, put the wooden box in her purse, and the key in her coat pocket, where she felt a piece of folded paper.

It was "the series of strange events."

"Well, here's one more." She wrapped the key in the paper, and put them both in her pocket.

As she drove away from the bank, she pulled the paper and the key out onto her lap. Heading down Divisidero, she turned onto Oak, 8th, and then onto 90, heading across the bridge. Stuck now in rush-hour traffic to Oakland, she realized she had been driving without thinking, and would likely be crawling along for an hour hour. *Where am I going? To Treasure Island, and Promised Land church*, came the reply.

She remembered what the musicians had said about playing again on Tuesday night, and realized she was likely going to arrive just in time for the meeting. *Whatever that is...I wonder if Maybell will be there?*

She took the key out of the paper, and rubbed it along her jeans, turning it over again to see the writing, "Tziyon, Tziyon, what are you?"

Finally, the traffic moved off the bridge, and she turned onto the island, and at exactly 6:55, parked in front of the church. The sidewalk was empty, and in the lobby, people were heading in different directions, the teenagers toward the gym, parents minus babies into the main room, and there was Maybell, heading in her direction.

"Well, hello, Miss McConnell. It is sho nice ta see you on this fine evenin. I was hopin you'd come back!" The old lady squeezed her hand, and Maura felt such love that she blushed.

"Thank you, Maybell. It's nice to see you, too. To tell you the truth, I hadn't even thought of coming tonight, I just found myself driving around, and well, here I am. I'm not sure what to do now." She looked awkwardly around, playing with the key in her pocket.

"I understan how dat is, Honey. I don't always know what I'm doin neither!" She winked at Maura and laughed. Before Maura knew it, she was laughing, nervously at first, but as Maybell just kept on, and was soon holding onto her belly, Maura tried to stop, but found the more she tried to control it, the more she laughed. Her cheeks and sides actually began to hurt, but it felt so good she didn't want to stop.

Maybell shook her head, and wiped her eyes with her

hanky, "Mmm, mmm, mmm, I declare dey is nuthin lak a good belly laugh!" Maura just nodded in a agreement, a grin plastered on her face, totally in awe of what was happening.

"Miss McConnell, would you lak to join me fo a coffee o tea? We gots us some o dat good dark roast, organic fair trade coffee, ah know you kids jes love it." Maura smiled at her enthusiasm. *She could be ten or one hundred and ten...*

"Sure, Maybell, I'd love that, but I insist on buying."

Maybell frowned.

"If that's ok?"

"Miss McConnell, when somebody wants to give yo a blessing, yo kin jes say, 'Why thank you!' I'm a whole lot richer dan you think! Dis is mah treat - do you good to jes receive it, no strings attached." They stepped up to the counter.

"Git anything you lak, Honey. Caitlin, I'll have a mug o dat chamomile tea please, wid honey."

"You bet, Miss Maybell, and what can I get you?" she asked Maura. Maura was distracted looking at her piercings, and the brilliant tattoos that virtually covered her arms and neck. She saw there was a theme from the girl's hands up to her shoulder: scenes of lions, giraffes, zebras, a rhinoceros, flamingoes, and parrots in incredible detail. It was mesmerizing.

As she gazed further up the arm, there was a man and a woman, standing before a beautiful tree, and up in the branches, a jeweled serpent surrounded by musical notes. There was a gate in front of this scene, and over it a sign, with something written on it. She stared, trying to make out the word, and suddenly it came into bold relief, set apart from the flowers and vines twined around it. TZIYON.

She put her hand to her mouth and gasped.

Maybell looked at her, unfazed, and Caitlin waited patiently for her to give her coffee order. Maura gulped and looked first at one, and then the other.

"You okay, Honey?" Maura took the key out of her pocket, and unwrapped it from the paper. She showed it to Maybell.

"Do you see what is written on this key?"

Maybell peered at it through her bifocals, and let out a whistle, taking a step backwards, while holding the counter like she was about to faint. And for about a minute, she just kept looking up, chuckling to herself, and shaking her head. But it was her face that Maura stared at. It shone like the sun.

"Where did you git dat?"

"It belonged to my grandmother, who recently passed away and left it to me. It was in a safe deposit box at the bank where I picked it up today."

The old woman paid for the drinks, and they walked to a quiet corner where there was a comfortable sofa and soft lighting.

As soon as they sat down, Maura, asked the burning question.

"Maybell, what is this key, and why is the word on it the same as the barista's tattoo?"

Maybell sipped her tea.

"Maura, why do you think I knows dat answer?"

"Maybell, I am feeling very strange, and confused at the moment. There are so many weird things happening to me. I feel like..."

Maybell leaned forward. "It's alright, chile, dey ain't nuthin to fear. You is safe heah."

"I-I feel like I am not really safe, Maybell. Ever." Her voice trailed off. "I have so many problems." She looked around to make sure no one was listening, and leaned closer. "And I'm starting to hear voices."

Maybell didn't flinch.

Inside, Maura was churning, desperately trying to hold back the twisted thoughts, unrealized dreams, and a lifetime of lies, that threatened to burst from her mouth.

But Maybell just smiled and sipped her tea, seemingly oblivious to her inner turmoil.

"Would you lak a cookie, Honey? I made some nice, soft molasses cookies today." She reached into her big leather bag, and put a colorful plastic tub on the table in front of Maura.

Panicking, Maura continued. "Maybell, I can't live like this anymore. I feel so lost, and I am not sure how to go on. My world seems to be falling apart, like there's nothing solid, and I don't know what is real anymore. I-I feel like I'm losing my mind!" She breathed in spasms, her heart, her words, her feelings now unleashed, and she prayed there was a beach where they could wash up to safety.

Maybell just patted her hand, "Honey, when I was a little girl, dey was an ole lady name Miz Gould, and she baked de mos deelishus molasses cookies you ever tasted. I allus said I would grow up one day, and make em fo mah own chilren, and I did."

She beamed with delight, and took off the lid, releasing the pungent odor of cloves, helping herself to a cookie. She held one out to Maura.

Maura was taken aback at the incongruity; either Maybell was kind of slow, or there really was nothing to fear.

"Why don yo jes take a break Honey?" Suddenly, the cookie looked absolutely amazing.

"Sure, I'll try one." She bit into a little taste of Heaven, as the aroma of molasses, and the sweetness of granulated sugar hit her tongue. "Wow, that tastes incredible, Maybell!"

Maybell pursed her lips in a happy grin.

"I is kinda proud o ma bakin. Glad you lak 'em."

Maybell sighed contentedly, and finally responded to Maura's question, and her fears.

"Miss Maura, seems lak you gots a lot o prolems, but de main thing is yo don't know Glaurius fo yoself, chile. Fo sho he is de answer to evythang, evy prolem you ever gon have."

Bewildered, and frustrated, Maura exclaimed. "'Know Glaurius?' What on earth does that even mean? I keep hearing stuff like this, but it makes no sense to me!" She shook her head.

Maybell nodded and chuckled, squeezing out her tea bag. "I bet you has, girl, i jes bet you has."

At that moment, Maura wasn't sure if she wanted to hit Maybell or hug her, as she sat there like Yoda, nodding, muttering and smiling, saying everything and nothing all at the same time.

Maura leaned forward again. "Maybell, do I seem normal to you?"

"Now dat is a question! As a matta o fact ah think you is prolly the sanest you bin in a long while, right at dis bery moment."

Maura sat back and sighed. "Well, I sure don't feel sane, or normal." She grabbed another cookie and pointed it at the old woman, for emphasis, as she munched greedily. "Maybell, I thought I had all the answers, and that I was really going places." She gazed out through the plate glass windows at the front of the cafe.

"Do you know who my father is? Senator Jim McConnell. Yes, we are people who are making the world in our image. Growing up, my father explained it all to me - what my purpose was - and it all made sense. See, it made sense, because I was in charge, part of the ruling class."

She thought about that for a second, and dropped her gaze to the table, her voice drifting off. "Yes, I was in charge..."

Maybell stroked the smooth sides of her mug thoughtfully, nodding as Maura continued. "An now? How you feelin now, Miz McConnell?"

Maybell suddenly looked like a head of state, seated across the small cafe table, her majesty hidden in a simple dress, her spirit profound, and timeless, filling the room.

Fear and shame prickled along Maura's spine, as she felt the pang of her egotism exposed for the ugly thing it was. She couldn't restrain the truth any longer.

"I-I feel like I've been a part of a gigantic hoax, like what I have believed all these years isn't really true or what's best at all, and there are greater forces at work that I don't understand, and can't control!"

Maybell let that fall with all its force, and remain untouched between them, not responding for several long seconds.

But the unconquerable smile appeared again.

"Yup, dat there is what you call a dee-lemma! Hehehe, cuz you sho nuf cannot control de world, other people, Glaurius, o any o dem nohedi - at least not yet."

"Nohedi? What is that?"

"Maura dey is evil spirits, an what's bin talkin to you, makin yo see thangs. At least it's mostly dem. You hear serafs I'm sure, too. Mebbe even seen o heard de Three I 'magine. Yup, all de talk 'bout ghosts an angels, an what-not, es all real."

Maura was all ears. "Really? So you're not freaked out by me saying I see and hear things?"

Maybell leaned back and chomped on a cookie. "Welcome to de spirit world, girl."

Maura's face contorted with turmoil, her logical mind battling the implausible thought.

"Tell me more about this spirit world Maybell. Have these things ever happened to you?

"Has what ever happened to me?"

"Have you ever seen things?"

"Don git me started chile, ah's seen a awful lotta things in my day. It's very common fo human beins ta see into de spirit realm. Fo example, lotta time lil chilren dey awful afraid at night, from sumthin dey sees and heahs, and no one believe dem hartly. But dey so skeered dey almost go crazy wid fear. But when dey knows Glaurius, dey jes say one word to dose evil spirits, and quick as lightnin, dey go!"

Maura felt like she was five again, alone in the darkness of the old Victorian, with the cold rain beating against the windows and running down the eves, surrounded by the creaking and moaning, footsteps and laughter, that performed for her ears and eyes only. Then she began to feel like Maybell could look right into her, and she started to quake with fear. She glanced at the old lady, not sure if was safe, or a threat.

"How did you know that?"

"What, Honey?"

"About what happened to me as a child?"

"Why Maura, I didn't, but I'm not surprised t'all. You is one o dem sensitive types. Aruni he out to destroy evy chile. Is you feelin skeered right now?"

Maura nodded her head like a little girl.

Maybell reached across the table for her hand. "Oh honey, das Aruni right there, dem nohedi is tomentin you! But it's ok, cuz I'm gon pray fo you, if dats ok?"

Maura nodded her head hard this time. "Yes, please, Maybell!"

Maybell cleared her throat. "By de power o Glaurius, I command all nohedi to go from heah right now, and to stop harassin Maura. You must leave, now."

Maura held her hands together as she'd been taught as a child, and her eyes clenched shut, trying to concentrate.

Suddenly, the oppression lifted, and all fear was gone, like the passing away of a summer storm, leaving the air fresh and clean. Amazed, she opened her eyes.

"What the...?"

Maybell took a sip of her tea and grinned. "Dat is de power o de King, Miss McConnell." She wagged her head back and forth. "Mmm mm mm, he is so strong!"

She explained to Maura.

"Maura, honey, you bin livin in the web o lies that the Prince o Darkness – Ole Lucifer hisself - has spun around dis planet. Don't you know you is a spirit in dat body o yours? He bin weavin a spell 'roun you all yo life!"

"Prince of Darkness? A spell? I-I've been taught that *Lucifer* is the real god – 'the one who brings light.'"

"So I haven't been 'seeing things' all my life?" Splintered memories of her life began to knit together.

"Girl, yo has bin taught a heap o lies! Ain't no light in dat ole goat 'cept razzle dazzle…And yes, yo *has* bin seein things apparently, cuz girl, yo is a seer! Dats a gift!"

She cleared her throat. "Dey is few grownups dat will

listen to de tales of children, so you gits ta thinkin you is crazy, and jes shut up, and live wid it. But dem nohedi is real, Glaurius is real, and his serafs is real. And Ba'al Aruni – Lucifer – is real!"

She cleared her throat. "Dey is few grownups dat will listen to de tales of children, so you gits ta thinkin you is crazy, and jes shut up, and live wid it. But dem nohedi is real, Glaurius is real, and his serafs is real. And Ba'al Aruni is real! But you is not gon hear 'bout dis in yo fancy universities, in de news, in de movies o no place where dey is civilized folks. No, all dem educated people, dey done educated demselves right into stupid. Ain't even smart enough to believe what dey seen wid dey very own eyes. So dey jes lose dey sight, and can't see nuthin no mo. But folks lak me, well we believe what we see, so we kin see mo and mo."

"What do you mean you can see 'more and more'? More and more of what?"

"Well, its lak dis, de mo you believe, da mo revelation you git. Glaurius will come to you and show you truths 'bout anything you wants to know. An dey is truths you kin *see*, and *feel*, and *know* - dat is believin at its very highest. Fo'git 'bout dat 'blind faith' bizness. Dey is no such thing. Knowin' by de spirit, now *dat* is faith dat sees!"

"So you know Glaurius?"

"I sho do, chile, I shorely do."

"And how can it be that this invisible world exists, while we are surrounded by the material world everywhere we look? Why doesn't everyone know about this? And how does it work - the two worlds together?"

"Well, Maura, once upon a time, the other world was all dey was. Actually, dis world was perfect - no pain o suffring, no death, sickness o disease - nuthin bad t'all. But den Ba'al Aruni, he tricked de first woman, tole her Glaurius was a liar and she couldn't trust him, tole her dey was a secret and Glaurius was keepin it from her. But dat was a lie, cuz Aruni, he hated Glaurius, and wanted to be God hisself. So she and her man dey believed de lie and when dey did, dey gave their power to Aruni. And oh how he has spun his tales and misery all dese years! He bin workin a long time makin up lies, and dey sound so *good*! Jes what people wants to hear, but it's all so empty, so meaningless. In de end, people is jes misrable all over de earth, from birth to death."

"And Maura, all de wise and powerful people, dey jes

pretend none o dis is true, lak dey is no God to answer to, lak dey is the be-all, and the end-all. And Glaurius, he don show up at the UN and say 'heah I is, now all you people pay 'tenshun!' No, it ain't lak dat. It is a secret fo those who wants to know de truth. To us, we kin see all we wants to see. So dis 'invisible world' as yo says, is right there, you just gots to have de right eyes to see it."

Maura realized it was the same story she had learned as a child at church. But somehow, it now seemed different, and completely plausible.

She leaned toward Maybell. "Maybell, how do I get these 'eyes'?"

"Miss Maura, das de easiest thing of all! You jes believe!" She started laughing again, holding onto her side, as if it was the funniest thing she had ever heard in her life.

"Maura, honey, if you wants to know the secret, you has to use the de key and open the door."

"The door? What door? And do you mean the key my grandmother left me?"

"You have a door inside you – the door of who you really are. And Korban is the Way – the key."

"Maybell, you're not making any sense."

"Ah know, ah know, jes holt on. It don make sense to your mind chile. Jes wait a second."

They sat in silence, and soon, Maura felt a warm and powerful presence fill the room, like an invisible, billowing cloud that released soft waves of power and light.

But the nohedi twisted the knife.

Suddenly, she remembered the horror of the morning, and terror streamed through her veins like ice, and she turned, stricken, to Maybell. Nearly hysterical, she croaked out the monstrous confession, "Maybell, I am a murderer. I have murdered my own child!" She frantically wrung her hands, as if trying to wipe something from them.

But Maybell quickly and firmly took them, looking her squarely in the eye. "Maura, chile, listen to me. This is the time to ask forgiveness fo all you've done. Tell Glaurius how sorry you is, and ask him to forgive you, and help you. Den you kin see through de eyes of truth, and git free in you mind, in your heart, and be done wit all dat fear."

Maura began to sob out loud, the anguish of a thousand years.

Finally, after what seemed like an hour, she was spent, and

saw that Maybell still sat there quietly, compassion shining in her eyes.

And she heard a voice in her head, *Don't be afraid. Let go of the lies, the walls. Your world is not real...*

She went with the impulse to surrender, and suddenly felt her inner world tumble to the ground, like a child's block-city: the fear, oppression and control, crashing down, down, down pieces flying in every direction.

Humpty Dumpty sat on a wall, Humpty Dumpty had a great fall...

The nohedi whispered back, *All the king's horses, and all the king's men, couldn't put Humpty Dumpty back together again...*

She wanted to sink into sleep, but was startled to attention, suddenly surrounded by a brilliant light. *The light! Turn off the light!* She fought panic at the sudden exposure.

Nowhere to hide! She discovered she was in a vast amphitheater, on a platform before a gleaming white throne, which was encircled with enormous wheels made of some unfamiliar metal or stone, and in the center of the wheels was a swirling, fiery rainbow.

The throne became a judge's bench, and she began to tremble in terror, her teeth chattering like skeleton bones, eyes wild with fright. The nohedi in the shadows whispered his unceasing accusations. *This is it, Maura. You have finally come to the end of the road; the thing you feared has come upon you, and what will become of you now?*

He feigned pity, *Poor Maura, what has become of all your grand ideas, your ambitious plans? Your 'New Age?' No, there is no peaceful oblivion for you when you die - no, you must pay!*

She wanted to scream, but there was no sound, and she stood paralyzed, staring at the walls, and the writing on them. As far as she could see in every direction, there were rules and laws – tens of thousands - an endless ocean of words and statutes, "Do this, don't do that." There were legal precedents, and the principles of various nations, school rules, and laws governing the workplace, relationships, Church rules, traffic laws, safety, and environmental guidelines - rules for every aspect of human existence, written in the granite walls.

As she whispered some aloud, they began to swirl around her madly, like leaves in a cyclone, and began shouting at her. She clapped her hands over her ears to stop the furious sound, and suddenly, it was again, absolutely silent, silent, except for the flickering sounds of the lapping tongues of fire.

In the quiet, she saw words illuminated in the base of the

throne that she had not seen before, and she approached to get a better look. "Love the Lord Glaurius with all you are, and your neighbor as yourself." The voice again spoke to her; *All of life can be summed up in these two commands.*

As she stood before the throne, she began to cry, deep sobs from within, and sank to her knees, her head in her hands. *I have not kept these laws!* After crying for what seemed like hours, she lay spent and empty on the cool marble floor, and through bleary eyes, suddenly saw that someone was kneeling beside her. She sensed he had been there for some time.

"Why are you crying?" The voice was like gentle, rolling thunder.

She sat up, and he turned to her, a brown-skinned man with a handsome face, but it was hard to capture his essence, or to know what he truly was, because she saw his face first like an eagle, then a lion, and an ox, and again, a man. Around him, were wheels of light that moved in all directions and brilliant colors sparkling like sunlight on diamonds, as power flowed out from him in waves.

"I-I don't know where I am, and I am afraid." She lied, and lowered her eyes, like a frightened child. He reached out, his strong hand, gently lifting her face to his.

"Maura, why are you crying?" *He knows my name!* His gentle voice wooed her to take a risk, and speak, to tell her fears, and she tried, but she couldn't look into his eyes; shame and guilt consumed her thoughts - the memories of her life, and failures re-playing in her mind, over and over again.

"All the words written on the walls - I have spent my life fighting the rules, but it's like the whole world is built on them. What does it all mean? And what is this place? Is this the throne of Glaurius?"

"Yes, Maura, and this is the way the throne of Glaurius appears to you in your present condition."

"I don't understand. Isn't Glaurius the great judge of all? Isn't he watching every move we humans make, to punish us?"

"That's your perspective of him right now, and yes, he does rule the earth, and watch over the affairs of men, and judge and punish. But there is another aspect of him that you cannot yet see. You see, your understanding, indeed your very nature is corrupt - dead even."

"You have not been awakened yet in your spirit, so you see him from the perspective of a broken reality, but when you are made alive, and the eyes of your heart are open, you will see the truth, and come to progressively know the many wonderful intricacies of his nature, and your own - and all this by the power of his great love. This is what we call 'The Kingdom of God."

But the ever-present nohedi whispered its lies again, which travelled the well-worn pathway in her brain. Maura looked around the walls, and began to shake.

"But the laws, I cannot stop thinking about them, and how many I've broken! I've done things I didn't even feel were wrong at the time, but now I feel afraid, like I am beyond hope. Is there forgiveness for someone like me?" She began to weep inconsolably.

"Maura." The voice drew her instantly away from the pain, and the nohedi's diversion, and this time when she looked, she saw the one in her dream. *Korban!* Her heart began to pound with longing.

Then she saw him in another place, a magnificent temple, lying on an altar, still and beautiful, his dark curls matted against his face, his blood running in rivers down the cut stones, splashing into the gutters below, and flowing out into the whole world. *There is one law, and one law-giver...*

She began to sob as she saw him there, his life-force ebbing away; she wept again for her failures, for the pain of her childhood, for the loss of family, and for the death of her dreams. It seemed she was crying for the entire planet, giving voice to the great sadness of the Earth, and all its children.

After some time, she was quiet again, and saw Korban now lying dead, in the deep dark womb of the earth. In the profound stillness, she heard the sound of her own beating heart. And as she listened, the sound of another heart joined in, filling the universe, drumming louder and louder. Then light pierced the darkness – a small shaft at first - but then, thundering like a locomotive, it exploded from the vault of the grave, laying bare the roots of the earth.

And as she watched, in awe, he rose from the realm of Death, and came forth, naked and glorious, glistening with new life, magnificent in the first rays of the sun. He turned to glance at her; *I am The New Man, the Superman...*

Maura fell on her face before him.

At that moment, the sound of whirring wings approached, and serafs appeared, clothing him in a white linen shirt and pants, and covering him with a many-colored robe. He came to her, speaking her name like a song.

She lifted her eyes very slowly, worshiping every part of him, spellbound by his majesty. And as she encountered this essence, this divine glory, she felt grief and despair fall from her like grave clothes, and life and hope come into the very depths of her soul. She reached out to touch the edge of his robe, and saw people and nations woven into the fabric. Korban extended his hand and raised her up, and she gazed into the eyes of the Creator of the worlds.

She whispered, "Please forgive me."

His look, and his answer penetrated to the depths of her soul, *I will have mercy on whom I will have mercy...*

Korban took both her hands in his, studying everything about her, stroking her hair, caressing her cheeks, his face rapt with love. She melted under his affection, struggling to stay on her feet, and he swept her into his powerful arms. She laid her head against his chest, and the pounding drumbeat of his heart.

She lay in his arms for some time, unable to see anything but his face, because of a bright, shiny mist, and pulsing, colorful lights that filled the atmosphere. But she heard music everywhere - a swelling melody that started as the hush of the tide, then throbbed out minor chords like waves breaking on lonely cliffs. A symphony of instruments she had never heard before, accompanied by voices, reached heights and depths unknown to earth, and played unseen, all around her; at the same time, it seemed to come from within Korban, as though his thoughts and emotions were being expressed through the music.

Turning to look up at him, her eyes fell on something hanging from his neck on a simple piece of rope.

*A key! It looks just like...*Korban looked into her eyes, and nodded his head, his handsome face wreathed with smiles, finishing her thought.

Mine.

He kissed her on the forehead.

And suddenly, interrupting the music and the moment, a single, long blast from a ram's horn sounded, and they were transported to the top of a mountain that had been split in two. Below, the landscape was a barren wilderness - nothing moved, the only sound, the moaning of the wind.

Then overhead, a great sucking sound began, and she saw a vortex of debris swirling madly above them, in a sky full of dark, terrifying clouds - clouds containing thousands of screaming winged creatures. It appeared as if they were trying desperately to hold back something very, very large that was pushing into the atmosphere, something trying to break in, against which the pathetic horde were no match.

The 'something' was birthing through a very small opening in the darkness, and suddenly, great streams of blinding light pierced the blackened wasteland, and in the blinking of an eye, the creatures, and the darkness vanished.

Maura gazed in wide-eyed wonder at the fiery radiance of the new star, robed in pink and scarlet. Trembling with life, it blushed and dazzled, suspended in the midst of the heavens.

Breathless, she turned her face up to his.

"What is this?"

"It's the beginning of the new Heaven and Earth."

Alarm mixed with wonder, as she asked. "Korban, is this really happening? Where are the old earth, and all the people?"

He smiled as he turned to her, his face full of the radiance of the sun.

"This is a vision of the near future; the old earth, and the people are still where you left them, dying to see this."

He swept his hand across the sparkling turquoise sky, as fresh winds washed over them, and she suddenly saw, ever-so-faintly, the outline of a glistening city.

"Tziyon," she whispered, with unutterable joy.

"The Promised Land." He sighed happily, and drew her to him, inhaling the scent of her hair. They stood in silence, as she basked in his healing presence and affection. After some time, he spoke.

"I have a message for you to bring to earth: the message of my Kingdom, and of my love for the world." He looked at her with great appeal in his eyes.

"A-a message? Oh Korban, how can I ever go back, after seeing all this - after seeing *you*?"

"Maura, you need to go back, it's not your time to come here yet." She buried her head in his chest, trembling.

"I have waited a very long time to see you face to face, and for my kingdom to come to Earth; I wanted you to see me, and to see the future with your own eyes, so you could believe while you are still in the old world; there is much to do, and some very difficult things ahead. And with all the unbelief and lies, it is necessary that you know in what - and in whom - you believe."

"And," he went on, "you can't stay because you don't possess your immortal body; you will be changed after you die, or if I return before then."

She stopped breathing for a second.

"Maura, death and Evil have no power over you now, because your seraf watches over you." He lifted her chin and looked into her eyes.

"Nothing can happen to you without my consent, and you will learn to master this fear of Death, and of Aruni. I do not know when your time will come, and I wouldn't tell you even if I knew; what a way to live – always fearful of the end! No, you will be fed and taught by my own spirit, so that you can live in joy and hope every day of your life, and laugh at the direst of circumstances – because you have power within, and a future you can see."

"Then you *will* go back with me? I can't do it without you!"

"Maura, I have died already, and have my new nature, so I cannot dwell on earth as I am. But I can communicate with you here." He reached out and placed his hand over her heart.

She held it there, her eyes closed for a few seconds, but then popped open in wonder. "I heard you! You told me the truth I need is in The Book of the Way!"

He laughed. "Yes, I did."

"Maura, I'm everywhere at all times, you need only to quiet your thoughts and activity and seek me, and you will find me."

"Like meditation – TM?"

"Yes. You will learn more from the people I have ready to teach you."

Her head hurt, and her heart was heavy at the thought of going back. *This is the craziest thing ever, but somehow I know things are going to be okay...*

"Can I ask you something Korban?"

"Of course."

"Hey, you already know what I'm going to ask, don't you?" She smiled, raising her eyebrow in question.

He nodded, smiling back, as he stroked her hair and twirled the ends.

"Why me, Korban? What is special about my family, and why did I receive the key? I'm not a heroine in any sense of the word, and as you know, I've done terrible, terrible things."

Her voice dropped off, as she looked away from him in shame, before continuing.

"Even the good I do is so people will notice me, and my goal in life has been to be powerful and important; I'm full of pride and resentment..." She paused again, her heart fill of memories. "And pain."

Korban looked thoughtful as she spoke.

"Maura, that right there, is why you *are* a heroine: you are smart, and have great courage, and when you know the truth, you are quick to embrace it, even if it reveals the darkest realities of your heart; I can trust people like you. That is an extremely rare quality – honesty. And as far as the things you've done, not only are you forgiven, I do not even remember what they are; I forgive and forget. And as for the pain, and the memories, and all the things that you have suffered, I will heal you, and give you peace and closure."

She looked at him with gratitude for the last part, and then astonishment as she thought about what he said about forgetting all she had done.

"Are you serious – you don't *remember?* How can that be? I can never forget the wrong things people have done! "

He smiled. "That is another thing that will change about you in time: you will learn to love as I love, and forgive and forget. "

"I can remember if you want to talk about something, but I wouldn't want you to continually re-hash all the bad stuff. There's no fun in that."

He began to laugh, and to her great relief, so did she.

"Maura, many in your family have been so welcoming to me over the centuries, and well, I just like you guys! You care about the poor, love the truth, and hate injustice and pretense – all things that matter to me."

"So we have a lot in common after all?"

"Hahaha, indeed, we do. We are going to be good friends."

She noticed they were now down the mountain, standing beneath a broad-leafed tree in a green field. Overhead, bluebirds flitted and sang, as they stopped beside a low, hand-stacked stone wall. Korban held her hand, playing with her fingers.

"Maura you - along with many others - have a major role to play in the events at the end of the old world. I know it seems hard to believe because there are so many people, you feel so small, and life is so complex, but I really do ultimately control everything."

He looked into the distance. "And people are absolutely everything to me."

She eyed him strangely.

"Even the ones who despise you?"

"Especially them. There is nothing I haven't done or wouldn't do to keep people from destruction; I really have only one enemy, Maura."

His face became enflamed with a mixture of grief and rage, and she turned away, unable to look at him, aware this was a battle far beyond her.

Then his face softened again, and the anger was gone, like the sky after a storm. He gazed lovingly at her, but seemed to be looking *into* her, as if at something in the past.

"And, my beautiful one, you are a reminder of a promise I made a long time ago, to a woman a lot like you – power-hungry and curious." They laughed at that.

"And for the record, the desire for power and knowledge isn't a bad thing. We *created* you to be inquisitive and have authority - but without wisdom, there's only trouble down that road. You know the story: Chevah, the first woman was deceived by Aruni, and everyone born from her enters the world blind and stumbling, with a bull's eye painted on their backs."

He went on. "I promised Chevah I would make everything right one day, and she would always have daughters who believed - and as she failed in the opening scene of this great drama, you are one who will rock the final act."

Maura stared in wonder at his words, and then feeling almost eager to return and get to work, she clapped her hands together.

"Okay, I'm almost ready. Just one last question."

He laughed at this, teasing her. "I doubt that."

She grinned. "Korban, what is the meaning of the key?"

He pretended to think very deeply, and then asked, "Well, my love, what do keys do?"

"They open things," came the reply.

"Yes, they do. Keys open doors, and unlock things. So what might you – or anyone – need to have opened and unlocked?"

"Well, lots of things, I guess. In a sense, every big idea is a door or key to some reality, some new understanding. All the things I've read or studied – or written – have revealed or exposed something, although now I know most of it wasn't very helpful, or at least didn't lead me to the truth." She grimaced slightly.

"But Maura, all those words came from hearts searching

320

for truth, and had a measure of truth in them - even if the writers didn't know about me, or about our Kingdom - because we have put this longing in every human being: to be reunited to us, and to exist according to their original design."

"So you are the key, then?"

"Yes, I am the key, the door, and the way – back to The Garden, to Paradise, and immortality."

She shook her head, as if to clear it so she could understand all that she had seen and heard. "Korban, there is so much I didn't know."

"Yes, my love, it is mysterious, this story – and there is much more to tell." He lifted her face to look into her eyes. "But would you have it any other way?"

She thought about the strange dream she had had of the writing in the sand, and tears started to roll down her cheeks, her emotions playing wildly. *It's almost time to go back.*

"Maura, you will become what you are destined for through struggle as well as joy."

"Like the butterfly."

He smiled, and took her hand in his, "Yes, like the butterfly."

They walked along the low stone wall, hand in hand, as the breath of Heaven's perfume wafted over them, and the enrapturing music never stopped. He stopped and looked at her, and in his eyes, she saw delight, mixed with the glory of future events.

"But before you go, I have something else to show you – something you must never forget."

She cocked her head, wondering what might be next, when suddenly she found she was ascending with him, into the sky. Gripping his hand tightly, she looked down as the meadow turned to mist, and rising from the mist she saw a great wheel made of glowing copper; it began to turn, slowly revolving, and in the wheel she saw thousands of serafs, all covered with eyes that looked in every direction.

When from the middle of the wheel, a blood-red rose appeared; she watched in amazement as it opened, displaying hundreds of intricately-layered petals. And driven only by his will, she and Korban moved effortless through the air, and into the center of the flower, where she saw they were joined by tens of millions of people, who had entered into that vast ampitheater.

Every face shone with a radiant happiness, and suddenly,

from the throat of each one in that innumerable gathering of humanity, a song arose in which Creation, too, joined: the majestic planets and blazing stars revolving in their orbits in space, all land animals great and small, gleaming fish and chanting birds, every plant and flower and tree, and every living thing, lifted its voice, and expressed in intricate harmony its ecstatic joy, like a melody plucked on the strings of a giant harp.

And with the song still ringing in her ears, Maura found herself staring again into the smiling brown eyes of Maybell Carter, surrounded by the sounds of steaming milk and laughing children, at a corner table in the Promised Land Café.

Epilogue

Ty and Maura have a few things in common: they both made decisions about life based on their cumstances, genetics, past experiences, and what was expected of them by others. They also lacked the close, healthy connection with parents who could give them direction, and provide safety and unconditional love. In each of their lives, this set them on a course to "look for love in all the wrong places." And finally, they knew nothing at all about a good God who loved them.

Maura was constantly harassed by destructive, demonic forces, and had no idea of their source. Like all of us, she did her best to make sense of life, and tried to "be somebody" and even wanted to change the world, but when her eyes were opened, she discovered that there was no promised land at the end of the road she was travelling.

Ty lived life at a frantic pace, seeking to hide the shame and confusion of his identity, and nothing in the elite world that he inhabited gave him ultimate purpose in life.

Psychologists have been debating for some time as to the nature of the personality – how we become who we are. There are those who believe that our family environment is the key factor in who we become, and others who say we are born with certain predispositions that determine our fate.

But long ago, a young Hebrew shepherd beautifully revealed the mystery of human existence.

"For I am fearfully and wonderfully made; you tenderly fashioned me in my mother's womb."

Yes, dear reader, God created you and me, and it was his good pleasure to do so.

When Korban (Jesus) taught the people of his day, he expressed the heart of God in an astonishing statement, "For God so loved the world that he gave his only son that whoever believes in him would not die, but have eternal life." That son is Jesus.

Did you get that? God's plan is *that you would live forever.*

But wait, there's more.

Do you want your loneliness replaced with a deep sense of belonging and purpose? Do you want to have a personal or family legacy, or change the world in even a small way? Or maybe you want to be a kind, forgiving and happy person, or operate in miracles, with the power to heal the sick, free people from mental illness, and open blind eyes. Or maybe you want to help the poor, and teach them to thrive…

The fact is, "The Superman," or "The New Man," was God's idea, and its reality has been available for two thousand years. Jesus Christ was the first New Man - a man with unselfish motives, abounding with moral goodness, and authority. And in a mysterious but very real way, his death and resurrection from the dead makes it possible for *anyone who believes* this, to receive the same power he has, and be just like him - that's actually the message that he preached. Jesus Christ is God, and the mystery of Jesus, the mystery of the ages - the secret of the universe - is that you can be like God.

And God gives this power to anyone who asks will turn away from their own understanding, and follow him…

So will *you* become a new man or a new woman, boy or girl, and know God, and serve the earth as He intends, or will you remain a mere mortal, with merely human power and ideas, at the mercy of unseen, evil powers and lies, doomed to spend eternity apart from God?

Let him awaken you to know see that he is the One your heart longs for, and that *you* are the answer to a dying world. Child of Light, it's time for you to discover what you were born for.

* * *

If you're tired of struggling with fear, or want to stop the cycle of climbing the ladder, destructive relationships, heartache, anger, and despair, if you are sick, dying, abandoned and poor, or rich and empty, Jesus wants to change you from the inside out, and reconstruct your life instead of you self-destructing.

If you want to know and encounter God, just say what you are feeling. Maybe something like this:

"God, I am so tired, so lost. I've tried to figure things out on my own, according to what I thought was best, but my life is a mess. I don't even know what's true, or where to turn anymore. God, if you're real, please show me the truth. Forgive me, and show me what to do."

When you pray this simple prayer from your heart, God will hear you, and you will encounter him like Maura, Ty and Lailah. And you will enter Heaven now – because his plan has always been for you to be his son or daughter, and your destiny has always been The Promised Land.

Mary Elizabeth Morin

Resources

If you've been impacted by this book and want to learn more, here are a wide variety of resources for you to check out - something for everyone!

josephprince.com
moralrevolution.com
new.jesusculture.com
kcm.org
lecrae.net
joycemeyer.org
ignitinghope.com
iamsecond.com
joelosteen.com
net-burst.net

ABOUT THE AUTHOR

Mary Elizabeth Morin has had a storied life, growing up in small-town New York and New England during the turbulent 1960s and 70s. She spent many years in the desert southwest, and Juarez, Mexico, and writes about nature, spirituality, and dreams. Her greatest passion is to see people and relationships restored. She lives in Redding, California with her husband, son and daughter.

Find her on Facebook at
www.facebook.com/promisedlandmedia

E-mail her at: mary.promisedlandmedia@gmail.com

www.ingramcontent.com/pod-product-compliance
Lightning Source LLC
Chambersburg PA
CBHW071848220626
47052CB00002B/20